KING SOLOMON'S CARPET

KING SOLOMON'S CARPET

—

RUTH RENDELL
WRITING AS

BARBARA VINE

HARMONY BOOKS
NEW YORK

Published by Harmony Books, a division of Crown Publishers, Inc., 201 East 50th Street, New York, New York 10022.
Member of the Crown Publishing Group.

Originally published in Great Britain by the Penguin Group in 1991.

HARMONY and colophon are trademarks of Crown Publishers, Inc.

Manufactured in the United States of America

Library of Congress Cataloging-in-Publication Data

Vine, Barbara
    King Solomon's carpet / Barbara Vine.
        p.   cm.
    I. Title
    PR6068.E63K54   1992
    823'.914—dc20   91-43668
                                                                              CIP

ISBN 0-517-58795-5

10 9 8 7 6 5 4 3 2 1

First American Edition

AUTHOR'S NOTE

Although there are vertical shafts which penetrate the London Underground from street level, and some which descend from higher than that, none is to be found in any building near Holborn Underground station, nor behind the Soane Museum, nor anywhere in the neighbourhood of Lincoln's Inn Fields.

It is not possible to travel from Kensington High Street to Notting Hill Gate on the roof of a tube train car. Or if it is possible it would be too dangerous for any sane person of any age to contemplate.

The rest of the factual information in this book about London Transport Underground is true.

To the men and women
who work for
London Transport Underground;
and to those
who make music in its tunnels

'I tell you,' went on Syme with passion, 'that every time a train comes in I feel that it has broken past batteries of besiegers, and that man has won a battle against chaos. You say contemptuously that when one has left Sloane Square one must come to Victoria. I say that one might do a thousand things instead, and that whenever I really come there I have the sense of hairbreadth escape. And when I hear the guard shout out the word "Victoria", it is not an unmeaning word. It is to me the cry of a herald announcing conquest. It is to me indeed "Victoria"; it is the victory of Adam.'

G. K. Chesterton, *The Man Who Was Thursday*

KING
SOLOMON'S
CARPET

I

A great many things that other people did all the time she had never done. These were the ordinary things from which she had been protected by her money and her ill-health. She had never used an iron nor threaded a needle, been on a bus nor cooked a meal for other people, earned money, got up early because she had to, waited to see the doctor or stood in a queue.

Her great-grandmother had never dressed herself without the help of a lady's maid, but times had changed since then.

Places had not changed much and the family still lived at Temple Stephen in Derbyshire. They still spent Christmas quietly and had a big house party for the New Year. They played games as they always had, Consequences and Kim's Game and a game her brother had invented called Closing Pepper Gate. Sometimes they took bets on the heights or depths of things and the location of things and the number of things.

One of the guests asked the others to bet on how many metro systems there were in the world. They asked him if he knew the answer, for if he did not how would they ever find out? He said of course he did, he would not have suggested it otherwise.

She said, 'What's a metro system?'

'An underground railway. A tube.'

'Well, how many are there?'

'That's what I'm asking. You name the number of your choice and put ten pounds in the kitty.'

'In the *world*?' she said.

'In the world.'

She had no idea. She said twenty, thinking that must be far too many. Someone said sixty, someone else said twelve. The man who had proposed the wager was smiling and, seeing his smile, their sister said a hundred, her brother-in-law ninety.

He won and got the kitty. The answer was eighty-nine.

'One for every year of the century,' someone said, as if it were appropriate.

'I've never been in the tube,' she said.

At first no one believed her. She was twenty-five and she had never been in the tube. It was quite true. She mostly lived in the country and she was rich. Also she was not strong, there was a little something wrong with her heart, a murmur, a valve that functioned less than perfectly. The older people called her 'delicate'. She had been told that having children might present problems, but nothing that could not be managed. She might want children one day but not yet.

It made her lazy, it made her rather self-indulgent. For instance, she never felt guilty about lying down after lunch. She liked having people about to look after her. It had never occurred to her to get any sort of job.

Since she was seventeen she had had her own car and when she came to London, a fleet of private hire cars at her disposal, not to mention the taxis that swept round the Mayfair corners. She had been married and divorced, had had fifteen lovers, give or take a little, had been to the United States seventeen times, to Africa twice, explored from a car or at a leisurely pace the capitals of Europe, twice circled the world, done the 'sophisticated' things but left undone so many ordinary things. And she had never been in the London Underground.

She had no intention of going into it. You heard such stories! Rapes, assaults, gangs, fires, trains halted through suicides, the rush hour.

Her brother, who was also her twin, said when they were back in London, 'I shouldn't bother. Who cares whether you have or not? I've never been in St Paul's Cathedral. I hate it, I'd like to destroy it.'

'What, St Paul's?'

'The tube. I'd like to raze it and plough over the site like the Romans did with Carthage.'

She laughed. 'You can't raze something that's already underground.'

'It runs under my flat. I can't stand it, I hear it in the early hours.'

'Move, then,' she said idly. 'Why don't you move?'

She rested after lunch and then a taxi took her up to Hampstead and a shop that sold a certain kind of ethnic clothes not available elsewhere. The shop was round the corner in Back Lane. She bought a dress made for a Peruvian bride, high-necked, tight-waisted, with big sleeves and a big floor-length skirt, white as a white rose, with white satin ribbons and white lace. They said they would send it, they got so far as taking her address, but she changed her mind, she wanted to wear it that night.

There was no shortage of taxis going down Heath Street and Fitzjohn's Avenue. She let them pass, came to Hampstead tube station and thought what an adventure it would be to go home in a train. Buying the dress had altered her mind. She was possessed by a reckless excitement.

This she knew to have its pathetic side. What would they say to her if they knew, these people who were obliged to use this means of transport day in, day out? The thought of their contempt, their disgust and envy, drove her in.

Some minutes were occupied in the buying of a ticket. She did not know what to ask for at the ticket window so she essayed the machine. It was a triumphant moment when the yellow ticket fell into the space behind the small

3

window, bringing her change with it. She watched what other people did, showing their tickets to the man in the booth, and she did the same.

There was a staircase. A notice informed the public that this was the deepest Underground station in London, three hundred stairs to the bottom. Passengers were advised to take the lift. The gates of the lift closed as she approached it. If she waited, surely another would come. It was then that she reflected how complicated a process it was, this travelling by tube. She thought of herself as intelligent and had been called so. How was it then that all these *ordinary* people seemed to manage it with effortless ease?

The lift came and she got into it fearfully. She was alone in the lift. Would she have to operate it herself and, if so, how? It was a relief when others came, others who took no notice of her but, if they thought of her at all, must think her as seasoned a traveller as they. An illuminated indicator told them to stand clear of the doors and then they closed. The lift went down of its own accord.

Down there in the depths, and she was very aware of how deep it was, a sign pointing ahead and then to the left said: *Trains.* Some people, instead of going ahead, turned directly left, thus indicating their sophistication, their experience, their refusal to be baulked of a short cut by official-dom. On the platform she was not at all sure that she was in the right place. She might find herself not being carried down to London but spirited away to distant unknown suburbs such as Hendon and Colindale.

The train coming in made a noise that was fearful and seemed dangerous. All her energies were devoted to appearing in the eyes of others as nonchalant. At the same time she watched them to see what they did. It seemed that she might sit anywhere she chose, that there were no rules to obey. She had never been very obedient in other areas of her life but in the tube she was a child again, learning,

4

wary, and without that presence which had always been there in her childhood.

She sat in a seat near the doors. To be near the doors seemed safest. She had forgotten this was supposed to be an adventure, an experience her life lacked. It had become an endurance test. The train started and she breathed deeply; with hands folded in her lap, artificially composed into an attitude of relaxation, she took long slow breaths. Her fear was that it would stop in the tunnel. She understood that she did not like tunnels, though this was something she had previously been unaware of. She did not have claustrophobia in small rooms or lifts. It was possible she had never been in a tunnel before, except perhaps in a car going quickly through some underpass.

But she was surviving. She was all right. The train came into Belsize Park and she looked curiously out at the station. This one and the next, Chalk Farm, were tiled in white and buff, reminding her of the servants' bathrooms at Temple Stephen. She occupied herself with studying a map on the opposite wall because she knew she would have to change trains at some point. Tottenham Court Road must be that point, an interchange from the black line to the red. This train would take her there, was bearing her there rapidly now, and at the station she would follow the signs, for signs there must be, to the Central Line going westwards.

They had reached Camden Town, blue and cream, another shabby bathroom.

It was unpleasant, what happened next. Such things happen in bad dreams, dreams of the recurring kind from which one awakens in panic and fear, though she had never dreamed anything like this. How could she, never before having been in the tube?

The next station should have been Mornington Crescent but it was not. It was Euston. It took her quite a long time to understand what had occurred and what she had done wrong. The map explained, once she understood how to use the map. By this time she was trembling.

The train she was in was one bound for south London, as perhaps all were, but it would be reached via the Bank instead of Tottenham Court Road, describing a loop through the City to do so. She had got into the wrong train.

All this time she had scarcely noticed there were other people in the car with her. Now she did. They did not look like the kind of people she usually associated with but seemed inimical, common, even savage, and with truculent, peevish faces. She told herself to be calm. Nothing irreversible had taken place. She could change at Bank and take the Central Line, the red line, from there.

At King's Cross a large number of people got in. This was the station where the fire had been, she had read about it and seen it on television. Her husband — she had still been married then — told her not to look.

'Don't get involved. There's no one you're likely to know.'

She could see nothing out of the window to show there had been a fire. By the time the train moved off she could see nothing at all out of the window, she could scarcely see the window, so many people were squeezed between her and it. She sat very still, making herself small, the bag with the dress in it crammed behind her legs, telling herself it was a privilege to have a seat. There were people, thousands if not millions of people, who did this every day.

One thing to be thankful for was that no more could get in. She had to revise this at Angel and again at Old Street. Perhaps a point was never reached where no more could get in, but they would be pushed and crushed until they died or the sides of the car burst with the pressure of them. She thought of a tired analogy she had often heard, people

6

in a crowded train compared to sardines in a tin. If things go wrong inside a tin, gases build up and the contents swell and the whole thing explodes . . .

After Moorgate she had to think how she would get out at the next station.

She watched what others did. She found it was not possible even to get up out of her seat without shoving people, elbowing her way, pushing past them. The doors had come open and there was a voice on a public address system shouting something. If she could not get out the train would carry her on to the next station, to London Bridge, it would carry her on *under the river*. That was what that band on the map was, that zone of blue bending up and back like a water pipe, the river.

Others got out and she was carried along with them. It would have been hard at that point not to be ejected from the train. She felt tumbled out, pushed and pummelled. On the platform the thick, sour air seemed fresh after the atmosphere inside the car. She breathed deeply. Now she must find the red line, the Central Line.

The strange thing was that it did not occur to her then to follow the Way Out signs, leave the station and go out into the street where a taxi could be found. It occurred to her later, when she was in the westbound Central Line train, but not then, not when she was trying to find her way to the interchange. All her concentration and all her thought were bent on finding where to go, on doing it right. The bag with the dress in it was crushed, her pale shoes were covered with black scuff marks. She felt soiled.

Once she went wrong. She waited for some minutes on a platform, a train came and she would have got into it if that had been possible. She could not have brought herself to do as some did, step in and squash her body against the bodies of those who formed the dense wad of people which already bulged from the open doors. The doors ground to a close. Looking up at the illuminated sign overhead she was glad she had not attempted to push her way in. The train was going eastwards, bound for a place called Hainault she had never heard of.

She made the transfer to the right platform. A great many people were waiting. A train came in, going to another place she had never heard of, Hanger Lane. She knew the direction was right, it would stop at Bond Street where she wanted to be. She began to feel that if she did this a few more times she would get the hang of it. For all that, once would be enough for her.

Entering the train was not so bad as entering the east-bound one would have been. It was possible to walk in without pushing or being pushed, though there was no question of finding a seat. Others stood, so she could too, it would not be for long. What she should have done was obey the voice that told her to pass right along the car. Instead, she stayed near the doors, holding on as best she could to an upright rail, the bag with the dress in it clutched in her other hand.

A man, quite young, was sitting in the seat nearest to the door. Of course he would get up and offer her his seat. She waited for this to happen. All her life men had given up their seats to her, at point-to-points and tennis matches, their window seats in aircraft, their centrally positioned armchairs in balconies overlooking royal routes. This man stayed where he was and read the *Star*. She held on to the rail and to her bag.

At St Paul's a great throng crammed the platform. She saw a sea of faces, each stamped with a kind of purposeful, hungry urgency, a determination to get into this train. As before, when she was on the Northern Line, she thought there must be some rule, some operating law, that would stop more than a limited, controlled number getting in. Authority would appear and stop it.

But authority did not appear, not even in the form of a disembodied voice, and the people came on in, on and on, more and more of them, a marching army, a shoving, crushing battering ram of men and women. She could not see if the platform emptied because she could not see the platform. A man, pushing past her, swept the dress bag out of her hand, carrying it along with him in his thrusting progress. She could see it still, made an ineffectual grab at it, seized only a girl's skirt instead and, relinquishing it with a gasp, saw its wearer's face loom close to hers, as distressed as her own must be.

The bag was bundled and squeezed, stretched and squashed, between the legs of the stumbling mass. There was no possibility of her reaching it. She did not dare let go but hung on to the rail, where another four hands also hung on, for dear life. Faces were closer to hers than faces had ever been, except those of lovers in the act of love. The back of a head pushed one of them aside and pressed so close into her face that hair came into her mouth, she could smell the less than clean hair and see the beads of dandruff. She turned her face, twisted her neck, found her eyes meeting a man's eyes, their eyes close and gazing, as if they were about to kiss. His eyes were dead, purposely glazed over, blinded to deny contact.

And then, as the doors groaned shut and the train moved, the fidgeting, the adjusting of positions, the shifting of hands, ceased and all became still. Everyone froze into stillness like people playing the statues game when the music stops. She knew why. If the heaving had continued, if there had been continuous restless movement, existence inside the train would have been impossible. People would begin to scream. People would begin to beat each other in their frenzy at something so intolerable imposed upon them.

They were still. Some held their chins high, stretching

necks, their expressions agonized, like martyrs in paintings. Others hung their heads in meek submission. It was worst for the very short, like the fat girl she could see between face and face and back of head, standing with nothing to hold on to, supported by those who surrounded her, her head under the men's elbows, a woman's handbag, clutched under an arm, driving its hard corners into her throat.

By now she had lost sight of the dress bag. Acquiring its contents had been the purpose of her outing, but she no longer cared about it. She cared about surviving, about remaining very still and suffering, enduring, holding on until the train reached Chancery Lane. There she would get out of the train and the system. She should have got out of the system at Bank, she knew that now. To lose the dress, the white Peruvian wedding dress, was a small price to pay for escape.

When the train stopped she thought they were there. She wondered why the doors were not opening. Outside the windows all was darkness and she understood they had stopped in the tunnel. Whether this ever happened without dangerous cause, whether it often happened, what it signified, of all this she had no idea. She would have liked to ask, speak into the face of the man whose breath, rich with garlic, fanned hotly into her nostrils. Her throat had dried. She had no voice. She was aware, more strongly now than before, of all the human bodies pressed against her, the elbows and breasts and stomachs and buttocks and shoulders, and of the hard glass panel against which her own side was crushed.

The heat began to increase. She had not specially noticed the heat before but now she did as droplets of sweat formed themselves on her forehead and her upper lip, as sweat in a single long drop rolled very cold and insinuating down between her breasts. Of that icy coldness she was very aware, but not as relief, rather as pain, rather as shock.

It grew hotter. The train gave a lurch, a kind of belch, and she held on, held her breath, waiting for it to start. It sighed and sank once more into immobility. The man close to her grunted. His face had gone very red and looked as if it had been sprayed with water. A drop of sweat ran down her forehead and into her eye. It stung her eye and she asked herself why this should happen. Why should salt tears not sting while salt sweat did?

While she was wondering this, holding on to the rail with a wet slippery hand, feeling the heat rise and thicken, the train belched again and this movement, much more powerful than before, shifted and heaved the people around her to enclose her in a kind of human tide. Her face now against a tweed back, she fought for breath, struggled and pushed, moaning as another icy drop flowed down her body and set off the pain.

It *seemed* to set it off, to trigger it, for as it slipped along her skin like a bead of ice, a huge pain took hold of her left arm, as if an iron claw had grasped it. She arched her back, tried to stretch her neck above assorted flesh and hair and smell. The train started, moved forward on a smooth glide, and as it did so the iron claws embraced her, like the appendages of a monster.

They embraced her and dragged her down, through shoulders and arms and hips and legs, to a conglomeration of dirty, trodden-on shoes. The train ran on smoothly towards Chancery Lane. The last thing she saw, as her heart that had the little something wrong with it collapsed, was the bag with the dress in it, stuck between a pair of trousered legs.

There was no room in the train. Not one more passenger could have squeezed in. Yet as she sank to the floor and died they fell back, they shrank back and made the space for her she had needed for life. For dear life.

At Chancery Lane the train was cleared and the body

removed. Remaining in the car was a large dress-shop bag, made of thick, strong paper with some kind of dark blue lacquer coating and a picture of a woman in unidentifiable national costume. They were apprehensive about opening it and sent for the Bomb Squad.

Eventually, much later, a wedding dress was found inside. A receipted bill with it gave the address of the purchaser. It was sent to her home and came at last to her family.

2

The young woman's death did not find its way into Jarvis Stringer's book.

Only accidents of a more spectacular kind would appear there, the first 'sledger' to come to grief, the over-zealous railmen attempting to close doors who were decapitated at tunnel portals, the victims of fire. He read the account of the inquest and of the later failed efforts of the family to bring an action against London Transport Underground. If they had been successful, the incident might have appeared in one of the chapters of disaster.

The girl's brother was later to claim acquaintance with him but by that time Jarvis was in Russia and his book half-finished. He started it while he was living with his mother in Wimbledon, before he moved to the School.

It was to be a complete history of the London Underground.

London has the world's oldest metro system [he began]. *It dates back to 1863, to a Victorian London of slums, of gaslight, of the powerless and the poor. Three-quarters of a million people came there every day to work. They came on foot, by river steamer and in horse-drawn omnibuses and drays. And there were those who could not come at all, they lived too far away.*

One man had a vision of a railway that would link all the mainline railway termini. His name was Charles Pearson and, though born the son of an upholsterer, he became Solicitor to the City of London.

'A poor man,' he wrote, 'is chained to the spot. He has not leisure to walk and he has not money to ride a distance to his work.'

There had previously been a plan for gaslit subway streets through which horse-drawn traffic could pass. This was rejected on the grounds that such sinister tunnels would become lurking places for thieves. Twenty years before his railway was built, Pearson envisaged a line running through 'a spacious archway', well-lit and well-ventilated.

His was a scheme for trains in a drain.

3

The house by the line was always called the School. Jarvis Stringer called it that, as he had done since he was a small boy. He was too young to remember when it had been a school, though his mother could, she had been there as a pupil. By the time Jarvis was five it was closed and abandoned and his grandfather had killed himself.

The building was a red-brick Victorian house in that West Hampstead street which runs parallel with the Metropolitan and Jubilee Lines of the London Underground. This large house, neo-Gothic in all respects but for its Italianate belvedere, stood about a third of the way between West Hampstead station and Finchley Road station, at which point the lines enter portals and dive underground. Its grounds were small for so large a house, no more than two shrubberies dividing it from its neighbours, and at the rear a stretch of lawn with trees ran down to a fence. Through the palings of this fence the trains could be seen rolling past, northwards to Amersham and Harrow and Stanmore, southwards to inner London. They could be heard too, a constant if sporadic singing rattle. Silence came only in the deep watches of the night.

These lines had been there for many years when Ernest Jarvis bought the house in the twenties, the Metropolitan Railway having been extended from Swiss Cottage to West Hampstead in 1879. Ernest was well off, having his share of the Jarvis family money, and there was no reason why he should not have made his school in some more attractive part of NW6, up in the neighbourhood of Fortune Green for instance. Even his daughter did not know why he had chosen a house overlooking the railways or for that matter why he wanted to keep a school at all. He did not particularly like children, though he liked trains. Jarvis Stringer's grandparents' qualifications for keeping a school were that he had been up at Oxford where he had read Greats and she had left Goldsmith's College halfway through her teacher training.

The mystery was that it was successful for more than thirty years. People sent their daughters to Cambridge School, dressing them up in the toffee-brown and pale-blue uniform Elizabeth Jarvis had selected. Perhaps Ernest had been rather clever in naming his school and Elizabeth showed great psychological soundness in the choice of that Cambridge-blue trim on the blazers and ribbon on the panama hats. Of course no one even hinted at some connection between this school for girls by the railway lines and the great university, but the implication was there. Because of its name and that pale blue the school enjoyed a peculiar indefinable distinction. A small kudos attached to going there, though the fees were never high. Studies were not taxing and little emphasis was placed on the passing of examinations. It seems to have been a fact, as Jarvis's mother pointed out, that no girl from Cambridge School, NW6, had ever got to any university, let alone Cambridge.

In 1939, when the new double tubes were constructed, branching off the Bakerloo system, Ernest spent much time away from the school watching the digging of the new Metropolitan Lines under buildings at Finchley Road. He saw the underpinning of the North Star Hotel and the rebuilding of Finchley Road station. Not many years later, during the Second World War, bombs fell in the street, destroying neighbouring houses but leaving Cambridge School intact. Elizabeth Jarvis said it was like St Paul's Cathedral, miraculously saved while all around it lay in ruins. Elsie Stringer thought the analogy unfortunate, but typical of her parents' attitude towards the school.

Jarvis came down from Cambridge with a degree in engineering; not a very good one because he had done no work. From his grandfather he had inherited a love of railways and the School. That is, his mother inherited the School first and never went in a train if she could help it. Jarvis wandered about the world as young people do, but instead of driving a van to India or observing political upheaval in Central America or getting into trouble in Africa he went to look at metro systems. He was one of the first passengers on MARTA, the Atlanta underground, when it opened in 1979, rode the new tube in Fukuoka two years later and in the following year watched the building of MMTA in Baltimore and the metro in Caracas.

It was while he was playing with his first train set, a fifth birthday present, that the news reached his mother of her father's suicide. Jarvis was in his bedroom and Elsie in hers, next to his. She took the phone call in there. He had heard the phone ring but did not listen to what was said. He was playing trains. Sometimes, when he thought about that day, as he did occasionally, it occurred to him that this was the first instance of railways being able to distract him from the pains of life. In future, it was always to be the same.

His mother came in, fell on her knees in front of him and pressed him to her. She was gasping and shuddering. She held on tight to him, murmuring, 'Oh, my darling, hug Mummy, hold on to poor Mummy, poor Mummy's had a terrible shock.'

Jarvis put up with it for a moment or two. Then he struggled to escape. He looked at her. She was very white.

'What's the matter?' said Jarvis.

'Poor little boy, it wouldn't be right to tell you,' she said.

She sat on his bed, shivering, hugging herself. Jarvis went on taking his train from London to Penzance, the

Cornish Riviera. In his imagination he was both engine driver and passenger. When they got to Plymouth he would be station-master as well. Even then he had a special devotion to subterranean tracks and as the train came to the Wellington tunnel (he and his parents had been on holiday to Cornwall that summer) he began letting out a series of long drawn-out hooting sounds.

His mother burst into tears. Jarvis hooted once more. But he was a tender and affectionate child and he saw that something more was required of him. He got up and stood by his mother and put his hand on hers. She had behaved like this when his grandmother died a few months before. He said to her, 'Is grandad dead?'

She was so shocked she stopped crying and asked him how he knew. Jarvis said he had guessed. He had also noticed that she was not just unhappy this time. There was something more. He sat on her lap and let her hug him. He judged five minutes was long enough for that, a lifetime when you are five, and since he had just learned how to tell the time he watched the clock over her shoulder. She went on sitting there staring at him long after he was back on the floor. By the time he had got the train to Exeter St David's, its first stop, people had begun arriving, notably his father in a taxi.

Ernest Jarvis had hanged himself. The school had begun to fail in the forties and fifties and the number of pupils declined to fifteen, to ten, to three. Long gone were the days when they employed four teachers. His wife taught the remaining pupils, three seventeen-year-olds, and, as if she had only postponed death until her duties were done, she died of a heart attack at the end of July, the day after the last girls left. Ernest had no wife, no occupation, very little money and a huge white elephant of a house that needed ten thousand spent on it.

Cambridge School had a bell which was never rung,

which had never been rung. It was housed in the belvedere, a word that Ernest insisted meant 'bell tower' even after his sister Cecilia told him its correct meaning of 'beautiful view' or 'beautiful to see'. He bought the bell in a shop in Camden Passage and hung it up, intending to ring it to summon laggard children to school. Then his sister told him gently that schools like his didn't have bells, a bell would lower the tone of the place and put off the parents of prospective pupils. The bell continued to hang there, the rope passing through apertures in the ceilings of the top, first and ground floors into a poky cell which was to double as cloakroom and bellringer's room. After a year or so the rope was taken up from the lower floors and wound on to a cleat on the top storey.

Ernest Jarvis did what he had to do elaborately, and it must have taken him a long time. The trapdoors which covered the original apertures and which had been closed for thirty years he managed to get open with the aid of a tool, a screwdriver from the appearance of the marks. Methodically, he replaced the screwdriver in a toolbox in the garden shed, though he was not known as a tidy man.

When he unwound the rope from the cleat the bell rang once. Perhaps he had forgotten that the bell would ring or he hardly cared whether it rang or not. Cecilia Darne, who lived round the corner, said she heard a bell toll once at about eight in the morning. Of course she also heard it toll again and then heard a broken peal, a dreadful stuttering ringing, some quarter of an hour later. Many people heard that but only Cecilia seemed to have heard that first single clang as Ernest, her brother, in freeing the rope from the cleat, gave it a tug which caused the bell to spring upwards and fall again.

He passed the rope through the now open apertures, down into the place where those toffee-brown overcoats had once hung and above them the brown felt hats with their Cambridge-blue ribbons. By November 1958 there was nothing in the cloakroom. A row of pegs on one wall faced a row of pegs on another, eight feet apart. A small window, rather high up in the wall facing the door, was glazed in frosted glass with a single pane above of the stained kind in a dark purplish-red. The stone floor was covered in very light brown linoleum with a pattern of black fleurs-de-lis. Ernest fetched a stool from one of the classrooms. It was a teacher's stool that had once stood behind a high desk. In the event, Ernest chose not to use it. He was getting on for seventy and had arthritis. Perhaps he did not trust himself to mount that stool and do what he had to do.

The stool was there when he was found. So, of course, was the chair, from his own sitting room, which he had considered more suitable for his purpose, kicked over and lying on its side. When Jarvis came to take over the house, although a good many people had been inside it and others had lived in it, the chair and the stool were still in the bellringer's room. The stool stood in the corner to the left of the window and the chair diagonally opposite it. They looked as if they had been arranged by some cleaner who had been sent in to tidy up and who did not know that in this room Ernest Jarvis had hanged himself. The rope, however, was no longer hanging down through the hole in the ceiling. Jarvis, coming there to take possession thirty years later, found a rope attached to the bell and its other end wound round the cleat. He wondered if it was the same rope but did not like to ask his mother.

Probably it was the same because hardly anything in the School had changed. Another aunt, Ernest Jarvis and Cecilia Darne's sister Evelina, lived there in Ernest and Elizabeth's living quarters until she died. Then Tina Darne, who was Cecilia's daughter but only a year or two older than Jarvis, persuaded Jarvis's mother to let her move in and start a commune. Tina stayed for no more than six months but some good, hard-working, idealistic people remained, the kind who are made for communes and communes for them, and they mended the window frames and grew vegetables in the garden. But none of these people changed the School. It was far beyond their means. By that time it needed not ten thousand spent on it, but forty.

Ernest had made a will when his wife died and left everything to his only child. 'Everything' was the School and £98 in the bank. Considering he had been in possession of a thousand a year from carefully invested family money, a very good unearned income in 1925, he had not done well. Perhaps he thought of this too when he climbed on the chair and made a noose at the end of the rope, a very neat noose with the rope bound ten times round the loop in even rings.

It worked. As he dropped and kicked away the chair the bell rang once. Poor Ernest must have kicked and jerked, for it rang again, a stuttering tremble of sound, and then was silent. A neighbour who heard the bell, a sound she had never heard in all her fifteen years in the street, puzzled over it for half an hour and then went across the road to the school.

Jarvis's mother told Jarvis his grandfather had gone to live with Jesus. She never explained the means by which this journey had been made, though Jarvis some time later overheard a conversation about suicide, his mother refer-ring to her 'poor father', and put two and two together. When he was fifteen his mother told him about the hang-ing. He had nagged her about why they did not go to live at the School, instead of letting all those other people live there, and at last she told him why.

'I could never bring myself to live there,' she said, and then, in a way characteristic of her, 'Besides, it needs thousands spent on it before civilized people could live in it.'

Civilized people, in her view, did not include her aunt Evelina or cousin Tina or the idealistic vegetable gardeners. She and Jarvis's father and Jarvis lived in a semi-detached house in Wimbledon. Jarvis disliked the whole suburban scene but there was not much he could do about that until he was older. Sometimes he went to West Hampstead and paid a visit to the School, to the commune, and enjoyed it very much and thought how much he would like to live there himself. When he slept there, as he occasionally did in the classroom on the ground floor known for some mysterious reason as the 'Remove', he could hear the trains run past the end of the garden and to him it was the most romantic sound in the world. Going home next day, he noticed as he waited on the platform for the tube to Baker Street, that the track sings as the train comes into West Hampstead, long before you can see it, and the silver lines shiver as it approaches.

There was a property boom in the seventies. This was nothing to what came ten years later, no more than a mini-boom, but prices began to rise and estate agents to rub their hands and gird their loins and look about them. One of them wrote to Jarvis's mother to tell her he could get a good price for Cambridge School. In the eighties estate agents actually called on Jarvis at the School to *beg* him to put the place in their hands. They bombarded him with letters and rang him up at least once a week. He always told them to forget it because the School was falling down, it was subsiding, and one day would crumble and disappear: the trains had shaken it to pieces. This was what the surveyor had told the first buyer to whom Jarvis's mother had offered the School in 1976. He had been going to convert it into flats but backed out of the deal nearly as fast as the second prospective buyer, who was a surveyor himself.

The commune moved to Devon, leaving behind them

some rhubarb growing in the garden which was still there when Jarvis moved in. At one point the local authority threatened to put a schedule of dilapidation on the place to force Jarvis's mother to repair it. His father died, two years later she remarried and went to live in France. She could see – anyone could see – that Jarvis was an eccentric. He was very different from the sort of person who gets a job and then a better job and promotion and a wife; two children, a boy and a girl, a house, a better house, a car and all the rest of it. As soon as he had any money he spent it on going to Central America or Thailand by the cheapest possible means to look at some new underground. He was gathering data for a book about world metro systems, a task on which he had been engaged for years. When he was at home he had begun living at the School, where he boarded up the broken windows and had the chimneys cleaned.

'You'd better take it over,' Elsie said, off to Bordeaux. 'It seems such a shame, that dear old place going to ruin. You could let a bit of it and live on the rent.'

She said this last doubtfully because she had seen the School as recently as Jarvis had and could not imagine any 'civilized people' renting it. But she worried about Jarvis having practically nothing to live on, as she saw it, though he never worried.

He had a little bit of money his father had left him. His mother got the Wimbledon house. Jarvis's money brought him in a tiny income, on which it was just possible to subsist if he walked everywhere, never went to the cinema, ate anything nice, smoked, drank, bought new clothes nor used the phone. Jarvis didn't much want to do any of these things, but he did want to go up north and admire the old Glasgow PTE, not to mention going back to ride once more San Francisco's BART, which tunnels deeply through the rock under the Bay. His income he augmented by writing pamphlets about railways, teaching an evening class in car maintenance – a subject he knew little about but which he mugged up from a handbook the night before – and, if things got bad, painting houses.

When his mother had gone, Jarvis got into a District Line train at Wimbledon Park, changed on to the Victoria Line at Victoria and on to the Jubilee at Green Park for West Hampstead. It was a long and awkward journey but Jarvis enjoyed it. He could never get tired of the tube.

Half an hour later he was crossing the footbridge from the northern to the southern side of the lines. The rails below him, steely and shining, made a wide silver river. The bridge, though reinforced with big steel girders which obstructed much of the view, had old lichened wooden boards across its central section and wooden stairs. Between the girders the back of the School could be seen, a rather forbidding, dark plum red with Gothic windows of a kind more suitable to a church. On either side of it, where the houses had been bombed, blocks of dull flats had been built during Jarvis's childhood.

A Metropolitan train roared up non-stop to Wembley Park and a slower Jubilee passed it, stopping at the platform below. Jarvis thought he would enjoy hearing the sound of these trains while he was writing his history of the London Underground. He went down the steps and through the little brick alley.

Cambridge School was cold inside and it smelt. Jarvis crossed the vestibule, a large high-ceilinged chamber with mock-medieval hammer beams, on the walls of which were incised on yellow pine panels the names of pupils who had in some small way distinguished themselves. A big iron lamp with branches, an electrolier, hung high above from the ceiling two floors up. The flights of stairs ended in galleries with pine balustrades and all the heavy, badly carved dark-stained woodwork was pine, as it might be in a church. The stair banisters had excrescences shaped like pew ends every few treads. Jarvis opened the case he had brought on the vestibule floor, carried the typewriter into Remove, where he put it on one of the desks, and took his clothes upstairs.

There had never been a first form at Cambridge School. New pupils began in the third form, and III in Roman numerals showed in worn black lettering on the door ahead of him. IV or Four was on the door to the right and round the corner on the left was the Handwork Room, the Headmaster's Study being on the extreme right next to the bathroom and opposite the Staff Common Room. All the woodwork in the School was pitch pine, now become either a fierce saffron yellow or a dark, almost sooty, brown. The floors were of the same wood, some bare, some covered in linoleum, and everything appeared in a state of decay. Jarvis thought he had read somewhere, or been told, that woodworm was most active in May, yet now in September those small heaps of ginger-coloured dust that lay everywhere looked fresh, and as he opened the door of Three a trickle of the same dust came down on his head.

He chose to sleep in Three because it had the best view of the Jubilee Line, unobstructed by trees, and as he came into the room and crossed to the window, he saw beyond the garden and the trees and the rhubarb plantation a silver train speeding southwards. There was a fireplace too, as there was in Remove and the other first-floor classrooms, Six and Upper Six, and in the Staff Common Room. At the moment it was warm, but soon it wouldn't be and he would need fires. He would need light too. The electricity supply had been cut off at least two years before.

Jarvis was an eccentric and in the opinion of many who knew him a very strange man, but he had a quiet way of getting on with things. He was not a procrastinator. No one could, with justice, have called him a layabout. When he had had his lunch, which he brought with him in the suitcase, a packet of salami sandwiches, a croissant with jam in it and a fruit-and-nut bar, he set off for West End Lane, to the Electricity Board and the Gas Board, to make inquiries about a chimney sweep, and put an advertisement for tenants in a newsagent's window.

But before he got to the newsagent's he met, coming out of Fawley Road with a small boy and smaller girl, his first cousin once removed, Tina Darne.

4

The trains ran down to Finchley Road all day and up to West Hampstead all day and others pounded through without stopping up into Buckinghamshire. The sound of the trains and the flash of their silvery sides through the trees was part of living at the School. The blaze of lights in the evening was part of it, and the singing and shivering the rails made. Only at night, in the deep of night between one and the dawn, was there silence and semi-dark.

You got used to it. Jarvis liked it and Tina did not mind. There was not much that Tina minded. The two bathrooms and the kitchen were communal, but Tina had her own bathroom and kitchen. No one had the Art Room, the Science Lab, the Handwork Room, the Staff Common Room or the Headmaster's Study, though there was a chance someone would one day. No one used the cloakroom where Jarvis's grandfather had hanged himself and no grown-up person ever would.

Where the wooden floors were not exposed they were covered in that brown linoleum with a pattern of black fleurs-de-lis. The great iron electrolier, with its arms and claws, still hung high above the entrance hall. It resembled a medieval instrument of torture, a rack or wheel. The lamps on it were fake candles, set in sconces like upturned lion's paws. All the windows had roller blinds made of a dark-green fabric so tough that the years of neglect had done nothing to decay or even damage them. They rolled up and down perfectly and their presence obviated the need for curtains. There was no central heating, only a collection of electric and oil and gas heaters, imported by tenants or discovered more or less in working order in the Handwork Room where all such things were stowed.

Tina had warned against putting that advertisement in the newsagent's. She thought it unwise. Arriving at the School with Jasper and Bienvida in a borrowed beat-up Ford van, its roofrack loaded with launderette bags of clothes and its inside with her sticks of furniture (sticks was the word), she told him the advertisement would only attract riff-raff. Jarvis grinned but could see the wisdom of it. There was riff-raff and riff-raff, your own being a different thing altogether.

'Asking around' was what Tina recommended. The moment she was settled in she would start asking around. Jarvis thought he had better get on with it himself because anyone Tina found would very likely default on the rent. Tina herself was not a risk in this area because the man she had lived with longer than any other was paying her £50 a week for the children's keep. It was not that Jarvis was asking much rent, in fact no estate agent would have believed what he was asking, but the whole point of letting bits of the school was to get enough for him to live on, indeed to get to Cairo and ride on the new 42.5 kilometre, 33-station ENR.

He went among the beggars who congregated in tube-station entrances, looking them over as they sat hunched and huddled on steps. It was not possible to give a home to all, so how could he pick out one or two? At the foot of the Piccadilly Line escalator at Leicester Square a drunk man squatted, singing hymns. Jarvis tried to talk to him but he was deeply suspicious, saw Jarvis first as a social worker, then as the press, swore at him and spat, landing a gob of spittle on his jacket lapel.

It was late but the platforms were crowded. When the train came in Jarvis had to stand. He changed on to the Jubilee Line at Charing Cross and at Bond Street four men

28

got in. They entered the train confidently, in a way that put Jarvis on the alert; they looked immediately to right and left, then having exchanged whispered words, split up, two going to one end of the car, two to the other.

Trouble in the Underground was something he had occasionally witnessed. It was usually late at night but not always. Once he had seen a girl set upon by a gang of other girls on a descending escalator. He was on the one going up. She was standing still, alone on the moving stair, when the others pounded past her, snatching her bag from her shoulder, a chain from her neck, the last one tearing the earrings from her ears. At the top, Jarvis jumped on to the down escalator but the gang had disappeared into a train coming in opportunely and their victim stood weeping, holding her bleeding earlobes.

Another time he had seen a tourist, a non-English speaker, make the discovery that his wallet had been taken, with his passport and everything he had. That had been in a train like this one, a Jubilee train heading northwards, and Jarvis could clearly remember the man's despair, his shouts and exclamations in a language no one understood. But if these men who had split into two parties were here for some heist or scam, they were being slow about it, for they sat calmly in silence, one of them in the seat next to Jarvis, a dusty-looking, very ordinary, middle-aged man in a voyeur's dun-coloured raincoat.

They all got out at Baker Street. But not to change trains, only cars. Jarvis saw them get into the next car and on an impulse he jumped up and followed them. The same thing took place at St John's Wood and now he thought he knew who and what they were. Perhaps what told him was the attention they paid to the drunk man who weaved his way, shouting and stumbling, down the car. Most people when confronted by that kind of thing pretend it is not happening, hide themselves behind newspapers, show an unwarranted fascination in reading advertisements, but these four watched the drunk man's progress, they seemed to monitor it. When he staggered out at Swiss Cottage the youngest and tallest of them went to the door, apparently to check that he did not re-enter the train.

'Are you Guardian Angels?' Jarvis always talked to people without reserve. If he was curious he asked.

The man in the raincoat turned to look at him, hesitated, said, 'A similar organization. We're the Safeguards.'

'Do you get much trouble?'

'It's been quiet tonight. In fact, it's been quiet all this week. Making up for last, I reckon.' The man in the raincoat said hopefully, 'You're not looking to join, are you? It's voluntary but there's what you might call a lot of job satisfaction.'

Jarvis, who was getting out at the next station, asked where they would be the following night; the man who said his name was Jed Lowrie told him the Metropolitan, the Hammersmith Line. On the ramshackle desolate station at Latimer Road he met them dutifully changing cars, but instead of joining the Safeguards, found himself offering Jed and Abelard, his pet Harris hawk, a home at the School.

Jed also had part-time employment in the Job Centre, and he turned pale when he heard the minuscule rent Jarvis was asking. The hawk installed in the old bicycle shed, Jed moved into Upper VI. Peter Bleech-Palmer, who was the son of Tina's mother's best friend, took V while he was waiting to share a flat with someone in Kilburn.

The research Jarvis embarked on for his book took him into the lower level concourse at Bond Street. He was conducting an experiment with the gales that blow through that station when he paused to listen to three buskers playing Scottish reels. One of them had the bagpipes, another a violin and the third a flute.

They finished a rendering of a Burns song and then the flautist put down his flute and began to sing in a fine baritone voice. He sang 'Scotland the Brave' and then 'So Far from Islay', he sang of exile and loss, of love of one's country and separation from it. The subject of his songs was as far from subterranean noise and heat and crowds as could be imagined. Jarvis was entranced. The only kind of music he liked was sung music and of that he liked all sorts – opera, lieder, folk, country, rock, jazz, soul, the blues.

'That was very good,' he said to the singer. 'I don't know when I've heard anyone sing that so well. Do you do requests?'

'Do we what?'

'You know, like in a restaurant or whatever. If I ask you for something will you sing it?'

'Depends what it is.'

The singer, who was a good-looking fair-haired boy, no more than twenty-three or four, looked pointedly at the hat, now reposing on the tiled floor. Jarvis fished in his pocket and among the coins found a pound.

'He'll sing the whole of the Don's part in *Don Giovanni* for that,' said the man with the bagpipes.

Jarvis laughed. He asked for an Irish song of love and loss. The singer sang it without accompaniment. Imagine accompanying that on the bagpipes! When he got to the line about its not being long, love, till our wedding day, Jarvis felt the old undefined longing and the tears pricking his eyelids, though the last thing he wanted was a wedding day or a wife or any permanent relationship, come to that. He thanked the singer and gave him another 50p, which he could ill afford.

A crowd had gathered, blocking the passage. Having understood what was going on, people were putting up their hands for requests. There was a scattering of applause as the singer began and the bagpipes skirled. Jarvis slipped away and on to the platform to feel the wind blow through, ahead of the train emerging from the tunnel. He knew that when they built the Jubilee Line they had had to put in a big fan shaft here to release the air or passengers might have been blown off the platform on to the line.

It *was* windy. Women's hair got blown about. Jarvis had once seen a poor girl's skirt blown over her head and been embarrassed for her. The passengers carried away, another lot came streaming in. He went back the way he had come, hearing the music ahead of him, and recognized the tune of a Geordie air. The crowd was still there, but someone in uniform was pushing his way through and starting to harangue the singer.

Jarvis, who was taller than anyone else there, said over the top of heads, 'They're not doing any harm. They're cheering us all up.'

'It's against the rules, sir,' said the man in uniform.

Being called 'sir', which happened seldom, always had a terribly softening effect on Jarvis. He could not help feeling how kind it was of a fellow human being to accord him such deference, that the speaker must have a particularly sweet and generous nature, must love and honour him, and he had to struggle against this, he had to resist cravenly agreeing with whatever was said that preceded that 'sir'. He just managed.

'Then the rules should be changed. It's very unjust.'

The man pushed his way back. He said to Jarvis, 'That's not for me to say, sir,' and, less pleasantly, 'nor you either.'

Seeing there was to be no more entertainment, the crowd began to disperse. The musicians were packing up their instruments. The one who had not yet spoken, or not in Jarvis's hearing, was swearing under his breath.

'Where will you go now?' Jarvis said.

The man with the bagpipes said in a phony refined accent, 'How about dinner at the Gavroche before we go back to our suite at Grosvenor House?'

'Come home with me and give us a concert,' said Jarvis. He added, 'I'll pay you. It won't be much but I will pay. It's for my book, the chapter on underground entertainers.'

They looked at each other. They seemed to confer silently. The singer said, 'OK. What have we got to lose? I'm Tom, this is Ollie and that's Mac.'

'Jarvis Stringer.'

They played for him and Tina and the children until they were exhausted. It was too late to go home after that so they stayed the night. Two of them never went home but stayed on. Mac had a girlfriend and a baby with whom he lived in a Bayswater hotel room provided by Westminster Council. Ollie moved into the Headmaster's Study and Tom into Four.

'I hope they'll pay,' said Tina.

'Tom's got a job as well,' Jarvis said. 'He gives flute lessons.'

Tina shrugged. 'Flute lessons? I don't believe it. Imagine that when I'm trying to get the kids off.'

Since Jasper and Bienvida never went to bed until Tina did but fell asleep wherever they happened to be, Jarvis hardly took this protest seriously. Tina occasionally said that sort of thing to try and sound like a normal mother. She sometimes pointed out, though not aggressively, that Jed's hawk Abelard on its perch in the bicycle shed screeched incessantly during the hours of daylight. He thought they probably had enough tenants now.

He had enough money to go to Cairo and he was off next week. From seeing one of the newest metro systems in the world, he wondered if he could fix it to go home via Budapest and see one of the oldest.

Pearson's plan to send people 'like so many parcels in a pneumatic tube' met with mockery from Henry Mayhew, the journalist and sociologist. Mayhew had written a four-volume work called London Labour and the London Poor *and had been an influence on Dickens. He was also the founder of* Punch.

'We have often smiled,' he wrote, 'at the earnestness with which he advocated his project for girdling London round with one long drain-like tunnel . . .'

Punch *itself laboured the irony:* '*We understand that a survey has already been made and that many of the inhabitants along the line have expressed their readiness to place their coal cellars at the disposal of the company. It is believed that much expense may be saved by taking advantage of areas, kitchens and coal-holes already made, through which the trains may run without much inconvenience to the owners . . .*'

To build it they diverted the course of three rivers and uprooted many thousand poor people living in the Fleet Valley. And this work was done by men inexperienced in the task. No one had done it before. At least they did not encounter what the builders of the Moscow Underground came up against many years later, a quicksand in their path.

The line from Farringdon to Paddington opened on 9 January 1863. Victorian notables, among them Mr and Mrs Gladstone, travelled on the first train. At their destination a brass band was playing. There was a banquet in the evening for 700 people but Pearson was not there. He had died six months before.

The Metropolitan Company had offered him a reward for his efforts. He refused it, saying, 'I am the servant of the Corporation of London; they are my masters and are entitled to all my time and service. If you have any return to make you must make it to them.'

Nobody says that sort of thing nowadays.

Pearson was a brave man and a liberal, an early anti-racialist. He campaigned against the ban on the admission of Jews to the freedom of the city and as sworn brokers. It was he who helped to have removed those lines in the inscription on the Monument which accused Roman Catholics of starting the Great Fire of London.

Tom Murray did not want to have a lot of girfriends, but

just one for good, one he could be deeply serious about. He saw himself as a man who fell in love, not one who had affairs. It had shocked him to discover, while a student, that at least half the men in his year had had no love or emotional experience at all. Their sensual lives consisted in picking up half-drunk girls in pubs and spending the night with them, perhaps only seeing them once or twice more, or never again.

He wanted a great love and thought he had found her, for life, when he was eighteen. Diana was a music student like himself, she was beautiful, warm, loving, a serious person. But her parents moved to the United States, she transferred to an American university, and after a while stopped answering his letters. For a long time there had been no one else for him because he refused to compromise. Then, just before the accident, he had met a girl whose looks reminded him of Diana. She was a pianist and he met her while they were both taking part in a young performers' competition. But while he was in hospital he lost her. She came to see him once, was shy and vague and noncommittal, later wrote to say it was best for them not to see each other again.

During the months of recuperation and the months of rediscovering himself as a changed person, a quick-tempered, irritable person, nervous and hypochondriacal, Tom thought of sex and love as remote concepts that were not for him, that were ridiculous for him to consider. It was as if he said to himself that he had enough to worry about without that. But once at the School, in his own place and with his daily occupation, he began to think again of this dream woman, and added to the old notion of what she should be, which Diana had personified, was an idea of her as his rescuer, as someone who would save him and make him whole again.

He could not live as Jarvis did, a detached life with only

casual human contact. It appalled him to think of living as Tina did, with one lover after another, apparently not even selectively, or as Jed, long separated from his wife and child, consoled by the society of a bird. He envisaged marriage, a lifelong commitment, growing richer as time passed. The face that came before his eyes was Diana's, soft-featured, full-cheeked, the mouth dimpled at its corners, the eyes large and dark brown, the hair a rich mass of chestnut-brown silkiness. She must be a musician or one who loved music. She must have that quality, without which no woman could meet his exacting standard, a gift of caring and nurturing, a loving, maternal sweetness. He found himself looking for her in the street, in the trains that took him down to his busking. He was lonely and longing for someone who perhaps did not exist.

Like most musical children, Tom first played the recorder. He picked it up in an hour or two and went on to the guitar. His mother had a guitar she had played when she was young, in the sixties. His parents had no piano, but his grandmother had a baby grand and he taught himself to play that whenever he visited her. Soon he was learning the flute.

He was one of those people who can play any number of musical instruments. It is said that they play none really well but this was not true of Tom who looked like becoming a child virtuoso of the flute. No one knew quite why this did not happen, why he remained good but no better than that, nor why he failed the audition for admission to a county youth orchestra. Tom himself said it was because he had to work hard at school at subjects other than music, he could not devote himself wholeheartedly to the flute. His grandmother told his parents it was due to his talent being dispersed. He had found he had a good voice and was taking singing lessons, and he went on flirting with the piano and a trumpet he had bought between practising his flute.

Tom was his grandmother's only grandchild and one day, when he was fifteen and staying at her house in Rickmansworth in order to have access to the piano, she told him she was going to make him her heir.

'I've made a will and left you everything, Tom.'

He did not know what to say, so he said, 'Thank you very much.'

'I'm not making any conditions, I've already changed my will, but I'd like you to do one thing for me. Well, two things really. I'd like you to go on to a university and do music, but I think you'll do that anyway, and I'd like you to stop playing other instruments. I mean, give up the piano and that trumpet you say you've got.'

'It doesn't do me any harm.'

'For my sake, Tom, because I ask you.'

Tom thought this a ridiculous reason for doing something (or not doing something), because a person who knew nothing about it asked you. But he said he would, making a mental reservation that at any rate he would stop playing her piano. He did not stop playing the trumpet or taking singing lessons. Not playing her piano might have meant not going to Rickmansworth but he still went. He went more often. The idea of being nice to someone because they were going to leave you their money was not pleasant; Tom often told himself this, but it was the reason for his going to see his grandmother.

He also told her lies. Apart from saying he had given up singing and trumpet-playing, he invented things, such as that his school had suggested he go in for the Young Musician of the Year contest.

About his acceptance by the Guildhall School of Music and Drama he did not have to lie. He thought perhaps all lying would now be over because he was about to rush

37

along the highway to success, fame and fortune. Tom did very well at the Guildhall where nobody told him he should stop singing, a piece of good news he passed on triumphantly to his grandmother. It was after he had been spending a Sunday with her that the accident happened.

The accident changed Tom's life.

When he went home to his parents' house in Ealing or to the Barbican, his grandmother drove him the mile and a half to Rickmansworth station, which is up on the northern end of the Metropolitan Line. Sometimes, in good weather, he walked. The evening the accident happened was fine and he could have walked. In any case, his grandmother would have driven him. But while they were out in the garden during the afternoon they began talking to the man next door who had a motorbike and was leaving for the City on it at seven. Tom had never before ridden pillion on a motorbike, but Andy the neighbour had a spare crash helmet. For some complicated reason he made this trip every Sunday evening. Tom did not much like the long train journey through Harrow and Northwood and Wembley down to Baker Street, and the changing and the waiting. He accepted the offer of a lift.

They were on a narrow winding road which skirted Batchworth Heath when it happened. The distance from his grandmother's house was just over a mile. Andy overtook a container lorry, the kind of thing that should never have been on that road, and hit a Volvo estate car coming in the opposite direction. Everything was going too fast except Andy and he had not been going fast enough.

Tom was thrown clear. He flew through the air and struck his head against a tree, his life being saved by the helmet. Andy died quickly under the wheels of the Volvo.

The six months Tom spent in hospital prevented his return to college. He had a broken leg, several broken ribs, a broken collarbone and a very badly broken left hand.

'Lucky you're not a pianist,' said the orthopaedic surgeon.

The man probably thought you played the flute just with your mouth.

But it was not the damage to his hand or the rest of the obvious physical damage that made a tragedy for Tom. It was what had happened inside his head. Or what he *thought* had happened inside his head, for those at the hospital who were supposed to know told him the brain scan showed nothing untoward. He had not fractured his skull. His brain was undamaged. How to explain to them that he was changed? This quick temper that flared at nothing, that was new. This irritability. These headaches. Above all, this loss of ambition, drive and – immeasurably worst – his lost music, his lost love of it, need for it.

Tom went home to Ealing at last. The little finger on his left hand would be permanently stiff and the hand, though almost entirely usable, was not the shape it had once been. More operations on it were proposed. Tom did not know if he would have them. He did not know if he could play the flute and he was afraid to try.

His father said he must apply to return to college.

'They'll make me do my whole second year again,' said Tom. 'That's what they always do.'

'You don't know that till you try.'

'I won't get a grant for an extra year and I don't suppose you'll pay up.'

His father said not to talk to him like that, so Tom walked out and went to live with his grandmother in Rickmansworth. His grandmother said if it was a fact he would not get a grant she would finance him but that he should find out. It was surely only a matter of writing a letter or making a phone call. Tom agreed but trying to compose the letter brought on one of his headaches.

Secretly, he began playing the flute. He only played

when his grandmother was out. It was a great day when he found, not so much that he could still play, but that he still wanted to. For all that, his ineptitude caused him to fly into rages. If he had had the strength he would have broken the flute, but his left hand was too weak to apply the necessary force. Because he had to have money he got a job working in a sandwich bar near Baker Street. Some people his grandmother knew had a little girl who wanted to learn the flute and Tom started giving her lessons. Her parents did not seem to mind that he had no qualifications and had not finished his university course.

Most afternoons when his shift ended, he caught a Metropolitan train from Baker Street up to Rickmansworth, the Amersham Line. But sometimes he went down into London instead and roamed about, especially when it was warm. He liked listening to the street musicians who played at Covent Garden.

Once he went to a Prom at the Albert Hall. At that time there were never any buskers in Baker Street station and the ones he saw were at Leicester Square or Green Park. They played rock, which to Tom was a meaningless cacophony. He got talking to a man called Mac he met while listening to Vivaldi in Regent's Park and they agreed to try playing something in one of the Baker Street concourses.

Mac had said something about his fondness for wind instruments without actually saying what he played. Tom was aghast when he saw the bagpipes. He brought Ollie with him. Ollie could just about manage on the violin. Tom told himself that beggars could not be choosers and if he jibbed at playing the flute in this company he could always sing. It gratified him to discover how popular his singing was.

He and Ollie and Mac made a good team, playing at various Underground stations all that autumn and winter until Mac left because he had found a place to live up north and they took Peter on. They met Peter at Cambridge School, where they were all living. He had lost his job because the club where he played the piano had to close and, though he was after another one on the switchboard in a hospice, he was for the time being at a loose end. Peter could play a lot of instruments, though none very well.

When Tom told his grandmother he was moving out of her house and confessed – because since the accident he had also stopped lying, could not be bothered with prevarication – that he had been busking at stations, she told him she was horrified, she was disappointed in him.

'I've been ill,' he said. 'I'll never be the same again, do you realize that?'

'We'll none of us be the same again,' she said. 'People change all the time. Some people change for the better. You're not ill, it's all in your mind.'

'Look, I'll never be a concert flautist. My left hand will never work properly. I've got to have money, haven't I?'

'You've got to have qualifications in this world before you can get money. Tom, I'm asking you, I'm begging you, it's not too late. Let's sit down this evening, you and I, and write to the Guildhall School. If there's no grant forthcoming I'll pay.'

'They won't take me back.'

'Then we'll apply to others. We'll apply to all the schools of music and polytechnics in the country.'

'Look, I'll go back one day. I'm young, I can go back any time I want. I know I've got to go back, I know I need qualifications. But first I need money.'

He moved out next day. She was very cold with him. At the station, where she drove him, though he had been in the habit of regularly walking there, she refused to kiss him.

41

'Why don't you just go? 'I'll be in touch,' he said.

His hand was nearly all right. One day, he thought, he would have that operation and then he would apply to go to a university with a music course. But he was very young, he was not yet twenty-three. A year to make some money in could be spared from all the time in the world.

They went where they liked, played where they chose. Opinion was that Tottenham Court Road was the best pitch, the Central Line area. Tom didn't know that at that station you had to book your pitch in advance, add your name or the name of your band to the list under the No Smoking sign. A lot of Scots came this way via the Northern Line from King's Cross and they were giving their Scottish concert in the concourse when a heavy metal band arrived and told them roughly to move.

The railway police and station staff were always telling them that but they had never had it from fellow buskers before. The drummer lashed out at Tom and caught him a glancing blow on the jaw and Tom had to be held back by Ollie to prevent him retaliating. That was when they all realized acting like this was only playing into the hands of the authorities and giving them a real basis for enforcing their petty laws.

It also showed Tom something else: that busking was not what his grandmother and a lot of others seemed to think, just another kind of begging, but a real *musical* means of living, something you had to book and arrange like giving a concert in a concert hall. Unlike the noise made by the strummers who called it pop or country, his was serious music.

That day he committed himself to being a busker. He was a professional musician and the concourses of the Underground were his auditorium.

5

This would be the second time Mike's mother had looked after Catherine. She lived on the other side of Chelmsford and Alice took Catherine there in the carrying cot on the bus.

It was high summer, a warm sunny day. The baby was awake but fell asleep as they reached the house. Alice's mother-in-law thought she was going to have an afternoon's shopping, it was what she liked doing herself, and she believed, without any evidence for this, that Alice had been longing to get to the shops on her own. Shops were what she had missed most when she herself had been house-bound.

Alice gave her the bag in which Catherine's disposable nappies were and a change of clothes and she put the two bottles of formula into the fridge. The thought came to her that she might never see this woman again. Or this house, or this immaculate kitchen.

'She won't need all that,' said Mike's mother, eyeing the bottles. 'How ever long are you going to be?'

A lifetime. For ever. 'Not long. Mike starts a fortnight's holiday tomorrow.'

'Well, I know that. You're not going to be gone a fortnight, I hope. Though I must say I don't know that I'd very much mind having this little sweet one for a couple of weeks to myself.'

You may have to. 'Mike will be home at six.'

Alice told herself to stop making these appparently inconsequential statements. They were an expression of her inner fears and hopes. Fortunately, Mike's mother took them as further manifestation of her confused mental state.

43

The baby was asleep. Alice thought she could not leave her only child, her baby daughter, that she might never see again, without holding her once more, without at least giving her a last kiss. It was not possible to do that. Even if it meant disturbing her, waking her so that she cried when put down again, she must be lifted up in Alice's arms, held close to her and kissed goodbye.

Alice leant over the carrying cot. She touched the baby's cheek with her finger, turned quickly away.

'I'll go then.'

'Don't worry about a thing. Have a good time.'

The bus back took her past her own mother's house. Alice purposely did not look out of the window. She and Mike lived in a flat, very small, in a purpose-built block near the station. They had been there for six months, the duration of their marriage. Alice went up to the second floor in the lift, let herself into the flat and read, for the ninth or tenth time, the letter she had left for Mike. It was not a note but a long letter explaining everything, as long and taking her as long to compose as the last piece of writing she had done, an essay comparing and contrasting Verdi and Wagner and their operas.

Alice crumpled it up and pushed it into the kitchen bin. He might find it there but she did not think he would. Instead she wrote, on the back of a supermarket bill print-out: *I have left. I always said I would but you didn't believe me. Catherine is with your mother, Alice.* When she wrote Catherine's name she started to cry, but the thought of how ludicrous it would be, how corny, if a tear got on the note and smudged the biro, stopped her. It was then she understood that it was not too late to stay. She need not go. So far she had done nothing irrevocable. She could go down into the town centre and look at the shops, have a cup of coffee somewhere, get back to her mother-in-law by four. See Catherine again and bring her home.

Her packed suitcase was in the back of the bedroom cupboard. More valued, infinitely more *needed*, was the violin in its case on the living-room floor between the television and the bookshelves. She had not played it since two months before Catherine was born. On an impulse, she opened the case and took the violin out, held it and held the bow without applying it to the strings. She knew she was afraid to play after so long and knew too that if she stayed here she would never play again. But the sight and feel of it nerved her. It gave her courage. She replaced it in its case.

The money she had drawn out, emptying her account, less than a hundred pounds but better than nothing, was already in her bag. It was much too warm to wear a coat but it would be imprudent to leave her winter coat behind, and nights were always cold. Alice took off the cotton dress which was what young mothers wore in Chelmsford to shop in, put on jeans and a black T-shirt, the kind of clothes she would always wear now, through an indefinitely stretching future. The heavy, dark-blue broadcloth coat would not go into the suitcase. She put it over her shoulders. Carrying the suitcase in one hand and the violin in the other, she walked the two hundred yards to Chelmsford station and caught the 15.53 to London. They had bought the flat because it was convenient for Mike's daily train.

Later her mother was to say, 'It's beyond belief, you left the baby behind and took the violin!'

It was some time since Alice had been in London. While at the Royal Academy of Music she had lived there but that, though not much more than a year ago, now seemed infinitely distant. A lifetime intervened, Catherine's gestation and her short existence. Liverpool Street station, in process of being rebuilt, was dirty and noisy and very large. Alice thought, as she looked for signs to the Underground, I am frightened. I am afraid of what I have done and where I am going. By where she was going she meant her uncertain, unpredictable future, not the hotel in Bloomsbury which was just a jumping-off ground.

Once, like many Londoners, Alice had carried in her head a basic tube map, at least of inner London, but she had forgotten it. Holborn could be reached directly by the Central Line, she discovered from a wall plan. I mustn't go the wrong way, Alice thought to herself as she made her way to the platform. I must remember I want a westbound train, not find myself heading off back into Essex.

She had reached London at the height of the rush. There was no hope of getting a seat. She stood against the glass partition by the double-leaved doors with the violin and the suitcase wedged behind her calves. By now her mother-in-law would be wondering what had become of her. She had not specified, but somewhere around four-thirty to five would have been a reasonable time to return. It was a quarter past five, she saw from the clock on Bank Station. Her mother-in-law would be looking at the clock too, perhaps walking up and down with Catherine in her arms.

A lot more people got in, and at St Paul's, just when Alice thought it was impossible for more to get in, five did. Someone pushed them from behind, pushed their backs with the flat of his hand, and the doors closed. The edge of the violin case cut into her leg. The coat felt insufferably hot, she thought she had seen people looking at the coat with amusement, but there was nothing she could do. There was nowhere to put it down. Catherine would be awake and would find Mike's mother unfamiliar. Suppose she cried because Alice was not there? Alice had not thought of that before. What have I done? She made a sound and suppressed it.

Mike's office was near Chancery Lane, that was his station, he must use this line. She had never thought of that before either. By now he would be in the train, the 17.20, that got to Chelmsford just after ten to six. He always got that train, he was entirely reliable, steady, though no older than she, designed for a good husband and father. A good father was what he was beyond everything. If he had been indifferent to Catherine, if he had not loved her at least as much, more, than she did herself, she could not have done it.

It should have been a relief to escape from the train at Holborn but as she crossed the platform and began to mount the stairs a feeling of confusion and disorientation took hold of her. At the top she stood leaning against the wall; her breathing had become strange. It was as if when she caught her breath she would necessarily break into a hysterical laughing and crying. She swallowed, forced herself to draw a long breath. The coat had made her so hot that she was sweating heavily. Sweat was actually running down her face like tears.

What happens next will seal my fate: the places I find, the letters I write, even the people I meet who point me this way or that. Alice set down the case and violin and wiped her face on her sleeve, wiped it on the rough wool sleeve of her winter coat. I am entering my true life, the life I was prevented from leading – well, that I prevented myself from leading by my stupidity, my incredible folly. Whatever happens to me now will be new, will be an advancement, an adventure, and it will not be Chelmsford. My life, which was held up, has begun again.

The sound of music met her as she approached the concourse where the escalators were. She walked on, towards the music.

In her time at the Royal Academy she remembered buskers in the tube, but they played rock or sometimes

47

jazz. The sound she was approaching, though hackneyed, its value almost destroyed by its popularity, was what the world called classical: an air of Mozart, a little night music.

Alice saw the musicians as she came to the end of the passage.

There were two of them, two men. One was playing a flute, the other a guitar. The guitar was not a suitable instrument for this piece and Alice could see that he was providing only a background strumming. His guitar case lay open on the floor in front of him and, as she watched, a woman coming down dropped a copper coin into it.

The man with the guitar was dark and smooth-faced, with longish hair, a sensitive mouth. He looked in his forties. His companion was much younger, perhaps no older than herself, fair, very good-looking, blue-eyed, with the sort of open face that persuades you its possessor must be gentle and kind. Alice had stopped to listen to them because this man, this kind-faced fair one, was quite a good performer.

She put her case and her violin down against the wall. The Mozart came to an end and she clapped. Someone always has to start the clapping and when she did a few others followed. A man put a 5p piece into the guitar case and then Alice put a 10p piece in. The fair man said thank you and he and the guitarist began to play Tchaikovsky. The music they played gradually grew familiar to Alice; it was music for the violin, the famous Violin Concerto, and it sounded very strange on the flute and guitar, so strange that it took her a moment or two to recognize it. They managed to render the melody, the tune.

Her instinct was to ignore the look the fair man was giving her, a look that was hopeful and inviting. She intended to pick up her cases and proceed with what she was here to do, go up and out into the street and thence to Streatham Street to find the hotel. But she hesitated. The

48

certainty that this particular music was being played directly at her and for her, that the fair man had seen her violin case and perhaps a look in her eyes of wistfulness, the fair man alone, for the guitarist seemed only there for support and back-up, decided her. Except that it was not really a decision, more an unthought-out reaction.

Alice squatted down, opened the case, took out her violin and bow and, hesitating only for a moment, walked over to stand by the others. The flute faltered, the flute-player stepped aside and indicated to her the place between himself and the hollow-cheeked man with the guitar. Alice caught a reassuring smile from the guitarist.

She began to play.

When Alice was sixteen her mother, angry with her about something, said in a fury, 'You needn't think being good-looking is going to be an advantage in life. It won't be. It'll be a burden.'

Even then she knew her mother said 'good-looking' when she meant 'beautiful', just as she said 'fond of' when she meant 'love'. And she also knew she was beautiful, enjoyed it, and that her mother, also beautiful, could see her own looks fading.

'You'll never know if people want you for your looks or for yourself. If you ever get to be a concert violinist, which I personally doubt, you'll always wonder if people want you on the platform because of your looks or because you're any good.'

'It doesn't work like that,' she had said loftily. 'You don't know anything about it.'

'You think it's going to be so marvellous having men buzzing round you, but it won't be for long, and then what'll you have when it stops?'

'My music.'

Alice, playing her violin at Holborn station, took it for

granted, she did not even have to think about it, that the man playing the flute beside her had invited her to play because she was beautiful. He wanted her to remain, to go on to Vivaldi and the Handel marches because her playing was good. She did not think it good, it was the first time she had played for weeks and the sounds she made disquieted her, but perhaps it was good enough for busking. She could not help observing that more coins fell into the guitar case behind her than had done before she began.

She had rolled up her coat and laid it on her suitcase. Playing had a liberating effect on her. She understood the true meaning of a phrase she had often heard but never defined: in her element. Incongruously, ridiculously, here in this Underground station, with musicians she did not know, playing to an unknown, only occasionally appreciative and ever-shifting audience, she was in her own element.

The fair man whispered to her, 'One final piece and then we'll call it a day. Can you do the "Entry of the Queen of Sheba"? They like that.'

'I can try.'

'You're great.'

She smiled at him. The guitar had no place here and the guitarist sat back with a grin, his back to the open case, and let them get on with it. They played it as a duet, perfectly teamed, at the fast pace the piece demanded, rollicking and dramatic. Alice ended with a flourish of her bow, held it high in the air and found herself laughing in triumph.

There was real applause this time, as at a real concert. She turned smiling to the flautist. For a moment she thought he was going to throw his arms round her and hug her, she was sure he had been thinking of it, but he hesitated and she turned away.

'You've done that before,' the guitarist said, scooping the coins from the case and into a large brown envelope.

'Not in the tube.' She giggled, pointing to a notice on the wall. 'Look. *Busking or playing musical instruments in the Underground, to the annoyance of other passengers, is an offence* ... It says you can be fined £50.'

'No one ever is. I'm called Peter and he's Tom.'

'Alice.'

'They never executes nobody nohow,' said the man called Peter.

'Other passengers aren't annoyed, you see. They love it.' This was Tom. 'It brightens up their dreary journeys. Look, you've a right to some of this.' He took the envelope from Peter. 'You've a right to at least a third, maybe more. You really drew the crowds with your playing.'

'And she's prettier than us.'

Alice shook her head. 'I don't want it. You keep it. I've got to go.'

She looked up the range of escalators. It was the gateway to life and one she suddenly had no wish to pass through, one she felt a gripping fear of passing through. But every day now would bring its own fear, a series of terrors. She must face them, get on with them, begin now. She put the violin back into its case, picked up the bundle she had made of her coat and thrust it under her arm as she hoisted up her suitcase.

'Well, goodbye. I really enjoyed that.'

'How about joining us at Green Park tomorrow?'

'I won't be there,' Peter said. 'Got to work.'

'What's this then if it's not work?'

'You know what I mean.'

'Have you got to work too?' Tom said, looking at Alice.

'No.' She felt like telling him who she was and what she had done, only he wouldn't be interested, he'd be embarrassed. 'I haven't got to do anything. I mean, I've really got to do *everything* and I start tomorrow.' He was nodding, looking as if he understood. 'I must go.'

'Where are you going?'

'Well, it's a hotel, a sort of hotel. A girl I was at school with, her mother runs it. You won't want to hear about this, it's boring. I'm going to stay there for a bit while I look round for a place.'

Tom said, 'Please come to Green Park tomorrow. Say you will. Please.'

She was almost amused by his vehemence. 'Why?'

'You're so beautiful to look at, isn't she, Pete? And you're a beautiful violinist. Are you really looking for a place?'

Alice lifted her shoulders, trying to seem indifferent. 'Who isn't?'

'I might be able to help. Come to Green Park tomorrow.'

She used one of Mike's worn-out expressions, immediately wished she had not. 'That's an offer I can't refuse.'

They went up to the street with her, Tom carrying her coat and Peter her case. Alice waved as they went back down, until they were lost to sight on their way to Bond Street and then, they had said, to West Hampstead on the Jubilee.

An hour had passed since she had thought about Catherine, about her and Mike and what would be going on at home. This now returned and it seemed that her meeting with Tom and Peter had been like a dream from which she was waking up to reality. It was very light outside, a shock of harsh brightness. London felt hot and dusty and the air smelt different from Chelmsford air, a compound of diesel and petrol fumes, exotic tobacco, oriental cooking and occasionally a whiff of urine.

She found the hotel. Mrs Archer told her that apart from three vacant rooms 'for the tourism', all the others were let off to the council, who put homeless people into them. These were mostly Somalis and Sudanis. Mrs Archer sniffed and shrugged her shoulders, admitting that the money was good.

It was not Alice's idea of a Bloomsbury hotel. Shabbiness she had expected, but not dirt and this air of something disreputable lurking though unseen. She was told where her room was and on the stairs – there was no lift – encountered a young woman in a black veil with a small pretty face peeping between the folds. Four small children trooped down behind her. Alice's room was tiny, with a single bed, one other piece of furniture apart from the wall cupboard, a small chair, and a narrow window that would not open. Later as she lay in that bed, after she had eaten a meal in a small cheap café in New Oxford Street, she squirmed between sheets of a kind she had never seen before, purple knitted nylon. It seemed to her as if every hair on her body, every roughness of skin, unevenness of toenail, snagged on the sticky, shiny fibres. She turned this way and that, imagining Catherine in her cot beside the bed in which Mike slept alone.

By five in the morning she had decided to go back, to return to them and forget music, blame her defection on a temporary post-natal madness. She slept, woke up at nine to find out her second mistake: that all hotels everywhere serve breakfast. The café which had provided her supper had coffee and Danish pastries on offer. Drinking the thin, bitter coffee, she reverted to the ideas of the night, to returning home, and before she had finished it was resolved on packing her things and making her way to Holborn station and thence to Liverpool Street.

The map of the London Underground, which can be seen inside every train, on all stations, on the back of the London A–Z guide, on tea-cloths on sale at the London Transport Museum, on posters, in diaries and in sundry other places, has been called a model of its kind, a work of art.

It was designed by Henry Beck and first used by London Transport on posters in 1933. They paid him five guineas, or £5.25 for it. It has been reproduced in millions and has served as the model for metro maps all over the world.

The last to carry the signature Henry C. Beck in the lower lefthand corner was issued in 1959. Today's version is irritatingly called by London Transport Underground a 'journey planner'.

It presents the underground network as a geometric grid. Some say that if you stood it up-ended on your roof it would look like a television aerial.

The tube lines do not, of course, lie at right angles to one another like the streets of Manhattan. Nor do they branch off at acute angles or form perfect oblongs. A true map of the London Underground shows the central complex as a shape suggestive of a swimming dolphin, its snout being Aldgate, its forehead Old Street, the crown of its head King's Cross, its spine Paddington, White City and Acton, its tail Ealing Broadway and its underbelly the stations of Kensington. The outer configurations branch out in graceful tentacles. The seal has become a medusa, a jellyfish. Its extremities touch Middlesex and Hertfordshire, Essex and Surrey. A claw penetrates Heathrow.

The Metropolitan Line, which was begun in 1863, had additions made throughout the 1860s and 1870s and in 1882 and 1884. The District Line, which was begun in 1865, continued to grow until 1902. Additions were made to the Central Line, first opened in 1900, in 1908, 1912, 1920 and 1946–9. The years between 1860 and 1884 saw the building of the Circle, for a long time called the Inner Circle.

The Northern Line was begun in 1890 but added to throughout the twentieth century until 1941. A new terminus and intervening stations were added to the Piccadilly Line of 1903–7 in 1933 and 1971. London's only entirely new tube line in recent times, the Victoria, opened in 1971, and the Jubilee, only a small part of which was new, the rest the partially transformed Bakerloo of 1905–15, was completed in 1979.

Since then the Docklands Light Railway has branched off the network to serve the redeemed areas of London's east river.

By eleven she was in Green Park Underground station with her violin, looking for Tom, lured to him by the sound of the flute reaching her as she descended the escalator.

'I didn't think you'd come.'

'I nearly didn't,' she said. 'I nearly went back to where I came from.'

He looked inquiringly at her, waiting for her to say more, but when she did not introduced the man he was with as Ollie, another guitarist. This was Ollie's last time, he said, he was going to live in France.

'They all move away,' said Tom.

'I expect I shall. I'll have to. I can't afford to stay in this awful dump I'm in for long.'

He started singing then and they accompanied him. Alice suggested he try the Don's serenade from *Don Giovanni*. They had no mandolin but Ollie's guitar would do. While he sang to the girl the Don wants to come to her window, calling her his treasure, asking her not to be cruel, at least to let him see her, he looked at Alice, turned his face away from the audience who had gathered and looked at her.

She was rather embarrassed but people loved it. A lot of coins were thrown into the guitar case and some of them were pounds. Alice had a poor opinion of her own voice, an uncertain soprano, but when Tom suggested the duet the Don sings with Zerlina she agreed. He sang in the words of the aria that she should give him her hand and put his out to her, but she pretended not to understand. People clapped. Ollie scooped out the money and found just a little short of £15.

'We usually bring our own food and eat it in the park,'

Tom said, 'but today we thought we'd eat a proper meal in a café with you.'

'But you didn't expect me to come.'

'I half did. I hoped you would.'

It was a sandwich bar like the one he had worked in. They made just enough money busking for him not to have to go back to that. Alice thought it sounded a hand-to-mouth existence. She did not tell them she had never had a job, had been supported by a husband she had left. When the coffee came Tom said she could come and live at Cambridge School if she liked.

'A school?'

'It used to be. It's just a house now where people rent rooms, only the rent's very low. There's a room free now Ollie's going. I asked the man who owns it and he said you could have the Headmaster's Study.'

She laughed. 'It sounds like a good address.'

'Say you will.'

'Leave her alone,' said Ollie. 'Let her make up her own mind. She ought to see it first.'

'Of course she'll see it. We'll go up there now.'

The Headmaster's Study was on the first floor next to Four. Alice, who had several times caught Tom looking admiringly at her while they were coming up there in the tube, and could not forget the way he had held out his hand to her while they sang the duet, wondered if having the room next to his was a good idea. But it was the only one available, since Jarvis did not want to let the other rooms on the second floor. The sound of the trains she was sure would prevent her sleeping at night. But she took it. The absurd rent lured her, it made her hundred pounds look less pathetic than it had when she checked into Mrs Archer's hotel.

Tom insisted on going back with her to Streatham

Street to fetch her suitcase and winter coat. On the return journey he told her all about himself and he held up his left hand for her scrutiny. It looked the same as the other one to her, except perhaps that the knuckle bone of the little finger was more prominent than the rest and the finger itself rather stiff.

'I think your grandmother was right. You should go back to college.'

'I don't mind you saying it.'

'That's what I've come to London for. I've got to go on studying. I want to go to Brussels, that's the best place. We ought to have a national conservatoire of music in this country but we don't.'

'I'll go back to college one day. I have this feeling I'll know when the time's right. I'll have to pay for it myself too, but I will. It would be wrong to rush into anything.'

She nodded, not taking in much of what he said. Being alone, as she soon would be, was a threatening thing. She did not want to find herself alone in that Headmaster's Study, where she would have to begin to think. For the first time since her escape she was very conscious of the fact that she had given birth only a month before and could even fancy she felt a pulling sensation where the fundament stitches had been. She was sore and uncomfortable, perhaps because she had been standing for so long and walking so much. If she was alone she was afraid she might begin to cry.

The last thing she wanted was for Tom to take her under his wing, to regard her in some sense as his find and his property, but that was what was happening. He said they must meet later, she must come and eat with him in his room and he would get a bottle of wine. Then he left her.

To avoid introspection she concentrated on her surroundings. Nothing remained to show that the headmaster had

had his daily being here, perhaps here conducted interviews with backsliding pupils, commended scholars. There was no desk, only a big bed someone had made up with whose sheets she did not know, an armchair and a table, a cupboard, a window through which the passing trains could be seen, tube trains and Metropolitan trains and the trains that went up to the Chilterns. She had seen a phone in the big hall they called the vestibule.

Her mind emptied. She sat on the bed and real life came rushing in to fill the vacuum. She thought of Mike starting his holiday today. He would be at his mother's and Catherine would be there too and they would be talking about her, that was all they would talk about. They would be saying she was mad and her behaviour beyond their understanding. Mike's mother would say she was mad and wicked. By this time, if not long before, they would have phoned her parents and talked it all over with them.

Alice decided to tell no one about it. She would keep it to herself. There was no point in talking about it to someone who did not know the personalities involved and could not appreciate the circumstances. She resolved on this but three hours later, having eaten Tom's Indian takeaway and drunk half Tom's wine, she was telling him her whole history.

Tom said, 'Why did you get married? Why didn't you have an abortion?'

He could not know it but to talk of aborting Catherine, who was a living child, a person, was like coolly contemplating murder. To talk of it now, that is. She had thought of it then.

'Everyone got at me,' she said. 'It's hard to explain because you think I'm strong.'

He had said so. She must be strong to leave like that, to make plans for leaving and carry them out.

'I'd just left the Royal Academy, I'd just got the results

58

of my finals. Mike was *pleased* I was pregnant. He wanted to be married and have a family and he said this way I'd have to marry him.'

'Did he do it on purpose?'

'No, it was my fault, it was an accident. I'd never thought of marrying him, he was just a boyfriend, he didn't even seem all that attractive after I got pregnant. Then my parents and his parents started on me. My mother said she didn't know what things were coming to when you had to make girls get married because in her youth it was always the boys who didn't want to.'

She thought he was going to start talking about abortions again. He only said, 'You didn't have to do what they said.'

'I gave in. I know it was weak. I was one of those people who're sick all the time in pregnancy, not just in the mornings, I was sick day after day for hours. I couldn't go out, I couldn't do anything. Mike was there every day, being nice to me and telling me not to worry about anything, he'd found this flat and his mother was seeing to furnishing it and they were making arrangements for the wedding. I just gave in, I hadn't the strength to resist them. A week before the wedding the sickness stopped and my mother said it had been psychological, she said that "deep down inside" – I'm quoting her – I longed for marriage and once I knew I was really going to get married I stopped worrying.'

'What would you have done if you hadn't got pregnant?'

'I was going to be a concert violinist.' She looked at him. 'I'm still going to be. That's why I ran away. That's why I left my baby.'

Her eyes filled with tears and she began to cry. Tom got up and went to sit beside her. He took her hand, then when she seemed not to mind this, put his arms round her. She sobbed and he held her close to him.

6

*A dark purplish-red, or burgundy, is the colour of the Metropoli-
tan, green of the District, yellow of the Circle, scarlet of the
Central, brown of the Bakerloo, dark blue of the Piccadilly and
black of the Northern. These are the colours of lines on Beck's
map and also sometimes of station trims and new station bucket
seats.*

*On the map the Victoria Line became light blue. When the
Jubilee Line was nearly finished there was some speculation as to
what colour would be used for it. Possibilities remaining were
pink, lime green, orange and mauve.*

London Transport Underground chose grey.

*Pink has been given, unexpectedly and without precedent, to
the Hammersmith branch of the Metropolitan.*

The days went by and Alice did not phone her mother.
Each day she had gone with Tom and Peter or just with
Tom down into the Underground and played her violin.
This, in spite of resolving not to do it again, not to lower
her standards, which playing pop classics against a background noise of trains and pounding feet and chatter, yells
and whistles and rival groups, seemed to her to be.

Standing there with the violin tucked under her chin
and the bow in her hand, she was removed from anxiety
and from thinking of Catherine. In a way it was as if she
was drugged. She felt set apart. The people who passed by,
sometimes pausing to give them money, were the others.
She and Tom and Peter were special and different, allied
by their music.

It kept her from worry and it kept her from settling
down to write those applications which would lead to

progress in her career of serious music. Alice had already told herself that it would be stupid to think about those applications yet. Apart from still being post-parturitive, she was in a state of shock – self-induced shock but shock just the same. The worst thing for her was to be alone. The best thing at the moment was to be with someone who admired her and was kind.

While Tom played his flute or sang, she played her violin, not much liking the sounds she heard herself making, sometimes even glad there was so much background racket and an undiscerning audience. But she had re-entered the world of music, she comforted herself with this; in the least expected way she was back in the life from which Mike and his family and marriage had threatened to cut her off for ever.

That night, after she had confided in Tom and begun to cry, he had comforted her, held her in his arms and kissed her. If he had not known she had had a baby only a month before he would have wanted to make love to her, she was sure of that. But she did not know if she would ever want to make love to Tom. Would she, come to that, with any man ever again? Alice's body felt cold and closed-up and stiff except where it felt sore and vulnerable, and her mind felt sore all over.

She slept badly. By the third day the silence from Mike and her parents and his parents grew uncanny. Yet how could it be otherwise when they did not know where she was? She asked herself which of them she should phone and found herself trembling at the thought of phoning any of them. His parents were impossible, her mother-in-law would just put the phone down. As she stood there in the vestibule, in front of the carved names of Cambridge School's distinguished pupils, all the Dorothys and Joans and Ediths and Hildas, the glass-panelled front door opened and an old woman let herself in. She said good morning to

Alice and Alice said hallo. She was thin and rather tall with a very lined gentle face and hair that was white but which Alice could see had once been blonde. She could also have told this was Tina's mother before Mrs Darne went off down the passage that led to the Headmaster's Flat. Alice thought it would be easier to phone someone like that than her own mother if you had done what she had done, but she could be wrong there. Appearances were deceptive and her own mother looked handsome and smart and had what people called a very sweet expression.

Still, it was her mother she must phone and that by default. Apart from other considerations, many other almost insuperable obstacles, in order to get hold of Mike or her father she would have to go through switchboards and in her father's case a secretary. She dialled her mother's number and nearly put the phone down when it started ringing.

When her mother answered, she said the stupid thing she always said to those who were supposed to be close to her, 'It's me.'

There was silence. Alice heard her mother's indrawn breath. More silence, nothing. She expected the receiver to be replaced.

'It's me. It's Alice.'

'I heard you the first time,' her mother said.

Alice waited. At least her mother had spoken.

'I think you must have lost your mind.'

'All right, I can understand people might think that,' Alice said. 'I had to leave, that's all. If I'd left it longer I might never have gone.'

'Then it's a great pity you didn't leave it longer. Who do you think is looking after your baby? Did you think of that? Are you going to condescend to tell anyone when you're coming back?'

'I'm not coming back.'

'Alice, you *are* coming back. You are having some sort of mental breakdown. The best thing will be to tell me where you are and Daddy will come and fetch you, or Mike will. Well, Daddy will. Mike's too angry and upset to do anything. You need to see a doctor. You probably need to be hospitalized.'

Alice had always called her mother Mummy. This would no longer do. 'Mother,' she said, 'I left because I want to be a musician, I don't want to be someone's mother and someone's wife. I don't love Mike, I don't even like him any more.' If she mentioned Catherine's name she knew her voice would break. 'I'm not going to tell you where I am. Not yet. But I'll tell you one thing. I'm a violinist now, I'm free to be that. I don't expect you to understand.'

Marcia Anderson gave her hard little laugh. It always made Alice wince. 'Mike saw you'd taken your violin. You left your baby and took your violin.'

'Goodbye, Mother,' said Alice. 'Give my love to my father.'

'I shan't bother, he's never going to speak to you again,' said Marcia.

Alice looked up at the lamp which was like an iron tarantula hanging from its web. Leaning her head back kept the tears inside her eyes. She thought, I'm not going to cry any more, it's stupid and awful, wanting to cry for everything. She stood there, leaning on the phone table, and started reading the names incised into the wood. She made herself read to keep from crying: Hilda Bevans, two credits, three passes in Oxford School Certificate, 1944; Marjorie Grace Pickthorne, one distinction, two credits, four passes in Oxford School Certificate, 1945. From behind the door of Remove came the regular faint clatter of Jarvis's typewriter.

The first trains were drawn by steam engines. The smoke and steam had to escape and passengers had to breathe. A civil servant home on furlough from Egypt said the tunnels smelt like a crocodile's breath. In the end they used a locomotive which diverted the steam into tanks behind the engine by means of a ducted exhaust. When the train emerged from the tunnel the tanks were opened and the steam released.

The point beyond Paddington Station chosen for the release of underground steam was in Bayswater, among the new terraces of five-storey houses then being built. In order not to spoil the appearance of Leinster Gardens, façades were put up where numbers 23 and 24 should be, at a glance indistinguishable from their neighbours but easily spotted by the observant eye.

I was first taken to see these 'houses' by my father when I was nine; I have often wondered since then why they had never become a tourist attraction. From the opposite pavement in Leinster Gardens, sandwiched between two hotels, the Blakemore and the Henry VIII, they present an appearance of early decay. It is possible to see that they had never been lived in, could never be lived in, though front door and portico are present and their ranks of windows, the spaces where the glass should be painted a dull blue. On that first occasion my father took me through Craven Hill Gardens into Porchester Terrace, showed me the blank brick back of the façades and lifted me up on to the wall so that I could look down into the shaft. I asked my father about the people in the adjoining houses, they must have lived in perpetual fog, and I remember he told me that perhaps they got their houses at a reduced rent.

Mrs Darne was coming back from Tina's. She had a shopping list in her hand which she put into her handbag when she saw Alice. They had already spoken, so this time Mrs Darne only smiled and Alice managed a faint smile back. Her mother's words rang in her ears. She was making an ineffectual effort to keep herself from trembling. Mrs Darne, she guessed, would be too polite, too gentlewomanly, to let herself notice. As the old woman reached the front door there came distantly but tremendously, with a long reverberating thunderousness, the sound of an explosion.

Mrs Darne said, 'Goodness, what was that?'

She had a voice and intonation exactly like those of the history mistress at Alice's school, an elderly lady, rumoured to be a baronet's sister.

Alice went outside with her. The sound was over and silence was back, or what passed for silence here. A train ran by. The front garden of Cambridge School was like a piece of meadow, long grass, willow herb, daisies and golden rod. A laburnum growing out of the midst of it was in flower.

'I suppose that was a bomb.'

'I suppose it was,' said Alice.

'There were houses all down this side of the street once,' said Mrs Darne, 'but they were bombed in the war. That was the night all our windows blew out. We had a Morrison shelter and we were under that, my husband and myself and his mother. Of course, that was long before Tina was born.'

'Perhaps it was just a car backfiring,' said Alice, 'or even thunder.'

'No, it was a bomb,' said Mrs Darne in the tone of an expert.

Alice went back into the house and upstairs to the Headmaster's Study. She had borrowed a small tape recorder from Jarvis and was going to record her own playing, a critical exercise that she had postponed from day to day. She took her violin out of its case, feeling afraid.

Accommodation was plentiful at Cecilia Darne's house where all those years ago a bomb had blown the windows out. It was a fine large house, built in the last decade of the nineteenth century of red brick and red tiles.

By Tina's standards and those of her friends, it was enormous. When she was in her teens she had even felt ashamed, having to confess to people she knew that she and her mother lived all alone in it instead of letting bits of it off as flats. But when Cecilia was married in 1940 and first went to live there it was thought a poor sort of house, semi-detached, shabby and in a dowdy district. The Jarvis family had all come down in the world, considering the money their Victorian grandfather, a manufacturer of bathroom fittings, had made for them, Ernest with the dwindling Cambridge School, Evelina nutty as a squirrel's cage and with her first sojourn in a nursing home behind her, Cecilia married to a Customs officer.

The house was called Lilac Villa, a name no one used, though the front garden contained several ancient gnarled lilac bushes. High-ceilinged large rooms filled the three storeys. On the top floor the bedrooms had pretty sloping ceilings and dormer windows peering out under eyelid gables. The front windows stared into a row of typical West Hampstead studios, red brick, balconied and with Gothic windows from a design by Burne-Jones. Tina had lived up there with her children when Brian threw her out, but ate downstairs because Cecilia was a good cook and the television was in the drawing room.

Tina never felt guilty about anything, but Cecilia was guilty all the time. She blamed herself for the way Tina was, though she did not know what she had done wrong, and she blamed herself for not trying harder to keep Tina in her house when she wanted to go off to Jarvis Stringer's. Cecilia was willing to do anything to make up to Tina for the deprivations of her childhood, though what these deprivations were she hardly knew. They must have been there because people only grew up like Tina when they had had a hard time as children. Perhaps she had been too old for parenthood, and then it was very sad for a girl to lose her father in her teens. Perhaps she should have had a brother or sister for Tina, though being well into her forties by then and having waited twelve years for Tina to come along made that impossible.

When Cecilia looked back to Tina's childhood it was always that particular day when Ernest Jarvis had hanged himself that she remembered. Tina was seven, very pretty and sweet, with long blonde hair. Even then she had found it difficult to get up in the morning, had begged and pleaded to be allowed to lie in a little longer, had gone back to sleep more often than not, the forerunner, Cecilia supposed, of her present practice of often lying in bed till noon. It was while Cecilia was running upstairs for the third time to tell Tina she must get up, she really must or she would be late for school, that she heard the Cambridge School bell utter a single toll.

The strange thing was that she knew it was Ernest's bell, the bell she had tactfully told him would be unsuitable for the kind of school he had in mind. She stood on the stairs by the open window, waiting for the next stroke of the bell, waiting in fact for this sign of Ernest's madness. It would not be too extreme to ascribe insanity to a headmaster with no pupils ringing a long-silent bell in an empty school. Besides, Cecilia had the example of poor Evelina before her and the recollection of a family rumour that a brother of that manufacturing grandfather had died in a lunatic asylum.

No second stroke came. Fifteen minutes were to pass before the bell rang a second time, succeeded by that awful rattle. Cecilia had closed the window and gone on upstairs to find dear little Tina up and dressed and trying to brush out the tangles in her golden hair. She had been a very affectionate child, climbing on Cecilia's knee to hug her, sitting with her arm round her father and her head on his shoulder. Cecilia sometimes wondered if this was the precursor of all that sex she seemed so fond of later on. She, Cecilia, though a loving, kind and humble woman, touched no one if she could help it and thought this reserve might be connected with her never having been much for sex. Of course she had touched Tina and kissed and cuddled her – too much or too little?

Tina said a terrible thing to her when she was seventeen, two years after her father died. It was in the late sixties, an awful time in Cecilia's opinion. Morals began to lose their meaning and people said anything that came into their heads, the sort of thing that used to appear in books as a row of stars or be written down on slips of paper and handed to judges in court.

'If you and Daphne had been young today,' Tina said, 'I suppose you'd have realized you were in love with each other and just lived together.'

Cecilia was speechless. She blushed deeply; Tina laid a hand on her arm and laughed merrily.

'Oh, Tina,' said Cecilia, 'what a terrible thing to say to me, what a really terrible thing.'

'No need to freak out,' said Tina in the parlance of the time. She held her mother's hot fidgety hand and stroked it kindly. 'If that's the way you are, that's the way you are. I don't suppose it's too late anyway. You look quite young for your age.'

Cecilia tried to gather together some dignity. She was near to tears. 'Daphne is my closest friend, Tina. We've been best friends since our first day at school, when we were five. I am very fond of her and I respect her as she respects me.'

Tina only laughed and shook her head. But the next time Cecilia saw Daphne Bleech-Palmer Tina's words came back to her and she was for a while shy and constrained. If they had not been in the habit of seeing each other so often, at least once a week and sometimes more, talking on the phone every day, that appalling suggestion might have driven a bolt through their friendship, eventually destroying it. But Daphne's dear familiarity, the pleasure of her company, the comfort of knowing pretty well what she would say in response to any remark, the whole warm, easy, *ancient* closeness that had subsisted between them for more than half a century, won over Cecilia's temporary, though profound, embarrassment. It had been deepest at the moment just inside the Bleech-Palmer front door when, as always, Daphne set her plump hands on Cecilia's shoulders and lifted her lips to Cecilia's cheek. The blood had run into Cecilia's face and she felt that its hot presence under her skin must burn Daphne's mouth.

But Daphne only smiled and, as also was customary, asked after Tina. They were both widows, so there was no husband's welfare to inquire about. Cecilia forced herself to show an interest in Daphne's son and Daphne's garden and after a while things grew easier. Their frequent meetings gradually heaped oblivion on Tina's remark and if Cecilia never entirely forgot it, it surfaced only when something was said that dug into that particular muddy accumulation. A piece, for instance, about homosexuals on the television, which was all too frequent, or some comment on the things Peter got up to.

One of them phoned the other every evening. Daphne, whom Cecilia suspected of being rather less well-off than she was herself, though this was not a matter to delve into, phoned her just after six on alternate evenings and she phoned Daphne on the others. The arrangement was to wait until after six because that was when the cheap rate started.

Cecilia always waited until after 6.30. She liked to watch the early evening news on BBC 1 and see it through to the end so that she could get the weather forecast. Daphne tended to phone her just after six, which meant missing fifteen or twenty minutes of the news, but Cecilia never said anything about this because she would far rather miss the news than hurt Daphne. She could always watch it at nine, though this was not the same. By nine she felt, knowing this to be illogical, that the news was stale and she had passed three foolish hours in ignorance of disaster or even, very occasionally, of something wonderful.

It was her turn to phone Daphne this evening. Cecilia sat in her comfortable drawing room on the sofa-bed that was always a sofa and never a bed – 'But you've got *five* bedrooms, Ma,' said Tina who had her eye on it – and turned on the television at twenty seconds to six. She had learned to time it so as not to hear the tail end of the terrible *Neighbours* music which, no matter how much you hated it, was a tune you could easily get on the brain.

The first item on the news was the bomb. It *had* been a bomb. It had gone off in a hotel in Leinster Place and would always in future be known as the 'Bayswater Bomb'. Two people had been killed, a waitress and a hotel guest, and five injured. If it had been timed to go off an hour later, probably it *had* been timed to go off an hour later but something had gone wrong, the hotel dining room would have been full and the results of the explosion much worse. Cecilia thought this would not be much comfort to the relatives and friends of the waitress and the guest. The waitress was only nineteen.

There followed a catalogue of bomb outrages in London in recent and distant years. No terrorist group had yet claimed responsibility. Cecilia reflected on how massive the explosion must have been for her and that beautiful girl to have heard it up here in West Hampstead. For some reason, perhaps because they had heard it together, she equated that girl with the dead girl in her mind and thought that if bombers could actually see the people they were going to kill, see that they were young and beautiful and full of hope, they might not do what they did.

She said it to Daphne when she phoned her after the weather forecast.

'That one doesn't work,' said Daphne. 'Look at the Nazis and the gas chambers.' She did not seem much interested in the bomb. Peter was being silly again. He had brought a boy called Jay to meet her, in exactly the way Arthur had taken her to meet his mother all those years ago. Then he phoned, he had just this minute phoned, to ask her what she thought of Jay.

'I told him he was being silly but he'd grow out of it.'

'I'm sure you're right.'

'He'll meet the right girl and then he'll feel differently.'

As Daphne said this there flashed into Cecilia's mind that conversation with Tina, that terrible thing Tina had said, and another thought, one that seemed to swim up out of the deep waters of her unconscious, the idea that she, Cecilia Darne, yes, she, had once long ago met the right girl, and here was that right girl talking to her now of something, oh, so akin to what Tina meant . . .

Panic was the feeling Alice had when, after several tries, she gave up attempting the Beethoven. She threw down the bow. She felt like throwing it across the room but managed to control herself. What was she going to do? Why hadn't she realized how hopeless she had become, how she had forgotten everything during those months of pregnancy?

She began pacing the room. Had that really been her playing? Not for a moment had she been able to deceive herself that she was anything but bad, truly bad. Buying that blank tape had been a waste, for she knew she would never dare play it back.

At the window she pressed her forehead against the cold

glass. The panic receded as she forced herself to make practical plans. It was no good harking back to the days of coming top in exams, the days of her violin teacher's delight in her, his saying that really he wouldn't be surprised if she was good enough for Brussels or Prague. A year of continuous musical training at a conservatoire and she would be fit for a top orchestra or even the concert platform. He would not say that now, he would be embarrassed.

She must find a teacher. Before she was fit for any audition she needed lessons. And lessons must be paid for. A train rattling by made her lift her head and look out of the window. You could see the station platforms from here, and the station itself and the bridge. Tom and Peter and Peter's new friend Jay were standing on the platform waiting for the southbound Jubilee train. She had told Tom she would not go with them today but now she wished she had. Being alone was the worst thing; when she was alone she thought about things and nearly all of them were bad.

If Tom wanted her she would go to Tom, just to be with someone, to have someone to hold her in the night.

She waved to him but he was not looking in her direction. Perhaps you could not even see the windows of the School from where he was. The silver train, drawing into the station, first hid him from view, then took him away. She watched it rattle down to Finchley Road.

Jay was no mean performer (in Peter's words) on the tenor sax but he was nervous and edgy about doing something which he said was against the law. It made them all laugh when Peter said that come to that, what he did with him was against the law since Jay was not yet twenty-one.

'Someone told me,' said Tom, 'that they never arrest you, they only move you on. They'd arrest you if you gave a false name or something like that or if you were just a beggar. I mean, you get people who blow a couple of bars on a mouth organ and then hold out their hands. We're real musicians.'

They were going to Oxford Circus for a change and had booked a patch. The Argyll Street entrance was full of real beggars, the kind that do not even have mouth organs. The beggars held out old caps, which made Tom resolve never to use a cap. A hat was all right or an instrument case or even a scarf with knotted corners. They set up at the foot of the first escalator. It was noisy and crowded, the concourses and passages full of tourists, hundreds of schoolchildren and students with backpacks.

Tom said he wouldn't play. Later on he would sing. The flute did not really go with a guitar and sax. Peter and Jay played the sort of music he disliked even more than he disliked rock, the kind of thing you associated with canned tunes in restaurants and supermarkets: 'La Vie en Rose' and 'Never on Sunday' and 'Un Homme et une Femme'. It hardly surprised him that people were not too keen on paying good money for that.

He found himself wishing Alice were with them then, wishing it quite fiercely. He *missed* her. Her lovely face came before his eyes and he thought how beautifully she had played on the few occasions she had come down here with him. The two of them should be playing here now, giving these commuters some real music, something they would love. Alice had been sent to him, in the midst of all his unhappiness and frustration and failure, this beautiful talented musician had been sent to him to save him. She was not Diana, she was not Diana's successor, but the perfection he had looked for and half-seen in both of them. The idea of a woman who would save him was not new, but it had become real, it was no longer fantasy.

He was falling in love with her. No, it was past that. He

thought he had loved her from the moment he set eyes on her. It was Diana's face but lovelier, as if Diana's looks had been enriched by life and sadness. A warmth, coupled with excitement, had filled him as she opened her violin case, took out the instrument and began to play. He loved the way her eyes lit when she heard the kind of music she liked well played.

Peter and Jay finished 'Some Enchanted Evening' and he told them which of his repertoire he would sing. That made Jay nervous again but Peter assured him they would manage, it was dead easy, a breeze. Tom sang a Burns song and then, because it went so well with the guitar, never mind the sax, Don Giovanni's pretty serenade. The coins started dropping into the guitar case.

When a railway policeman came to move them on, an officious, spiteful man, Tom thought, they went two stations down the Central Line to Holborn. The best pitch was free from 3.30 onwards. Peter suggested keeping on until half an hour into the rush hour but no longer as it looked like being particularly crowded today. Someone who put 20p into the guitar case also left his *Evening Standard*, possibly as part-payment or just to be rid of it.

Huge type on the front page announced a bomb disaster in west London. Tom read just enough of it to see that it was a long way from West Hampstead and no one he knew had been killed or injured. The IRA perhaps or some Middle Eastern group, there were plenty of them. Looking about him at the great press of people, the escalator that was a river of people flowing on and on, the crowds that streamed down the stairs so that if a train was held up there would be room for no more to squeeze on to the platform, he wondered why a terrorist group had never thought of putting a bomb in the tube.

Perhaps they had and it had been kept dark. Tom turned his eyes from the paper and started singing the song from

Don Giovanni that is always called the Champagne Aria. It was very fast and wild and Peter and Jay, laughing, gave up their attempts at accompanying him.

In another part of Oxford Circus, a station where three lines converge, where there are fourteen escalators, four and a half miles of passages and platforms and through which nearly 200,000 passengers pass each day, a man was taking photographs.

People do not like being photographed on their way to or from work. They are not on holiday on a beach. Most of them did nothing about it but hurried on, some scowling, one, a child, making a face at the camera, holding up his hands as if they were big ears and waggling his fingers.

The photographer was a dark young man with a beard and very blue eyes. He was dressed in black – black jeans and sweater. He began handing cards to some of the people who had let him take their picture. The cards had nothing on them but apparently meaningless hieroglyphics and they were thrown to the ground to add to the litter that so distresses London Transport.

He turned his lens on a man who came striding through the concourse, his collar turned up, his hat pulled well down. Hat and collar together were insufficient to hide an exceptionally ugly face, among other unattractive features a spoonbill nose and inadequately repaired harelip.

The man went up to the photographer.

'I want that film.'

The photographer smiled. He seemed pleased, satisfied, *relieved*.

'I said I want that film.'

'You don't want your lovely face on record?'

'That's right. Now give me that film, please.'

People passing turned to look. This was more interesting than being snapped and given a card.

'I'm at least as strong as you,' the photographer said, and thoughtfully, 'maybe stronger. But I'll give you the film gladly on one condition. That you'll come up and have a drink with me.'

He opened the camera, took out the film and handed it with another smile to the man with the spoonbill nose.

7

The identity of her children's fathers was unknown to Tina Darne. She knew they had different fathers and she knew that in each case there was only a certain number of possibilities, but beyond that all was obscure. It was her big secret. Tina had no moral sense about this question, no feeling that children ought to know who their fathers were or should be fathered by the men their mothers lived with or were married to. This seemed to her so much humbug. The reason for her secrecy was that if Brian thought there was any doubt about Jasper and Bienvida's paternity he might stop paying her the £50 a week child support.

One of those who must never never know was Tina's mother. Tina regarded her mother as a kind of insurance policy and her house as a bolthole. Finding out the truth about Jasper and Bienvida might finally militate against Cecilia Darne's view that a child should always be able to find a home with its parents. Tina had found a home with her parent, her father having died when she was fifteen, on every occasion when other roofs had failed her. The last time was for the three months before she encountered Jarvis in Fawley Road. Brian had thrown her out for what he inaccurately called adultery.

Tina had never been married, though her mother had never given up hope, and did not give it up now, that a wedding would one day take place. Cecilia Darne had loved Brian. He was the first responsible man her daughter had ever known. She thought it quite wonderful that this kind man, who was not married, who had a job, who was on Lambeth Council's housing list, actually wanted Tina to go and live with him. It was the first step, she believed, in the direction of marriage, for Mrs Darne – necessarily with a daughter like Tina – had moved with the times. Those views she had been taught in the twenties while a young girl, that men do not love or respect, still less marry, women who have 'given themselves' to them, she had been obliged to revise. She saw it happening all around her. She read about it and saw it on television.

Indeed, it now seemed to be the case that men did not marry women unless they had had sexual relations with them beforehand. Brian would marry Tina, it was only a matter of time. Perhaps he would wait until a baby was on the way, for Mrs Darne had not failed to notice that these days extramarital pregnancy, once a horrible disgrace, was often the loudly publicized occasion for a wedding, with the bride, far from ashamed of herself, carrying all proudly before her.

Brian Elphick had been on Lambeth's housing list for twelve years, having insinuated himself on to it when engaged to a woman he never married. Now he lied to the housing department about having lived all that time with an old aunt, since dead, and got a friend who kept a garage in the dead woman's street to swear to having seen him there daily. The flat he was offered was in a nasty area and in a tower block but neither he nor Tina minded about that. Cecilia Darne was very happy for Tina.

She had never heard of Peggy Guggenheim, nor of her boast that she had slept with every man she had ever known. If she had discovered that Tina could have said much the same she would have been deeply upset. Tina might have told her mother this, during one of their evenings of confidences, but it had never occurred to her, she being neither proud nor ashamed of it, nor even thinking it very out of the ordinary.

Thus Jasper's father might have been the man who was painting the flats and who came in for a cup of tea, or the old lover whom she happened to run into in Denmark Hill, or the neighbour who was moving out of Flat 16 and who came up to say goodbye while his girfriend was packing their furniture into the rented van. The only certainty was that it was not Brian, for Brian had been away during that crucial week of Tina's cycle, doing an electrical job in Aberdeen.

For Brian to be certain he was the father of any child of Tina's, for *anyone* to know he was the father of any child of Tina's, he would have had to keep her for months on an island inhabited only by the pair of them. Brian wasn't even away when Bienvida was conceived, but ill with flu and not inclined for sexual activity. He begged her not to miss the party they were invited to on his account, so she made him a hot drink, turned on the TV and, making no bones about it, said she would be back in the morning.

Tina got drunk and remembered very little of what happened after midnight. She woke up in bed with a man with a red beard, but from the snide remarks and sideways looks of those fellow guests who were still there in the morning gathered that he had not been her only partner of the night. Bienvida had red hair when she was born but later on it turned dark, so that told her very little. Brian never seemed to notice that the children were very odd-looking to be the son and daughter of a pair of fair-haired blue-eyed ectomorphs. Nor did he draw any obvious conclusions when he kept on coming on Tina in bed with other men. But after three such encounters he said he realized this was because after eight years she had stopped loving him and he made his famous remark about adultery.

Tina went back to mother. There was nowhere else to go.

The only woman Peter Bleech-Palmer had ever slept with

was Tina Darne. It might be truer to say that Tina slept with him. They were very good friends, which neither Daphne nor Cecilia could really understand, though for some time, especially before the advent of Brian, both mothers had hopes of their 'making a match of it'. Peter was a pianist, had a job as a pianist, and always seemed to have money, which made Cecilia see him as a potentially good husband. She was unaware that the job was in a 'gay and/or straight' bar in Frith Street.

When Tina and the children moved into the School, Cecilia felt both dismay and guilty relief. Had she driven poor Tina away by hesitating about paying for the installation of a bathroom? What would happen with Jarvis? Cecilia did not dislike Jarvis, she did not dislike anybody, but she feared and distrusted him as a bachelor with no regular job, no real income and a home which she was convinced would be sold to the property developers.

Notwithstanding experience and observation, she was still somewhere inside her convinced that if a man and a woman lived under the same roof, even if the roof covered a very large area, they would soon be cohabiting in a sexual sense. She was not to know that Tina, sticking to her principles, had long ago slept with her cousin Jarvis. Just once. Neither of them had any desire to repeat the experience. Cecilia could also vividly remember Tina's first venture at the School and the founding of the commune, the reputation it earned in a place which, after all, was only a stone's throw – within easy bell-sound – of her own house.

In those days there had been no children. Cecilia worried about those children. Another old belief of hers and one which died hard, which refused to die, was that no man will willingly take on another man's children.

'I worry about the children,' she said to Daphne.

'Do you know what they call them in America?' asked Daphne. 'They call them grandbabies.'

'Well, yes, kiddies, grandbabies, I worry about them. They run about so and they make a lot of noise, you know how children do, and I'm afraid Jarvis will get tired of it. I mean it isn't exactly his house but it's more his than anyone else's, if you see what I mean.'

'Except his mother,' said practical Daphne. 'Jarvis Stringer isn't that sort. I don't suppose he notices. He's always got his head in the clouds or down a tunnel.'

'I've never liked that house, that school, whatever they call it. It should have been pulled down after my brother died. Do you believe violent death leaves a kind of surge of energy behind it which is really what's meant by ghosts?'

'No,' said Daphne.

'Perhaps you're right. I know I always feel uncomfortable there. I always feel something's going to jump out on me from behind a door.'

Daphne laughed. 'That something would be Jasper or Bienvida.'

'I don't like going there,' said Cecilia. 'It's partly on account of the bell. Wouldn't you think my niece Elsie would have had it taken away? Jarvis never does anything that isn't to do with trains but I can't understand Elsie. And that's another thing. It's bad enough with the trains where I live but the whole house – the School, I mean – it shakes when the trains go by. It's like an earthquake, or what I imagine an earthquake would be like.'

But she continued to go there regularly, somewhat more often than she went up to Willesden to see Daphne. To go past the School and over the railway bridge was one of the ways of going shopping in West End Lane. Cecilia had passed Cambridge School several thousand times and been inside it several hundred times but she had never got over her feelings of loathing it. She had an obscure feeling that other passers-by would not notice the bell up there in the shadowy interior of the bell chamber. It was almost concealed by the small columns which held up the campanile roof, merely a shinier darkness in the dark. She told herself that if she did not look up she would not need to see it and after a while this not-looking would become habitual, but in the event she could not prevent her eyes from turning up to the campanile.

As she walked along, passing the blocks she still thought of as the 'new' flats, she caught sight of her grandson Jasper disappearing, in company with three other boys of similar age, into the narrow alley which led to the railway bridge. Jasper, at nine, was a sturdy, broad-shouldered, dark-haired boy, very handsome, with strong regular features and eyes of a curious shade of dark violet-brown.

Cecilia thought it remarkable, an instance of the inexplicable ways of nature, that a child could be so unlike his parents, but she thought no more than that. Reflecting in her vague kindly way that it was very nice for Jasper to have friends of his own age to play with in the holidays, a lot better than in the days when he had lived in that tower block in Walworth, she was still thinking along these lines as she entered the gateless gateway and found her eyes irresistibly turning upwards to the bell. It must have been the bell, a school bell, which brought into her mind the realization that this was still term-time, not holidays. Why was Jasper not at school?

Cecilia was about to let herself in when the young woman called Alice, who had been there when she heard the bomb go off, opened the door to her. Alice, Cecilia had often thought, was the prettiest girl she had ever seen. She put her in mind of a favourite painting her father had possessed, a portrait of Mary Zambaco by Burne-Jones, and which had hung in the hall of the family home in Hendon. It had passed to Evelina in the days when a Burne-Jones was not worth twopence and goodness knew what Evelina had done with it. Alice had the same swan-like neck, delicate features and full soft mouth, only her hair instead of red was a dark chestnut-brown.

'I'll just go and tap on Tina's door,' she said to Alice.

The place was a lot cleaner than in commune days. It did not look too bad. The smell was gone. From somewhere in the back Cecilia could hear that sound she had never been able to identify and had not liked to ask about, a regular screeching as made by a bird in a zoo. In this house, since commune days, she had always felt shy. She liked to go quietly, not ask too many questions, never to interfere. She was conscious of being a misfit, and that was a great understatement. It was partly her age, of course, she was an old woman by anyone's standards, but her attitude to life too and her clothes, her grey tweed skirt and green Viyella blouse and green and grey check cardigan, her stockings and 'court' shoes, the powder on her nose, lipstick on her thin old lips and the perm in her hair.

In the passage she encountered the man who always smelt of meat on the turn. Cecilia could clearly remember the days before refrigerators were in general use – she did not have one until 1952 – and remember too the smell of the joint by Sunday lunchtime if you had been imprudent enough to buy it on Friday. This man smelt far worse than that. Celilia, saying good morning to his 'hi', wondered if he had some dreadful disease.

She tapped on Tina's door. It was ten past twelve. Cecilia always left coming to Tina's until noon was past because she did not want to find her daughter in bed. Had she done so she would not have said a word, would not have looked a word, would simply have sat on the bed and talked to Tina for ten minutes instead of the two of them sitting opposite each other in armchairs. But if she came and found Tina up she could pretend to herself that Tina had been up for hours, and was a normal person and a proper mother.

83

What she in fact found Tina doing pleased her greatly. In Ernest and Elizabeth's awful old kitchen, which had last had a re-fit in 1926 and in which Cecilia herself would not have so much as peeled a potato, though nothing would have made her say so, Tina was baking a birthday cake for Bienvida. Cecilia would have been very surprised indeed if she had been wearing anything but jeans and a sweater or T-shirt, and she was not. What pleased her enormously was that over these garments Tina actually wore one of the patchwork aprons she had made and given her years before, with little hope of their ever being used.

The radio was on, whatever it was that shrieked was at it full-blast, and from somewhere upstairs came music that sounded as if it proceeded from a violin. Someone was hammering in the cellar. As Cecilia sat down she felt the earthquake rumblings that came when a train passed by.

'Where are you off to then?' said Tina, laying a rather floury hand on Cecilia's sleeve.

Cecilia had nearly got over feeling embarrassed when she mentioned Daphne. 'I'm meeting Daphne for lunch in D. H. Evans.'

'My God, can you still do that? I remember you taking me there to lunch when I was small and I threw up in the lift.'

Cecilia remembered it too. That word 'small' reminded her of her grandson. She was always careful while here to cast her inquiries in the form of statements and she said, choosing her words meticulously, 'I expect Jasper was a bit off-colour this morning so you felt it wiser not to send him to school. I'm glad he's well enough to be out with his friends.' As she uttered these words she thought they sounded snide and insinuating, sarcastic even, though she had not meant them like that. She had only wanted to know without seeming to criticize.

However they sounded, Tina took them in the spirit

84

they were intended, laughed loudly and said Jasper must be playing hookey in his lunch hour.

'Do they let them do that?'

It had occurred to Cecilia as soon as the words were out of her mouth that five minutes to twelve, which was the time when she had seen Jasper, was rather early for a lunch hour to begin. Indeed, it would have had to have begun much earlier, her grandchildren's school being a good fifteen minutes' walk away, on the other side of West End Lane. But of this she said nothing, watched Tina putting her cake into the filthiest, blackest, greasiest oven she had ever seen, while waiting for an answer to one of her rare inquiries. By the time it came she had almost forgotten what the question was.

'Oh, it's an awful school. They let them do anything, they can't control them. The kids hate it but what can I do? The teachers are always on strike and I don't blame them, poor things.' These statements, terrible to Cecilia's ears, were made in tones of the utmost placidity.

Her anxiety must have shown in her face. Tina uttered another peal of happy laughter, put her arms round her mother's shoulders, squeezing her, and using the pet name Cecilia loved, treasured and secretly longed to hear, said, 'Don't you worry, little mum, my kids'll always be all right, that's the way they are, they're like me. Off you go and have your nice lunch with Auntie Daphne and give her my love.'

Moved, Cecilia said, 'You know you can always come back to me to live, Tina. You know that, don't you? It's always your home.'

'Don't push your luck,' said Tina. 'I just might do that one day.'

Walking towards the station, having promised to bring back with her all sorts of expensive food items Tina had requested from Selfridges' Food Hall, Cecilia thought how much she liked living on her own and that at seventy-six she was too old to have Jasper and Bienvida running around her, fond of them as she was, not to mention Tina's boyfriends and the odd hours she kept and her lying in bed till noon. It embarrassed her to meet men – to herself she called them 'strange men' – coming down her stairs in the middle of the morning, putting their heads round the door and saying 'hi' to her. But she would put up with all that to make Tina happy and give the children a secure childhood. She would smile and be lighthearted and welcome them all back and have a bathroom put in on the top floor.

There was only one person she could have happily shared her home with and that was Daphne Bleech-Palmer. But Daphne had her own house in Willesden, a house Cecilia was sure she would not be willing to leave, though it was far less nice than Cecilia's own, being part of an ugly white brick terrace. It was a measure of Cecilia's character that, unlike most people, she experienced no *schadenfreude* about this, felt no secret pleasure in the superiority of her circumstances over her friend's, but sincerely regretted Daphne's inferior home and reduced income.

Cecilia went down the steps at West Hampstead station and stood on the lefthand platform waiting for the train to come down from Kilburn. She did not need Jarvis to tell her of the phenomenon of the shivering platform at West Hampstead as a train approaches, that and the singing of the rails, because she was accustomed to the point of no longer noticing it. The half-erased graffiti on the silver train she did notice, without being able to identify it as man-made. Cecilia attributed the marks to some kind of metal fatigue or rust.

A notice inside tube trains reads as follows:

In an emergency assistance can be provided more quickly if you operate the *red alarm* when the train is at a station. Only operate the *red alarm* between stations if it is *essential* to stop the train immediately.

There is a basic misunderstanding of human psychology here, for it is only between stations that you would wish to press the red alarm at all. Surely, if the train were in a station when the emergency occurred, you would get out and run away as fast as possible.

The trains on the Jubilee Line, at least beyond the confines of inner London, are seldom crowded at midday during the week. Only three other people shared the car with Cecilia. One sat at the extreme righthand end of the car, another at the extreme lefthand end and the third in the middle by the doors, facing the platform. Tina would have plumped herself down in the nearest seat even if this had been next to a passenger but Cecilia, conforming to usage, sat in the emptiest area of the coach, on the platform side with her back to the window. Having no book or magazine with her, she read from the opposite wall an advertisement for duty-free goods obtainable at Heathrow, one for travelling very cheaply by boat to Holland, another was deciphering an invitation to office temps couched in a kind of code, when the train drew into Finchley Road.

Only two passengers got into the car, a man and a bear.

Cecilia saw the bear and thought for about five seconds that it was real. Then she saw the man's face through the open mouth and immediately turned her head away so that she appeared to be looking at something of consuming interest outside the window. Anything of that sort, people in fancy dress, people in obvious disguise, caused her intense embarrassment.

The train started and soon plunged into the tunnel.

There was no longer anything to pretend to look at out of the window. Cecilia turned somewhat fearfully back and saw that the man and the bear had gone to the far end of the coach where a woman not much younger than herself sat alone. The bear was in front of this woman and half-squatting, its paws raised, in the attitude of a begging dog.

Cecilia could see that the man with the bear held it by a chain looped round its neck. He was a young, dark-haired man with a short dark beard and he was curiously dressed in a black overcoat that came nearly to his ankles. It was the kind of coat her father had worn all those years ago to go to business. She thought that she would leave the train at the next station, Swiss Cottage, even if this made her late for her meeting with Daphne, due to take place at one.

The woman whom the man and the bear were tormenting — for this was how Cecilia saw it, as torment — at least had the good fortune to be possessed of a magazine, which she was now pretending to read while the bear cavorted in front of her. It was pretence, Cecilia knew, for no one could help feeling an embarrassment so deep as to amount to actual dumb fear in the face of such a performance. Well, not exactly no one, she corrected herself, for she knew Tina would not be embarrassed or afraid. Tina would very likely laugh and clap or even stroke the bear.

This was what the bear-leader seemed to be asking of the passenger he now approached, the man who sat in the seat next to the doors. The man, middle-aged, wearing a suit, complied with a nervous smile. He put out a hand and smoothed the bear's shaggy head, giving it embarrassed pats, while looking up at the bear-leader as if to say, Is that all right? Is that enough? Will you leave me alone now?

The bear sprang at him with a growl. It was what an unreliable dog does when stroked by someone who is afraid of it. The man jerked backwards with a cry. Cecilia heard herself gasp and at once put her hand up to her

88

mouth. The bear-leader gave a tug on the chain, pulling it until the bear nearly fell over backwards.

'I can't bear it,' he said to the passengers, his eyes swivelling the length and breadth of the coach. 'I knew there was trouble brewin'. Geddit? Brewin? Bruin?'

The train, to Cecilia's extreme relief, drew into Swiss Cottage. She began to get up but by now the man and the bear had moved themselves into the open area of the coach between the pairs of doors. They had in fact stationed themselves in front of the doors which were the kind which open only if you press a button either from outside or inside. There was no one on the platform, or no one in front of the doors of this car. In order to open the doors she would have to get past the bear, say 'excuse me' to it, or actually push it. She dropped the inch or two down into her seat again as the train began to move.

Embarrassment had now been succeeded by fear. Embarrassment, she thought, *was* fear but of a very reduced kind, just as they say an itch is pain to a very mild degree. This new feeling was real fear, not so much of physical injury as of humiliation, that being most easily provoked in someone of her age and sex. It had not escaped Cecilia's notice that to many people, even today, old women are objects of ridicule. Her heart began to beat fast and heavily. She could hear it, as if it were not in her chest but something outside herself.

The man and the bear, who had had their backs to her, now turned round and the bear began a clumsy lolloping in her direction. Cecilia, with pounding heart, opened her handbag in a desperate effort to find something with which apparently to occupy her eyes. She could find only her chequebook and the small, leather-bound directory Jasper had given her for Christmas and into which, to gratify the child, she had painstakingly copied the addresses and phone numbers of friends accumulated throughout a lifetime. But it was as if her grandson had saved her life with his gift. She busied herself with putting on her glasses. The bear was in front of her now, dropping down into that squatting or begging position it had adopted to torment the other woman passenger. Cecilia opened the small red book and the first name she saw was Bleech-Palmer. The handwritten words swam before her eyes and her heart thudded.

The bear growled and grunted. Cecilia turned the pages of her address book, she turned them slowly, she scrutinized them as if they fascinated her. All the time she was resolving not to raise her eyes, not to look at the bear. The other passengers took no notice. She did not blame them. She had appeared to take no notice when they were persecuted, she had not intervened. If the bear attacked her they would very likely even then not intervene. Her hands had begun to shake and now her whole body trembled. The bear laid a paw on her knee.

Cecilia did not scream. Afterwards she wondered how she had kept silent, holding her breath, listening to the drumming of her heart. Through the tweed of her skirt, her pure silk lace-bordered slip and the nylon stockings she wore, she felt the hairy thing, hot-heavy and disgusting. She could not move, she could no longer turn the pages, but she kept her eyes down. Her flesh shrank away from the paw's touch, as if gathering and compressing itself on to the bone.

She supposed afterwards that the bear-leader took pity on her, or had grown bored. Instead of jerking on the lead, he gave a mighty push to the bear's head and the man-animal rolled over backwards. It rolled over with its paws and hind legs in the air, showing the dirty leather pads under its splayed feet. Cecilia found she had clenched her fists and was driving her nails into the palms of her hands. The bear began picking itself up as the train came into St John's Wood.

By this time Cecilia had forgotten all about not pushing past the bear to press the button and get out. She would have pushed past anything, a snake, a Rottweiler, a sabre-toothed tiger. In the event she had to step over one of its feet. The bear-leader laughed, a throaty giggle. She clutched her shopping bag and her handbag. As she reached the doors they came open, the button pressed by two people outside. Cecilia got on to the platform. She could see only through a watery mist and realized after a moment's panic that she still had her reading glasses on.

The train moved away, taking bear and bear-leader with it. Cecilia was shaking all over. She sat down on one of the grey bucket seats to calm herself, to get her breath, but instead she began to cry.

8

The birthday party was of a kind which Cecilia would have wondered at, had she been invited to it, for although a few of Bienvida's classmates were present in its early stages, by seven it had become a celebration for the grown-ups. Bienvida and Jasper were of course still there. No one noticed that Bienvida, her grandmother's grand-daughter more than her mother's child, had at some stage gone back to the Headmaster's Flat and changed into dungarees to keep her Oxfam dress of nylon organza from getting dirty. She was a tall, very thin child with the dark curly hair, aquiline features and wild poetical eyes of the Irishwoman. Jasper, her elder brother, had refused from the first to dress up for this party and wore his school jeans and Western shirt, though school had not seen him that day.

Bottles of wine were produced just after seven. Jed had provided some of it, Peter brought the Beaujolais Nouveau and the rest came from Tina's current boyfriend, who worked in the Grog Blossom shop. None of the children had wanted birthday cake, which Tina had mistakenly made with fruit and nuts in it, so they ate it as their second course.

It was a fine warm evening, vermilion streaks of sunset even reaching this eastern skyline. Jarvis had set up a trestle table on that terrace where pupils had once assembled for the annual school photograph. Around it sat Peter Bleech-Palmer, Jay Rossini, Tom, Alice, Billy the Grog Blossom man, Tina and himself.

From their feet stretched away the plain of shaggy grass, a wild lawn of weeds, buttercups, dandelions and lady's smock in full bloom. All the trees, so large now as to enclose this garden, excluding the sight of other houses, so that but for the complex of railway lines it might have been in the country, were in late summer leaf. The soft twittering hum came from birds going to roost. There were more birds in this London sanctuary than many country gardens and the cries of the hawk had not yet driven them away. The trains, running up and down from London to Stanmore and back, could only be seen through the foliage as a series of silver flashes, but their singing rattle made a constant background music.

There was no wind. The air was still enough for candles to be lit. In the fading light Tina, wearing greenish-blue Indian cotton with silver alloy chains of Kabul turquoises and coral round her neck, began lighting yellow wax candles set in saucers. As the wicks burned, a strong perfume of sandalwood came from them. But this was not enough to keep away mosquitoes, which started to arrive and drift towards the flames. Peter had brought his guitar and he and Tom began to play. When Tina and Billy began to dance Jarvis asked Alice but she shook her head, smiling at him. She was beginning to feel committed to Tom, she wanted to dance with no one but him.

The children's seats at the table had long been empty. Jarvis's train set, the one which had diverted him from his mother's grief on the day her father hanged himself, was laid out on the floor in Lower Six, a classroom on the top floor, and Jarvis had told Jasper he could play with it whenever he liked. Jarvis still occasionally played with it himself. Jasper, while dimly understanding that this was a very generous offer on Jarvis's part, considered himself too sophisticated for train sets. But he went up there now, with Bienvida trailing behind him, from an obscure feeling that he ought to show Jarvis this offer was appreciated. He was also bored. Jasper knew he was allowed extreme latitude in almost everything he did. He also knew 'allowed' was not exactly the word but that it was more a question of not bothering. No one kept an eye on him. Sometimes this pleased him and sometimes it made him feel frightened, though he could not have said why.

He could have wandered unchecked all over north London if he had had a mind to it, but this was supposed to be Bienvida's party and he and Bienvida were supposed to be there. It had, of course, gone the way of all their parties he could remember and turned into an excuse for grown-up drinking, talk, dancing and all that cuddling and kissing stuff he inescapably associated with his mother.

He and his sister went into Lower Six and contemplated the train set in silence. It was just a train set, indefinably old-fashioned. They looked out of the window and down on the merrymakers. Peter had taken the flute from Tom, Tom was dancing with Alice and Jarvis capering with Jay, while Tina and Billy were half under the table in a clinch so tightly intertwined as to seem to make one person of them.

'Shit,' said Jasper. 'She's off again.'

Bienvida, being two years his junior, asked wistfully if he thought she would ever go back to Brian. If she had been speaking to a school friend she would have called Brian Daddy but this was not acceptable to Jasper. Early in life he had put away childish things.

'I doubt it. Don't put that idea into her head, Bee. I like it here. There are things I specially like about living here, never you mind what they are, they're just things I like. So don't go telling her she ought to go back to that dump in the sky.'

Bienvida said nothing, though her wild and wary eyes looked wilder.

'They will be all over gnat bites,' said Jasper.

His duty done – that Jarvis would never know one way

94

or the other made no difference in Jasper's estimation – he went back on to the landing which by now was in darkness. Faint light from the open doors of Five, Lower Six and Upper Six made it possible to see, shedding pale blurry patches on to the corridor floor. Bienvida pressed the light switch but the bulb was long used-up and no one had replaced it. The skylight in the ceiling looked as if covered by a dark purple cloth. Up here once, Bienvida had seen the full moon appear in that purple square and a pointed cloud cut a segment from it like an eclipse. Since then she had sometimes looked for the moon again in that dark, usually empty space but had never seen it.

Jasper stood looking at the bell rope which came out of a small square aperture at what was the base of the campanile. The end of the rope was wound round a cleat high up on the wall above the door to what had once been the Science Lab. It was far out of the reach of grown-ups as well as children, except that Jasper did not really think anything was out of his reach.

'There must be a hole in the floor under here,' he said to his sister, scuffing with his toes at the worn grey and red runner which one of the commune people had laid along this corridor. 'And there must be another hole in the floor outside the Handwork Room.'

'Why must there?'

Jasper had got down on to the floor and was grubbing about under the carpet. His fingers felt the division between the old floorboards and then the cross-cut which marked the edge of a trapdoor. He scraped with his thumbnail the metal hinge. 'Because the rope used to come down through here so they could ring it in the cloakroom. They never did ring it but they meant to. Shall I tell you why they never did?'

'I don't know where the cloakroom is,' said Bienvida.

'It's that room no one ever goes in. Down the bottom

95

between the way out to the veranda and the toilets. Shall I tell you why no one ever goes in?'

'Not if it's very frightening.'

Once more on his feet and staring up at the bell rope, Jasper said, 'D'you know what I'd like? I'd really like a cigarette.'

'You'll get lung cancer.'

'Have you ever heard of anybody of nine getting lung cancer?'

Jasper opened the door of Upper Six and looked inside. Putting the light on would be too risky, but the curtains were drawn back and by now their eyes had become accustomed to a darkness in which could be made out the shapes of furniture and smaller objects, a darkness of monochrome and black spaces and faintly gleaming edges. Jed's room had a raunchy, hot, savage smell. So might smell the den of some great carnivore, thought Jasper, where the floor was stickily carpeted in dried blood and littered with licked bones.

He fumbled about on the table, felt in the pockets of the odorous hawk-training jacket which hung on the back of the door, told his sister to try the cupboard. She opened the door a little fearfully, but giggling now. Her giggles became a scream, a short sharp shriek like the sound the hawk made.

'Shut up, will you?' said Jasper. 'What's got into you? D'you want them to hear you down there?'

But the music must have drowned Bienvida's cry. Jasper looked out of the window and down into the candlelight. . No upturned face met his eyes. His sister clutched his arm.

'I put my hand into something horrible.' She talked in her ghoul voice. He could see the whites of her eyes and the big dark pupils rotating. Both children were always asking each other: Shall I tell you? Shall I? Shall I tell you what happened, what I saw, did, shall I? 'Shall I tell you what it was I put my hand into, Jas?'

'Yeah, OK, what was it?'

'A dead person's stomach. Like he'd been cut open and died and I put my hand in all among his intestines.'

'Oh, come on,' said Jasper. He had found the cigarettes and matches with them, up at the end of the windowsill between a pile of books and a plant pot. A cigarette between his lips, he struck a match, lit it and held the lighted match up inside the open cupboard.

'It's not a dead person's stomach, it's those day-old chicks he gives Abelard. They're all messed up together in a bowl.'

'Yuck,' said Bienvida. 'They're dead, aren't they?'

'Of course they're dead. Shall I tell you what happened in the cloakroom, Bee?'

'Yeah, OK, what was it?'

They returned to the landing and sat on the stairs. 'One day I'm going to ring that bell,' said Jasper, puffing away.

'What happened in the cloakroom?'

'An old man that wasn't our grandfather but something like that hung himself. In the cloakroom. I heard Tina telling Tom about it. He hung himself from the bellrope. It came all the way down there then.' Jasper extended his narrow brown neck in which the Adam's apple had not yet appeared and in the near-dark clasped his hands round his throat. The throttling sound he made, accompanied by a frenzied rolling of the eyes, expelled the cigarette from his mouth and sent it halfway down the stairs.

It took them a few moments to find it. By then the fleur-de-lis patterned linoleum which covered the stairs was singed and smelling. Bienvida had started giggling and clutching at Jasper, alternately nervous and hopeful, terrified of the corpses and ghosts he fed her, but always hungry for more. Holding hands, they came down the stairs in an exaggerated parody of the grown-ups' dancing, shaking skinny hips, flicking their free hands, the glowing end of Jasper's cigarette describing parabolas in the darkness.

Below them the vestibule was lit, dimly, by the electrolier, in which only two candles had bulbs in them. Someone must have come indoors to turn that light on. Jasper laid a finger to his lips and tried the cloakroom door. It was not locked, as he had feared it might be. Taking Bienvida by the hand, he drew her inside. Absolute darkness and a new smell in here, not rotting meat or burning lino but something sour and cold. If a wet stone could smell it would smell like this.

They had been inside no more than thirty seconds, Bienvida trembling all over the way she did from terror and excitement, when they heard the voices of Peter, Tom and Alice, as these three people crossed the hall and went upstairs together. Jasper dropped his cigarette end on to the floor and trod it out.

'We'll sleep in here,' he said. 'We'll get our sleeping bags and a torch and things and sleep in here.'

'Not tonight.' Bienvida's voice was faint with the horrifying enormity of it. 'Not *now*.'

Jasper said impatiently, 'Of course not now. I'm not planning on going to bed yet.'

In quest of further adventures, experiments, discoveries, he emerged from the cloakroom, his sister behind him and holding on to him, and padded along the passage towards the long disused kitchen regions and the cellar stairs.

Dancing with Tom, Alice nearly told him what had happened that day. He was kind and understanding. He had asked her to talk to him about the things that troubled her, but she could not. People were enjoying themselves, Tom was laughing, she was afraid of casting a blight. Now was not the time to tell him how she had tried to phone her mother, had dialled the number and her father answered.

Bravely, Alice made herself say who it was and her father put the phone down. That had unnerved her. She phoned her mother again at a time her father could not be there; she had to know about Mike and Catherine, what was happening.

'Mike's sister's looking after her, what's-her-name, Julia.'

'Mike's not going to let her adopt Catherine?'

'What do you care?' said Marcia Anderson. 'You've made it pretty clear you couldn't care less.'

'Would you like me to give you my address, Mother?'

'Suit yourself. I can't say I know of anyone who wants to write to you.'

She told herself she deserved it, but that did not make the punishment less. She held Tom close and pressed her cheek to his. After a while she drew away again, determined not to seem inviting, and they danced in silence. They were to be friends, not lovers, she had made up her mind to that.

The mosquitoes broke up the party. They came in a singing swarm. Peter was the first to say he was going indoors; he took one of his bottles of wine with him and Alice and Tom followed. He came up with them to Four on the first floor, Tom's room. This irritated Alice. Peter might have supposed that they were lovers from Tom's ardour and her acquiescence, might have thought it not just tactful but a requirement to leave them alone together. If she and Tom had been two men he would have been discretion itself, she thought. He behaved sometimes as if heterosexual love were an improper or even immoral exercise and if his presence could disrupt it, so much the better.

Still, they were not lovers and never would be. She had drunk very little, a small glass of wine while they were eating and another ten minutes before they came in. Mike had once called her a natural non-drinker, one who enjoyed neither the taste nor the effect. But in Tom's room, when

Peter had poured the wine into two mugs and an inch into a glass for her and she had tasted it, she found she liked this wine that had a taste of how elderflowers smell, reversed her decision and asked him to do as he had offered and fill her glass. It was a Riesling from Yugoslavia. She was experiencing no unwelcome change of consciousness, no lightness in the head. They talked. Peter sat in the armchair, she and Tom on the bed. A corn-coloured moon climbed up the sky outside the closed window and Tom turned off his lamp so that there was no competition for the warm moonlight.

Peter picked up the wine bottle and looked at her and this time she didn't put her hand over the top of the glass. Tom said he had had enough so she and Peter drank it. Peter kept looking at his watch because he was on duty at midnight. Since giving up playing the piano in the Soho bar, he had had a job as a receptionist and switchboard operator in a hospice in Kilburn. When he had had a few drinks, though not otherwise, Peter talked about how he knew he ought to have the test to find out if he was HIV negative, as he hoped, as he desperately hoped, but he had not had it yet.

At a quarter to twelve he left. Alice was drunk. There were two conflicting thoughts in her mind. One was that it was horrible and she would always regret it if she made love to Tom only because she was drunk, the other that here was the opportunity to get it over, make a start, break the ice. She was drunk, so she didn't care. She wanted to, she quite wanted to, she might as well.

Tom didn't expect it. She watched him. He was so handsome, probably the best-looking man she had ever seen, anyway the best-looking that she knew, fair, tanned, slim, features like an actor in a Western, like the hero. He had got over expecting her to turn to him, pull him close to her, lie beside him. Sometimes he said he knew it would happen one day. He would wait. Love did marvellous things, he said, and one day love would do that.

He must expect her to get up off the bed and kiss his cheek, say good-night, see you in the morning, go out quickly and close the door behind her. She did get up. She was not very steady on her feet and she kept thinking how she had resolved not to do this, but her thought processes were blurred and hazy.

She started to take her clothes off. He made a sound behind her, an intake of breath, nothing more. She took off her clothes and turned round in the moonlight. Tom was quite still, looking at her. Because of the way he was looking, his parted lips, his wondering eyes, she felt desire, a flicker of it, the first sign, the first time for months, a movement like a string being plucked where she thought her womb was.

The bad thing was that when she woke in the morning she could remember nothing about it. She had woken in the night, she could remember that, and at first not known where she was. She was lying on the edge of the bed far from Tom and had not known it was Tom's bed and Tom's room or that she was not alone, but had been cast at once, as usual, into that incredulous panic where she was asking herself, how could I have left Mike? How could I have abandoned Catherine? I can't have done that, I can't – how could I? And then Tom had moved. His hand had reached for her and a sigh of relief at finding her had come from him and she had turned deeply into his arms to let him hold her there. The panic was absorbed by his warmth, the hard resilient muscles of his body, absorbed and drawn and sucked out of her.

But the morning – in the morning there was nothing. There was mild headache and muzziness but no memory. It sickened her that she could have made love with Tom and be able to remember nothing of it. She only knew that they had made love at all by the sticky wetness in between her thighs and on the bedsheet.

Birds were singing in the garden trees. It must be a blackbird she could hear in the pear tree. Her room was not far from Tom's and on the same side of the house, but she could not remember hearing birds before. The dawn chorus, her mother called it, though it was not dawn but nearly eight.

Tom was awake and watching her. She turned her face to him and smiled, feeling pain as she moved her head. Her massy hair, which she usually plaited at night or at least tied back, was all over the pillow and herself and him, covering his shoulders as well as her own. She felt a different kind of guilt. She was so ashamed of not remembering what had happened that she felt she must compensate him in some way, so she kissed his mouth and stroked his cheek.

A little breeze blew in. At some point he must have got up and opened the window. That was why she could hear that thrush, that blackbird, that cuckoo.

He said softly, 'I love you so much. You've made me very happy.'

She said she was glad. If only she could remember.

'You know how I said you could save me and only you. Well, it's starting. I can feel it. I'm starting to feel like I used to.'

'I couldn't save anyone, Tom. I can't even save myself.'

'Perhaps it's easier to save someone else.'

She put up her arms to him and he began to make love to her very gently and slowly. She thought about Mike. Thinking about Mike now was wrong, was disgusting, but she could not help herself. She thought how rough they had been with each other, how savage almost, sometimes in an odd way wanting to be done so that they could begin all over again. Tom made love like he played the flute, with slow, studied precision. He was patient and controlled. She put aside the guilty thought that he made love as if he had studied it as he had told her he once studied keyboard fingering and Bach's Innovations. It was strange that an impulsive, warm person could be such a calculating lover.

His care was wasted. It made her impatient. She kept her eyes open, looking at him, though his were closed. He was so good-looking, wonderfully handsome and young and sweet, and that should have been enough, but it was not. She smiled at him when it was over because there was nothing else she could do.

The birds went on singing. He began talking to her about birdsong, about bird music, really. After a while he made tea and brought it back to bed and they talked in a way she never could have with Mike, or anyone she knew, about Garstang's book on the songs of birds and about Haydn's Bird Quartet and Wagner's bird music in *Siegfried*. Tom had perfect pitch and a wonderful recall and he could sing whole passages from Boccherini's aviary music.

This was having something in common with your lover, she thought, remembering the way it had been with Mike, who was interested only in banking and golf and what he called making a home for one's family. She seemed to see a distant future in which she and Tom were together in their own home, a house where music was made, and with perhaps their own children. But that idea killed the vision and she could only put her arms round him again and hide her face against his chest.

Jed would have been at the party if it had not been his duty evening with the Safeguards. They were a group of three men and a woman, patrolling the Central Line trains westbound from Oxford Circus. By the time the train reached Ealing Broadway they had been in and out of every car and as the train returned they followed the same routine.

The woman had a car at Ealing in which she would drive them all home after the last train was gone. They rode in five westbound trains and four eastbound trains, observing how the crowds began to thin, especially in those heading for inner London, encountering no trouble beyond some pushing and shoving by teenage boys and a smoker in the third car who put out his cigarette without protest when one of them asked him. The smoker was black. The only other black person in the car accused them of being racist, which made one of the other men indignant and started an argument.

The last train going westwards disgorged its passengers at Queensway and Notting Hill Gate, five only at Shepherd's Bush and one lonely traveller at White City.

'I believe we're the only ones left,' said Jed as they stopped at East Acton, a rather dark little station that looked as if it might be out in the country.

At Ealing Broadway they found they had been. Walking along the empty platform, away from the empty train, they felt like the four last people on earth.

9

An American was responsible for electrifying the London Underground.

He was a monopoly capitalist from Chicago called Charles Tyson Yerkes. (The name should be pronounced to rhyme with 'turkeys'.) He came into control of the District Underground Railway in 1900 but he had no particular interest in trains or the tracks they run on. He was interested in making money.

Yerkes had been an embezzler in the United States and had served a prison sentence. He was thrown out of Chicago and fled to New York where he built a palace and filled it with Old Masters. In London he gradually took over the Underground system and came to control every line except the Metropolitan. But first he had built his own power station at Lots Road in Chelsea, and another at Neasden, and electrified the District Line.

London Transport Underground still draws its power from Lots Road, the vast elegant power station that overshadows Chelsea Harbour.

In no other British rail system are the sections of a train called cars. They are variously named coaches, carriages or compartments. But cars are what they are called on the London Underground, just as they are in all American trains. Were they dubbed cars by Yerkes, the crooked tycoon from Chicago?

When Yerkes died in the Waldorf-Astoria Hotel his empire was taken over by the son of a Derbyshire coach-maker, Albert Henry Stanley. He had been President of the Board of Trade in the 1914–18 War and was later created Lord Ashfield. He was godfather to a child born in a Bakerloo Line train and gave her a silver christening mug when she was named Thelma Ursula Beatrice Eleanor. T.U.B.E.

'I hope people will not make a habit of this,' said Lord Ashfield, 'as I am a busy man.'

When Jarvis first rode the Bay Area Rapid Transit system, or BART, in San Francisco, there were carpets on the floors of cars and closed circuit television in operation. He had never seen anything like it before and he was astonished. This was in the early seventies, when he was very young.

The massive car in which he sat was twenty-five yards long. The whole system had been constructed to stand up to earthquake pressures. But Jarvis's greatest pleasure came from knowing that this line, whose builders had had to work in compressed air because of the high water-table in downtown San Francisco, passed through the rock under the deepest bay in the world.

In those days he had been a smoker. On leaving Powell Street he had lit a cigarette and within seconds a disembodied voice was booming at him to extinguish it and at the next station put it out the door on to the track. Jarvis had complied. So entranced was he by all this technology that he half expected the same voice to thank him.

Jasper smoked for show. He didn't much enjoy it, but enjoyment was irrelevant. It was something people of his age were not supposed to do and that was enough for him. Another thing he was not supposed to do was be tattooed. His tattoo had been done the previous winter by a Chinese man in Harlesden, who specialized in non-fade colours, fluorescents and airbrush fantasy.

No one ever saw Jasper naked, since he skived off going swimming with his school and Tina was never present when he bathed, but he intended, one day, as a treat or reward, to show the tattoo to Bienvida. It was on his back, between his shoulder blades. The Chinese man had wanted to do a Celtic torque in plain black, very fashionable at the time, but Jasper's wish was for something less austere. He chose a lion done in tawny red, prowling among turquoise palm trees and blue and purple flowers. He could only see it himself by standing with his back to one mirror and looking in another. He was very interested in discovering whether the tattoo would grow as he grew and he thought he already detected some enlargement. Having it done had been painful and quite expensive. When he got a passport of his own, if they still had the sort Jarvis had by that time, he was going to write 'lion tattoo on back' under 'distinguishing marks'.

Jasper often went to school but nearly as often did not. His school was a big red-brick Victorian building to the east of Kilburn. There were not enough teachers, those there were harassed almost beyond bearing and driven from pillar to post, and no one ever seemed to know who Jasper was, still less remember his name. A great many obscure languages were spoken and some children remained silent because no one else spoke their language.

It was not long before Jasper made contact with the boy who wrote the sickness notes. Damon could copy anyone's handwriting and had been told by their class teacher, in a burst of anger, that he would go far, perhaps as far as the Scrubs for forgery. But she never seemed to make the connection between these skills and the sickness notes, apparently in parents' hands, which her pupils brought to school after prolonged absences of two or three weeks. She was busy and tired and underpaid and fed up.

Damon had given Jasper measles, glandular fever, two bouts of flu and two colds since Easter. He and Jasper and others, schoolfellows or street acquaintances, spent their days on the streets or in the Underground. At first they had taken to the Underground because it was warm, later for other reasons. Jasper thought of a way of smoking in the trains.

They clutched each other and fell about, it made them laugh so much. Jasper laughed until he thought he was going to be sick. Prudently, they had got into the Jubilee

Line train at Finchley Road, in case someone they knew might be on the platform at West Hampstead.

In the train, in a car with only two other people in it, Jasper held up his cigarette in the middle of the space where the doors would meet when they drew together, and let them close on it. The cigarette was held in place quite tightly with the end outside and filter tip towards him. When the train started Jasper put his mouth over the tip and realized he couldn't light the cigarette because the end was outside. This was what started him laughing.

There were five of them. They laughed and pushed each other about. A boy called Lee fell over and rolled about on his back with his legs in the air like a dog. Damon rubbed Lee's stomach with his foot the way you would a dog's and Lee screamed because it tickled. All the while the cigarette was in between the doors, being carried along with them to Swiss Cottage.

In the station Jasper forgot for a moment that the doors were the kind that need to be opened by pressing the button and wondered why they didn't open. He had his cigarette firmly between his lips because he didn't want it falling on the floor, or worse, on to the track. Damon pressed the button, the doors parted and Jasper, making sure no one was watching, lit his cigarette. He held it up there in his fingers and let the doors close on it. In order to stop it going out he drew hard on it and exhaled billows of smoke into the car.

They were hysterical and hiccupping with so much laughter. Of the two passengers, both women, one had turned and given them a glare, the other pretended nothing was going on. Jasper knew she was pretending, though he could not have said how he knew. Damon and Lee lit up cigarettes of their own at St John's Wood, which they placed between the doors, and Chris and Kevin were going to do the same at Baker Street. But there a braver adult, entering and pushing them aside, saw what was going on and drove them out of the train.

All five of them had tickets. It might just be possible to get past the ticket collector at West Hampstead without paying but at Finchley Road there was a nearly impenetrable barrier of ticket gates. Jasper and his companions were of a size to creep under gates and had done this until they were caught. They walked along the platform and made their way to the Metropolitan Line, thus entering, though they did not know it, the oldest part of the system.

The London Underground is the second largest metro system in the world. Its length of 422 kilometres is exceeded — just exceeded — only by New York's network.

The Metropolitan Line grew fast in the 1860s and 1870s, the District Line joined it and it spread its branches out into the open countryside to the north-west of London. But it was still a steam railway and remained so until after the turn of the century.

These were cut-and-cover railway systems. By 1890 a different kind of underground railway, a tube, had been tunnelled out through the green and yellow clay (incidentally providing materials for millions of bricks), and this first line passed under the river from King William Street to Stockwell. It was known at first as a subway, a name thought of as an American term for an underground system, but later on was named the City and South London Railway and became the first tube railway in the world.

Another remarkable thing about it was that the trailer cars were pulled by electric engines. Although the passengers in the 'sardine box railway' had to sit facing each other on long benches in light too dim to read a newspaper, they could breathe. The days of fear of a subterranean death from suffocation, at least if you lived in south London, were past.

The buskers were at Leicester Square, deep down at the level of the Piccadilly Line. Peter had borrowed a xylophone from a dying patient at the hospice and with Alice on the violin and Tom with his trumpet, they were attempting the foxtrot from a Shostakovich jazz band suite.

Alice was learning how to make a receptacle out of a scarf and had folded a cheap silk square into a bonnet shape. It had started filling with coins when they played the popular Eine Kleine Nachtmusik. This odd Russian jazz, rendered on unsuitable instruments, was nearly as successful. She could not see how much was in the scarf, only that there were a lot of pound coins among the others.

Tom was exultant. He kept saying how their fortunes had taken a turn for the better from the moment Alice began playing with the group.

'It's you, you're magic. You're our lucky charm.'

She smiled at him but pulled away when he tried to kiss her. Kissing in public, holding each other, even holding hands, was not something she would ever consent to. But she was starting to feel that making music underground might not be too unacceptable a way of living, it might be preferable to certain compromises, when an unpleasant thing happened.

For a while people had dropped coins into the scarf in passing but since Tom began to sing, starting on his Mozart opera repertoire, a small crowd lingered. Among them was a boy of about fifteen, who suddenly bobbed down, snatched the scarf and ran.

Alice could not go on playing. The bow flagged in her hand and she heard herself exclaim. Tom gave chase. He went running off after the boy down the tunnel, dodging people and cannoning into others. After a moment or two Peter followed him. They came back empty-handed. What had happened was what always seemed to happen when there was trouble underground. A train – which, as Peter said, the law-abiding might wait ten minutes for – arrived and bore the boy away in the nick of time.

Alice burst into tears, she could not help herself. Anyway, she knew, and perhaps Tom knew too, that it was not just this theft which had made her cry, not only this isolated setback.

'We've got to have money,' she told Tom as they went home together in the Jubilee train. 'We'll need money for our educations.' She surprised herself, the words came out, she had not thought about them or thought at all about this subject. But now they were spoken she knew she had been right. This was what they had to do.

'What educations?'

'We've got to go on, you and I. You said I'd save you and that's the way I'm going to do it. I'm going to see you get more education. And I've got to have violin lessons. I've got to find a teacher because I'm just not good enough, I'm utterly out of practice and I need help. You have to finish your degree and you know you say what stops you is money.'

'We make money playing in the tube.'

'We've just lost everything we've made.'

'It's never happened before.'

'We never make very much, Tom.'

He took it as a personal reproach. She saw him blush, the way Mike might have done if someone told him his salary at the bank was inadequate. And as Mike also might have spoken, crossly and defensively, he said, 'It'll get better. I've got plans.'

'We need real money,' she said. 'I think I'm going to have to get a job.' She corrected herself, 'Well, we're going to have to get jobs. I've got to do what I set out to do, Tom. I've given up too much just to let it go.'

'You can be what you like,' he said. 'You can be anything you like. I wish I had untold thousands to give you. I love you.'

She never knew what to answer when he said that. It made her feel awkward and she looked away.

The Metropolitan and District Lines, though hugely expanded, still operated by steam in 1895, the date of Conan Doyle's The Bruce-Partington Plans. *This story depends for its interest and a good deal of its plot on the existence of the District Line.*

It would no longer be possible to do as Oberstein and Colonel Walter did and place a dead man on the top of a train from a window in west London. The train carrying the body of Cadogan West gave a lurch as it passed over the points and the curve in the rails just before Aldgate Station. The body was thrown off on to the track and the investigators with the exception of Sherlock Holmes were deceived into believing it had fallen from a carriage. It could not happen today. This was at Gloucester Road, or near it, and though the tall buildings are very close to the line here, they are not close enough for anyone inside to reach or even touch a passing train.

Illustrations from Sherlock Holmes stories decorate the platforms at Baker Street, but The Bruce-Partington Plans *is not among them.*

Can this be because London Transport was afraid it might give passengers ideas?

The cars in Underground trains have a door at each end as well as the double- and single-leaf doors for passenger use. The end doors, with sliding glass-panel window for ventilation, are *not* for passenger use. Notices attached to them make this plain. Above all, they are not to be used when the train is in motion.

It is here, where the doors are, that cars are linked together. The linkage is tight and the space between the doors is a few inches. Outside the train, at the foot of each door, is a step or running board, again no more than inches wide. On the body of the car, on each side of the door and on what might be called the architrave, are two handles. The roofs of the cars are ellipses, the curves somewhat shallower than in the days of Charles Tyson Yerkes or, come to that, Sherlock Holmes.

At Ladbroke Grove a boy called Dean Miller, whom the rest of them knew and had teamed up with on the platform at Royal Oak, opened the door at the end of the car and climbed up on to the roof.

There was no purpose in this. If Dean had a motive for doing it he did not say what it was. But they had no need of motive or purpose. It was enough to do it.

This is a very old part of the Metropolitan, called the Hammersmith Line, nearly 130 years old, the line running out in the open via Latimer Road, Shepherd's Bush and Goldhawk Road to Hammersmith. There are no tunnels and no low bridges to encounter on the train's journey to Latimer Road. As Ladbroke Grove is left behind, the chimney of the old brick kiln at the now demolished Ruston Mews can be seen, the street once called Rillington Place where Christie the multiple murderer lived, killed women and immured them in his garden and the cupboards of his house.

But this was unknown to Dean Miller, it having happened twenty-seven years before he was born. Spreadeagled on the roof of the car in a scissors or St Andrew's Cross position, he concentrated on holding on and not losing his balance as the train gathered speed under the shadow of the Westway and rocked past the desolate terraces of north Kensington. He had done this before, but not here. He had done it on one of the western stretches of the Central Line from North Acton to Ealing Broadway, a rather more hair-raising experience than this. For one thing, it had begun to rain as soon as he had climbed on to the car. The train had halted for a full five minutes on the western side of West Acton and all that time Dean had been lying on the roof in the rain. He heard later that a suicide had thrown himself on to the line.

It was not raining this time and the train went through to Latimer Road unhindered. Dean climbed off the roof and let himself into the car the way he had come. Surrounded by the others who made a protective wall between him and the rest of the passengers, he stood there brushing himself down.

Jasper said, 'What was it like?'

'It was OK,' said Dean.

'Would you do it on one of the underground bits?'

'Would *you*?'

Having brushed the most obvious dirt off his clothes, Dean sat down. He broke off and ate a piece of Mint Crisp from out of the platform chocolate machine Kevin offered him as a tribute to his prowess.

'You couldn't do it where it's, you know, really tube. Not unless you're less than nine inches through. You'd get your head knocked off.'

This led to an attempt by Chris to measure the chest depth and head size of the others. But since he had no tape measure he could only estimate, by a very rough and ready method, that Lee being the thinnest was the only one to qualify. Lee gave him a shove, there was some pushing and tripping up, Kevin fell over into Dean's lap and a woman at the other end of the car shouted that if they didn't behave themselves she'd find someone at Goldhawk Road who would make them.

The easiest course was to leave the car, which they did by the end doors, and they were still walking in single file through the train when it came into Hammersmith. The Metropolitan has a different station here from that used by the District and Piccadilly Lines. They made the change-over and came back into London on a District Line train from Richmond. At West Kensington Lee wanted to get out on to the roof and sledge to Gloucester Road but Dean, who had assumed the position of expert adviser, said he wasn't sure about the tunnels. He thought you would have to keep well over to one side of the car roof to avoid being struck by the side of the tunnel arch as the train came into Gloucester Road.

But which side? He found it hard to remember whether you had to position yourself on the left or the right side. They all got out at Gloucester Road and tried to check it out. Chris said it was obvious you would have to be on the right side. Not if you were in a Circle train though, Kevin said. Then it would be the left.

No one felt like risking an attempt on Gloucester Road to South Kensington. They changed platforms for the Circle going clockwise and, told by Dean that it was a safe stretch, at Gloucester Road both Chris and Damon climbed out on to the roof of the car. The train stood a long time in Gloucester Road station, for no apparent reason. Passengers went to the open doors and looked up and down the platform, trying to make out why they were stuck there, but no one looked up on to the roof of the car. No one ever does.

Before the train started Damon came down. He didn't say anything. He just shook his head.

'Chicken,' said Dean.

'I was not.'

'You were.'

'I was not chicken. I was cold. It's cold up there.'

Jasper thought of going up in his place. He immediately felt excited. Then he felt sick. Once he had thought of it he knew he would have to do it. If not now, tomorrow. If not tomorrow, next week. He would have to do it. But he wasn't going to climb up there now and once up there see some obstruction ahead, some tunnel rim that might be just too low, so that he had to get down again and come back in like Damon had. And get called chicken by the expert.

He wished the train would start. When the train had started he wouldn't be able to go up there. It felt dead, marooned, abandoned, as if it would never move. As the chugging of the motors began, on a sudden unexpected surge, he felt as relieved as any forty-year-old traveller in a hurry to keep an appointment. The doors gave their preliminary sigh and closed. Jasper knelt up on the seats with the rest of them to observe out of the window their progress to Kensington High Street.

There was not much to see. The train immediately entered the tunnel – a tunnel cut just beneath the surface, of course, not the deep tube. There was probably a space eighteen inches deep or more between the roof of the car and that of the tunnel. It was dark but not black-dark as inside the tube. You could see the dirty brown cables strung along the walls. Where the Circle runs through the cut-and-cover, in most stretches of it, are open shafts for ventilation. There are two of these on the stretch between Gloucester Road and Kensington High Street and, as the train passed under the first one, they all cheered. Daylight suddenly burst upon them, sunlight, and up there for a moment blue sky and white clouds and a tall whitish building.

The darkness made this a more hazardous stretch than that undertaken by Dean Miller, or if not more hazardous, more frightening. 'Scary' was Kevin's word for it, an American word he said, and they all agreed that, yes, it was scary. You could never be absolutely sure, Jasper thought, that up there in the tunnel roof there wouldn't be some great iron bar or post sticking down to within an inch or two of the top of the car. You wouldn't be able to see, or avoid it if you could see.

They cheered again when the train passed under the next, much bigger shaft, again the sunshine came flooding in and again you could see the sky and brickwork and even trees. A moment or two of renewed darkness and then the train was coming into Kensington High Street. Covered in

116

dirt, Chris came quickly back into the car, showing no pride in his achievement, but giving Damon a glare of contempt.

'What got into you? Were you chicken?'

'I was not,' said Damon.

'You were scared,' said Chris. 'There's nothing to be scared about. It was OK. It was great.'

'I was not scared.'

'Chicken, chicken, chicken,' said Dean.

Damon hit him. They rolled on to the floor. Someone down the car said it was a disgrace and the school holidays were too long and someone else said, pity the poor teachers. At Notting Hill Gate, as they were leaving the car, they found their way impeded by a uniformed official of London Transport Underground that the woman who said the holidays were too long had got hold of and was complaining to.

The official was saying, 'Now wait a minute, you just wait a minute,' and put his arm out right across the open doorway. Jasper ducked underneath it and started running. They all knew there were no television cameras here. It would have been a different matter at Oxford Circus, say. Damon and Chris followed him. None of them looked back to see what happened but galloped for the interchange to the Central Line.

This involved an escalator going deep down. Instead of standing on the treads, they ran down. Jasper wondered if the man in uniform had actually seen Chris on the roof of the car, had had a phone call from Kensington High Street that someone was on the roof of a car, or if he knew nothing except what that woman was telling him. Buskers were at the foot of the escalator, not Alice and Tom and Peter, but two men with a saxophone and an electric guitar, playing rock. Jasper looked back up the empty moving stair.

On the eastbound platform Dean and Lee were already waiting for them. They had doubled back and got out of the single-leaf door of the car. Now there was only Kevin unaccounted for. He came rushing on to the platform just as a train bound for Debden came in. Nothing had happened, he had been given a warning, that was all. They all got into the train, though Dean's idea had been to head for Epping, but it was as well to be on the safe side.

As soon as they were in the train, in a rather crowded car where there was no chance of a seat, Jasper understood what he had to do. This was it. When the train had emerged from the last tunnel on the Central Line between Stratford and Leyton, issuing with little more space to spare than toothpaste squeezed out of the nozzle of another kind of tube, somewhere past that point, though he was not sure yet where, he would climb out on to the roof of the car.

He stood between Kevin and Damon, holding on to the upright, saying nothing. He intended to tell no one about this, just to do it. The car remained crowded as far as Holborn and then the passengers thinned out. Jasper got a seat. He was not yet of an age where polite altruism is practised among friends, a situation in which one denies oneself comfort and offers it to another. Such a thing would not have occurred to Jasper or to any of them. A seat became vacant and he sat down in it.

In the back pocket of his jeans he could feel the rather squashed packet of cigarettes. When he had done his roof ride and the sick feeling had been replaced by a feeling of triumph, he would have a cigarette. The closed doors would hold it for him and he would smoke it on the way back as he had smoked that earlier one on the way down from Finchley Road.

They came back on the Northern Line, a tall handsome

man in a long overcoat and a man whose face was mostly hidden by an upturned collar and a hat pulled well down. It was a train bound for Mill Hill East that they got into, so they were obliged to change. They did so at Euston. But instead of waiting on the same platform for an Edgware train, they made their way up to the British Rail terminus, and in the men's lavatory the bear got into his bear suit. Outside, in the concourse, the bear-leader passed the chain round the bear's neck, made a noose of it, and led the bear back to the Underground.

Money was never short with the bear-leader. It was not for money that he had the bear dance to amuse commuters. He made no attempt to re-enter the system without paying but bought two tickets from the machine while the bear waited meekly with bowed head. As they descended the escalator they were once more the centre of attention. No one looked anywhere but at them, not at the advertisements or each other or the tube map, but at the man and the bear.

In the passage leading back to the northbound platform of the Northern Line they stopped in a corner, the man got out his mouth organ and the bear began to dance. The rich ignore the simplest things in the area of earning, making, keeping, *regarding* money, and the bear-leader forgot to put any receptacle for money on the ground in front of them. He had no hat and certainly he had no handkerchief, but the bag in which the Semtex was would have done, or the square scarf which, under the brown hairy suit, was still knotted round the bear's neck.

It scarcely mattered, since only one of the passers-by gave them anything. This was a man who perhaps gave to all tube buskers indiscriminately, without even looking at them, for he tossed a 5p piece on to the ground as he strode past. The coin bounced, spun and rolled away into the corner.

The bear said, 'Put the bag between us and open the top of it.'

'Remember what's inside.'

'That won't matter. You could throw a fag end in, throw a lighted match in. It needs percussion to go up. Black powder now, that would be something else again.'

'I'm learning,' said the man with the mouth organ.

They were bound for Epping because Dean lived there. A self-appointed leader, he made the rules without being explicit about them or even explaining that there were rules. He wanted to go home and therefore the others must come with him. What happened to the rest of them when he left them on Epping's still rustic station, at the extreme eastern end of the Central Line, was their business or misfortune. Jasper sensed some of this and vowed not to go along with it in the sheeplike fashion of the others.

Cars in London Transport Underground are seldom entirely empty. Even in the slack times, between rush hours, there are usually several people in each car, even on these distant tentacles of the lines. In their car, after Snaresbrook, only the six of them remained. Jasper had begun to feel hungry. It was lunchtime and past. He had about a pound on him, in small change, which would buy no more than a chocolate bar and a couple of packets of crisps. But Kevin was a notorious thief and always had money. The idea of Kevin's rewarding him for his prowess with a real lunch somewhere acted as a spur to Jasper, but he did not really need a spur. He was prepared, determined, ready.

A woman the same age as their combined ages stepped into the car at Woodford and quickly stepped out again when she saw Lee swinging from the passenger hand-holds, Damon and Kevin sparring on the floor and Chris doing something to a continental ferry advertisement with a red felt-tipped pen.

It was getting greener outside the windows, not exactly country but a lot of trees and leaves and green grass among the buildings. At Debden they would have to change, if they were going on further with Dean Miller. Jasper was not. Loughton was the place he thought of as the station at which to de-train and seek food. He was suddenly aware of the sun, of bright sunshine pouring into the car.

The platform at Buckhurst Hill was empty, or empty at their end. The station looked sunlit, deserted. It looked like somewhere waiting for a film to happen, Jasper thought, like a Western on television where two gunmen will come out of the badlands and hold up the mailtrain on the Santa Fe railroad. By that time he had opened the door at the end of the car. Behind him Dean said, 'He's going to sledge,' but Jasper did not look back.

He climbed up the door of the next car, using the handles and window frames as footholds. It was easy getting up there. What he had not anticipated was that the top of the train would be so smooth. Curved, yes, he had expected that, he had known he wasn't going to find a flat plateau, but something to hold on to he had expected, a double ridge perhaps, pipes or cables, not what was in fact there, nothing more than shallow flanges at the tops of the double-leaf doors. Nothing would have made him do a Damon and slink back. He squatted, then lay down, he edged and wriggled along and had his fingers round those curved shallow indentations when the train started.

It gave a lurch and Jasper, his heart in his mouth, felt his body jerk and slip. He held on, digging his fingers into metal, as if the metal were soft and would give. The train pulled out, heading for Loughton along the green valley of the Roding. Under his prone body the roof felt hot. September sunshine had been shining on it ever since Leyton. Now the sun stroked Jasper's back, laid a burning hand on the nape of his neck. He spread his legs and tensed his fingers. He was in control now, he had the measure of this car roof, this train, the knack of getting a grip on it.

In spite of the heat, he understood why it was called sledging. This was what it must be like on a toboggan roaring down the snowy slope of a mountainside. A great exhilaration filled him. The train was going fast, rushing along now, and the clatter of it sang in his ears. He bounced a little, pleasantly, not alarmingly. Why had no one said it was like this? Why had no one told him how marvellous it was?

Jasper would have liked to yell and sing and shout, if he had dared lift up his head. He would have liked to stand on the roof of the train and leap along from car to car like one of the bad guys in that Western. But he dared not move, not this time, not yet, and he held on tight, lying there with his body ten times more thrillingly alive than he had ever known it.

A great joy possessed him as the train bore him on, on, on through the sunshine, down the line to Loughton.

IO

Yelena Donskoy lived not far away, over the other side of the Finchley Road, in Netherhall Way. Alice could easily walk there, carrying her violin. The money she had left of the hundred pounds she had brought with her would not even cover the first lesson.

'I'll give you the money,' Tom said. 'You ought to know that. What's mine is yours.'

They were sitting in the garden, on the grass on Jarvis's blanket. Tom had a toy xylophone someone had given Bienvida and he kept playing short snatches of melody. Alice touched his hand.

'I do know. You're good to me. But I'm going to have to get a job.'

He could only think of music. To him it was inconceivable she or he or anyone with her training and aspirations could seek any work but the most menial outside. Working in a sandwich bar was all right, that was like an actor 'resting'.

'Teaching, d'you mean?' he said. His own teaching job had come to an end. The child had failed her flute exam and the parents blamed him.

'I mean a secretarial job.'

He played a long trill on the rainbow-coloured plates. 'You can't be serious.'

'I think I could do it. I've got a degree and they say it doesn't matter what you've got a degree in as long as you've got one. I used to work for my father in the holidays and I got quite good on the computer.'

Hearing about her degree had begun to irritate him. It seemed to throw his own deficiencies into relief. She was beginning to know that look of his, sarcastic, petulant, the eyebrows up and head a little to one side.

'But *why?*'

A train came up from Finchley Road. She waited for it to pass. 'Tom, I haven't enough money to pay Madame Donskoy for even one lesson. I know you'll give it to me but you can't go on giving it to me, can you? You haven't got it. I think I could earn quite a lot and it wouldn't be for long – maybe a year. It would be easy to travel up and down from here, so close to the tube.'

'I don't believe I'm hearing any of this. We make money busking and we have a good time, don't we? We're playing real music and getting an audience. We made £21 yesterday.'

She did not say it aloud, but thought, between three people for a day's work. Tom banged away at a single note on the xylophone. Sometimes he looked like a little boy, his lips pushed out.

'I thought you liked playing the violin.' It might have been Jasper talking.

'I like it too much not to do the best I can with it.' She tried to talk briskly. 'I haven't been quite honest. I'm not thinking about a job, I've applied for one. I've got an interview on Friday afternoon.'

He sat up. She could see he was furious. In a quick violent gesture he hurled the toy hammer he was holding across the garden.

Alice pretended to take no notice. She began talking steadily about how she had hoped her father's partner would give her a reference. But her father still refused to speak to her and when approached through her mother as intermediary, said that if it was in his power he would like to see to it that she never got a job anywhere ever again. She wrote direct to her father's partner. Jarvis was going to give her the other reference. He knew nothing about her secretarial skills but, as Tina said, he would give anybody a reference for anything, he was kind.

Tom was not looking at her, he seemed not to be listening. When she tried to take his hand he snatched it away. She got up and went to hunt for Bienvida's xylophone hammer in the bushes.

A disquieting thing happened. Having found the hammer up by the fence which separated the garden from the railway line, she had to go back to him. She sat down cautiously. He was kneeling, she thought he was getting up, but suddenly he threw his arms round her and held her so that she could hardly breathe. It was public here and she hated the idea of people seeing but she let herself go limp in his arms.

'I love you so much, darling. Don't quarrel with me, we mustn't ever quarrel.'

Nobody in Bienvida's class at school ever had tea. They had crisps or chocolate biscuits and cans of drink when they got home from school, but not tea, not the kind of thing she got at her grandmother's. Bienvida knew nothing of the English tradition of tea, bread and butter and sandwiches, biscuits and cake and a pot of tea served at four o'clock. She was too young to have read about it and no one had told her, but she sensed, when she had tea at Lilac Villa, that this was how things should be, had *used* to be, and was something surely specially appropriate for people of her age when they got home at four.

Other things at Cecilia's Bienvida also much approved of. She was a child who liked washing her hands before meals, perhaps because she had never been told to do so. She liked sitting in a clean room, at a table with a cloth on it, or on the chintz sofa, watching *Neighbours* on her grandmother's television. She liked talking with Cecilia, though much of what she said to her was lies.

Bienvida told the lies less for her own protection than for her mother's. And in the hope of making Cecilia happy and making her believe existence at Cambridge School was orderly and smooth-running and what Cecilia herself would call decent. So when her grandmother asked her, putting the question optimistically, as one expecting the answer 'yes', if Jasper was attending school regularly, Bienvida replied that he was.

'He does go to school, doesn't he, Bienvida?'

'Yes, of course he does,' Bienvida said with as much earnestness as she could muster.

'Because he's a clever boy and he needs education.' Cecilia hesitated, went on vaguely, 'He would need it even more if he weren't clever, but I'm sure you know what I mean.'

Bienvida, eating homemade sponge cake, butter-iced and scattered with chocolate vermicelli, said she did know. She sat very upright at the table, enjoying the soapy smell of her clean hands.

'I expect you go to bed at the same time, don't you, even though he is two years older than you?'

This time Bienvida did not have to lie. She replied that this was true, they did go to bed at the same, forbearing to add that it was seldom before eleven and might be at midnight. Rather gracefully, she changed the subject by asking if she could have another piece of cake, another piece of this *delicious* cake, a grown-up adjective which made her grandmother smile.

Cecilia, in spite of the smile, felt miserable and ashamed of herself. It was very wrong, she had always maintained, to question innocent children about their mode of life behind their parents' backs. If she had heard of anyone else doing it she would deeply have disapproved. But she could not help herself. She could not help herself though she was not entirely, or even halfway, deceived by Bienvida's lies.

She even knew what kind of lies they were, designed to protect her and Tina and keep them happy and caring for one another, and she loved Bienvida even more for this.

Knowing they were lies should have kept her from further questioning. It inhibited her but could not quite stop her. She felt her way round the burning question, the one that might have the terrible answer, she danced round it, pouring Bienvida more weak sugary tea, plying her with chocolate chip cookies. Was Jed still there? That noise she heard while visiting the School, was that really a bird he kept?

'It caught a magpie,' said Bienvida. 'It killed it.'

To Cecilia's horror, her dark eyes, often tragic, filled with tears. How to comfort her? What to say? There was of course nothing to say, there was no comfort. But Cecilia's speculation that she might have in the freezer the kind of ice-cream that is called a Dracula stopped the tears falling. And Cecilia, coming back from the kitchen with this dark-red frozen confection in a glass dish, returning to Bienvida who sat quiet and sad with her hands folded, could not proceed to her most important question, her ultimate, momentous and awesome question. She could not bring herself to it. It was not possible for her to ask this innocent and gentle child, whose eyes were too wary and too sad for her age, if her mother's boyfriend Billy was living with her and sharing her bed. However she put it, whatever circumlocutory terms she used, she could not ask it and retain her self-respect. As it was she could feel in her mouth the sour taste of disgust.

It was a distance of no more than two hundred yards to the School but Cecilia walked her home. It was daylight, it was on the whole a 'nice' district, Cecilia thought Bienvida an obedient girl who would remember about not speaking to strangers, but nevertheless she walked home to the School with her. She always did. She had read too many newspaper accounts of abducted and murdered children, seen too much evidence on the television of the peril children were in.

At the School gates she left Bienvida and watched her until she disappeared round the back of the house. She might have gone in with her, the child had even asked her if she was coming in, but Cecilia never called at the School in the evenings. Besides disliking the place, she was afraid of what she might see. Daphne had told her she imagined much worse than could possibly be happening, drinking and even drugs and the place in a mess and Tina with some man, perhaps in bed with some man. Oh, no, that's nonsense, Cecilia had said, I don't imagine that at all, but she did.

When she got back Cecilia went upstairs and looked at the rooms up there. A pang came to her when she remembered how she had obliged Tina to 'live' downstairs while sleeping on the top floor. That this had really only been so that she could see as much as possible of her grandchildren did not really make it any better. Her motive had been selfish. It was pleasant upstairs, with fine views from the rear windows. You could see as far as the Heath. A bedroom each for the children, a living room, and the fourth room she would have converted into a bathroom and a kitchen, as she should have done long ago. Tina could have the big bedroom on the floor below. This reminded Cecilia that Tina probably was not sleeping alone, probably never would sleep alone. She did not think she could stand having Tina's boyfriend, any boyfriend of Tina's, to live in her house.

It came back always to this: she loved Tina and the children, but she could hardly bear having Tina live with her. Why were human beings made this way, that they did not want to be – or did not want constantly to be – with the people they loved best? Except when they were in love, of course.

Cecilia, clearing away the tea things, closing the window

because the evenings were cool, was visited by a faint memory of being in love. She was dancing with Frank Darne, wearing a backless dress which her own mother had not approved of and into which she had inserted a cover-up panel of silk. It was to be a long time before she and Frank were married, they had been engaged for years, and by the time of their marriage she had grown very used to him, was very fond of him and secure with him. The bed part she had not much cared for, though as long as it did not hurt it was bearable. But at that dance, all those years before, as she felt his hand on her bare shoulder and saw the soft strange expression in his eyes, she had had such an odd thought: be mine, she had thought, come to me so that I am you and you are me, let us be lost in each other.

After all this time she remembered it. She often remembered it. But it had not lasted long, nor come again. And of course she had not spoken those words aloud. Theirs had not been a passionate relationship, or she supposed not, having known no other to judge by. He had been good to her, a good husband and father.

Cecilia looked at the grandfather clock which had belonged to Frank's mother. A quarter to six. It was Daphne's turn to phone. She put on the news just to get the headlines and sure as fate, regular as clockwork, the phone rang at two minutes past. While she had been waiting she wondered what everyone would say to the preposterous idea of her moving out of this house, leaving it to Tina, and going to live in Willesden with Daphne.

Because a light was on up in the gallery but not downstairs, the electrolier cast its spider shadow on the vestibule floor. A window open somewhere caused the chain of the electrolier to vibrate ever so little and this kept the spider on the move, creeping across the floorboards, sometimes making a little sideways jump, crab-fashion.

Bienvida did not much like it, she had not liked the way the spider feet ran across her own as she went across the vestibule. The cloakroom, even on her own, was preferable, even though she expected to see a ghost.

She had made up her mind what it would be like, an old man with a white beard, a kind of Father Christmas in mourning, for its garments would be dark and diaphanous. It might have a noose slung lightly about its neck and, although she could not think where she had got hold of this idea, a scythe in its hand. Waiting for Jasper, sitting inside her sleeping bag and with a blanket round her, she trembled with a fear that was not entirely unpleasurable.

It was dark outside the little high window with its clear panes and its single ruby pane, and there was no light in the cloakroom. There was no bulb holder and only a piece of frayed flex coming out of the ceiling. Bienvida had brought pillows and cushions, two candles and a box of matches, two chocolate bars called Twirls and a doll named Caroline. She had wanted to be called Caroline for as long as she could remember and, failing to persuade anyone to call her this, had bestowed the name on the doll.

It was late, nearly a quarter to eleven, and Jasper had promised to be there by 10.30. It would be the first night they had spent in the cloakroom, having decided it would be wisest to wait for an evening when Tina had gone out. Tina would come back very late, creep into the Headmaster's Flat and avoid going near their bedrooms for fear of waking them. Bienvida had told her grandmother that Tina always came to look at them before she went to bed, but Cecilia, though longing to believe it, did not really do so.

It was hours since she had seen Jasper. While it was still light he had gone down to West End Lane, to the Indian shop on West End Lane bridge, to buy two cans of Coke and a comic. The Indian would most likely refuse to sell him cigarettes, or Bienvida hoped so. She disliked the smell of tobacco smoke in her bedroom. It was now totally dark, but for the square shape of moonlight cast on the floor from the small window high up in the wall. Bienvida lit one of her candles and placed it in the neck of a milk bottle. The light made the room more creepy, not less. Before, she had not been able to *see* the darkness but now she could, she could see the big dark spaces that looked solid, that looked like black crouching furry things, where the light did not reach.

Jasper came into the cloakroom before things got too bad. He had a torch he had 'borrowed' from Tom's now unoccupied room and a camera that was Jarvis's. Both children were getting into the habit of stealing things, here in the School and outside. They stole and were not found out, so it seemed easier the next time. Jasper had paid for his Coke at the shop on the bridge but not for the Smarties which he took from the counter while the Indian man had his back to him at the till.

Though in some ways this was a good opportunity, it was too dark in the cloakroom to show Bienvida his tattoo. It was also rather too cold to take his clothes off. He got into his sleeping bag, peeled the tops off the Coke cans and passed one to his sister.

'If we see anything,' he said, 'it will probably be at midnight and it'll be a sort of bundle hanging from a rope in the middle there.'

'I don't want to see it,' said Bienvida.

'Yes, you do. You want to see it. I'm going to take a photograph of it. It should come out all right with the flash. Shall I tell you where I went sledging today?'

'Yeah, OK, where did you?'

'I went on top of the train from West Hampstead to Finchley Road.'

Bienvida said nothing. The idea of riding on the tops of

tube trains did not attract her, nor was she altogether sure that she believed everything Jasper said. She helped herself to Smarties, or rather she picked out four orange Smarties. Those were the only kind she liked. Bienvida had noticed that the orange ones had milk chocolate inside them and tasted of orange whereas all the other kinds, though of different colours, red, green, mauve, yellow, brown, tasted the same and only of the plain chocolate in their centres. It was one of the mysteries of life that exercised her mind.

'I'm getting into training for the going-through-the-tunnel part,' said Jasper.

'You could get killed. You could get your head chopped off.'

'I said I was getting into training. It's a matter of keeping your head.'

Jasper laughed immoderately at his own joke and then repeated it in case Bienvida had missed the point. She had but she wasn't going to say so and smiled obediently. They ate the Twirls and finished the Coke. Jasper said it was two minutes to twelve and time to blow the candles out. Nothing would be seen by candlelight. He had his camera at the ready but all that happened at midnight was the entry into the house of Jarvis, Tina and an old friend of Tina's from the past.

By the time Jarvis had gone into Remove to make himself a cup of tea with the electric kettle he kept there and Tina and her friend had said good-night to him and gone into the Headmaster's Flat, both children were asleep. Tina was careful not to make a noise but she did not look into the children's rooms.

The Church of St Mary Woolnoth in King William Street was built in 1727. A Roman temple of Concord once stood on the site. The name of the church had nothing to do with wool but was a distortion of that of Wulfnoth, a Saxon prince, who had erected a timber church here and dedicated it to St Mary of the Nativity.

*A later building was badly damaged by the Great Fire of
1666. Nicholas Hawksmoor built the present church. Its ceiling is
painted blue with stars to resemble the night sky as it must have
been when the Romans looked up from the open space of an
atrium.*

*The first tube tunnel, in those days called the City and South
London, was tunnelled through beneath here. The Company had
parliamentary sanction to demolish St Mary Woolnoth and
would have done so but for the great public outcry. Bowing at
last to pressure, they underpinned the foundations of the church
and built Bank station on top of them.*

*An angel's head over the station entrance commemorates the
saving of the church.*

*A recorded voice warns you, as Central Line trains come into
Bank, 'Mind the gap, mind the gap, mind the gap, mind the
gap, stand clear of the doors, please.' The gap yawns at your feet
but it is not the only one in the system. There is quite a wide gap
between car and platform at Holborn on the northbound Piccadilly
Line, but no warning voice.*

*It is true that the gap at Bank is the result of the curve the line
must make, but not that it describes this curve to avoid passing
under the vaults of the Bank of England.*

Tina and Jarvis had gone out together some three hours
before to a pub in St John's Wood. The purpose of Jarvis's
visit to this pub was to meet a man who worked at
Intourist and who had very nearly guaranteed him an
investigative trip to the Soviet Union where, rumour had
it, there was a metro boom and eight new systems were
either being built or planned. The purpose of Tina's visit
was pleasure.

The Russian was late. Before he arrived Tina had spotted
someone she knew standing at the bar. This was a neatly
made, dark-haired man of medium height, aged perhaps
forty. She introduced him to Jarvis as Daniel, whom she

had last seen ten years ago when she happened to run into him on Denmark Hill. Jarvis noticed particularly Daniel's eyes, which were a very dark violet-brown, the colour of the heart of a pansy. They reminded him of someone else's eyes but he could not remember whose.

After he had drunk two vodkas and found fault with the brand provided by the pub, the Intourist man began whetting Jarvis's appetite with a description of the new little metro at Kuibyshev and the possibility of a visit to the earthquake-resistant system at Tashkent.

'In the Soviet Union we have the best metros in the world. All of them conform to the high technical standards of the Moscow system.'

Jarvis was not sure that he believed this, or even that the Moscow technical standards were high. He wanted to see for himself.

'In Erevan, for example,' said the Intourist man, 'the tunnels have been designed to withstand earthquake up to force ten on the Richter Scale.'

Jarvis thought the same could have been said of the Bay Area Rapid Transport in San Francisco. The next time he caught sight of Tina she was up to what he had once or twice before seen her engaged in, a kind of courtship ritual. She and Daniel were sitting on opposite sides of a small round table, holding right hands in the manner of people performing the move called the cobra in arm-wrestling and who are about to perform a trial of strength, but not doing this, not tense or combative but relaxed and absorbed in each other, their eyes held in unblinking contact, their lips slightly parted. While he watched, their mouths met in a kiss and drew away.

When the pub closed and the Russian had gone, they returned together in one of the last tubes to run northwards that night. It took a long time to get to St John's Wood station because Daniel kept stopping to kiss Tina under the street lamps.

While they waited on the platform Jarvis told them about King Solomon's carpet. This magic carpet of green silk was large enough for all the people to stand on it. When ready, Solomon told it where he wanted to go and it rose in the air and landed everyone at the station they wanted. He said the tube reminded him of this carpet and elaborated his theme, but they were not listening.

In a double seat, they held each other in a clinch from St John's Wood to Swiss Cottage, to Finchley Road, to West Hampstead. They walked to Cambridge School with their arms round each other. Jarvis, who was not much troubled by sexual feelings, who was celibate for months or even years on end, eyed them tolerantly and with about as much interest as he accorded to photographs of such efficient but relatively unexciting metro systems as those of Brazil.

Back at the School he offered them tea but they were too deeply entranced with each other even to answer him. He put on a light in Remove but soon turned it off, filled his kettle by moonlight, and watched from the open door the shadow of the electrolier hopping and tripping across the vestibule floor. Presently it became still and he knew that the open window somewhere had been closed.

The last train had passed along the line to Finchley Road and the last one had gone up to Kilburn and all was still and silent. Jarvis thought of how, with luck, he would soon be in Leningrad where the tunnels have been bored through the clay nearly as deeply as those under Hampstead Heath.

11

During the Second World War the London tube became a deep
shelter.

Heavy raids began on 7 September 1940. People bought low-
value tickets and refused to leave the Underground until the all-
clear had sounded. During that October an average of 138,000
people sheltered in the system and sheltering was eventually
allowed in all seventy-nine deep tube stations.

The station now named Archway was formerly called Highgate. The opening of a new Highgate station at the top of the
Archway Road, a very deep one, was delayed after the outbreak
of war so that it could be used solely as an air-raid shelter. It is
one of the deepest in the system. Passengers in trains rushing
through non-stop from Archway to East Finchley on the Northern
Line saw whole families sleeping on the platform.

Shelterers sleeping on the platform at Russell Square on the
Piccadilly Line heard during the nights a soft, continuous roar
coming through the tunnel. This was the snoring of sleepers on
the platforms at Holborn, next station down the line.

The British Museum hid its treasures in the tunnel between
Holborn and Aldwych.

The worst wartime disaster was at Balham on the Northern
Line at eight in the evening of 14 October 1940. A bomb
penetrated the northbound station tunnel at its northern end,
rupturing water mains and sewers. Water and gravel rushed into
a station by then plunged in darkness.

Those still alive were evacuated through emergency escape
hatches. Sixty-four shelterers and four railwaymen died. Later,
when it was all past, seven million gallons of water were
pumped out of the hole the bomb had made.

The day before Balham, nineteen people were killed and fifty-

two injured by a bomb at Bounds Green on the Piccadilly Line. The day before that, a bomb killed seven people at Trafalgar Square on the Bakerloo Line, and on the day after one person died after a bomb fell on Camden Town on the Northern Line.

At the Bank, on the evening of 11 January 1941, fifty-six people were killed and sixty-nine injured when a bomb cut through the concourse just below the street. The station collapsed and was closed for three months. A story, widely believed, that a hundred people trapped inside were never brought to the surface but walled up in a subterranean chamber, is almost certainly not true.

They were a legal firm who occupied the two top floors of a building to the north of Lincoln's Inn Fields. The brass plate on the façade of the house proclaimed them as Angell, Scherrer and Christianson, Solicitors and Commissioners for Oaths, and an incised arrow pointed in the direction of a narrow alley where the entrance door was.

Holborn was the nearest station, a few minutes' walk away. Alice took the Jubilee Line to Bond Street and the Central back to Holborn. She started work as secretary to James Christianson, whose room was on the top floor.

Tom became very angry when she told him she had got the job.

'I didn't think you meant it.'

'Of course I meant it. I need the money. You need money too. We've said we'd help each other with money and you've helped me. I'm very grateful that you've helped me pay for my lessons. Now I want to help you, I want to make you some return.'

They were in her room, the Headmaster's Study, finishing their evening meal. Tom had bought a bottle of wine, which Alice did not think they could afford. It was painfully clear they could not afford luxuries, yet Tom bought wine almost every night. He had emptied his third glass of it and in a sudden, unexpected and violent gesture, hurled the glass against the wall. Alice gasped with fright. It was the first instance she had seen of his temper.

'I don't want your fucking gratitude,' he shouted at her.

'I'm sorry, I only meant we agreed to sort of share things and do things together.'

'Is that what you call going off and getting this job? Doing things together? Sharing things means making music together, it means doing what we've always done, how we found each other. Do you remember how we found each other?'

The way he put it she found embarrassing. 'Of course I do, Tom.'

'It was at Holborn. In the station. I'll never forget it, I'll remember it all my life. You'll go through there on your way to this job of yours and you won't even think of it.'

She was picking up the pieces of broken glass. She went to the bathroom for water to try to wipe the wine trickle off the old wallpaper. When she came back he appalled her by falling on his knees at her feet and begging her to forgive him.

'I love you so much.'

'I know.'

'I want to do everything for you. It drives me mad that I do hardly anything, I feel so frustrated and impotent.'

'Hardly that.'

She wished she had not made that remark, a cheap crack, the kind of thing Mike used to say. It resulted in his taking her in his arms, urgently demanding that they make love. With Mike, Alice had often agreed to love-making for the sake of peace, though she might not feel like it and knew she would not enjoy it. When she left she resolved never to live like that again, yet here she was taking off her clothes and getting into bed with Tom, returning his kisses, running her hands over his body and even simulating sounds of pleasure and excitement.

Not doing so would mean being alone in the nights, without Tom to hold her. Waking in the night was still an awful thing. She thought about Catherine and she thought about failure at her music, what would become of her if she could not make it any further, if it turned out after all that she was only fit to become a teacher of children taking their first violin lessons.

Her own lessons with Madame Donskoy did not please or encourage her. They terrified her. She found herself constantly waiting for the Russian woman's approval. She would watch that broad, jowly, truculent face for some sign, not of appreciation, not of pleasure or even complacency, but just not of disgust. Possibly Yelena Donskoy was not disgusted, did not hate what she heard, but it was just that her old face had naturally fallen into those grim lines, as age had made the cheeks droop and pulled down the corners of her mouth.

No word of praise ever came from her. The most frequent sounds she made were grunts. She would adjust Alice's fingers. Sometimes Alice thought she made an absurd fuss about the way the violin was actually held, something she had not come across in a teacher since she first held a bow when she was twelve.

One day she said something that made Alice's blood go cold.

'It is very amusing how you find in this country grown-up men and women struggling with technical matters which in Europe would have been mastered when they were ten.'

'Do you mean violinists?'

Alice wished she had not asked this question. Madame Donskoy gave her horrid smile and looked sideways so that Alice could not help feeling that she herself would not have been dignified with that title, that no pupil who came to this murky, dark, stuffy house would have been.

Sometimes they had tea. Whether it actually came out of a samovar Alice did not know. It was cold, stewed, milkless, brought in in a jug. They drank it in a room where the chairs and tables were all draped in plush rugs or shawls and where there was a lot of greenish-blue and crimson Venetian glass. Yelena Donskoy talked about the German violinist Anne-Sophie Mutter for whom she had an extravagant admiration and Yehudi Menuhin whom she claimed as a friend.

Tom wanted to come and meet Alice after the lesson was over. His excuse was that it was not safe to walk home down Frognal and Canfield Gardens after dark. Alice let him. It was only once a week and if she permitted this she felt she was on firmer ground for resolutely refusing to let him come for her at Angell, Scherrer and Christianson.

Brian Elphick took the children out every Saturday. He always asked them what they would like to do.

'Go to the London Transport Museum in Covent Garden,' said Jasper promptly.

Brian agreed wholeheartedly. He had expected to be asked to take them to a funfair and took this as a sign that Jasper was beginning to develop an interest in things apart from ghosts, comics and junk food. In the train going down to Baker Street, they decided on the Transport Museum, a trip up the river, lunch at McDonald's somewhere and a visit to a cinema that was showing a double bill of two of Bienvida's favourite films: *Dumbo* and *The Belstone Fox*.

Inside the museum Brian watched Jasper examining tube cars, paying special attention to their roofs, with all the concentration of a foreign railway engineer on a fact-finding visit.

Bienvida, at her self-appointed task of making the best of things, or of giving the impression that this was the best of all possible worlds, said, 'Daniel is a cook in a restaurant. He cooks really nice food for us. Did you know?'

'Is he married?'

'Oh, no,' said Bienvida, who hadn't the faintest idea. 'I expect he'll marry Tina and take us all to live in a new townhouse in Mill Hill.'

Without Alice, busking in the tube concourses lost much of its charm. It also lost much of its income. Alice hated to hear this but Tom knew that a great many of the people who passed them, in the tunnels and at the foot of the escalators, only dropped a coin in the hat because Alice was a beautiful girl.

Peter still went with him, but not every day. He did not always feel like performing underground in the mornings when he had been working at the hospice all night. Peter, anyway, was never quite well, had a rash all over his face and neck and was starting to lose weight. Jay was crippled by shyness and afraid to be with Tom without Peter. Terry had disappeared somewhere, like they all seemed to.

The first time Tom went alone into the Underground with his flute he felt vulnerable and rather shy. He felt awkward. It was late afternoon, just before the onset of the rush hour. He set up in the corner of a bend in a passage at Oxford Street, laying his jacket on the ground behind him, something which always made him feel he had a claim on this particular tiny piece of the Underground system. Instead of a hat, instead of the knotted scarf which had proved unsafe and a let-down, he had his open flute case. Telling himself not to feel self-conscious – had he not done this dozens of times in company? – he put the flute to his lips and began to play.

First he played the little air from *The Magic Flute* by which Tamino fetches the beasts out of the forest. The thought came to him that he too was trying to summon beasts from a jungle, these people in this subterranean place, many of whose faces looked to him bestial, mad or very wretched. Some, on the other hand, looked happy and pleased with themselves. He was trying to summon them to pay a little, a very little, for his music.

Someone dropped a 2p piece in, someone else a five. Tom played the solo parts from one of Mozart's flute concertos, but the competition soon started up, a three-piece band with electronic instruments, including a raucous saxophone, by the sound of it not more than fifty yards away.

Where the passage turned at right angles some yards ahead of where Tom stood, was a pair of double doors set in the wall. The tunnel was hung with posters, all brightly coloured, but these doors were of a shabby matt grey. As Tom began to play a selection of English folk airs, an arrangement of Alice's, these doors opened. They opened inwards and Tom had caught a glimpse of a dark cavern, a black vault whose floor seemed to slope downwards, before a man in uniform came out and quickly secured the doors behind him.

Tom had never before considered that what he saw of the Underground system might not be all of it, that there might be secret and hidden ramifications. It was rather a thrilling thought that appealed to the child in him. The man who had come out of that hidden hallway saw Tom, gave him a glare and hurried past.

No more than five minutes had gone by, during which he once again played the little air Mozart wrote for Tamino, then Alice's arrangement of Papageno's bird-catcher song, when two railway policemen arrived. At first they were quite pleasant, merely asking what he was doing there and if he knew playing in the Underground contravened a London Transport by-law. But Tom found himself growing angry at an alarming rate. The presence of the police had driven away his audience, the passers-by who, at last, pleased by the light tuneful airs, had started dropping real money into the flute case. But the worst thing was that the rock band round the next corner was still pounding and grinding away.

One of the policemen asked Tom for his name and address.

'I don't see what that's got to do with you.'

'I'm sure you won't mind giving your name, sir.'

Being called 'sir' did not bring the same delight to Tom as it did to Jarvis. 'Wolfgang Amadeus Mozart, Salzburg,' Tom said.

He had underestimated them. They took him away and searched him, sent him off with a caution.

His takings amounted to less than a pound. He put the money into his pocket, cursing the police, wishing he had some way of getting back at them. He could feel a headache starting. They had made him come up here and if he wished to return he would have to buy another ticket. He decided to get a bus home and passed up the steps out into the sunshine. Tom, like most of the people who crossed the ticket hall at Oxford Circus, did not notice the observations room or the six television screens it contained, though it was built of glass and open for all to look at.

Inside the room the assistant station-manager was watching the screens. Two were for the Central Line, one for the westbound platform and one for the eastbound, two for the Bakerloo and two for the Victoria. A train was leaving the northbound Victoria Line platform but otherwise all the screens showed empty tracks. While his eyes followed the departing train, the corner of his glance was caught by one coming in on the Central from Tottenham Court Road. He turned to watch the westbound Central Line screen and saw a man and a bear step out on to the platform.

It was not his first sight of them. They had appeared on

these screens before and once he had come across them busking in the entrance to one of the Victoria Line platforms. The bear danced and the man accompanied him on a mouth organ. The assistant station-manager pointed them out on the screen to one of the station staff who had just come into the observations room.

'I saw a dancing bear when I was on my holidays. In Greece. It didn't really dance, just jumped about.'

'That isn't a real bear,' said the assistant station-manager.

'They put hot trays under them to make them jump up and down. That's how they're trained. Cruel, really. We wouldn't do a thing like that here.'

'It's a man, not a bear. You might go down and see they don't start anything.'

He went down. The man and the bear were not playing the mouth organ and dancing but making the interchange to the Bakerloo Line where, on the northbound platform, the assistant station-manager saw them appear on his screen. He assumed that his staff member had driven them off and he watched them get into a train. When he first saw the man and the bear their behaviour and appearance had alerted him to the possibility of some danger associated with them. But they were only buskers, beggars, the kind they called hippies when he was young.

Three days later, at the slackest time, early afternoon, Jasper, with Damon and Kevin, came down into London on the Jubilee Line, changed on to the Bakerloo at Baker Street and on to the Circle going clockwise at Embankment. There were no automatic ticket gates at West Hampstead but a staffed barrier, which sometimes made it possible, if the man at the barrier was otherwise occupied or even temporarily absent, to slip through. But today the man was there, his eagle eyes on them from the moment they came into the ticket hall, and he continued to watch them as they reluctantly put their money into the machine and took out minimum-fare tickets. Jasper was short of money and the collection of coins to make up 50p that he had put into the machine were almost the last he had. Brian's pocket money, bestowed on the previous Saturday, was gone and the ticket money had been all that remained of the £5 Daniel Korn had given him to keep out of his and Tina's way last Monday evening. If you do not go to school but spend your days drifting about London, money does not go very far.

He had never stolen money, only things, but the idea was not entirely unacceptable. The woman sitting opposite him, who had got in at Regent's Park, had placed her handbag on the seat next to her. Jasper eyed this handbag longingly and he could see that Kevin was doing the same. But they were not alone with her in the car, there were two men up the other end. Someone would press that orange alarm button thing if they tried anything.

In the Circle train Jasper began to feel nervous. The other day he had heard his grandmother say to Tina, apropos of some dangerous activity she thought (erroneously) that he might be up to, 'They have no fear at that age.'

Jasper said nothing, but inwardly disagreed. He had a lot of fear, as much often as he could handle, though of course he could hardly tell how much *more* he might have when he was grown-up. He was afraid now. But there was nothing to be done about that, he was committed to it and had to go on.

Chris had ridden the section between Gloucester Road and Kensington High Street. Jasper's plan was to do the next bit, Kensington High Street to Notting Hill Gate and on to Bayswater. No one, except possibly Dean Miller, had travelled more than one station. Practice had taught Jasper how better to maintain his grip on the roof of the car but it was still, as he saw it, the essential problem. They made the surface of those cars so smooth, so curved and slippery-smooth. It was as if they did it on purpose. As Jasper came to think of it, he saw that it probably *was* done on purpose. He reflected regretfully on the old car he had seen in the museum, relegated now to use by British Rail on the Isle of Wight. The roof of that had all sorts of handholds and footholds, ridges and flanges and overlapping bits to hang on to.

A lot of people got out at South Kensington and the train waited there, though no one got in. Damon kept saying he wanted a Dairy Milk bar out of the machine but he was afraid the train would go off without him. Of course, by the time the train did move he might have bought chocolate for all of them and, come to that, been out into the street and back.

It gave Jasper a bit of a shock to see a railman, a guard perhaps, come in by the door at the end and walk through the car. He had come to think of those doors as for *their* personal use. The man looked hard at them, glared at them, as he passed on his way to the door at the far end. Grown-ups, Jasper had found, especially male grown-ups, reserved a special sort of look for people of his age when they were in a group: condemnatory, harsh, threatening. He wondered how old you had to be not to get it any more. Perhaps quite old, perhaps it only increased as you got to be a teenager.

Kevin said, when the man had gone, 'Suppose you'd been getting out on the roof when he came.'

'I wasn't, was I? So you can't suppose I was.'

'Oh, yes I can.'

'You can't.'

'I can.'

'Shut up, will you?' said Jasper. 'I'm going up on the roof at the next station. Is anyone coming with me?'

Damon wouldn't. Damon it was who had lost his nerve and come down last time. His eyes met Jasper's and Jasper saw fear there. He was not going to say anything, he would leave it to Kevin to start chicken-calling. But he did think how strange it was that a daring forger like Damon should not be afraid of writing his aunt's signature on a cheque but be scared stiff of riding on the roof of a tube train car.

He asked his question again, out of politeness really. Company on the roof would not be congenial and he was glad when Kevin said, no, not this time, they'd leave him to get on with it. The train came into Kensington High Street, Jasper opened the door at the end of the car and climbed out on to the roof.

He could see the heads of the passengers getting into the train. No one saw him. No one looked up. He lay down, wriggled along and stretched out, gripping with his fingers the edge of the shallow depression above the double-leaf doors. The station was open to the sky, a cloudy whitish sky, and to the right loomed a large red-brick building. Jasper could see ahead of him the opening to the tunnel, which looked quite large. It looked as if there would be a yard or more between him and the inside of the tunnel roof.

For all that, he wished the train would start. More people kept arriving on the double platform of this rather big spread-out station, but no more got into this train. They wanted the District Line to Wimbledon or the Circle going east. He felt a dryness in his throat, a slight constriction like the beginning of feeling sick. It would be better when he was actually in the tunnel. As the doors closed he felt the vibration through his body, a kind of tingling. The train moved off quite smoothly, heading for the opening and the darkness inside.

It became dark very quickly once the car he was on

passed into the tunnel. The smell was sharp, oily, gaseous. He turned his head and looked to the right side, then to the left, but he could see nothing. The lights from the car did not reach up here and the brickwork and cables which could be seen from inside the train were invisible out here in the dark. It was a straight run, so keeping his hold was less of a problem than it might have been.

The darkness was awful. Jasper had not really anticipated such deep, intense, *furry* darkness. It was as if it was not (as he had once heard a teacher say) absence of light, but something solid, a darkness not airy but made of something, cloth perhaps, which lay on him and wrapped him. A dirty smelly blanket of dark swaddled him in thick folds. He thought of lifting his head, his eyes seeking the light, but he remembered the roof which might not be so high here, which might come down lower. At this point it did not do to think about projections sticking down from the tunnel roof like those things you got in caves, stalacmites or stalactites, poles or iron spokes. He would not think of them.

Then light showed ahead, then light burst with a wonderful unbelievable brightness overhead, as the train passed under a shaft. But it was very short, a brief brilliant gap, before a dark mouth swallowed the linked cars again. Dean had told Jasper there would be a second shaft, a much bigger one, and he could already see the distant glimmer of it far ahead. The train rushed into the light, into a long shaft planted like a garden and, high above, a bright white sky shining down. There was a bit more tunnel, but not much, and then the train was braking and shuddering, Jasper feeling the withdrawal of speed, a trembling through his legs.

Notting Hill Gate.

Yellow brick arches on either side, like the supports of a bridge. Stairs going up from the platforms. It was too near the surface to have an escalator here. While they waited in the station, he turned his head and looked back the way they had come. Though he had sometimes felt while in the tunnel that the roof was in places frighteningly low, the exit from it, a red brick arch, looked quite high above the top of the train where he lay. Jasper felt a surge of exhilaration. It had been easy, it had been *great*. He would go on to Bayswater, maybe even on to Paddington. Later he might think about doing the long stretch from Baker Street to Finchley Road, where the Metropolitan trains charged at high speed past the old ghost stations.

The doors closed. The train trembled and slid into motion. Jasper dug his fingertips into the shallow curved flanges above the doors. He felt the car begin to rock a little at the gathering of speed and he lifted his head for a glance at the tunnel mouth ahead of him.

It was not a brick arch like the one they had come through but a steel girder. Not a curved portal, not an arch, but a metal overhang that seemed to scrape the top of the first cars as they passed under it. There it hung, a curtain of green-painted steel, a half-descended guillotine, a killing barrier to break off anything that protruded above the surface of a train roof, or sever a head. And it was one of a series, five or six of them, green metal traps.

Jasper stared. The first overhang was still a long way ahead but it was coming closer, closer, as the train speeded up. He thought, it'll chop my head off. A kind of paralysis took hold of him. He seemed glued to the car roof, rigid, his back arched and his head up, no hands, his hands numb. Ahead, the green wall of metal awaited him, it would not suddenly rise up, it would not yield and give way or slide open like a supermarket entrance. It was not made of that green sponge stuff his grandmother stuck flowers in. It was iron-hard iron and it would sweep him from the roof and fling him on the brick walls, spread him on the posters, shatter him on the air. But first would come a blow like a hammer with a head on it twenty feet wide.

Fear galvanized his body and he drew up his legs, he was on all fours, quivering there like a runner on his marks. He let out a yell and leapt. He slithered and then sprang into a mob of lifted faces, open mouths, round like Os.

Not to hit his head or break his legs, not on top of anyone, not on to the platform, but into the hairy arms of a bear. The car whose roof he had ridden on disappeared under the green guillotine.

12

Later on, when Jasper was telling Bienvida about it, he said he thought he had died. He thought he was dead and the bear was one of the creatures that inhabited wherever it was you went to when you died. Sometimes he had told her stories of an afterlife and an afterworld inhabited by bears and wolves and pterodactyls.

At the time he did not think much. He was all sensation, fear, amazement, relief and more fear. In the bear's arms he was at first terrified and no less so when he saw the grinning face between its jaws. The bear set him down and his instinct was to run away up the stairs and out into Notting Hill Gate. It was official retribution he was afraid of, of some uniformed man taking hold of him. One of those Victorian errand boys, trying to get into the false house in Leinster Gardens, would have feared being grabbed by the ear. Jasper was afraid of being taken by the shoulders and propelled along at a run. To some office, some police station, some court with a judge.

He was grabbed, but not by a man in uniform. By an ordinary member of the public. Or so it seemed. A man who was with the bear, who had said something to the bear while Jasper was held aloft, took him by the arm in a strong squeezing grip. Jasper wriggled. The man held on. He said to Jasper, 'I want to talk to you.'

These words had no strange ring for Jasper. They were what a certain kind of adult said. It had not escaped his notice that whereas grown-up people have some reticence when it comes to reproving each other for bad behaviour, no such restraint affects them when children offend. You did not have to be someone's mother or father or teacher in order to tell him off. He supposed the tall man with the piercing eyes and the beard and tied-back hair intended to tell him off, to ask him if he wanted to die, if he understood the dangers inherent in sledging, and then to hand him over either to a station official or else one of those policemen who it seemed actually worked for the Underground. He wriggled again, tried a swift twisting movement.

'Let me go.'

A woman in the crowd, a crowd which had begun to lose interest now he wasn't dead, injured or meeting violent retribution, said, 'He ought to get into serious trouble.'

There was a murmur behind her and someone else said they didn't know what things were coming to. The man who held him said to Jasper, 'The least you can do is say thank you to Bruin.'

Someone laughed. Jasper said, 'OK. Thanks. Can I go now, please?'

The man did not slacken his grip. He had a ring on one of his fingers which dug into the flesh of Jasper's upper arm. They stood there all three of them, as if waiting for the next train. The crowd had begun to depart through the exit and a fresh lot was appearing.

'I said I wanted to talk to you.'

'You're hurting,' said Jasper.

'Maybe, but if I let go you'll be off and I want us to have a talk. I'm not going to tell you off about what you were doing, if that's what you're scared of.'

'I'm not scared.' Jasper wasn't going to have that. 'I don't want the police coming, that's all.'

'Neither do I,' said the tall man, and for some reason this made him smile. 'Neither do I one bit. I think you and I see things in much the same way. We see eye to eye.'

'Three of a kind,' said the bear.

A train was coming in. It emptied and re-filled. The tall man told him to look as it passed under the green girder.

'You'd have made it,' he said. 'You weren't in any danger. It just *looked* too low. You'd have had a good two feet.'

Jasper, regaining his confidence, looked at the departing train and was less sure. 'You weren't up there. How would you know?'

This time the tall man did more than smile. He laughed. 'Come on,' he said. 'Let's go.'

The hard hand relaxed as they mounted on the escalator. At the top it was removed altogether. Jasper, who had been struggling to run away, now no longer wished to do so. Child of a child-abusing world, he was fully aware of what people thought when they saw a man manhandling someone of his age. The tall man would be aware of it too, and that was why he had removed his hand. This made Jasper feel powerful. He swaggered a little as he came off the escalator and into the ticket hall. In the underpass, where the stairs go up to the north side of Notting Hill Gate and the beggars congregate at the foot of them, the bear went into the Men's and came out again as a man with a scarf covering his chin, a hat shading his face and carrying a plastic bag full of bearskin.

They took Jasper into the pizza house. He had forgotten about being hungry, but he was now, voraciously. The bear who was a bear no longer queued up to get their food and Jasper and the tall man sat down at a table in the corner. It was very warm after outside and Jasper took off his jacket, placing it on the seat beside him. The tall man had a black beard and a black moustache between which his lips showed narrow and red. The ring on his finger was done in two sorts of yellow metal. He wore black jeans and a T-shirt striped black and yellow like a wasp's back and over them a wide-open black overcoat that reached nearly to the floor.

While they waited for the food to come, he said, 'My name is Axel Jonas. What's yours?'

'Jasper.' He hesitated a moment before giving his surname. This was because he was not always certain which it
was. It had usually been Elphick but lately people called
him Darne because that was the name his mother called
herself by. Jasper had a brief recall of Brian in the Transport
Museum, of the pocket money, of how kind he always
was, and said, 'Jasper Elphick.'

'You can call me Axel. The bear's name is Ivan. He has a
surname but for reasons of his own he likes to keep it
dark.'

'Why does he dress up like a bear?'

'For his amusement,' said Axel, 'and mine.'

Jasper thought his voice very cold when he said that. It
reminded him of the tone of an interrogator in a spy film.
But he was not in the least afraid. The pizza house was half
full, there were people everywhere and it was broad daylight, a bright, cold, brisk autumn day. There was nothing
to be afraid of.

Ivan came back with a loaded tray. He was still wearing
his hat and scarf. Jasper noted with some surprise that he
had brought exactly the same food and drink for each of
them. He could not remember this ever happening before
when he had been taken out to meals by adults. They, for
instance, had always wanted beer or wine as well as salads
and coffee and such uneatable, undrinkable things as that.
He and Ivan and Axel all had a ham and mushroom pizza
each and a can of Pepsi-Cola each, and the pizzas were all
equally large.

So far Ivan had uttered no word since remarking that
they were three of a kind. In order to eat he unwound his
scarf and tipped back his hat. He was not only the ugliest
person Jasper had ever seen, but the most peculiar-looking.
His was not really a human face at all, it seemed not to
have the normal human features and proportions. The eyes
were small, sunk in flesh and very wide apart. The curious

nose was quite straight until it came to the tip where it branched out into a kind of platform. The bit between this nose and his mouth was about twice as long as on most people and bisected by a narrow white vertical scar. It looked as if there had been a split there from nose to lip and someone had very neatly sewn the opening together. Jasper had never seen anything quite like that before. Axel's black hair was tied back with an elastic band but Ivan's, poking out under the hat brim, was loose, curly, rough and brown, not unlike the bear's pelt.

All these details were carefully noted by Jasper the better to describe the whole scene to Bienvida later on. He had made up his mind that a request was going to be put to him. If they did not intend to reproach him they must want something from him and Jasper, streetwise child that he was, a knowledgeable innocent who, peering into scenarios of sexual adventure and violence and drama as he had done, knew everything and knew nothing. He supposed Axel and Ivan wanted him to go home with them so that they could do something to him. Do perhaps something like what he had more or less seen Daniel Korn doing to Tina. Or take photographs of him without his clothes on. Jasper, somehow, knew about this too. But the pizza house was full of people and he was a fast runner. Only he wanted to eat his pizza first.

Axel let him do so. He let him eat half of it and he and Ivan ate half theirs and then he said, 'Have you done much of that? Riding on top of tube trains?'

'A bit,' said Jasper cautiously.

'Where have you done it?'

'What d'you mean, where?'

Axel did not answer this. He said, 'There are a lot of old stations in the Underground, aren't there? Stations that aren't used any more?'

'Ghost stations,' said Jasper, eating the second half of his pizza.

'Is that what they call them? Have you seen them?'

'You can see some of them on the long bit between Baker Street and Finchley Road. On the Metropolitan. They used to have names but I don't know what they were.'

'But you've seen them? You've seen them from the top of a train?'

Jasper had not. It was perfectly possible to see these gloomy deserted platforms from inside the cars but he decided not to tell Axel this. He said an economical, 'Yes.'

'I want you to tell me if you think it would be possible to get on to these stations. And if you got on to them, could you get out on to the street?'

He talked like a schoolteacher. This was new. Previously, he had talked like an ordinary person, like one of Tina's friends, but now he spoke like the man whose class at school Jasper had been in last year, and whose chilly and hectoring manner had been in some part responsible for his truancy.

'I don't know,' he said.

'OK. Does the train slow down when it passes these stat-ions?'

'It goes very fast all the way to Finchley Road. It goes at high speed.' Having told his lie, Jasper was in no mind to make the untruthful boast less of an achievement. 'What d'you want to know for?'

It was apparent at once that Axel was not going to tell him that. His face closed up. It became dead. Jasper did not particularly like that expressionlessness, that stony stare. He turned his eyes to Ivan and Ivan said in his funny whistling voice, very intensely, very *penetratingly*, 'What he means is, is there a way you could climb up and like get into the street, up a manhole or whatever?'

Jasper said it again. 'I don't know.'

'Or could you get out of the train on to one of these –

what-d'you-call-'em? – ghost stations, and get off again on another train?'

'I told you,' said Jasper. 'They don't stop.'

He was beginning to feel a loss of nerve. Various memories from his intellectual intake, television and comics, were showing him what he might do. Refuse to say any more until he had another pizza. Ask for payment of another kind. His throat dried up when he thought of that, his appetite went. In this climate of dwindling courage, he found himself with an idea, a means of escape.

It involved no more than a simple statement. He made it, watching them.

'Jarvis could tell you.'

Axel said sharply, 'Who's Jarvis?'

'Just a man,' said Jasper carefully. He no longer wanted another pizza. His hunger was gone. 'Can I go now?'

'Wait a minute.'

Axel unfroze in a strange, unnerving way. His face came alive again and he smiled. His teeth were white and clean and even. Jasper thought of telling Bienvida about him, about his black beard and red mouth and white teeth and the hair tied back with a shoelace. Of course lots of men wore their hair tied back but it was often thin or they were bald. Axel's hair looked like a man's in a costume of the 1700s he had seen in Madame Tussaud's with Brian, thick and dark and glossy as a blackbird. Jasper would not have been surprised if the two teeth at the sides of Axel's front ones had been pointed like Dracula's. Perhaps he would tell Bienvida they had been.

'Who's Jarvis, Jasper?'

A deep breath in and Jasper said, 'I haven't got any money to get home with.'

'Can't you walk?'

'Not to West Hampstead.'

'Ah,' said Axel. 'So you live in West Hampstead. And does this Jarvis live there too?'

Jasper was silent. Suddenly the scene in the pizza house had become like television. He saw how foolish he had been to suspect these men of doing the sort of things to him he had half-seen men do to women. If he had known the word he would have said he had been naïve. This was crime, this was something bad and big.

'Who is Jarvis? Does he live with you?'

'He might,' said Jasper. He had heard that on television too.

'He's your mother's boyfriend.'

This was Ivan, speaking flatly. Jasper was incensed in the way we are when we discern complete misunderstanding.

'He's not!'

'Never mind that. Why would he know?'

'He knows about the tube. He's written books.' Jasper, thinking fast, planning, let fall a piece of information he thought useless, that he thought mere stalling. 'He's our cousin.'

'I'd like to talk to him. Where d'you live in West Hampstead?'

Jasper's plan of asking for money before he disclosed information had never really got off the ground. He was afraid to do it. Even surrounded by the customers of the pizza house he was afraid to do that. He reached for his jacket, which had fallen on to the floor. It was filthy from the top of the tube train car. He put it on, saying he was cold. Axel Jonas was watching him.

'Funny way you've got of showing your gratitude,' said Ivan.

'You said I wasn't in danger,' said Jasper triumphantly. 'You said I had lots of room, you didn't save me from anything.'

He sat, darting quick looks from one to the other of them, and then he jumped up and was off. He was off like the wind, out of the pizza house, weaving his way between the people on the pavement, ducking under arms, leaping across the street in defiance of a green light and traffic, down the stairs past the shabby sprawled beggars and into the underpass.

They would follow him. For some reason they wanted Jarvis, they wanted what Jarvis knew. He had a good start though and he was tube-wise. It was a disadvantage to have no money, but not all that much of one for him. He simply went under the ticket gates. He dived down at the point where the law-abiding put a ticket in the slot and then plunged under the closed leather-bound jaws.

Left or right? Right was the Circle Line and the way he had come. They would expect him to go that way. For quickness, it made no difference whether he took the Circle to Baker Street and the Jubilee to West Hampstead or the Central to Bond Street and then the Jubilee. But they would expect him to take the Circle. He ran down the two escalators that led deep into the tunnels for the Central Line. There were more trains on this line, it was a better service.

If they came on to the platform there would be no escape for him. He ran as far down as he could get, put people between himself and the entrance, perhaps fifty people. He had barely reached the end of the platform when a Liverpool Street train came in. If they got in and walked through he would have no defence. Perhaps he should get out at Queensway, throw them off the scent. But that would be bad if they got out too, for there were no escalators at Queensway, only lifts. He thought of being trapped in the lift with them.

If they were on the train. As far as he knew they were not on the train. He got out with extreme care at Bond Street, feeling like a marked man. A child is marked, a child is distinctive, he has no disguise for his youth, his grace, his smallness of stature. Jasper felt small, he felt like an animal. His heart raced a bit. He couldn't walk, he had to run. The winds of Bond Street were blowing, meeting him on the stairs, whipping down the escalator.

They were not following him. He waited for the Jubilee train coming up from Green Park and he thought, could they have got to Green Park before me, could they be in that train waiting? But it was impossible. It could not be done. In a taxi maybe, early on a Sunday morning, but not on the London Underground at any hour, not by taking the Circle back to Gloucester Road and the Piccadilly to Green Park, which would be the only way.

He entered the train with all the caution of an old-time spy who has an assignation at a Berlin checkpoint. His imagination showed him the film, half-real, half-surreal, where the fugitive, safe at last, savouring relief, steps into the waiting limousine to find his two enemies there before him, smiling broadly. Two people only were in the car, a black man and a white woman, both with a weary down-trodden look. A throng followed Jasper in. He thought, I'm OK now, it's all right now. What would they have done anyway? Nothing. They would have done nothing.

Once at West Hampstead, he considered going home by a circuitous route. It was rather early to go home at all, not yet three. He could go round by West Hampstead Mews instead of the street where the School was or the bridge. It seemed to Jasper that the thing to avoid was leading them to Jarvis's house, to the School.

But they were not following him. He got off the train, on that very exposed platform, and concealed himself behind one of the free-standing signboards on which were a tube map and cinema advertisements. A lot of people got off but Axel Jonas and surname-less Ivan were not among them.

They could of course be following on the next train. Jasper went up the steps. He had no ticket to hand in and no money and the ticket collector was at the barrier. But so was a line of people. Jasper joined the queue, and to his relief, more people came to stand behind him. He hoped very much for a passenger in front to get in an argument with the ticket collector and divert his attention. His luck held and the woman two in front of him produced an out-of-date travel pass. The ticket collector scrutinized it, Jasper darted to the side of the man in front, under the woman's arm, and ran. Bellows of 'Come back here!' pursued him.

He hid in the Indian's shop. They would not keep up the hunt for more than seconds. The ticket collector couldn't leave his post. Jasper contemplated a shelf of cereals, another of cat food. He could smell the chocolate laid out on the counter where the till was and his mouth filled with saliva. The Indian was watching him with hatred, with a longing for revenge, as one of his prize unproven shoplifters.

Jasper sauntered out. More people were coming out of the station. They might have come off the train from Stanmore or the train from Embankment. You couldn't tell. Axel Jonas and Ivan No-name were not among them. But suppose he had missed them? Suppose they had come off a train he knew nothing about while he was in the Indian's shop? Jasper was almost positive they had not, that there had been no intervening train. But he experienced, perhaps for the first time in his life, that feeling of irrational unease when we know something cannot have happened, we are ninety-nine per cent sure it cannot have, it is against all reason and nature and probability, and yet we are anxious, we dread, we shiver for that one per cent.

Jasper turned down Blackburn Road and went over the bridge. From there he had an excellent hawk's-eye view of both platforms. A train came down from Kilburn and almost at once another up from Finchley Road. They were not among the passengers getting off but Jasper was still wary. He came off the bridge through the little brick alley and began a circuitous way home via Priory Road and Compayne Gardens.

He did not know, in any form of words or any mental picture, that his grandmother's house was a sanctuary for him but it was so. His body knew it and his instincts, the animal part of him that is drawn to its warren or its dray. Consciously, Jasper knew only that he would be safe there and get something nice to eat.

When Jed went down to Kent to take the falconry course they had not told him the hawk would shriek all day. It stopped when he fed it. In the night it was silent while he was out with the Safeguards. It was silent when it perched upon his wrist in the jesses and he walked it up to the Heath or, as had once happened, he took it in the train up to the countryside beyond Barnet. Once back on its perch, unfed because when well-fed it would not wish to fly and hunt, the shrieking resumed.

That it might disturb his fellow residents did not trouble Jed. He had an inner conviction that they did not hear it as he did. Once, fifteen years before, he had been a respectable householder, married and with a small child. The night crying of the child had been terrible to him. He had never been able to let her cry but had picked her up and walked her and fed her, in spite of his wife's admonition, his wife's anger. The crying pierced his soul. But he knew that others, everyone but himself and his wife, were unmoved by the sound. One dreadful night of crying his mother was staying with them. She slept through it, she heard nothing. In the morning she was cheerful, happy, astonished to hear that her grandchild had not slept peacefully through the night.

So it was with the others, he was sure. They did not hear it. Only he heard it. When he came home from work at five he keyed himself up as he approached the house, he prayed that there would be silence, that at last the hawk had understood, had complied, had resigned itself. But there was never silence. From a long way off he heard the thin shrieking like a whistle of wind on the air. And he thought of that phrase of his, absurd in the circumstances, melodramatic, meaningless really: it pierces my soul.

How greedily it fed! He felt he was starving it, he was depriving it of the one thing that made life liveable. A few minutes after he had gone indoors again, the shrieking began. Jed sat in his room, in Upper Six, in his smelly jacket where meat juice, blood, had stained the pockets and the lining, in the smelly room where there was no refrigerator and the day-old chicks, yellow, a little slimy, festered in their bowl, and thought how he loved the hawk. Abelard. He loved no one now but he loved Abelard. He was starving the thing he loved and submitting it to a slow torture.

In the shed in the garden it continued to utter its regular piercing cries.

Jarvis, in Remove, typed the last line of the first half of his history of the London Underground. He could leave it now and return to it in three months. In two weeks' time he was going to Russia. It was not a very good time of the year to go to Russia, for winter had arrived. But Jarvis, in pursuit of metro systems, had been in Washington in August and Helsinki in January, and was not deterred by the prospect of snow and low temperatures.

Among other things, he was looking forward to seeing the Pushkinskaya station in Moscow where chandeliers hang from the ceiling in the low-level concourse. One thing only was making him anxious, and, sitting in Remove at his typewriter, feeling the faint tremor of the floor as a train passed by, he fretted at the prospect of being refused permission to see the work in progress on the new Underground in Omsk. He *must* see it. At the moment he had no proof that such a system was even being built in Omsk. It might be only a rumour and his Intourist friend could not – or would not – confirm or deny. At least, he must go there and find out.

Bienvida came home from school and entered by the back door. Abelard was shrieking. She knew Jed was in because she could smell the smoke of his cigarette. She had seen Jarvis through the window in Remove. But she felt alone, she felt the empty spaces of the house, indifference to whether she was there or not breathed through those spaces.

Bienvida changed her clothes. She put on a dress. Everyone wore jeans or tracksuit trousers at school and Tina said she would feel out of it if she had a skirt on, so Bienvida wore jeans. But she liked dresses, she felt more comfortable in them, and the one she put on, of green and blue plaid with a white collar, had been bought for her in Marks and Spencer's while she was out shopping in Oxford Street with her grandmother and Auntie Daphne. Over this she put on her school coat and she carried a pink plastic shoulder bag that had been Jasper's birthday present and which he had stolen from a department store at the Brent Cross Shopping Centre. She was going to her grandmother's.

The first thing she said when she got there was that Tina was at home doing the ironing. It was an invention she had arrived at on the way to Lilac Villa, having dismissed 'having a cup of tea with two ladies' as a fiction too incredible to be swallowed by anyone who knew her mother. She was pleased to see Jasper. While Cecilia went to make sandwiches for them Jasper said, 'Shall I tell you what happened to me today?'

'OK, if you want.'

'It's very frightening.'

'I quite like being frightened sometimes.'

'I thought I'd died,' said Jasper.

'Yes, but you hadn't.'

He told her about the sledging and the bear who turned out to be a man and turned into Ivan without-a-surname and about Axel Jonas. Both children had seen the film version of *The Phantom of the Opera* and Jasper said that must be what the Phantom's face was like when he took the mask off for the girl to see: like Ivan's. He said that Axel Jonas was a vampire with those funny sort of teeth.

'What's a vampire?'

'Like Dracula.'

'What, like Dracula sticking his teeth in a person's neck and eating their blood?'

'Absolutely,' said Jasper, 'only you don't eat blood, you drink it or suck it.'

Bienvida shrieked like Abelard. Jasper, quite recovered from his experiences, enjoying himself, started laughing. In the kitchen, Cecilia heard them, heard what she thought of as their happiness, their merriment, and told herself all things were well, all things worked together for good, Tina was settling down, was a good woman, was being a good mother at last, all would be well.

After 6.30, after she had watched the early evening news, she would make her phone call to Daphne and tell her of the children's visit. She would tell her, if she could slip it in without sounding like one ridiculously occupied by trivia, of Tina's dutiful attention to the ironing. And then listen to poor Daphne's recital of Peter's latest doings, how he was 'being silly again'.

The two of them were in the cloakroom when the doorbell rang. Tina had not yet come back. Jasper and Bienvida now used the cloakroom as a den. They had accumulations of bedding there, Jasper's radio, a kind of mini ghetto-blaster Brian had given him, some bags of Japanese rice crackers neither of them much liked but which Jasper had stolen from the Indian shop, candles, matches, Jasper's cigarettes and a bottle of Lucozade, half-empty, Jed had put out with the rubbish. Bienvida had rescued this as a present for Jasper because someone at school had told her it had cocaine in it.

'Not cocaine, *caffeine*,' said Jasper. 'You'd better tell your friend so she doesn't make the same mistake again. But I'll drink it. I quite like the taste.'

Bienvida could read perfectly well but she liked Jasper reading aloud to her. What Jasper was reading to her was a book he had found under his mother's bed, on Daniel Korn's side, *Count Oxtiern* by Donatien Alphonse François, Marquis de Sade, in the mistaken belief (understandable in the light of the cover illustration) that it was a treatise on vampirism.

They heard the doorbell ring and someone go to answer it. The footsteps sounded like Alice's. From the cloakroom a conversation on the doorstep or even in the front vestibule could not be heard. Jasper drank some Lucozade and resumed his reading.

Whoever was at the door had come in. Jasper could hear Alice's voice and he heard her speak his mother's name, he heard her say 'Tina'. Then the man with her spoke. He spoke in the voice of Axel Jonas and Jasper, falling silent, felt another strange new sensation, the illusion of his bones turning to water, as if his legs had melted.

13

At Hammersmith station Tom was waiting for her in the
ticket hall. He had suggested they play there for an hour
and he had brought her violin. He handed it to her as if
they had made some prior arrangement.

Alice resented Tom's bringing her violin. It seemed to
her an act of possession. She imagined him going into her
room and looking for the violin, opening the cupboard,
finding it there and lifting it out, touching her things,
pushing things about to find the case, then carrying the
violin about with him, leaving it on the dirty floor in the
Underground concourse with his and Peter's jackets and
the flute case. She resented his taking for granted that she
would want to go back to being a busker.

'Why do you want me to?' she said. 'We won't make
much. We'll be lucky if we make as much as your fare
home.'

'You used to like it.'

'I didn't exactly *like* it. It was all there was.'

They had walked about for a while, arguing. Alice
thought Tom ought to get a real job, though she did not
say so. She said she would not be very pleased if someone
from the office saw her playing her violin down there.
That made Tom laugh.

'You've got very respectable all of a sudden, darling.'

Alice hated being called 'darling'. It was what her father
sometimes called her mother. She thought of it as a possession word, an ownership word, exclusive to wives or
wives designate, besides being old-fashioned. But again she
did not say so. Even as she did not say so, she realized there
were many things, an increasing number of things, she did

167

not say to Tom. When they first met she had told him everything.

She did as he wanted and went down into the underpass with him. Using her violin case as a receptacle for their takings seemed a sullying, a desecration, but he nodded and smiled encouragingly at her when she put it in front of them, so she left it there. The underpass was dark and dirty and there were stains and patches of grease on the floor that she shuddered to look at too closely. Footsteps echoed hollowly from a long distance away.

'I'll tell you why it's a good place to play,' Tom said. 'Women are scared of going through here. Seeing us here will reassure them. They'll feel more confident, they'll be grateful and their gratitude will make them generous.'

But there were no women. All the passers-by for a long while were young men who behaved as if Alice and Tom were not there, as if they were no more than the concrete uprights, the peeling walls of this dark underground passage. For a long time only one coin was dropped into the violin case. When Alice peered at it she saw that it was foreign, a Dutch guilder.

She would not have believed it possible to recognize a hand. One man's hand is surely very much like another's. But the only other hand to drop money into the case that evening she thought she recognized, a man's left hand, with a wedding ring on it.

Tom was singing love songs, an artia from *Falstaff* and then 'Ein Mädchen oder Weibchen' from *The Magic Flute*. She looked up and the bow became motionless in her hand. The man who had dropped the money was walking away, his back to her. Around that back were the straps of a baby harness. It was Mike.

Alice's heart felt as if it had ceased to beat. It started again with a sensation in her chest like nausea. He had not seen her. He had dropped the money into the case because, perhaps, he always did this when he passed buskers. How would she know? She had never known him well, had forgotten most of what she knew.

Where was he going? What was he doing in Hammersmith? She followed him with her eyes, watching him hungrily as he walked away through the underpass. A feeling of relief came to her that she had not seen Catherine, but it was immediately succeeded by a longing to see the baby, by an impulse to run after him.

Tom stopped singing. 'What happened to my accompanist?'

She must tell him. 'Nothing,' she said.

Mike had gone, had disappeared up the steps. He must be on holiday, visiting some friend he had made since her departure. She said to Tom, 'Let's go.'

'We've only been here for twenty minutes.'

'It's a bad place. No one's going to give us anything. Let's go home.'

In the train he took her hand. 'Something's upset you. What is it, darling?'

'I don't want to play down there any more,' she said. 'Not anywhere in the tube. It damages me. Every time I do it, I play worse.'

'You once called it your element.'

He was angry and when they got home he went to his room and she to hers. Alice tried to put Mike out of her head by thinking of Brussels, of going to Brussels to study when she had enough money. Then she began to think of Tom. The money she was making would send him back to university to do his final year. He would be here and she would be in Brussels. She thought of the money she had earned as buying off Tom, or paying him off like a redundancy payment or love's golden handshake.

When the doorbell rang she did not at first consider going down. Others were surely in the house, Jarvis perhaps, Tom certainly, Tina and the children, though in the Headmaster's Flat you could not always hear the bell. It rang again and Alice thought, as she had done once or twice before at the sound of the bell, it could be Mike, it could be Mike come to find me. A rapid fantasy showed him recognizing her after he had passed, following her home.

Did she want him to come? She supposed that, perversely, she was hurt by his not wanting her, though she did not want him. No letter from him had ever come, no phone call, no message even. It was galling to have discovered that his indifference to her was as great as hers to him. The worst was his passing her by this evening, not knowing her, not recognizing her playing nor her hands, nor her body, nor bent head.

The doorbell rang again.

Alice went downstairs. The front door had stained-glass panels in it and through them you could see a caller's height and shape. She could see enough to tell it was not Mike. Disappointment dropped through her, as if her heart had lost its balance and fallen. How could she be disappointed not to see the husband she had left with such relief?

She opened the door. The man who stood on the doorstep was tall and thin and dark. His face was like a monk in one of El Greco's paintings. Alice, who knew nothing about painting, had once told a friend who was an art student that all the young men in El Greco's paintings had the same face. The art student had been cross and said that was nonsense, that was ignorance, but still Alice saw them as all the same, all narrow and pale, with dark eyes, with dark pointed beards and dark hair and expressions of controlled hunger.

This man had that face and expression. He looked at her for a moment in silence and she stood looking at him, feeling that he might do some sudden violent thing.

Instead he said, 'Is Tina in?'

Alice said, 'I don't know. I'll see.'

She left him standing there, went down the passage to the front door of the Headmaster's Flat. There was no bell, no knocker. She banged on the door with her fist. While she waited she thought, he might have said that to get into the house and steal something, and when she went back, having got no answer from Tina, he was in the hall. He was standing with his back to her reading the list of names incised into the pitch pine panelling, the Ediths and Dorothys with their pathetic Matriculations.

Turning round to face her, he said, 'Are you a teacher here?'

She shook her head. 'It's not a school any more.' She felt a little afraid now that he was inside. He had closed the front door behind him. 'Tina's not in. Can I give her a message?'

For some reason that made him smile. 'You can give her this.'

It seemed to be a letter. The envelope was not sealed.

'Jarvis not in either?' he said, and added, 'My name is Axel Jonas.'

She was relieved. He was not an intruder, there was nothing sinister in his behaviour, he was a friend of Jarvis. He knew Tina. Yet his knowledge did not extend to awareness that the School was no longer a school. He surprised her by reading her thoughts.

'I've never been here before.'

She nodded. 'You can wait for him if you like, but he may be very late.'

'Where is he?' His voice was suddenly louder, rougher.

'How should I know?'

'Are you his girlfriend? His wife?'

'I just live here,' she said. 'I have a room here. Two or three of us have rooms here and Tina and the children have the flat.'

Again that intuitiveness of his surprised her. He was looking at the door marked Remove. 'Can I wait in there for Jarvis?'

'Well, it *is* his room . . .' She hardly knew why she said that. He already knew. Jarvis must have told him. 'Who is it you want to see? Jarvis or Tina?'

He made no answer. He opened the door of Remove and stepped inside. Alice went back to Tina's front door and pushed the envelope under it. She hardly knew what to do. Perhaps she should fetch Tom, ask Tom what to do about this Axel Jonas who had made his way into the house and was now alone in Jarvis's room with the door shut. A great impatience with Tom took hold of her. She did not want him fussing about. Somehow, she knew he would be proprietory in the presence of this man. He would call her 'darling' possessively.

Alice did nothing. She wondered what she would do if she opened the door of Remove and found Jonas looking through Jarvis's desk or reading his papers. She would not know how to act. It was best to do nothing, dissociate herself from all of it. She went down to the kitchen because she had had no evening meal, had eaten nothing since lunch. There was nothing in the fridge but some stale cheese, a re-corked bottle of Bulgarian red wine. She ate some cheese with white bread. The house was very quiet. It was as if it was empty.

Listening to the silence, protracted now, lasting a whole ten minutes, Jasper came out of the cloakroom, followed by Bienvida. They crept out. There was no one in the hall, no unmasked Phantom, no Dracula. The two men had come and, failing to find the boy they were searching for, had left again.

The security of his own bed had become very attractive to Jasper in the past half-hour. In the cloakroom, he had made contingency plans. If it looked as though Axel Jonas was searching the house for him, as it seemed from the one sentence clearly heard that he would be, 'Where is he?', they would sneak up the stairs, go to the second floor and ring the bell. Pursued by Axel Jonas, he would ring the school bell, toll it out over West Hampstead for help.

'It would be better to phone the police,' said Bienvida.

This he ignored. He could see she was shivering, she looked as if she was going to cry. She said it again as they approached the front door of the flat.

'We could phone the police, Jas.'

'I shall never phone the police as long as I live,' said Jasper recklessly.

Snivelling a bit, Bienvida produced her key and they let themselves in. On the doormat was an envelope he immediately recognized. The letter inside it, one of Damon's forgeries, asked his teacher Miss Finch to excuse his absence on the grounds of glandular fever. Jasper knew what had happened. The letter must have fallen out of his jacket pocket in the pizza house. Axel Jonas had been here merely to bring it back. On the other hand, it meant the man now knew his address. There would be no need to toll the bell tonight but they would remain locked inside the flat, to be on the safe side.

'Stop crying,' he said. 'It's going to be OK.'

'It's not.'

'Look, if you'll shut up I'll show you something. I'll show you my tattoo.'

'You haven't got a tattoo.'

'Want to bet?'

He took off his sweater and his T-shirt. Bienvida contemplated his back with awe. She stuck out one finger.

'It's *beautiful*. Would it be all right if I stroked the lion?'

'Do you mind?' said Jasper. 'No, it bloody wouldn't be all right. You can look all you want but don't touch. And don't go telling anyone I haven't got a tattoo on my back.'

★

173

Tom intended to prepare a surprise, something to make up for his behaviour to Alice. He had quickly become contrite about her. He should not have taken her to that squalid place where harm might have come to her and he could not have protected her. No wonder she had been upset.

His swings of mood troubled him but he would not think about that now. The room was cold, the electric heater warmed it inadequately, and it seemed it would be a good idea to light a fire in the grate. Accordingly, he went on a hunt for coal.

Although he had never seen it or even been told such a region existed, he was sure a house of this size and this age must have a cellar. If they had a cellar, old people such as his grandmother kept coal in it. He went down in the direction of the kitchen and the various other 'usual offices', bootrooms and sculleries that were in this part of the building, and opened one door after another. The fourth door he opened gave on to a stairway. Tom went down, pressed the light switch and found it worked. A light bulb of low wattage came on.

Coal there had been once upon a time. An area was closed off with low wooden walls. Inside it was deep in soot and a kind of coke-like gravel but no coal remained. There was no wood either nor indeed anything in the cellar, which looked as if no one had been into it for ages.

He gave up the fire idea and went out for Chinese takeaway, which he set out on the table in Four and opened a bottle of white wine. Then he tapped gently on the door of the Headmaster's Study to summon Alice. He smiled proudly, ushering her in, showing off his surprise. The room had warmed up, a fire was not necessary.

Alice was no longer hungry. She could only think of the money he had spent on this food, this wine. He made a pittance busking in the tube, *she* made the money, you could say this unnecessary food had all been bought with *her* money. She did not say it. She kept thinking how she must not hurt him, how she had done too much hurt already to others, she must not now hurt Tom.

The face of the man downstairs, the man who was surely still downstairs waiting, she could see like an after-image when she had been looking at something bright and had closed her eyes. It seemed printed there on some inner screen, a pale grave face with eyes that were not grave but bright and searching. An urge to see him again, to find what he was doing down there, made her unable to relax. She would have liked quiet in which to speculate about him. Tom made her feel impatient with his questions as to how she liked the wine, did she prefer Chinese to Indian, shouldn't they do this more often, go out to eat some-times.

'We are supposed to be saving money,' she said.

He shrugged. The hurt in his face which should have restrained her only provoked exasperation. She hardly ever noticed his hand any more but now she found herself looking at it, the very slightly distorted knuckles, the stiff little finger. It brought her an inward shudder, though it was not in any way grotesque, it was not even very obvious.

He said in a colder voice, 'I've never told you about my grandmother, have I?'

'You've said you had one. Why?'

'My grandmother's rich. When she dies she'll leave me her money. Perhaps you think I shouldn't talk like that – I mean, they call it waiting for dead men's shoes or some-thing, don't they? – but it's only realistic to admit she's going to die. She's eighty.'

Yes, and she might live fifteen years, thought Alice. Women do, some women. She did not say it aloud. She said what he had predicted she would: 'I think you shouldn't talk like that.'

'I keep upsetting you today, don't I, darling?'

'I don't want to sit in judgement on you. Who am I to judge anyone?'

'You can judge me. You can say anything to me.'

It was just not true. The idea of arguing about that made her feel weary and exasperated.

'Tom, will you excuse me, please? Will you please not ask any questions? There's something I have to do downstairs?'

Of course he asked. 'What do you mean, something you have to do?'

His voice was the same but she could hear the temper rising in it. She was getting to know him well.

'I'll explain later. Please, Tom.'

He lifted his shoulders in a shrug that was at the same time baffled and bitter. Alice ran downstairs into the dark hall. She put no lights on. There would be lights on inside Remove and Jarvis there and Axel Jonas gone. Telling herself this, she knocked on the door before opening it.

He was sitting in Jarvis's armchair with only a table lamp on, reading or looking through a book. When he saw her he got up. He laid the book down on the desk and came towards her. Alice had closed the door. She had been going to say, had been rehearsing on the stairs what she would say, that he must go, she should never have let him come in here, that it was wrong for him to be in Jarvis's room, however much a friend of Jarvis's he might be.

'I've been hoping you'd come back,' he said.

'Have you?'

'But you're too late. I have to go. What are you called?'

'Alice.'

Her name had a curious effect on him. Even in the half-dark she could see his face change and a look of pain, of disbelief, cross it. The expression was almost immediately wiped away. His eyes which she had supposed dark grey she saw were blue.

'Alice,' he said, and repeated it. 'Alice.'

He came very close to her. She found herself unable to move. He did not embrace her. He took her face, her chin, in his hand, and brought her mouth to his mouth. She felt his mouth smiling as it approached hers, then not smiling but kissing deep, as the hand that held her face tightened its pressure on her jawbone.

Alice did not put up her hands. She stood, being kissed, joined with him at the mouth only as he let his hand fall, kept his lips on hers, his tongue pushing her lips apart and entering her mouth to search it. It endured while her brain became a red screen of slowly turning indefinable images. It was over abruptly with a kind of shock of loss. She was shaking, she thought she would fall. His voice came from a long way off. Her eyes were closed and to open them involved an effort, a difficult process to be learned anew.

'We'll meet again soon.'

Afterwards, she wished, wished passionately, she had gone to the door with him, spoken to him, asked what that meant, that meeting again soon. Instead, she stood there, opening her eyes on to the dimly lit room. Doors must have closed but she did not hear them. She came slowly out of Remove into the empty hall, went back to switch off Jarvis's light.

She was not thinking, she was only feeling, not yet asking herself what she had done, if she had done anything. Tom's door was closed. She prayed he would not open it and put his head out as she passed. He did not. As she came to the Headmaster's Study she heard people let themselves into the house. She stood and listened until she heard the voices of Tina and Daniel Korn. If she had not gone down and encountered Axel Jonas again, if she had not encountered him in the half-dark and returned his strange kiss, Alice knew she would have spoken of him to Tina, would later or tomorrow have mentioned him to Jarvis. Now she would not.

In bed in Lilac Villa, Cecilia lay awake. This was unusual. The pattern of her nights was that she fell asleep quickly, woke at four and remained awake. Daphne had told her, she having got it from Peter, that finding it hard to get to sleep is a sign of anxiety, waking too early a sign of depression.

Cecilia did not think of herself as chronically depressed but rather as one who tried to look on the bright side of things. The bright side at present would be to bask in the good things Jasper and particularly Bienvida had told her that day. How, for instance, they would be going out with Brian again at the weekend. Brian, who once used to meet them outside at some prearranged place, now actually came to call for them at the School, had a cup of coffee in the Headmaster's Flat with Tina, was on pleasant conversational terms with Tina. Bienvida had even suggested it as likely Tina would accompany them when they all went to the Tower Bridge exhibition on Saturday.

This did not sound like Tina. Cecilia admitted it, faced it. She did not believe everything Bienvida told her, perhaps believed less than half. That Brian and Tina would get together again, might even *marry*, was Cecilia's dearest wish. She was thinking once more about what to do with her house. A possibility might be to make over the house to Tina on condition she lived in it with Brian. And then she, Cecilia, would move in with Daphne.

But she knew it was not in her nature to make such a condition, even if it were possible, legal, workable. She had long ago made a will, leaving everything unconditionally to Tina, her only child. Tina would not agree to any such conditional arrangement, she was sure, and sure too that it was wrong even to attempt to manipulate people in this way. At least the children had not mentioned other men in Tina's recent life.

Cecilia allowed herself to imagine Tina's wedding to Brian with the children in attendance, a page and bridesmaid. Such a ceremony would have seemed very shocking to her once, but she had adjusted to things, she had adapted. She knew there were many people who lived together and had children and then married with the children there at the wedding. Daphne and she had discussed it, though more in connection with Peter than Tina. As she dreamed of Tina settling down, so Daphne dreamed of Peter ceasing to love men, moving in with the right girl and later marrying her.

But thinking of Peter brought to Cecilia a sense of great fear, of impending doom, as she envisaged for her friend terrible unhappiness coming to her through her son. She tried to re-direct her thoughts, lying there in her bed in the big, dark empty house, and found them straying to Daphne's own wedding, so long ago but so clearly remembered, at which she had been a bridesmaid.

Daphne's new husband had given her a present, as was correct, but Daphne herself had chosen it, a cameo brooch, the cameo carved from deep pink and very pale pink coral. Several times over the years Cecilia had thought of giving this brooch to Tina but she never had. It was not the kind of thing Tina wore, with her preference for Indian or African jewellery. One day perhaps Bienvida would have it.

Thinking of the brooch made Cecilia wonder where it was, made her put the light on and get up and begin searching for it. At last she found it in a box in a dressing-table drawer in one of the spare rooms – perfectly properly put away, neatly packed in pink cotton wool, tidy as all her things were. But she reproached herself for having hidden it away there, for years perhaps, it was possible it had been there for ten years.

She brought it back to her own bedroom and put it in her jewel case, no longer in its box but pinned to the velvet padding with which the case was lined. This move, this nocturnal act, brought Cecilia a deep satisfaction, a sense of having restored things to order and righted an obscure wrong. She fell asleep at once.

14

Hooded, his feet still and steady in their jesses, Abelard perched on Jed's wrist in the far corner of the Piccadilly Line car. It was a Saturday and they were going up to the end of the line, to Cockfosters.

Jed had decided it would be unwise to go back to Hampstead Heath at present. He had had some strange looks while flying Abelard up on the Heath behind St Columba's Hospital. Believing it to be an unfrequented part, he had nevertheless encountered several groups of people. One woman had actually spoken to him and in a censorious way, asking him if he knew there were more than 150 different kinds of wild bird inhabiting the Heath, and that these were protected species.

He would not have dreamt of setting Abelard on to anything but pigeons and rabbits, but it was true he could not always, or even often, control what the hawk did. There had been, after all, the incident of the magpie that had so distressed Tina's little girl. Up at Enfield Chase he would have more scope, more space and solitude.

The tube car had been full as far as Wood Green, but gradually the passengers had got out and now he was alone but for one other man, a black man in the uniform of London Transport Underground. This man had been sitting two seats from Jed, had looked curiously once or twice at the hawk, but after a while had moved away to the other end of the car. Jed knew this was because of the rank smell that came off his hawking jacket, a foul reek that repelled people but seemed to comfort Abelard and keep him quiet.

At Cockfosters he got out, holding Abelard, poised,

silent, hooded, on his wrist. When the hawk was quiet like this Jed felt a deep warm love for him, the kind of love he could not see as different from what he had once felt for a woman and a child. He wanted no other companion, required no more response than Abelard showed by simply *being* there, remaining perched on his arm, without attempts at escape.

But the week gone by had been terrible. No more terrible than all the weeks preceding, it was true, but no less either. The dreadful cries had begun at dawn, ceased only at feeding time when Abelard fastened upon his food, his meagre ration of food as Jed saw it, and had begun again before Jed left for work. The cries met him as he returned. He was afraid to ask the occupants of the School if they ceased at all during the day. He did not want to know the answer.

Jed weighed him. He knew that if the bird were overweight he must withdraw even the rations he was having – an ounce would be too much, half an ounce ominous. But he prayed for Abelard's weight to have declined so that he could feed him well and suppress that screaming. Yesterday had been a good day, a happy day, the weight loss considerable, surprisingly high, and oh, there had been such pleasure, such loving delight, in doubling the ration of steak pieces, in watching those flashing eyes, that gobbling beak. It was a quiet, contented hawk, sleeping on its perch, that he had left to go out and join the Safeguards on the southbound Victoria Line duty.

Together they made for the Triangular Wood. There were rabbits and Jed released Abelard from his jesses, watched him fly, swoop, circle and at the prescribed whistle, return to his hand for the chick reward.

The day was mild, damp, grey. Only the oaks still kept their leaves, brown and shrivelled. The grass was a bright sharp green from autumn rains. Abelard swooped into the misty sky, pursued a pigeon, obeyed Jed's command to fly to the tall trees at the far end of this grassy clearing. Or did his best to obey. To Jed's sensitive eyes, his flight seemed impeded by something indefinable, seemed stayed, clipped for an instant, before he attained the low-hung branch that was his destination.

Concerned, Jed began walking towards this tree, and as he approached, summoned the hawk. He felt a tremor of anxiety. But as Abelard flew towards him, came unerringly to his hand, he saw with relief the un-crippled, sure winging, the smooth flight of a strong young bird.

Each time the phone rang Alice expected it to be Axel Jonas. He knew Jarvis, so he must have the phone number of this house. He had told her they would meet again. She began answering the phone, running downstairs when she heard it ring. It never was Axel. The only calls she got were from her mother.

Her mother was 'coming up' to London, to do Christmas shopping. She wanted Alice to meet her for a talk.

Alice expected some kind of trap. Her mother would not be alone, would have Mike with her, or even Catherine. She was glad now that Mike had not recognized her when she and Tom were in the underpass at Hammersmith. It was a wonder to her that she had ever fancied she missed him or could return to him. Music was all-important. Even Tom took second place to that, and Axel Jonas was nothing to her, just a man she had allowed to kiss her because she was in a disturbed state and hardly knew what she was doing.

The day before the meeting with her mother, on her way to work in the morning, she saw a man she could have sworn was Axel Jonas in the crowd on Holborn station behind her. But when she looked back again he was gone and she thought she must have been mistaken. That evening she had a lesson at the house in Netherhall Way. Alice was nervous and could not concentrate. They had tea and Madame Donskoy talked about Anne-Sophie Mutter and then she said, 'I find it very amusing how some people want success without the ability to reach it.'

Madame Donskoy always said she found the kind of thing amusing that others would say they found tragic.

'Are you talking about me?' Alice asked.

'We have a saying in Russia that if the hat fits you, wear it.'

'We have a saying in England like that too.'

Tom did not ring the doorbell when her time was up. She had not mentioned going to her lesson, but he was waiting under the tree just outside the gate and the man's figure, stepping out in front of her, made her jump.

'Carry your fiddle for you, lady?'

'Oh, Tom.'

'I worry myself sick to think of you out alone in the dark.'

She did not say it would soon be dark at the time she came home from work, for that would be to re-open the question of his meeting her. They walked back through the dusky shadowy Hampstead streets, overhung with trees, pale lamps showing between autumn leaves, Tom's arm round her waist.

'I'm meeting my mother tomorrow,' she said. 'In the perfumery department of Dickens and Jones.'

'I don't believe it.'

He said that rather too often and it had begun to irritate her.

'She wants us to have a talk.'

'Alice,' he said, 'Alice, don't let her make you go back. Don't let her talk you into anything.'

The intensity in his voice made her shiver. His voice was like a weight laid on her shoulders.

'Who would want me back?' she said lightly.

'Anyone would want you.'

The meeting with her mother was not happy for either of them. They had lunch together in the restaurant of a department store where a young woman sat on a small dais, playing a violin. Alice thought she played rather well, too well, and would have preferred to be made to wince and cover her ears. She told her mother about the violin lessons to show she was serious about what she was doing. She thought of adding a fiction about Madame Donskoy advising her to apply to the Britten–Pears School in Aldeburgh for a fortnight's intensive course with some great virtuoso, but decided against it. She did not want to tell lies to her mother as well as to Tom.

'Things are all working out very nicely for you, then.'

'Things are working out.'

'Don't you want to know how your baby is?'

'It's better if I don't know, isn't it? It's better to cut myself right off.'

'Don't you think you did a wicked thing, walking out like that? Couldn't you have explained your feelings, talked about it?'

'If I'd done that I never would have gone. I'd not have had the courage.'

'I've seen Mike a few times,' her mother said. 'He never mentions you, it's too painful for him. He's thinking of selling the flat and moving in with Julia and her husband. Catherine and Julia's baby are nearly the same age. She'll soon forget she had any other mother, if she hasn't forgotten by now. Julia's a wonderful girl, she's a wonderful mother; she may not be much to look at, but where do looks get you?'

Alice felt like saying, to Oxford Street listening to someone playing Tchaikovsky better than she did. Marcia said that with her looks she'd probably found herself someone else by now. Or had there been someone else before she left?

'I'd like to have a bet on with you.'

Her mother had never offered to bet on anything before and Alice was surprised.

'I'd be willing to bet a great deal of money, a thousand pounds, say, that you never make it to the concert platform. No, I'll take that back. That you never make it into any orchestra. There you are, that's fair. A thousand.'

When at last Axel Jonas phoned her it was at work. She was in her office next to James Christianson's. She could hardly believe it when he said who it was. Her mouth dried but she managed to ask him how he got this number. He said it was from someone who knew them both and she guessed that was Jarvis. Axel refused to be more specific. He suggested a meeting at a pub in West Hampstead, the Railway or the Black Lion, he seemed to know all about it.

'That would be too near home.' It was her first step on the road of deceit.

The silence which greeted this seemed to her to be full of laughter. It *was* silence, but somehow warm with mirth. Then he said very lightly that they could go to this place in Kensington, near where he lived.

'I don't have your curious passion for travelling great distances to get a drop of brandy.'

She wondered why she wanted to meet a man who made her feel foolish. There was no way of explaining to him that she did not want Tom to know without implying that she expected more from their encounter than he intended. And did she? What did she expect? At least she could find out why he wanted to meet *her*.

'It's not usual to ask a man that when he invites a woman out.'

He said it coldly, in a tone of reproof. It was as if she had committed some breach of good manners. After he put the phone down she decided not to go. She did not know the man, she had barely spoken to him. What was a kiss? Her mother's generation might take a kiss seriously, but not hers.

It was very hard to be free of Tom, who wanted to be with her in all her waking and sleeping hours. Alice contrived a lie about mending the breach and visiting her mother and father in Chelmsford.

'I'll come with you,' Tom said. 'I'd like to meet your parents.'

'It's bad enough for them that I've left Mike,' Alice said. 'Have you any idea how they'd react if I turned up with another man?'

'They're going to have to get used to it, aren't they?'

'Not yet,' she said, hardly knowing what she meant by that.

Tom had broken out with one of those bursts of temper. This time he smashed a plate. When she flinched and gave a cry, he flung out his arms and swept the dishes off the table. She tried to get out of the room and he barred her way, accusing her of not caring for him, of treating him the same way as she had treated her husband. Alice told him she did care for him, which was true in a way, and he denied it and raged some more, then collapsed in tears, in her arms, something which had not happened before.

She had an urge to discuss Axel Jonas with someone. If she talked about him to Tom that would be the end of it. Mention him to Tom and there would be no meeting in a Kensington pub, no going miles for a drop of brandy. He was Jarvis's friend. She thought of talking about him to Jarvis, but when one evening on her return from work she encountered him in the vestibule, she realized she would have to explain how she had met Axel, how she had admitted him to Remove in Jarvis's absence and, above all, why she had not mentioned this before.

Instead she said, when he asked her if she found the journey very bad from Holborn in the rush, 'I didn't know you knew where I worked.'

He looked at her inquiringly, as well he might. 'Tina told me.'

'Ah. Of course.'

'I was interested,' he said, 'because your building's next to the one with the shaft coming up inside it. It's a big shaft that used to have a staircase in it to the Central Line. When they put the escalators in they took out the stairs and extended the shaft for ventilation. You could see that shaft opening from your office roof if you looked.'

She should have remembered his obsession with underground trains, his general lack of interest in anything else. He answered her inquiry without knowing he had done so, but left her even more in the dark as to how Axel knew the phone number of Angell, Scherrer and Christianson. She went upstairs. Lights were on in the galleries but not in the vestibule below, and when she looked down she saw Jarvis still standing there, as if caught in the toils of a monstrous spider, where the unlit electrolier cast its shadow.

She had made up her mind quite definitely not to meet Axel. There were enough complications in her life without this. She would not go and, in case he phoned her at the office again, she would ask the girl who ran the switchboard not to put him through. He would not come to the School again, she would never see him again. In a week or two he would be forgotten.

On the Saturday she got to the pub in Cheval Place before Axel did. He kept her waiting for fifteen minutes. She had bought herself a glass of wine, drunk it, was on the point of leaving. She was almost relieved he hadn't come. Now there would be no more deception, decision-making, doubts, inner inquiries, resolutions.

When he arrived he made no apology. He said, 'Oh, hallo,' as if they had known each other all their lives, met here every week at this time.

He wore the same shabby, narrow black overcoat that came nearly to his ankles. His beard had been trimmed, his face was very pale. The thick black, slightly wavy hair was tied back with a piece of thin black ribbon. Alice thought he looked like some peripheral character in a television drama about Freud. He bought her another glass of wine and himself a brandy. She noticed he wore a heavy, solid ring, made of alternating bands of white and red gold, on the forefinger of his left hand. He had not been wearing that ring when first they met, she was sure of that. Alice felt strange about it. She thought it was all right for men to wear rings but not sometimes to wear them and sometimes not, and not on the forefinger.

He asked her, astoundingly, how Jarvis was. She did not know what answer to make him.

'He's going to Russia next week,' she said.

'Ah, the secret agent.'

'He's going to see underground railways.'

'The man who watched the trains go by.'

'Yes, you could put it like that. He'll be away a long while. He's going to look at new metro systems.'

'Good old Jarvis.'

She drank some wine. 'Who are you?' she said. 'What do you do?'

'I'm a photographer. Oh, and I'm a bear-leader.'

'I don't believe it,' she said, like Tom. Why did she pick up men's speech patterns?

He started laughing. 'Which bit don't you believe? I'm a psychologist by training really, only I've never practised. As a matter of fact, I've never been a breadwinner.'

189

'That I believe. What did you mean by a bear-leader?'

'I and this dancing bear did an entertainment in the tube. Not a real bear, you understand. A man dressed up.'

'But I saw you!' she cried. 'I was part of a group busking in the tube and I saw you!'

The coldness returned to his voice. It was a low soft voice that could be very warm or very chilly. 'I imagine thousands did,' he said. Cold now, his voice dull, 'I'm mad, you know.'

'So I see.'

'No, you don't think I'm serious. But I mean it. I am mad. I am insane.'

'They say,' she said lightly, 'that if you know it you're not.'

'I'm afraid that's not true. It's the worst thing, being mad and knowing you are.'

He was looking very hard at her. She thought, with an inward shiver, he's right, he is, he *is* mad. I'll go, she thought, I'll get up and run out of here. He laughed, a warm, delightful, reasonable laugh.

'Come, let's go, I'm going to give you lunch.'

She expected a cafeteria, or at best a wine bar. He took her to an exclusive restaurant in Walton Street where the management, with extreme politeness, offered him a choice from a selection of ties before they were shown to their table. Axel chose one, not exactly meekly, but with a bland smile. Alice felt insufficiently well-dressed, was very conscious of her jeans, her shabby blouse and cardigan.

They had champagne, then more wine. When she was halfway through it Alice understood this was going to be the most expensive meal she had ever eaten. She remembered how she had reproved Tom for spending money on Chinese takeaway.

He talked to her about Jarvis. They had met through Ivan, 'the bear', with whom Axel shared a flat, and who had been at university with Jarvis. His manner was conversational, interested, quite gentle. He asked her about the house, about Cambridge School, how long she had lived there, who else lived there. He had, he explained, no idea that Jarvis had become a landlord.

'It's how he lives,' she said. 'It's where he gets his income.'

She told him about the rooms, with their classroom names or numbers still on the doors, and about who lived where. He listened. Then he seemed to lose interest. He talked about her. She must tell him about her music, about her ambitions.

While she spoke he watched her closely. Being analysed must be like this, thought Alice. Axel seemed to listen and weigh every word, sometimes his lips moved into a half-smile, sometimes the extreme gravity of his expression returned. She was again struck by his priestly look, the contemplative gaze, the visionary's eyes. What he had said about being mad now seemed absurd. When the meal was finished, when he had paid with an American Express gold card – another surprise – she began to wonder about this priestliness, this casual coldness. What would they do now? What would he expect of her?

He had told her he had a flat 'just round the corner'. The man called Ivan lived there too but might not be there now. Alice, who had once thought she could handle this kind of thing, simply did not know what she would do if Axel looked at her in a certain way and spoke in a certain tone and asked her if she would like to come back with him to where he lived. She remembered the kiss. But the man who was walking beside her up Beauchamp Place might not have been the same man as he who had taken her face in his hand and brought her mouth to his mouth.

Still, she supposed they were walking in the direction of

his flat. She walked. He no longer spoke to her. At the top, in Brompton Road, he stopped, turned and looked at her and she was mesmerized. Her legs had grown weak. She was staring at him, her hand up to her mouth.

It all happened very quickly. She hardly took it all in. He had hailed a taxi, opened the door for her and as she stepped in, instead of following, was instructing the driver to take her to the street where Cambridge School was in West Hampstead, and pressing a fiver into his hand. She sat back in the cab, shaken. He must have said goodbye, she must have said something, but what it was she could not recall. It had been a shock, yet what had she expected?

A promise of some kind of future, an arrangement made for another meeting. He walked off without looking back and she knew she would never hear from him again.

He phoned her at work the following Thursday. She had rehearsed what she would say if this happened, but by Thursday she had abandoned hope or fear. Already she did not know whether in connection with Axel she felt hope or fear. She had intended to say no, it's impossible, I'm sorry, I can't, but said instead, yes, all right. They were to meet in the same place, the same pub.

That second Saturday she awoke very early. It was deeply dark. Jarvis's leaving for Russia had awakened her, his soft and careful closing of the front door. No taxis for Jarvis. He would take the Jubilee Line train from West Hampstead to Green Park and the Piccadilly Line that goes all the way into the terminal at Heathrow. The British Airways flight BA 872 departed for Moscow at 9.15.

Alice wondered what she would wear for Axel. She had nothing, she possessed no nice clothes. Her best were what she wore for work. It humiliated her that she cared, that she even concerned herself with how she looked for this man who teased her, who used her, who would turn up late in a shirt without a tie and a coat a derelict might wear for begging in a tube entrance.

Tom slept quietly beside her. He was so handsome, it was a pleasure to look at him. No woman who could have Tom would look twice at Axel. Alice got up and quietly drew back the curtains to let in the grey light of a winter dawn. Tom slept on. Light never woke him. She began working through her poor wardrobe, trying to find something flattering to wear for Axel.

This time he was early, he was there when she arrived. His brandy was on the table in front of him and for her was a glass of champagne. He got up and took both her hands in his and she felt the heavy red and white gold ring on his forefinger bite into her palm.

Almost the first words he said to her were, 'I wish we could meet later in the day. I rather dislike making love in the afternoon.'

She blushed. The blood did not just come into her face and heat it but rushed there and beat. She took her hands away from him and sat down.

He was laughing at her, again making her feel foolish.

Tom had promised Alice he would apply to the various schools of music, of which she had prepared a list. He had made this promise more than a week before but had done nothing about it. He could not imagine himself at college again, in a learning situation, and with students of twenty. It was different for Alice, who already had a degree, who needed no further formal education but could, if she so chose, apply for auditions with orchestras. Tom had dropped out of his music school because he was ill, his head hurt him and he could not concentrate, and when people spoke less than sweetly and ingratiatingly to him he flew into a rage. Would it be any different now? His head no longer hurt but he was sure he was no better able to concentrate and once more he was giving proof of his rages nearly every day.

He even felt angry now because Alice had gone to see her parents for the second week in succession and had once again refused to let him go with her. Her visiting her parents on her own unnerved him. He was afraid they might persuade her into all sorts of things – if not to return to Mike, to continue her education, to pursue that crazy idea of hers of going to study in Brussels. They might even offer her money for this. Tom knew he had to get hold of money himself.

Another James Galway he would never be. He would never be a Thomas Allen. He was rather proud of this piece of self-knowledge, of confronting it and bearing it. All those talents of his, his playing and his singing voice, had been crippled for ever on that night in the dark road at Rickmansworth. He looked at his poor hand, tried to bend the little finger and, failing, was overcome with self-pity.

If only his grandmother would die! He did not need Alice to tell him he should not talk like that, think like that. He had been fond of her once, still was. As he waited at the School for Peter and Jay to come and collect him, Tom thought that instead of going down into the Underground with them, he might go instead to visit his grandmother. Why should he not say to her, you have promised me the money one day, give me some of it now? She could only refuse and she might not refuse.

He would buy a place for him and Alice to live in, and then, if Alice wanted this, go with her for a year to Brussels. He thought of how she would love him if he made this possible for her. When they came back he would start a business. He would go on busking in the tube, busking in the tube was what he liked doing, what he really enjoyed more than anything he had ever done, but he would start a business too. Something connected with music. Tom had been good at woodcrafts at school, he was deft with his hands, and he thought he could learn to make violins. He had a pleasing picture of life with Alice ten years hence, the house full of violins made and in the process of being made, Alice second violin in some northern orchestra, or perhaps she had given that up to have their babies. Outside the house, in the suburbs of this north country town, he would hang a wooden sign with a painting on it of a violin. He had been good at art at school too.

Instead of taking her to the same restaurant, or any restaurant at all, Axel ordered sandwiches at the bar. He said he was tired. He had been up at six to see Jarvis off at Heathrow. There were several of them, all old friends, who met at the terminal for a coffee. Ivan had been there too but he had had the sense to go home to bed.

'I've got something to tell you,' he said to Alice, but would not specify what.

It was not very pleasant in the pub, smoky and crowded. They had a tiny marble-topped table and a small iron chair each, but were crammed into a dark corner. There was no possibility of sitting anywhere else. Axel came back with cheese and pickle sandwiches Alice did not much want to eat, more brandy for himself and another glass of the pub's champagne.

She kept thinking of what he had said about making love in the afternoon. It was the most extraordinary remark anyone had ever made to her. She thought about it, wondering if it was a joke or if he had really meant what he said. And when, looking up, she caught his eye, she had the uncomfortable feeling he knew she was thinking this. It could not be true but she felt he knew what she was thinking all the time.

'What were you going to tell me?' she said at last.

He seemed genuinely puzzled. 'Was I going to tell you something?'

'You said you were. You said you had something to tell me.'

'Oh, yes. Yes, of course. I wonder how you'll react.'

He was looking at her, she thought, like a biologist at some vivisection victim, cool, interested, without the least empathy. His expression changed quickly. It was sensitive, it was almost *tender*. He put out the hand with the ring on it and reached for her hand across the table. Instead of taking her hand he stroked the fingers. He smiled a rueful smile.

'I hope you'll be pleased. Will you pretend to be pleased even if you're not? Will you, Alice?'

'I don't know,' she said, like a little girl.

'Oh, come, you do know, you must. Yes or no?'

'Yes.'

'I'm coming to live in your house.'

She said nothing. For a moment she thought she had misheard or that it was an expression, a slang term or euphemism, for something else. It was like saying, when you turned someone out, that you were showing them the door or giving them the keys to the street.

'I'm sorry. I don't know what you mean.'

He repeated what he had said, with an edge of exaggerated patience. 'I'm coming to live in your house. In the house you live in. I'm renting a room — well, two rooms.'

'But you can't. It's Jarvis's house.'

'Oh, Alice,' he said, and the fingers again stroked her fingers. 'What do you take me for?'

She shook her head.

'What did you think I meant? Did you think I was going to become a squatter? Naturally, I asked Jarvis. Well, as a matter of fact, Jarvis asked *me*.'

'Why do you want to? You've got a place to live.'

'I can't go on sharing with a bear.' He laughed a little. She stared at him. Her hand felt as if it must melt under that feather-light stroking. 'I can't share with anyone. Alice, you promised to *pretend* to be pleased.'

Had she promised? She was stunned by his announcement. She did not know what she felt.

'I shall be taking the Fifth and the Art Room,' he said. 'He says they're vacant.'

He would be above her and Tom, up on the second floor with Jed and the train set and the bell. It would not always be afternoon. She felt herself redden again and he saw it. She could tell that he saw it from that small twitching smile of his. It was a long time since she had noticed the presence of anyone else in the bar or smelt the smoke or heard the bursts of laughter. They were alone. She felt very weak and very vulnerable. He tightened his hold on her fingers and grasped them.

'What do you believe in, Alice?'

She felt her way, anxious to know what he meant. 'God, do you mean, or some principle or what?'

'Whatever you like.'

'Music . . .'

'Ah, I thought you'd say that.'

'How about you?' She whispered it.

'I? Well, I believe in love. Everlasting love, love beyond the grave. Revengeful love and retribution.'

He brought her hand to his lips and kissed it lingeringly. 'And now you must forgive me, I have to go.'

She could hardly believe what she was hearing. She heard herself whisper, 'No, no, please . . .'

'But, my dear, I have an engagement I absolutely must keep.' She hardly recognized the affected drawl. He laughed at her bewilderment. 'Oh, Alice, don't look like that. I believe you *are* pleased I'm coming to the School.'

'I am pleased,' she said numbly.

Once more he hailed a taxi, opened the door and handed her into it.

15

Cecilia Darne had once said of her neighbour's cat when its flank was grazed by a car that it had learnt its lesson and would now avoid the streets. Bienvida repeated this rather sententiously.

'I'm not a cat,' said Jasper.

His sister did not know what he meant. She had remarked to him that she supposed he wouldn't do any more sledging after his scare.

'Anyway, cats don't ride on top of tube trains,' said Bienvida, who was beginning to see the falseness of her analogy.

'No, but I expect rats do,' said Jasper. 'I expect they come out of holes in the roof and ride on top of a train to get to the next station. They could go for miles like that.'

They talked about rats for a while and about mice. Bienvida had found that if she put breadcrumbs on the cloakroom floor in the evening, when she came back later she stood a chance of seeing as many as a dozen mice feeding. One ran across Jasper's hand while they were sleeping down there and he woke up yelling, but no one else in the house heard him. For weeks he had kept away from the Underground. He had even gone fairly regularly to school. Once he had dreamt about that last roof ride and in the dream he had not jumped off in time, there had been no man in a bear suit to catch him, and the green metal overhang that Axel Jonas said was not low enough for him to hit his head on was only an inch above the roof and rushing towards him as he woke up. In another dream Axel Jonas had been on top of a car with him, struggling with him to throw him off on to the live rail. Jasper had resolved never to go back, never to risk that again.

But time changed things. After a while, even Cecilia's neighbour's cat most likely ventured once more to cross the street. He never spoke about it to Damon. The others, who did not go to his school, he had not encountered since that last fateful ride. He had no need to discuss it with anyone. He dwelt on it alone. What exercised his mind, what tempted him, was that long run from Baker Street to Finchley Road, that run which was the same distance as on the Jubilee but without two intervening stops. He had told Axel Jonas he had already done it.

If he had not told Axel Jonas this he would not care so much, it would not matter, he could forget it. But, as things were, it was as if he had to make that lying boast into truth. He had to do it and then he could stop. Like one of those tennis players whose ambition is to win Wimbledon, once he had done it he could retire.

Calling on Tina at the hour she herself appointed, the 'safe' hour of noon, Cecilia saw a tall, dark young man with a beard and a shorter man with a hat and scarf on unloading furniture from a rented van. There was a metal structure that might just be a bed and a thing Cecilia thought might be called a futon and a lot of cameras and photographic equipment. A number of boxes and suitcases stood on the pavement outside the School gates.

Cecilia recognized the bearded man as the one who had tormented her in the train. She therefore assumed that the other one had been the bear. It was a shock and she had to curb a natural instinct to turn and flee homewards. Her heart was pounding but she watched them as she approached, as she went up the path and from the shelter of the School porch. They did not recognize her, she was sure of that. She might not have been there for all the notice they took of her. However, Cecilia was used to that and did not even mind much. She knew very well that the least noticeable, the most invisible and indifferently regarded of all human beings, is an old woman.

After a moment or two she decided she must be mistaken. One dark bearded man looks very much like another. There must be hundreds of tall thin young men with black beards in London. As for the other, she had never really seen the bear's face, she had not dared to look between those jaws. She was glad she had been sensible and not allowed panic to prevail. Having given them one more glance to confirm her certainty they were not her tormentors, Cecilia let herself into the house. Seeing the two men struggling up the path with the bed frame, she left the front door open for them.

The children were at school. At least, they were not there. Cecilia preferred to believe they were at school. At this quiet noontime, finding Tina in her kitchen seated at the table drinking coffee and reading the *Guardian*, she could make herself believe all was well. When Tina looked up like that and smiled and said, 'Hallo, Ma. Hi. How's tricks?' she could not suppress the hope that this remark would be followed by, 'I've got something to tell you,' and then by the longed-for announcement: 'Brian and I are getting married next week.'

No such announcement was made. Easy-going, calm, taking life as it came, Tina got up and made her mother a cup of coffee. She talked desultorily about this new job that had come her way and which she might take. Over the years Tina had talked of taking jobs, sometimes with enthusiasm, but she never had taken them. There was a broad streak of happy-go-lucky, philosophical placidity in the family, which showed itself in Jarvis as well as Tina, and perhaps in Jasper, though it had by-passed Cecilia and her siblings and showed no sign of coming out in Bienvida.

'I want you all to come to me for Christmas, Tina,' she said after her daughter had finished outlining the dubious advantages of working part-time in a nearly new old-clothes shop. 'You could come on the Eve if you liked and stay over and then the children could have their stockings.'

'Yes, well, OK. I mean we'll come on the Day all right. We don't have to decide anything now, do we?'

Tina never wanted to decide anything like that now. Spontaneity was what she liked. Turning up as a surprise. Cecilia did not persist with that one. She was approaching what Daphne, who watched and always had watched a lot of panel games on television, would have called the $64,000 question. She skirted round it.

'Daphne will be staying as usual, of course, and Peter will try to come for lunch.'

Tina said nothing. She was scraping red varnish off her nails, using the tip of her right thumbnail as a tool, and dropping the peelings into the dregs of her coffee. Cecilia tried at first to pretend this was not happening, tried neither to look directly at Tina, nor ostentatiously away. Because she could not actually not think about it, she tried telling herself it was not filthy and disgusting but a normal thing to do, what thousands of young women did, and she must be a fussy old bigot even to notice it. She breathed steadily for a few moments and said, 'I thought of asking Brian too.'

'Asking Brian what?' said Tina.

It was not in Tina's nature to make things easier for anyone. She did not know when things were hard. They were never hard for her.

'Asking him for Christmas, Tina.'

'Oh, did you?'

'Do you think he would come?'

'I don't know. You could ask him.'

Cecilia left it. She was going to meet Daphne at Brent Cross Shopping Centre, where they intended to do their Christmas shopping. She went there by bus. There is a station at Brent Cross on the Northern Line, but in order to get to it from West Hampstead, no more than two miles away, it would have been necessary for Cecilia to go down into London on the Jubilee, change at Baker Street on to the Circle, at King's Cross on to the northbound Northern (the Edgware branch) and finally reach her destination eight stations later. Jarvis, in his youth, had made a plan for an underground link between Golders Green and Kilburn with intervening stations called Child's Hill and West End Lane, but this was never more than a dream, and he did indeed dream about it, asleep in the hotel in Dnepropetrovsk, as he often dreamed of non-existent or fabulous lines and of whole apocryphal metro systems.

Axel Jonas had been living at the School for two days before Alice knew he was there.

She had said nothing to Tom about his imminent arrival. She had said nothing to anyone. As soon as she had time to herself, Tom having gone out to buy food, she opened the doors of the rooms he was to have and looked inside. She had never been in either before. The windows of each were hung with dark green blinds as were all the windows in the School. Five contained a table and a wooden upright chair. In the Art Room the easels were still there and a long table with chairs round it. There were framed pictures on the walls, some of these, reproductions of what Alice vaguely knew to be famous paintings: a red-headed girl in a white dress and an angel holding a lily, the portrait of a young woman with a long white neck, a church with an immensely tall spire and trees round it.

From the windows of Five you could see the garden, the backs of factories beyond the railway lines, the silver trains scarred with vestiges of graffiti, the same view as from her own room. The Art Room gave on to the street, the row of leafless plane trees, the houses with paper chains glimpsed behind the windows and lumps of cotton-wool 'snow' stuck on the glass. It was dry and cold out there, the cold light wind ruffling litter and leaves along the gutter.

Alice was expecting a phone call. It was two weeks since she had spoken to him. Each time the phone rang she expected it to be Axel and she ran down to answer it before Tom could. But it was always Daniel Korn or Tina's mother or Peter. Tina only answered the phone if there was no one else in the house. She took the attitude that if she was wanted, some intermediary would fetch her, or if there was no one there the caller would ring back when there was. Tom, on the other hand, answered the phone a lot. It was very likely for him, for his 'work'. Alice noticed, with increasing disquiet, that Tom was beginning to take the attitude to busking in the tube of a man running an important and lucrative business from his home.

'Jay knows a really good guitarist he thinks he can persuade to join us,' he said to her one evening two days before Christmas. 'It'll be a distinct asset if we can get him.'

She raised her eyebrows.

'I've got to give some serious thought to how we're going to handle the competition. These rock bands, however basic, always have really sophisticated amplifying equipment. At the moment we just don't stand a chance against it.'

They were in the Headmaster's Study. Tom had his elbow on the table and his chin resting in his hand. He was frowning with the effort of concentration. A lock of fair hair had fallen across his forehead and he pushed it back, combing through it with his fingers.

'There's no question who makes the better sound. People want our sound, they love it, you can see that. It's a fallacy that people aren't hungry for art, for good music. They are. But what's the use when it's drowned by a hundred decibels of saxophone? I've got to make it my aim as soon as we've got over Christmas to do something about amplifying our sound.'

She reminded him that they had no food in the house, they had to go out and buy food.

'We can eat in that Chinese place.'

He said it indifferently. He said it as might that up-and-coming businessman he sounded like, a man who was succeeding in his career and making money hand over fist. Alice told herself not to remind him, as she longed to do, that she was earning £800 a month and he, if he was lucky, eighty. The music school application forms remained as they were when they arrived, unopened, untouched.

'As a matter of fact,' he said, 'I'm getting up the nerve to ask my grandmother for a loan to buy the necessary equipment.'

They had come out on to the landing or gallery at the top of the first flight of stairs. It was one of the colder days of a mild winter. Tom was one of those men who never wrap up, who always wear a short jacket, simply turning up the collar in the wintertime. Alice, very glad these days that she had brought it with her, wore her winter coat. She had jeans on, boots, a woolly hat and gloves, and round her shoulders the big blue and red shawl she had bought, her sole extravagance. Her bright brown curly hair fell down her neck and over this shawl like some additional warming garment, a cape or veil.

Tom had begun talking about what he called, in an awful pun, the second string to his bow. He had discovered a course, taking place in Cambridge, where they taught violin-making. Making violins would not only be lucrative, but therapeutic. He could imagine the feelings of peace and serenity and accomplishment working quietly at this splendid and useful craft would bring him.

Alice had put her hand through his arm but withdrew it when she saw who was coming up the stairs. Her heart expanded and slowly turned over. It was not a feeling she had ever had before. It did not exactly hurt but it was on the edge of hurting. Once more in its rightful place, her heart began to beat with heavy drumstick blows.

He was coming up slowly, his head lifted, his eyes turned towards her. He wore his long dark overcoat and with it a black scarf, long enough to measure his own height twice. It was not tied round his neck but its two ends hung over his shoulders and down to his feet like some kind of vestment.

Alice did not know what to do. There passed through her mind the idea that he had come to find her, perhaps even to take her away. Or, worse, *not* to take her away. She thought, suppose he comes up to me and *kisses* me in Tom's presence. Axel stopped and looked at them before mounting the second flight. That is, he looked at both of them. His eyes had not left Alice's since she first saw him there.

He said, 'I'm Axel Jonas, a friend of Jarvis's. I've come to live here.'

Holding out his hand, Tom went towards him. He said his own name, then hers, looking over his shoulder at her. They were shaking hands, Axel's eyes continuing to meet hers blankly, without recognition, without *apparent* recognition.

She took his hand. It was cold, she could feel the cold through her woolly glove. A shiver went through her, a strong galvanic movement he must have felt pass between their joined hands. Alice took hers away. She felt Tom must see what had taken place, for it seemed to her a small silent drama, the air around them thick with concentrated tension, with Axel's studied control, her suppressed fear and, yes, her longing.

But Tom was smiling pleasantly. 'We were just going out to eat,' he said.

Axel inclined his head.

'Don't hesitate to ask, will you, if there's anything you want to know. About the place, I mean. Well, about anything you have problems with.'

'I won't hesitate,' Axel said, and Alice thought he said it meaningfully, she thought there was a special meaning underlying those words that referred to her. He would not hesitate, not now, he would not delay.

He passed on up the second flight, and Tom, halfway across the vestibule, looked back and up the two flights and up the two galleries to see which door he opened. Alice was now reluctant to go out. From being fearful and rather shocked, she had become excited. The idea was inescapable that Axel had come here for her, had moved in for her sake, to be near her, under the roof she was under.

She could not eat. She fidgeted to be back. While they were in the restaurant and on the way home she hoped Tom would mention Axel, just say something about him, even that his arrival was unexpected, even something disparaging about his appearance. She was already afraid to speak of him first. But Tom was uninterested. Tom only wanted to talk about his musical projects and their future.

'Is there any future in busking?' she said at last, awaiting the explosion, the anger.

He only grinned. 'Oh, we shan't be busking for ever. Or not in the way you mean. When we've made ourselves famous down there we'll come up into the light. Jay's got a good contact with a journalist who's going to do a piece on us for the *Evening Standard*. What would you say if I told you we could be the resident trio in Covent Garden in a year's time?'

She said nothing. On the way back, just outside the front door, she said, 'What did you make of that man we met when we were coming out?'

'What man?'

He had forgotten or had never cared.

Alice lay awake a long while, thinking about how Axel must have come for her. One of his rooms was directly above the Headmaster's Study, the other above and at the front of the house. She listened for a movements overhead, heard nothing. In the morning the house was silent, there was no one about. It was a Friday and her last day at work before Christmas.

Now that Axel had come and had seen her she expected him to phone her at her office, but he did not phone. Tom was in Holborn tube station when she went down there and they travelled home together. He had had a good day, attracting discerning travellers with less well-known Christmas carols, singing 'Lullay, lullay' and 'Personent Hodie' and 'Love Came Down at Christmas', his personal takings amounting to over £10.

Alice had convinced herself Axel would be in the vestibule when she arrived. He would be standing as he had done that first day they met, reading those old-fashioned girls' names engraved on the pitch-pine panel. The hall was empty, the whole house felt empty. She and Tom ate their meal in the Headmaster's Study, listened to a new recording she had bought of a Brahms concerto. They often listened to music together, but never after eleven at night and were always discreet about the sound. Alice had never worried she might be disturbing anyone but now she thought of Axel, half-expecting him to come to their door and ask them to turn the stereo down. From that evening she could date her perpetual thinking about Axel, from that evening he was never really absent from her thoughts. He was the air she breathed, the sounds she heard, his face superimposed on the faces of others, he figured in the dreams she dreamed.

There was nothing she could do about it. He was *there* in

her head. That he was not there in the flesh was a perpetual burning, trembling anxiety. He might as well not have been in the house, perhaps he was not in the house. Her thoughts narrowed to a point that contained one tiny seed of purpose: to go to the door of Five or the door of the Art Room, to knock and open the door and go in and find him. She never did this, only thought incessantly of doing it.

Among the things left behind in Underground cars have been: a brace of pheasants, several Christmas turkeys, £1,500 in cash and a suitcase containing a full set of Masonic regalia.

Travellers tend to leave more things behind at Christmas time. At Liverpool Street last year four bags of Christmas groceries were handed in as lost property as well as a baker's wooden tray of sandwiches.

Every train is cleaned at night. On the Central Line every train is litter picked at the end of each journey. At Oxford Circus eighty sackfuls of rubbish are collected each day. This is mostly made up of takeaway boxes and freebie magazines. But what clutters the tunnels is human hair, shed softly, imperceptibly, invisibly, by the millions who use the system.

The fluffers go into the tunnels by night when the power is off. Their task is to pick clean the spaces between the rails. It is not a hazardous occupation, but tedious, sinister and sometimes frightening. There can be no trains running on those tracks, for the power is off. You know for certain no trains can run. But if a train passed through the tube there would be no more than nine inches space between its sides and its roof and the tunnel wall.

Imagine you hear a train coming. There is nowhere to go, no escape. And you do hear trains coming. What you hear are the driverless Post Office mail trains running along their own parallel tunnels, and you know it, but do you suppose you always know it when you are in the tunnel in the depths of the night?

In the Tokyo underground staff are employed exclusively to collect into baskets sleeves torn from passengers' clothes in the crush and the shoes they have left behind.

On the evening before Christmas Eve Jed took Abelard to the vet. The vet heard about the trouble Abelard was having with his flying, how he seemed not always to be able to succeed in reaching the highest branches, how he had lost feathers from his right wing, and made an appointment for Jed to see a specialist bird vet at a veterinary college. He stressed how important it was to keep the hawk warm.

Jed brought Abelard indoors and put him on the perch in Upper Six with the oil heater on. He went out at eight to meet three other Safeguards, a man and two women, on the northbound Northern Line platform at Tottenham Court Road. All was quiet on the first run up to High Barnet and back again, but on their second time out a crowd of teenage boys came 'steaming' through the train. They kicked a woman's bag out of their way, emptied the contents of a suitcase over the floor and pushed an elderly man over when he tried to stop them. Jed got out and alerted the driver who put a phone call through and two London Transport police officers were waiting to board the car the boys had reached at Kentish Town.

There was peace after that until one of the women Safeguards, Maria, found a suspicious carrier-bag left in a corner of the second car. They speculated it might be a bomb before turning it over to the assistant station-manager at Tottenham Court Road, but Jed thought it was most likely a Christmas turkey someone had forgotten.

Abelard was sleeping on his perch when he got home and the room was warm and cosy.

Tina took the children to her mother's house late on the morning of the 25th. She did not go on the Eve because she was out celebrating with Daniel Korn until some time in the small hours of Christmas morning. At Cecilia's for lunch were Tina, Jasper and Bienvida, Brian Elphick, Daphne Bleech-Palmer, Peter Bleech-Palmer and Jay Rossetti.

It was a real sacrifice on Brian's part as he had been invited with his girlfriend to spend the day with her sister and brother-in-law at their house in Chigwell. But he was a nice man with old-fashioned ideas about what constitutes duty and obligation. Bienvida and Jasper knew all about the girlfriend and had often met her but Jasper was not specially interested and, like the majority of males, though not all, hardly ever talked about people to other people. Bienvida on the other hand had been very interested, but had lived up to her well-known reputation for discretion and never mentioning anything that might cause trouble. She had not said a word about Brian's girlfriend to Cecilia and had even prepared herself to deny this woman's existence in the unlikely event of her grandmother's inquiring.

Tina had a hangover and cold, which combined to make her morose. It put an unfortunate blight on things, Tina's cold, because Jay became inordinately distressed about it, fretting that Peter might catch it, even suggesting that they should not stay for lunch. Daphne could take only so much of this before saying, 'It wouldn't be the first cold he's had, I'm sure. He used to be very prone to colds when he was small. You want to worry about Cecilia catching it, she's the one who gets bronchitis.'

But Jay persisted. Peter had to sit as far from Tina as possible and every sneeze provoked an exclamation of dismay from him. Anyone but Tina would have been made to feel uncomfortable. Jay took Peter away in a taxi as soon as lunch was over.

The London Underground does not run on Christmas Day.

Brian had his car and ran Tina and the children home in it. The distance was very short but they had their presents to carry and Tina's head was killing her, as much from drink the night before as from her cold. They met Axel Jonas coming out with a man in a hood pulled down to hide his face but, not knowing them, they concluded they must be friends of Alice and Tom.

When they had picked up the wrapping paper and folded the best bits for use again next year – if there was a next year, as both of them these days mentally reserved – when they had wrapped the turkey in clinging plastic and put it into the fridge, Cecilia and Daphne sat side by side on Cecilia's sofa and watched a video. It was *A Passage to India*. They did not say much to each other. Like a long-married couple, they had said it all and there was not much left. To say something kind, pay a small compliment to the other, was the wish of each as it was on most days when they met. Accordingly, Daphne said what a dear little girl Bienvida was and how pretty she was going to be, and Cecilia said how much better Peter was looking.

Cecilia had read the book. She found her thoughts wandering a little. On the whole she felt very happy. It was always a joy to have Daphne to stay, to bring her morning tea in bed, knowing exactly how she liked it without having to ask, a very little milk, one level teaspoonful of sugar, to draw back the curtains, ask the question out of which long ago Daphne had made a joke that had become a ritual for them: 'How did you sleep?'

'On my left side, dear, and under your very nice warm quilt.'

Cecilia turned her attention back to Mrs Moore and the Marabar Caves.

16

The only one of them to catch Tina's cold was Tom. Alice went back to work after the Christmas holiday with a sense of freedom because he was not down in the Holborn concourse when she left for home. A man with drums, a man with a guitar and a girl singing Tammy Wynette songs were there instead.

She was thinking, as usual, about Axel Jonas, seeing his face in every crowd, on every Underground platform, in photographs when she looked in a newspaper. The man himself she had never seen since that meeting at the top of the stairs, but she had heard his footsteps above her head, and the previous evening had heard him behind the closed door of Remove. Tom was in bed in Four, his own room, nursing his cold. It was late but there was a shop open all night in West End Lane. Alice went out to buy aspirins and coming back saw through the big bay window a faint light, like the moving beam of a torch.

It went out and she could almost have deceived herself that she had imagined it. In the hall she listened outside the door of Remove. She could hear sounds from within, not footsteps but of objects being moved, papers pushed across a wooden surface, wood sliding on wood. Or she imagined that was what she heard, she was not sure.

That it must be Axel she knew. Neither Tina nor Jed would take any interest in the contents of Jarvis's room. But if it were Tina or Jed she would have opened that door and asked them what they were doing. She thought of walking in upon Axel in the dark and knew she was afraid to do that, she was simply afraid of what might happen. Instead she went quickly upstairs, turning off the lights behind her. Making a hot drink for Tom, dissolving aspirins in a glass of water, she thought, but it's all right, he's Jarvis's friend, Jarvis has given him permission to be in there, though she knew this was not at all what was worrying her.

Later, she heard him come upstairs. To reach the second flight he had no need to pass her door but might have gone straight on up. His footsteps came along the gallery and stopped outside her door. She knew he would try the door and, finding it unlocked, come in. Her breath held, she waited, rigid with fear, she did not think she had ever in her life been so frightened. Never in her life had she hoped so much.

He stood there for a long time. It must have been a whole minute he stood there, and a minute can be very long, before moving away to the upper flight of stairs. She heard his door close above her head and a sweat broke out over her body. She could not have said if she was relieved or bitterly disappointed and she had no idea what she had been frightened of.

Not for the first time she went over in her mind the conversation they had had in which he said he was mad. He had said it quite seriously and calmly, as someone else might have said he was asthmatic or accident-prone. And now she was inclined to think, as she had not at first, that he had used the expression as people do when they mean wild or eccentric or quixotic.

He had said he believed in love. She remembered his expression as savage when he said that, but perhaps it had not been, perhaps that was the invention of her own memory. He believed in everlasting love, love beyond death. Why had he told her if he had not meant he could come to love her like that?

Contrary to what most people think, there is not much crime in the London Underground.

For instance, Brixton police deal with three times as many robberies as London Transport Police.

The commonest crime is 'dipping', another name for stealing wallets and handbags and picking pockets.

The Countess Teresa Lubienska, a Polish woman of seventy-three, was stabbed in a descending lift at Gloucester Road in 1957. It was quite late at night, a Friday in summer. In 1983 a booking clerk at Balham was murdered with a sawn-off shotgun. It was not shot or a bullet which killed him, but wadding propelled from the gun. Twenty-three suspects were interviewed but the killer was not found.

In the same year a vagrant called Kiernan Kelly tried to push someone under a train. He was charged with attempted murder and while locked in a police cell at Clapham with two others, garrotted one of his companions with the man's own shoelaces. Kelly claimed he was guilty of many murders and was sentenced to life imprisonment in 1984.

Most assaults on the Underground are caused by drinking. Telling someone to put out a cigarette may result in getting knocked down.

The man who rushes about crowded platforms trying to push people off on to the line is known to the police, with a sad lack of inventiveness, as the Wild Man from Borneo. His hair is long and bushy and his clothes dirty. One of his victims fell over the edge but came to no harm. The 'juice' runs through a rail on the wall side.

No one has ever been murdered inside a London tube train. If anyone has been raped, it is not known.

Indecent assault is common enough. The police call it 'bustle-rumpling'. It is hard to say how much of it is deliberate and how much the result of a sometimes unbelievably close proximity in the rush hours.

There are of course men who find the crush they curse an opportunity for fantasy made flesh.

★

Alice went into Holborn station and down the escalator. The sound of music ahead surprised her because it was Tom's music, taken from his repertoire of popular classics, Mozart's little night music giving place as she approached to a Strauss waltz. It could not be Tom unless he had made a swift recovery. She turned the corner and saw ahead of her, grouped in a deep curve of the tunnel wall, Peter with his guitar and Jay with his tenor sax, a bear waltzing with lumbering steps, and Axel mouthing the jew's harp he had made from a comb and a sheet of paper.

'It's not one of those amazing coincidences,' Peter said. 'We knew you'd have to come this way.'

They had not stopped playing. The bear had not stopped dancing. Only Axel abandoned his instrument, screwing up the paper and putting the comb into the pocket of his long dark coat. He looked at her, smiling slightly. She moved to stand with her back to the wall so as not to obstruct the flow of people. It was disquieting, what had happened. She had a fleeting sense, soon dispelled, that they had all known each other for years, had in some way conspired, were laughing at her gullibility and her discomfiture.

But Peter, finishing the waltz with a long trill on the strings, murmured to her, 'They kindly offered to take Tom's place. We met them when we called for him. The bear's been quite a success.'

The bear heard and pawed at her, shaking its heavy head. Alice could just glimpse the man's face between the jaws, an ugly, ill-made face with a spoonbill nose. He caught her looking and turned sharply away. She tried to smile but the bear's antics amused her no more than they had Cecilia. Then Axel was pulling him away, calling him Bruin and telling him to bear himself in a more seemly fashion. Jay picked up the hat and emptied the money into a bag, saying Peter was tired and they should call it a day.

They went, heading for the Piccadilly Line. The bear stepped out of his bear suit but, instead of revealing himself fully, appeared in a hooded anorak with the zip done up high enough to cover his mouth. When he left them to go northwards, he walked with the loping stride of a big animal. She was alone with Axel, though surrounded by throngs of people. They stood on the Central Line platform, up against the wall papered with reproductions of British Museum antiquities.

'I've talked to your lover,' he said. 'Your Tom.'

She thought his voice censorious, a little reproving, and again, looking up into his grave face, his sad penetrating eyes, she saw him as priest-like, as a stern cleric. It was an impression enhanced by the clothes he wore, the dog-collar effect of a round-necked dark sweater over a white T-shirt, the long dark scarf. Her instinct was to deny the relationship, to repudiate Tom. She only said, 'I gathered that.'

'We had a talk. It was most interesting.'

He sounded like a blackmailer. She thought his voice had a dry edge of menace. She heard a shrillness in her own as she asked him, 'What do you mean?'

A slow smile was spreading across his face. 'What do you think I meant? Oh, Alice, Alice, you thought I'd been telling him tales out of school, didn't you? You thought I might have mentioned clandestine meetings and a certain kiss – am I right?'

No one else could make her blush like that. She hated him for doing it. Her face was hot and the blood throbbed. The way he was standing now she thought one of the worst and most intimidating positions a man could stand in with a woman, he in front of her, pinning her against the wall with a hand on either side of her but not touching her.

He held his head on one side, he seemed to be listening, or *feeling*.

217

'Train's coming.'

She could hear nothing, feel no vibration.

'It's colder,' he said. 'Can't you tell? And the air's moving. Your blood pressure's dropped.'

'How do you know?'

'Jarvis told me.' He dropped his hands. 'I hate the tube, it's my enemy.'

'You can't call a *thing* your enemy.'

'Oh, but you can if it's acted like an enemy, if it's done you wrong.'

His eyes glittered as the thrill and rumble, a long way off, began to shake the lines. The train came out of the tunnel with a roar. The cars were full already but no one got out. Alice got in, was crushed up against the next person. It was going to be one of those home-goings when the station staff had to push backs in before the doors would close.

She managed to squeeze herself against the glass partition. Axel stood pressed against her. He could hardly have done otherwise than be pressed against her, it would have been the same for any man who had followed her in. She was very aware of the length of his body, of this long, enforced embrace, for it was long and enduring simply because, instead of diminishing at the next stop the crowd increased until not one more person could have been squeezed into the car.

The train slowed in the tunnel between Tottenham Court Road and Oxford Circus and came to a stop. There was someone crushed against Alice on her left and someone on her right but she was not aware of them. Or, rather, she was aware of them but as solid obstructions rather than human beings, pieces of furniture perhaps. Only Axel, his chest against her breasts, his hips touching hers, their legs pressed together, seemed alive. She could feel his heartbeat, which seemed to her to quicken its pace, to increase and increase until it was pulsing very fast. She tried to regulate her breathing as might someone who is anxious or afraid, but her breath came shallowly.

He was much taller than she, and her eyes were on a level with his mouth. She thought he was looking at her but would not lift her head to see. She closed her eyes. He would only have had to move a little to kiss her eyes. The train moved. She thought then that he was standing like this, about as close to her as one human being could be to another when they were upright and clothed, not because he desired it but because he had no choice. He was pressed up against her as impersonally as any stranger might be in this overcrowded train.

When at last she lifted her head to look at him her eyes met his. His head was bent. Immediately he closed his eyes. His face was full of suffering, not the exasperation, the discomfort and distress that showed on other faces, but a kind of despair.

She shivered. They fought their way out at Bond Street. The Jubilee Line train northbound was nearly as congested, but this time she and Axel were separated, two other bodies squashed between theirs. It felt cold on the wind-swept platform at West Hampstead after the hot fug of the tube cars. Tom would have put his arm round her to warm her but she did not want Tom. She foresaw an evening of sitting at his bedside, nursing him, that was what he liked, bringing him things to eat and hot drinks, while he talked about becoming the king of the beggars, the greatest street musician of all time, the great fiddle-maker, the Stradivarius of West Hampstead.

She said breathlessly to Axel, 'Can we go somewhere and have a drink?'

He had not spoken since before she saw him close his eyes and saw the pain alter his face. 'I don't like the pubs round here.'

His response, cold, indifferent, as if it were entirely a question of place, not of their being together, crushed her. She tried to match his tone with her own. 'All right.'

'I shouldn't go in the tube,' he said. 'I don't know why I do. It must be masochism.'

'Sometimes there's no choice.'

As if she had not spoken, he said, 'The real reason is I need to refresh my memory. I have to *know*. I could forget and I mustn't do that. I have to know what it was like.' He turned to look at her. 'We can have a drink in the Art Room.'

It was so unexpected it brought the blood up into her face. She was glad it was too dark for him to see. A dampness that thickened and darkened the air laid a cold touch on the skin. The pavements were a sticky wet. Cars ruled the streets here, there were few people on foot once beyond the area round the stations. Axel took no notice of her as they crossed the bridge and descended the steps. They might each of them have been alone, two separate home-going commuters who happened to be walking parallel. And by the time they came to the gate of Cambridge School he had gone on ahead of her, was several yards ahead of her, so that she was seized by a sudden dread that he would unlock the front door and step inside and shut it behind him before she could get there. Instead, he held the door open and stood aside for her to pass through ahead of him.

It had begun to look as if Jasper's plan was destined to fail. The plan, that is, to extend the bellrope and re-open the traps in floors and ceilings so that the rope once more passed down into the cloakroom. While Jed alone – and intermittently the hawk – lived on the top floor, it had not seemed too difficult a task, particularly now that Jarvis was away. The presence of Jarvis in Three made passing a rope down outside his bedroom door a dangerous venture. But Jarvis was gone and Tom and Alice's rooms were on the other side of the house. Upstairs the rope would have to be conducted down very close to Jed's door, but on the darker, righthand side of it and Jasper was pretty sure Jed had no cause ever to walk in that direction.

The day before, Tina had told Jasper there was a new tenant in the house, someone who had taken Five and the Art Room. She told him with no particular purpose in mind, she was only making conversation. Jasper was not pleased. The presence of someone else up there would interfere considerably with his plans. Of course it depended, as Bienvida had pointed out, on the sort of person it was. A woman like their mother would not notice, a woman like their grandmother would notice and would care. A man like Jarvis or Brian or even Daniel Korn would care, though Tom would not.

Bienvida, holding the doll called Caroline, and Jasper with a torch were in the passage outside the door to the Science Lab to the left of the top of the upper flight of stairs. There was no light on up here, only on the two lower floors. It was dim but not really dark. They had rolled up part of the runner and prised open the trapdoor with a screwdriver left behind by Daniel Korn when he had put up a shelf for their mother in her kitchen. Jasper had his new torch which he had bought with the money Cecilia gave him for Christmas. He shone it down the hole, which was a dark and dusty nest of old raw wood and cobwebs.

'You can see where the other hole is in the ceiling down there. It'll be dead easy to do if no one comes and stops us.'

As he spoke they heard the front door open and close. Part of the purpose of their visit to the top floor was to try and see the new tenant. Since Jed was in the garden with Abelard, their mother out and, so far as they knew, Alice in Tom's room with Tom, it seemed likely that this was who it was. Quickly, Jasper closed the trapdoor, Bienvida rolled back the carpet, and they retreated into the darkness of the passage.

Jasper expected the newcomer to switch a light on ahead of himself, to switch it on from the foot of the stairs, in which case he and Bienvida would have ducked behind the Science Lab door and watched through the crack. No light came on, though footsteps ascended, two sets of footsteps.

The woman was Alice, walking ahead and quickly in the direction of the Art Room. The man was tall and dark with a beard and wearing a long dark overcoat. Jasper at once recognized Axel Jonas and clapped his hand over his mouth to keep himself from crying out.

There was a sink in the Art Room and running water. Axel took a bottle of whisky out of the cupboard under the sink, and three glass tumblers, one of which he filled with water. A bulb without a shade, hanging from the centre of the ceiling, was the only light and it was of low wattage. The room was very cold and felt damp. Axel pushed on the switch of an electric fan-heater with his toe.

He gave Alice one of the tumblers, poured in two inches of whisky and a dribble of water. She disliked whisky, would never have had it from choice. He made himself a drink in the same way, identical quantities in an identical glass. The only chairs were upright ones of shiny pitch pine. He indicated one to her, cocking his thumb, and sat down in another, the table between them. Things could hardly have been less comfortable, the air still icy, the fan roaring and the dim lightbulb slightly swinging in the breeze it made.

They kept their outdoor clothes on. Alice was about to take a sip of her whisky when he put out a hand to stay her, said, 'No, we'll drink to each other.'

Their tumblers touched with a ringing sound surprisingly clear and musical in such cheap glass. His face was grave, almost sad.

'To someone else's lover.'

She did not know what to say. 'To you.'

The whisky that felt cold in the glass was hot in her mouth and went down her throat like a trickle of flame. She could not suppress her shiver, nor keep from defending herself.

'I didn't tell you I hadn't – got someone. I didn't deceive you.'

She expected him to smile but he didn't. The whisky had gone straight to her head. Her head was already swimming, she was already made a little reckless.

'Why do you expect me to tell you everything about myself? You've told me nothing about you.' She recollected that he had, just a little. 'Well, things I don't believe, things no one would believe.'

'What things?'

'You said you were mad, you said you hated things, the tube. Are you really a photographer?'

'Those are my cameras over there.'

There were two of them with other photographic equipment on a table under the painting of the girl. She looked, nodded.

'All right, but the bear ...' She tried to laugh it off. Something Tina had said came back to her. She had been quoting her mother. 'Do you think I look like her?'

She had displeased him, she could tell at once. That dead, glazed look concentrated his face.

'No. Not at all. Has someone been telling you that you do?' It must have been the meekness in her eyes as she nodded that made him kinder. 'She is Mary Zambaco by Burne-Jones. He was in love with her. You can tell, can't you? Perhaps you do look a little like her.' His face smoothed and his eyes lit. 'There is a resemblance.' As if to himself he said, 'I wonder if that's why I like you?'

She was enormously pleased; more than that, it was as if she had suddenly been made excitingly happy. It no longer seemed important or even relevant to ask him about the bear, about why he wanted to come here, about his idle, unemployed existence. He read her thoughts again.

'I told you I was a psychologist. You know they're all mad. If you had heard of Freud doing something like that, walking about Vienna with the Bear Man, you wouldn't find it at all incredible. Why don't you believe in me?'

'I do,' she said. 'I'm sorry. It just seems so strange.'

'It is strange.'

He got up and fetched the whisky bottle. She murmured, no, no, and put up her hand to cover the glass. He took her hand by the wrist and moved it away, mechanically, like someone pushing a handle. Another two inches of whisky went into her glass. He poured more than that into his own. She was staring up at him, caught as she had been at their past meetings by something mesmeric in his dark blue gaze.

She said breathlessly, 'I want to ask you something else.'

'I may not answer.'

'You won't mind answering this. How did you get my phone number at work? Jarvis didn't give it to you, he couldn't have, he didn't know the name of the company, only that I work in a building next to where a shaft goes down into the tube. You know how he's always thinking about trains and tube lines. You hadn't met Tom then. You didn't even know Jarvis let rooms.'

He had never returned to his chair but had been standing in front of her with his hands on the table. When she named Tom she saw his fingers press harder on the wooden surface and the knuckles whiten. For a moment he did not speak.

'I'm sorry but I would like to know.'

His voice seemed different, softer, more thoughtful. 'I followed you. I followed you from here one morning.'

So it *had* been him.

'You followed me?'

He smiled faintly, 'Why not? Aren't you glad I did?'

Her head swam. She pushed away the glass. 'I don't want any more to drink.'

'Are you cross with me?' He did not sound as if he cared, was only curious.

'No. No, I'm not cross. I don't understand you. I don't know what you want, what you're doing here.'

'I want you,' he said.

He pulled his chair round, sat on it and put his hands on her arms, not her shoulders, but her upper arms, gently pressing and stroking through the thick winter clothes. It was absurd the clothes they were wearing, but the room had not warmed, in spite of the blasts of heated air. She turned her face slightly from him, twisting her neck. He did what he had done before when he kissed her, took her face in his hand and held it, moving his fingers across the skin, feeling the bones, as if he could not see, as if he were blind. His own face he brought close to hers, closer and closer till the lips touched without kissing.

She could not bear the feel of those heavy clothes, but loosened her scarf and pulled her coat apart. His tongue touched her lips and licked them apart. It was rough, like a cat's. He held her by the neck, very lightly and softly, his fingers stroking the fine, thin skin at the back of her ears. She was growing weak, her bones made of limp string. The kiss was slow and exploratory, almost without pressure, boneless, their mouths made of silk. She found herself sliding backwards on the absurd hard wooden chair.

He opened her coat and her cardigan and her blouse, delicately, sweetly, not touching her skin, undressing her the way an expert lady's maid was supposed to do. When she felt his fingers they were miraculously warm in that cold room. He kissed her breasts, rubbed his lips against her skin, held her breasts in both hands delicately, like someone touching flowers.

She managed to say, 'Let's go to your room.'

Afterwards she thought it was like one of those fairy stories or myths in which the cantrip is upset by the wrong word or prohibited act. Psyche looks at the sleeping Eros and spills on him the hot oil from her lamp. The new young princess dares ask her husband where he goes when he leaves her by night. But it is enough, it destroys the moment, the spell is broken.

She had spilt no oil, broken no prohibition, done no more than speak and at first it seemed a wise thing, a necessary thing. It had been impossible for her not to say it. He lifted his head, remaining for a moment perfectly still. Then he drew her clothes together across her bare breasts. He caught her for a moment in an embrace of held shoulders and cheek against cheek. The casualness of that, the *economy*, should have told her. But she was carried away, transported on desirous wings, unable to think, unable even to breathe deeply. She leaned on him as he led her to the door. His arm was round her shoulder, holding her against him, but at the door he took it away. He laid a finger on his lips, opened the door.

It was still dark up there. The children had gone. The house was silent and might, for all Alice cared, have been empty. Opposite them was the door to Five, his other room. He took her hand in both his. She was aware, incredulously, that he was shaking his head, smiling at her and shaking his head. He rubbed her hand, like someone comforting a child.

'Not here,' he said. 'We can't here. Not with your Tom downstairs.'

Alice could only look at him.

'Think. Be reasonable. It wouldn't do, not in this house.' He was whispering. 'You'll understand that if you think about it.'

226

She found a voice, a shaky one. 'How can I *think*?'

'Not with your Tom ill downstairs.' He gave the hand he held a little shake and gently let it fall. Now they were not touching, had stepped apart, or he had stepped away from her. 'Things become – sordid. They become sordid very easily and I should dislike that. We'll find a way.'

'How will we?' she whispered.

He said, as if he spoke about some noble cause, looking beyond her, 'We shall overcome.'

He left her standing there. She could not have believed he would go like that, would leave her, but he did. He moved across the passage to the door of Five, put his hand to the handle, turned it, so that for a tiny instant of time she thought he had relented, that his arm would come out, his hand grasp her, draw her in. He stepped inside without looking back and closed the door. The ghost of a smile on his face she must have imagined.

She wanted to hammer on it and scream. Instead she went downstairs and, knowing she must go to Tom, must go to him within minutes, delay no more than half an hour, but not yet, not yet, let herself into the Headmaster's Study and fell on to the bed.

17

One of the ghost stations – Marlborough Road, or perhaps Lords – was the point at which the northbound Metropolitan train came to a stop. Nothing remained but the platform itself and the wall behind it which, shorn of its coloured posters and notices, maps and advertisements, hardly looked as if it had ever been a station. The half-hearted light of a January afternoon seeped on to the track here, bleaching sections of the dirty concrete to a paler shade of grey.

Lying on top of the third car from the head of the train, spreadeagled, by this time expert at holding on, Jasper reflected on Axel Jonas, who had asked him about these stations and if the trains ever stopped at them. He had said no. This was the first time it had happened in his experience. But he had no intention of telling Axel or even of speaking to him. That the man was living at the School he now knew and by this time was fairly sure he had not come there after him.

Since that first encounter on the top floor, while he and Bienvida had been considering the future course of the bellrope, Jasper had seen Axel three times: on the stairs, in the back garden where the black-bearded man was contemplating the screeching hawk in its cage and out in the street, returning to the house from the Finchley Road direction. On none of these occasions had Axel taken the least notice of him. Not only did he appear not to recognize him, but not even to see that he was there. Jasper, who one way and another had come across some very peculiar people in his chequered existence with Tina, had decided Axel was mad and to give him a wide berth.

The train gave a lurch and started to move. Jasper's anticipated thrill of riding at breakneck speed non-stop to Finchley Road had been rather spoiled by the stop. He had grown sophisticated, he could even think about other things while sledging. Inside the car below him were Damon, Kevin and Chris. Dean Miller had not been seen since the Epping trip. One or more of them intended to sledge on the southbound train going back. Jasper, climbing down and jumping for the platform without going back inside the car, encountered them all at the chocolate machine.

He was half-inclined to leave it and go home, take the short-cut by that footpath running parallel to the British Rail track from Frognal to West End Lane. His grand-mother had told him not to walk along that path alone, it was a notorious danger spot, and never after dark. It was not yet dark, though it soon would be, but Jasper paid very little attention to his grandmother's advice in matters of this kind. He thought he had a good chance of finding himself alone in the house apart from Bienvida, who did not count, and that this would be an opportunity to make some progress with the bell.

Not exactly an argument but a discussion was in progress as to which of them should travel back to Baker Street on the train roof. Chris pointed out that Damon, though willing enough to accompany the others and watch them do it, had never actually sledged himself.

'I'm not scared,' Damon said. 'It's just that I don't want to.'

'Everyone *wants* to,' said Kevin.

'I don't.'

'What do you come for then if you don't want to?'

Damon said nothing and Jasper said he was going home. He had done what he set out to do, he had ridden the car roof on the long fast stretch and that was it, he might not sledge any more. All good things come to an end, as Brian had once said to him and Bienvida after a Saturday visit to the cinema when they had watched *Dirty Harry* round twice.

'What are you going to do then?' said Chris as if there were no other options on earth, as if the only possible hobby or interest or sport or leisure activity open to them was tube-train sledging. 'What are you going to do?'

Toll a bell every morning at eight o'clock, Jasper might have said, make it my bell, the famous Jasper Elphick bell that rings across Hampstead day in day out without fail. Of course he did not say that. He did not say anything. He was at an age when it is not required to announce plans to friends and invent excuses and explain things before taking a formal farewell, it is not necessary to arrange a next meeting, bid them take care of themselves, send love to their nearest and dearest, shake hands or kiss, look back and wave when departing. It is not even obligatory to say, 'I'm off then,' but only to walk away.

Jasper had actually begun to walk away and to think about how he was to get through the barrier without a ticket – they were very vigilant at Finchley Road – when a voice came over the public address system. It was an Indian speaking with a strong sing-song accent and the vagaries of the system made it sound as if the speaker had his mouth full of stodgy carbohydrate, but the gist of the message could be made out. There had been an 'incident' on the line between here and Wembley Park. Considerable delays could be expected and passengers going south were advised to take the Jubilee Line.

Every year about two hundred people try to kill themselves in the London Underground. Half this number is successful.

Even those who cannot dive, who would not dream of diving into water, dive, not jump, in front of the oncoming train.

A London hospital is investigating the possibilities of training London Transport staff to spot potential suicides on the platforms. They would be taught to observe unusual behaviour, a lingering on platforms when train after train has passed through, a preoccupation with the lines, a final positioning at the tunnel portal.

If they were going back on the Jubilee Line Jasper thought he might as well go with them. That train would stop at Swiss Cottage, where it might be rather easier to escape without a ticket and which was not much farther from home. And perhaps Damon, who lived somewhere in the Belsize Lane area, Jasper thought it was, would get off with him.

The taunting of Damon was still going on and Jasper did not much like it. Of course he was used to it, heard it or something like it every day and all day, it was what life was about in his sub-adolescent world, someone finding your weakness, whether it was that you were too short or too tall, fat or had freckles, spotty or had red hair, black or Indian or had an accent or a funny mother or strange father or were too poor or too rich. But this was different, this seemed to get to the inside of Damon and to attack an essential part of him that was unseen and deeply buried. And whereas all those other things, like fatness or red hair, their possessor could not help, Damon you might say was responsible for his own lack of courage and it was a lack of something else that made him unable to be brave.

Jasper did not think of these things in these terms. He was only just ten years old. But he felt them. He did not like the look on Damon's face, which was a cornered, puzzled, childish look, as if Damon were much younger than he really was and as if he might be about to do the unthinkable and cry. The skin of his face had become pink and puffy.

In spite of the delayed trains on the other line there were not many passengers transferring to the southbound Jubilee.

They found themselves in a car with only two other people, a man and a woman, both elderly. Jasper had noticed before that people tended not to get into the cars where the four of them were if it could be avoided. This he found gratifying. He had three cigarettes in a packet and he lit one, holding it up between the doors as they closed.

Kevin, who had been quiet for a while, said to Damon, 'You're wet. The seat of your jeans is all wet.'

'It is not,' Damon said, but he looked just the same, not at first understanding the implication. Then he did and he went red.

Chris gave a crow of laughter. 'You ought to have Pampers on.'

These, Jasper thought, were a kind of disposable napkin for babies. He had seen the TV commercial. He took a draw on his cigarette and said, 'Leave him alone. Why don't you piss off?'

The train still hadn't moved.

'He's a baby,' said Kevin. 'He's chicken and he's a baby. A baby chick. Cheep cheep, baby chick.'

Chris said, 'Cheep, cheep,' too and, standing up and hopping about, began making little flapping movements with his hands. They both cheeped and flapped and hopped. The train doors opened abruptly and Jasper's cigarette fell out on to the track.

Jasper swore. He reserved his worst language for moments of extreme stress. 'Fuck off, the pair of you,' he shouted at them. 'Fuck you, fuck off!'

This roused the elderly man to action. He came lumbering menacingly down the car, got hold of Kevin with one hand and Chris with the other, started bellowing threats into Jasper's face. The doors closed, the train started and stopped again. No one noticed Damon go swiftly to the end door, open it and go outside.

★

The event which caused the delay on the Metropolitan Line – a man had died when he threw himself in front of the southbound train leaving Preston Road – held Tom up when he returned from his grandmother's, but did not affect his outward bound journey. From the station at Rickmansworth he had to take a taxi, there was no other way. It did not trouble him overmuch.

Lately, Alice had been buying all their food. She had a standing order on her new bank account to pay Jarvis's rent for both of them. If they went out to eat she paid and he had noticed that recently she had paid without complaining. Obscurely, he felt that Alice should pay. She had taken this job against his wishes, kept it although she knew he disliked it and nagged him about doing things he did not want to do. She must pay the price of that. What money he earned was his to do as he liked with and if the taxi cost him £5 it would be worth it.

By chance, or perhaps because it was the only way to get there, the taxi went along the very lane where his grandmother's neighbour had taken the corner too wide, crashed into the oncoming car and been killed, where Tom himself had been hurled off the pillion and struck his head on a tree. The tree was still there. Its smooth, silky greyish trunk was not even scarred. Seeing it all again started one of Tom's headaches, or a headache started. Whether there was any connection he could not tell.

He began thinking about how different things might have been if instead of accepting Andy's offer he had let his grandmother drive him to the station. Andy would no doubt still have been killed, his wife a widow, his three small children fatherless – or had he taken that curve so wide only because of the additional weight on the back? It was useless to speculate about that, perhaps useless to speculate at all. He, Tom, would have taken his degree, perhaps been auditioned and accepted by a celebrated orchestra. And he would never have met Alice.

Or would he have, because that was meant, his fate? Other contingencies would have rearranged themselves to make that meeting happen, not in a tube concourse, but in some musical situation, perhaps at Snape or on the concert platform. Meeting Alice had saved his life, he had no doubt about that, no hesitation. Yet he knew that if he did not have money he would lose her. She had not said so but he reasoned that this was what it was about. As soon as she gave up that job she would look to him for money. Success and money, he had to have those things. Fame would come, or start to come, with the appearance in print of the article the journalist who had come that morning was writing about him.

The journalist, a woman, an old acquaintance of a friend of Jay's, had turned up at ten with a photographer. Tom had wanted Alice to take the day off work so that she too could be in the picture, playing her violin, but Alice had refused.

'I wouldn't want people to see me like that,' she had said.

He grew angry at once, in the way he did. 'What does "like that" mean? Why wouldn't you? Who are these people who mustn't see you playing in what's going to be the great street orchestra of the nineties?'

'My parents, for a start,' she said. 'Mike, if you must know. My employers. I'm a *serious* musician. I think I've done enough damage to my musicianship already. How can I get to study in Brussels if I've had my photograph in the papers playing with people like Peter and that Jay?'

'Jay is a very good musician.'

'OK, you tell that to your journalist but count me out.'

The journalist asked about Tom's education and he told her about the accident, making quite a lot of the brain damage he now really believed he had sustained. He said it had diverted his talents along new paths and made him see that classical music should not necessarily be confined to that played by the Royal Philharmonic or listened to on compact discs. The people got rock and jazz live but were starved of *real* music. He had a dream of cities where an orchestra played in every square and a trio on the steps of every public building.

Tom did not know if this was really his dream, he had thought of it on the spur of the moment. The journalist wrote it all down and recorded it on tape as well. He told her about busking in the Underground and when she asked him if he knew this was against the law, said, 'What law? Some London Transport bye-law?' and laughed derisively.

She quoted, she had it all off pat: '"No person while upon the railway shall, to the annoyance of any other person, sing, perform on any musical or other instrument, or use any gramophone, record player, tape recorder or portable wireless apparatus."'

'Well, that's the clincher, isn't it?' he said triumphantly. '"To the annoyance of any other person"? People aren't annoyed by what we do. They love it.'

He told her about his ideas for amplifying, about wireless systems and 'hard-wired' sound, true diversity receivers and the elimination of 'drop-outs'. She said, surely that was only for rock and he said, why so? Imagine Beethoven coming through a really up-to-date VHF wireless system. She asked him if he had any hobbies, other interests, and he told her about the violin-making. He exaggerated a bit and made it sound as if he had already mastered the craft.

Photographs were taken of the three of them with their instruments and others of Tom alone. The journalist said, 'You're very good-looking, aren't you? I hope you don't mind my saying that.'

Peter, who had developed a strange black humour lately,

suggested that the best way to take *his* photograph was in a white cloak and carrying a scythe. The journalist gave a nervous laugh and seemed not to know what to say, for Peter did resemble a walking skeleton these days.

Tom's grandmother looked younger than when he had last seen her. That was two years before. He had phoned her to tell her he was coming but she was not warm towards him, she was not welcoming. Her kiss was a brushing of her dry, powdery, sagging cheek against his own.

She asked him if he wanted lunch, not to expect too much, she hadn't gone to any trouble, he would have to have what she usually had. Tom did not believe this, he thought it just the kind of thing people of her generation said, and he was rather taken aback when only cheese and crispbread appeared on the kitchen table, a couple of bananas to follow, and the kettle put on for instant coffee.

His headache was the kind that is not a constant pain, or rather, that *is* a constant pain but with sharp running shafts of intenser pain as well. These, though not visible, though not of the migraine type, nevertheless felt like lightning flashes leaping down his temples or jumping across the crown of his head. He asked his grandmother for an aspirin and she gave him two dissolved in water.

Their conversation for the first half-hour had been about her, her house, her garden, her occupations and her friends. Tom had asked the questions and she had answered. Half-way through lunch she had had enough of this and asked him abruptly if he had gone back to college.

'It took me a year to get over the accident,' he said. 'I couldn't face going back. I couldn't have faced studying.'

'I know that,' she said. 'You were living here. Had you forgotten you were living here?'

He had. It came to him for the first time that she was displeased with him.

'That was over a year ago, Tom. While you were here you told me that when you were better you'd apply to go back to college.'

'How could I?' he said, with as much bitterness as he could muster. 'Do you know what they make you do? I was nearly at the end of my second year but they'd have made me start at the beginning of my second year and do it all over again. And you don't suppose they'd have given me another grant, do you?'

He had underrated her. It had never occurred to him that she might have made it her business to find out these things.

'Of course I suppose it, Tom. That's just what I do suppose. It works like this, you apply and they'll give you a grant for your final year. Once you're into that you apply again or your head of department does: in your case he or she would explain how you'd been ill and say what a good student you were, and the chances are, the very good chances, Tom, that they'd give you a grant for your second year as well. I went into all this after you left here a year ago. I thought I should. I expected you back, you see, only you didn't come back.'

He muttered that he was sorry. He took courage, looked at her and said he had hoped, using a circumlocutory phrase, that she would finance him.

'But you don't need me to do that,' she said. 'You'll get a grant.'

'That's not quite what I meant. I'm not going back to college. It's too late.' In spite of her cold stare, her increasing look of incredulity, he told her about his street orchestra, his need for amplifying equipment, for a studio, for auditioning and engaging musicians. He told her about Alice, who was going to be a great violinist, but needed money for her studies.

His grandmother was silent. He had the impression she

had too many things to say, that her head was full of inquiries and reproaches and expressions of doubt and bewilderment, but that she sensed it would be useless to say them. She was too old and too tired to say them. The one thing she did say was really all that was necessary for both of them.

'What makes you think I've got money, Tom? I haven't any money. I've just enough to live on.'

He blurted it out. 'But you told me you were leaving me everything in your will!'

'Everything is this house.'

'You made me think – well, I had the impression, I mean, I thought you were rich, well-off, whatever you call it.'

She got up and cleared the table. She carried things piece by piece to the sink without using a tray. When she came back the third time and lifted up the cheese board, she said, 'I've left you this house in my will. I don't approve of will-shaking. You've treated me very badly, you've used this house as an hotel, you came in one day and said you were taking your things, you were moving out but you'd be in touch, but you never got in touch. I'm eighty-three years old and I shan't live long, but I don't intend to change my will because I doubt if at this stage I'd find a beneficiary much better than you. Admittedly, it would be hard to find one much worse.'

He had gone red. He knew he had behaved badly to her and he said he was sorry, but he had not been well, he often did not know what he was doing, he was not well now.

'Well enough to expect me to sell my house to pay the costs of setting up a street band,' she said.

Tom denied it. He was genuinely upset and filled with unaccustomed guilt. He felt that he had behaved badly and could not justify it, that she was right, had the whole of right on her side, and there was nothing he could say but repeat that he was sorry. If he could have had the time over again he would have acted differently. It is rarely that we feel like this, very seldom indeed that we actually feel, without making excuses for ourselves, without inner justification or compensatory reasons, that we have done wrong. For it is such an unpleasant feeling, this negation of the complacent ego, that we seem for a moment to be looking into a black pit where all nastiness is possible and into which we may so easily fall, to squirm there among the rest of wicked humanity.

Tom's grandmother told him he could not afford a taxi back to the station and she drove him herself. She drove slowly, pausing too long at road junctions, reacting sluggishly to hazards, as very old people do. He kissed her but she did not move her face while he did so. Although she nodded and even managed a small smile when he said he would phone her, he thought they both knew they would never see each other again.

Axel was waiting for her in the alley. Alice started at the sight of him. She was excited and strangely horrified, for she had not seen him for a long time, only heard his movements above her head while she lay awake at night. He looked steadily at her, smiled slowly, then turned his face to the door from which she had come. A single lamp at the far end lit the alley.

'So this is where you work?'

She said, and she thought what she said was stupid, 'It's not very interesting.'

'That depends on what interests you.'

Did he mean herself?

'We'll have a taxi.'

'All the way home?' she said, appalled at the cost of it.

'I'm not so wedded to the subterranean as your Tom is. I think I told you I go into it only for a purpose.'

She had no idea what he meant. A taxi came when she was beginning to think it was hopeless. She knew that when they were in it he would manoeuvre her into one corner of the seat and put himself into the other so that there was a yard between them, she was certain of that, so that when he sat close to her and took one of her hands in both his, she felt herself begin to tremble.

'Are you cold?'

She shook her head.

He closed the glass partition between them and the driver, resumed his seat pressed up against her. That austere face, Slavic, pale and dark, white and black, was redeemed by the eyes that were as blue as some pretty blonde girl's eyes. His should have been brown, sombre and brooding, but they were cornflower blue.

He said, 'That building we were in, your office, is anyone there in the evenings?'

She was astonished. She thought, in a moment I am going to be cruelly hurt, punished, humiliated. I am going to learn the secret of him, why he came to Cambridge School and got to know me. There is something in that building that he needs, some document or object or instrument, and that was the whole purpose of knowing me, to get his hands on that.

'Do you have a key?'

'Why?'

'Why do I ask?'

'Yes, what is it you want?'

He began to laugh. She watched him stonily. 'Oh, Alice, Alice,' he said, 'what are you thinking? What plots and secrets do you suspect me of now? Your face tells me you think I'm going about things in this clumsy way because I'm desperate to lay my hands on the *papers*.'

That he could have read her mind so thoroughly made her blush. She turned her face from him like an offended child. He took hold of her chin in that way he had and turned her face to him.

'I want to be alone with you. I want to make love to you, didn't you know that?'

The driver's head was unmoving, shielded from them by the glass panel. She had heard somewhere or read that it was illegal for taxi drivers to have the means of seeing the back seat.

'Don't you want to make love to me?' he said.

'Yes.' Her voice was very low.

He lifted her chin again. 'We have nowhere else to go.'

She did something she had never done before to anyone, took hold of his hand and bringing it to her mouth, covered it with kisses.

The man who had shaken Chris and Kevin and admonished Jasper did not seem to know the purpose of Damon's exit from the carriage. Jasper was not sure that Chris and Kevin knew. They might all simply have thought he was getting away from them, sneaking into the next car. Jasper knew he had climbed out on to the roof.

It was the best thing he could have done, in Jasper's opinion. The ride to Swiss Cottage accomplished, he would have overcome his fear of sledging and at the same time have put an end to further taunts from the others. The only drawback, from his point of view, was that Damon would take up the stop time at Swiss Cottage in climbing back into the car and the two of them, instead of getting off, would have to go on to St John's Wood.

Jasper went and stood by the end door, looking up through the glass panel at the roof of the car ahead. He could see nothing, not even Damon's feet. The train had now been standing in the station at Finchley Road for five minutes and seemed stuck there. The doors were closed but they opened once more and half a dozen people got into the car. They got in but they all avoided the end at which Jasper and Chris and Kevin were.

'He's not chicken,' Jasper said, and Chris said, 'OK, he's not.'

Kevin said nothing but took from his pocket the eight-ounce Dairy Milk chocolate bar, the comfort of which he had been saving for just such a moment as this, and began tearing off the wrapping.

Once more the doors closed. As the train left the station it would enter the tunnel and remain underground all the way to the terminus at Embankment. Jarvis could have told Jasper a lot of things about the construction of the various lines in this area of the Metropolitan, Jubilee and erstwhile Bakerloo, the feats of engineering, the threading in and out of tunnels, the displacement of subterranean tracks and insertion of others, but Jarvis had never talked to Jasper about the London Underground, he did not think he would be interested. And Jasper, though he certainly travelled on the Jubilee Line more than on any other, though this was the way he came every time he went to inner London, had not noticed – the average passenger does not notice – what Jarvis remarked every time he made this journey, that here the train must run downhill as it begins its descent under the Metropolitan line to the deep level.

Jasper sat down. He had a low opinion of people who ate chocolate bars without offering pieces of them round and he gave Kevin a contemptuous look. The train started. Jasper knew that the tunnel roof here was reasonably high above the roof of the cars, but it was a tube, not a sub-surface cutting. Just the same, Damon should be safe enough all the way to the river, though Jasper hoped, just for the sake of getting home, that he would come down before that.

The mouth of the tunnel received them, and for the first time Jasper was aware of the downward gradient, that the train was descending. Perhaps he noticed it because he was concentrating so hard on everything to do with the train, the behaviour of the train, because he was so aware of Damon, who was unpractised and had been afraid, on top of the car ahead.

He was concentrating but he was unprepared for what happened. Everyone in the car was unprepared. The train braked and gave one of those shuddering lurches which, if people are standing, are enough to knock them over. No one was standing in their car but at the second lurch they had to hang on to the seat arms to avoid being thrown on to the floor. One of the women cried out.

Time seemed to cease and there was silence. It endured and it did not. This might have been ten seconds which passed or ten hours. Afterwards, Jasper could not have said, except that the former was more likely. He was petrified by the silence, a silence that seemed outside this world and beyond time. His hands had fastened themselves to the arms of the seat and he had grown numb, his whole body was numb, but his brain raced.

From outside, up ahead somewhere, suddenly, came a scream, the like of which Jasper had never heard before. All the terror of every frightening thing in the world was in it. And it went on and on. The people in the car jumped up. Jasper stayed where he was. Jasper *saw*. He saw it come past the window, a mass of something dark and twisted, fighting the side of the car and screaming. He saw a foot stamp at the glass as the train tore it away and plunged on down into the deep, leaving the dying scream behind.

18

It was on the top floor of the building, under the flat roof, a small room with one small window, containing a single bed, a sofa that would make into a second bed, an electric fire, a small mirror on the wall, a piece of worn carpet fitted to the floor, a blanket in the cupboard and two pillows and two duvets encased in Tesco covers. It was known as the emergency room. Down the passage was a kitchen, small, with not much in it but a kettle and a gas ring, pots and pans, cutlery. A fridge and an oven had been considered unnecessary luxuries.

London is full of such rooms in its offices. They are for the use of those executives who live in the far reaches of the Home Counties and who cannot get home when British Rail is on strike or incapacitated by storms. Two directors of the company Alice worked for shared the emergency room on the night at the end of January when a gale hit London and trains stopped running into Surrey and Sussex. Martin Angell slept on the single mattress on the floor and James Christianson on the bed base. Late in the evening James Christianson went out to buy bread and coffee and Martin Angell had to let him in again because he had no keys. It was found that only two complete sets of keys to the building were in existence. James Christianson, foreseeing another such emergency, entrusted Alice with the keys to get two more sets cut.

Alice had three more sets cut.

It was not the kind of thing she did. She had never done anything like it before. She knew that she was mad. Reason, morality, ethical behaviour, all that was lost, was thrown to the winds. The amount she was learning about herself, what she was capable of, made her tremble. It was almost a criminal thing to do, this making extra copies of keys given her by someone who trusted her. She wondered what criminal thing she would stop at. Was there anything?

If he said, steal that, she would steal it. If he said, kill Tom, would she do that? He wouldn't say it. She clung to that. She thought, this is the way people are who fall under the spell of some murderer and join with him to do murder, just because he says to do it. It was not quite the condition they called *folie à deux* because that implied that each obsessed partner affected the other. She did not think that what she did, thought or wished affected Axel at all.

She had almost forgotten Mike and Catherine. They had become shadows in her past she had left behind. Tom was still there, like an unwanted husband. That was how she had begun to think of him. He thought she rejected him because of all his failures, his refusal to go back to college, to get a job, his inability to get money from his grandmother, his lack of money. It was better for him to think like that than to be faced with the truth.

She asked herself if she was in love? Was this being in love or was it an obsession, and what was the difference? It had one good effect on her. She was playing better.

Madame Donskoy did not utter any of those laudatory remarks made by foreign female music teachers in books. She did not say, I have taught you all I know, now it is in your hands. Or, it is you who should be teaching me. Nor did she enter that other familiar scenario, take her own violin and play so exquisitely that Alice was stunned and shamed and able to see the hopelessness of her own aspirations.

What she did say was, 'That was not so bad.'

It was praise. Perhaps it stimulated Alice to do better, or perhaps it was the reverse of what happened to poor Sibyl Vane when she lost the ability to act as a consequence of falling in love with Dorian Gray. Whatever it was, she thought she played faultlessly, but when the lesson was at an end, and it was the last but one, Madame Donskoy only talked about Yehudi Menuhin and some recording he had made with Stephan Grappelli of music from the twenties and thirties.

Alice wrote off to the Britten–Pears School about the chances of being accepted on a two-week course.

On the night of the storm, when the Underground trains ceased to run and Tom, caught with his flute on an escalator that stopped halfway up, had to walk home, she played her violin for Axel in the Art Room. He invited her. It was cold and the wind howled outside, rattled the windows and tore branches off the trees. Something crashed through one of the windows in Remove and in the morning Tina, going in there, found it was a tile blown off the roof of the flats opposite. Axel ignored the wind. He behaved as if it were a normal calm evening.

When she came to the door of the Art Room she hesitated and then she knocked. He laughed because she had knocked on the door.

'What did you think I would be doing?'

She never said much to him. She had begun to find it hard to speak to him. He took her in his arms, or rather, in his hands. It was the first time she had seen him without that long overcoat. His extreme thinness surprised her. She felt his bones against her as he ran his hands down her body and an erectness hard as bone pushing against her belly. It had become a commonplace that her desire was often strong enough to make her feel sick.

Why was he in such control, smiling, casual? She had believed self-control was harder for men and he was obviously excited. He only laughed, shifted her away from him and opening her violin case, handed the violin to her.

'Play for me.'

'I don't know what to play.'

He gave her one of those strange sidelong looks of his, the blue eyes shining. 'Something romantic.'

There was an arrangement she had once made and learned of the Great Waltz from *Rosenkavalier*. He knew the piece. She saw him mouthing words, the line about no night being too long with him. '*Mit mir, mit mir, keine nacht ist zu lang.*' It was too apt. Her unsure fingers shook. She heard the discord, saw him wince, and wanting to weep, kept her self-control but ceased to play.

'I'm not on form tonight.'

He uttered a devastating monosyllable. 'No.'

There was a little love-making after that. He touched her and kissed her and smoothed her body and laughed and sent her away on the usual grounds that more must not take place under the same roof with Tom, even though Tom was not under it just at the moment.

She had given him the keys.

She fretted about the ugliness of the room, the sordidness of the whole business, all these prevarications and illicit keys, and she asked herself again why a hotel room would have been sordid but this was not. Perhaps Axel could not afford a hotel room, but she did not think this was the case, she thought he could afford it. Sometimes she thought that Axel was, secretly, rich.

There were people that she had read of who found that a sordid element added an extra thrill. She did not know if Axel was one of them, but it would not have surprised her to find that he was. It might of course be only the slight danger of being here that excited him. This skulking in an office building, praying for people to go home, watching the street from windows, making up that bed with bed-linen others had used, all this seemed to her of a desire-killing squalor. But it did not kill desire.

He was late. She had known he would be late but was no less fearful for knowing it. Already she knew he was the kind of person who would enjoy keeping someone who longed for him waiting. She might be indifferent to keeping Tom waiting, but she never enjoyed it or gloated over it.

She went down to the bottom in the lift and walked back up the stairs, leaving the lift down there for him. It was a way of passing the time. At the top, in the bedroom where the twice-used sheet was carefully folded back on the bed, she thought about Catherine. Her child seemed very remote to her, a tiny doll at the far end of a tunnel. At the same time she felt there was something unreal about her ever having had a child. She had dreamed it and dreamed her short marriage.

Alice put the sheet back and pulled up the duvet. The bold invitation offered by that open bed shamed her. Besides, if she covered up the bed, closed the door, abandoned hope, he might come. She went downstairs again, looked at the open doors of the waiting lift, returned up the stairs. I won't wait for ever, she thought, I'll wait no more than another half-hour, but she knew she would wait, she would wait all night.

At the top she thought she heard footsteps above her, someone moving about. It did not occur to her then that it might be Axel, that he, like her, might have used the stairs. She knew no one had used the lift, she had seen it down there, she would have heard it come up.

Outside the room she stood listening. All the lights downstairs were out, she had turned them out as she came up. She thought, love should never be like this, planned for, arranged, *contrived* for, but spontaneous, a natural consequence of loving. He won't come anyway, I shall never see him again.

And then he walked out of the dark passage. He came from the one direction she did not expect.

'Well, and there was I thinking we'd missed each other,' he said. 'After all the trouble we've been to.'

He was not the sort of man to kiss a woman when he met her. He never will, she thought. She closed the door of the emergency room and locked it. There was nothing to say and she had meant to keep silence. She expected him to be grave and deliberate, intense as he had once been, but he was talkative, he was laughing, not as if he anticipated some great happiness but as if it had already taken place.

He had seen Tom. Coming from the Covent Garden direction, he had actually seen Tom through the window of a café. Perhaps Tom was on his way here.

'He has never been here. He doesn't know where it is.'

'I'll fight him if I must but I'd rather not.'

She thought of saying something then about not understanding, about thinking he respected Tom. Wasn't that why they were here and not at home in his room or hers? But she did not say that. He had sat down beside her on the bed and, no longer laughing, no longer euphoric, but grave and speculative, had taken her face in his hands.

She said the words she had once thought she would never say.

'I love you.'

He stroked her heavy hair, drew his fingers along the curve of her jaw, one long, cool forefinger across her throat and down to the parting between her breasts. He parted her blouse and lifted it away from her body.

'So you told me before. Would you like to prove it?'

The London Underground is not an enclosed complex, accessible only by way of the stations. Apart from the stations, nearly 300 of them, there are ways in and ways out.

The ways out, mostly, are ventilation shafts to let out bad air and let in good. Travellers would feel like passengers in an aircraft do when their ears pop if there were no vents in the tunnel to release pressure.

Blowholes covered with a grating were once a way of providing passengers with relief from sulphurous air. The Central Line put in 'ozonizers' that sucked air into the stations, but the salty tang which was the result clung to travellers' clothes and made them smell as if they had come from the seaside at Southend instead of Oxford Circus.

In modern times spent air is fanned out and fresh air let in through station entrances and staircase shafts. Fresh air is pumped through shafts enclosed in staircase wells and through special shafts, sunk for the purpose. In the long stretch on the Central Line between Mile End and Stratford, the Old Ford fan shaft has a spiral staircase inside. If the power failed between these stations, the distance might be too great for the train to coast to the nearest platform. In such a case the passengers could be led through the train and into the tunnel and up the staircase in the shaft.

It comes out in the street. Late one night in 1969 sixty people escaped up the shaft when the power failed.

The round tower at Regent's Park on the Bakerloo is the top of an escape shaft. On another long stretch, the Victoria Line between Tottenham Hale and Seven Sisters, is the Nelson Road fan shaft. This too contains a spiral staircase.

A stairway shaft, no longer in use for climbing up or down, was extended to the roof of an office block over the station site at Notting Hill Gate. Such shafts pass up through the centre of many office buildings in London. Their purpose is ventilation. All these office blocks belong to London Transport.

Every station in the central area of the Central Line has disused tunnels and shafts. The lighted stations, busy with people, bright with advertising, noisy with the roar of trains, are surrounded by dark, disused passages and ranges of shafts.

Some of these shafts once contained lifts, now replaced by escalators, some staircases. You can look up through the inside of *these enormous cylinders and see in the dimness the old Edwardian tiling, a yellow and brown design, spiralling the circular walls, following the course of what was once a staircase.*

Among the passages are signals and communications rooms. The automatic signalling systems are safe and efficient. Passengers on London Underground are safer by comparison than on any other form of transport.

According to London Transport Underground.

It would not have been possible to keep Damon's death from Cecilia. It was in all the newspapers, it was a front page story. Besides, Cecilia watched television. The secret they hid from her was that he had been Jasper's friend and that Jasper had been there when he died, had been in the train from which he fell.

Two officials of London Transport Underground went to see Tina. One of them was the group manager of the relevant stations on the Jubilee Line. They were sore and resentful because Kevin's mother, whom they had called on first, blamed them and told them things should be managed so that children could not climb on to the roofs of trains. Tina did not blame anyone. It would not have occurred to her to blame herself and as to Jasper, she said that boys were boys and that was all there was to it. She knew it was wrong of her to say so when that poor woman who was Damon's mother had lost her son, but all she could think about was her relief that it was not Jasper.

An inquest was held. There was to be an inquiry. Bienvida said, if Jasper had to appear at the inquiry would his name be in the papers? Having tea at Cecilia's, the doll called Caroline on her lap, she had told her grandmother firmly (without being asked) and irrelevantly that Damon was no friend of Jasper's.

'He never goes in tubes,' she said. 'He doesn't ride on the tops of trains and he doesn't know anyone who does.'

Cecilia understood with a sinking heart that the reverse of all this must be true.

The gale blew part of the roof off the bicycle shed, so Jed brought the hawk back into the house. Abelard was no longer capable of flying any distance. Jed did not know what to do about him. He worried about the bird's weight, that if he did not fly he would gain weight and perhaps never fly again, so he restricted his food even further and Abelard screamed. Sometimes Jed thought he could see misery and despair in the hawk's eyes, a desperate craving for food, as if there passed through his small, limited avian mind a knowledge that all there was in life for him was food and if he could not have it, or have enough of it, the stretching years ahead would be a slow, unrelieved torture.

The day of the appointment with the eminent bird specialist at the veterinary college came and Jed took Abelard up to Cambridge. Abelard perched in his jesses on Jed's wrist and the dignity with which he sat there filled Jed with pride. The other passengers in the Underground to Liverpool Street and then in the British Rail train could not see that he was incapacitated, that his wing would let him down as soon as he was released into the air. After a while Jed hooded him because he was afraid Abelard might start to scream. He was always afraid Abelard would start to scream.

The wing was X-rayed. The eminent bird vet handled Abelard very gently. He looked at the X-rays. He examined the wing again and this time it did not seem to Jed that he was gentle, but probing and pushing among the striated brown feathers with hard, searching fingers, though the hawk made no protest.

Abelard was once more on Jed's wrist and once more hooded and the bird vet said, 'It's bad news, I'm afraid.'

'He's not going to fly again?'

'I doubt it.'

The explanation which came was of a virus that had affected the wing, that had damaged the muscles and nerves beyond repair. 'It's no one's fault. It's nothing you've done, just one of those things.' The bird vet astonished Jed because he showed that he had not understood at all. 'They're expensive birds, you'll have paid a lot of money for this one. Seven hundred? Eight hundred? It looks like money down the drain.'

'Isn't there anything to be done? I mean, an operation, anything.'

'It's gone too far for that. Mind you, I doubt if it would ever have been possible. There's only one thing to be done. I can do it for you if that would be easier. You just leave him here with us.'

'Thank you, but I'll take him back.' Jed thought that if he did not go quickly he might break into tears. 'I can take him to my local man.'

'That's all right, then. It won't hurt. I mean, it won't hurt keeping him a bit longer, he's not in pain; he'll never be in pain, he simply won't fly again.'

Jed had to give them a cheque before he left the building. He hoped he had enough in his thin bank account to cover it. Once out in the street he took the hood from Abelard's head and they walked along together to catch the bus to the station.

Death had visited Jasper, had camped beside him and looked him in the face. He had not believed in death before, had not known it existed except as a remote incredible concept, more distant and less real than ghosts, less explicable than God.

Until now he had known that there were dead people in his past but he had not known anyone who had died. Brian's parents were alive and well, were not really old

253

yet, and his grandfather Darne was dead long before he was born. Jasper had not thought people did not die, he knew they did, he had been told so, but not the people *he knew*. They could not die. They might confront something that people called death but at the decisive moment it would be averted, it would be deflected as in films and dreams. It was as if, at the moment of their extremest, most fearful danger, some force would put out its arms and grab them and sweep them to safety.

He had been afraid for Damon, but not he now knew afraid that Damon would die. That had been too big for him to think of. He did not know any longer what he had thought might happen instead – injury, perhaps, or simply retribution. And when he thought back to those minutes before the accident, remembering it with a kind of cringing misery, he felt stupid that he had not known, had not anticipated, he felt as much of a fool as he had one day when he turned round in a crowd to speak to Bienvida only to find he was addressing some quite different girl.

There was no one to talk to about it. Soon after it happened a woman came to the School to see Tina; she was from the social services or London Transport or somehow both, Jasper didn't know, and he heard her telling his mother he might need something called counselling. He was not asked. Tina said, perhaps, why not? – it might be a good idea.

'It's a very viable concept in cases of accident witnesses,' the woman said.

Jasper thought counselling might mean being taken into the care of the council. There was someone in his class at school who was in care because his father had left, his mother could not cope and his brother had been killed in an accident. It did not seem too far removed from his own situation. But when he asked Tina, all she said was, 'I never heard such a load of crap. Where do you get this stuff from?'

There was no one he could talk to. He doubted if he could talk about it to Kevin and Chris even if he got to see them, but he did not get to see them, they were separated from him either by chance or by adult design, he did not know which. Their surnames, their addresses, he had never known. They were lost, swallowed up by London somewhere, and he knew he would never see them again.

He would never again go in a tube train. Well, perhaps one day when he was old, after years and years. He did not even like seeing the silver trains from the back windows as they rattled down to London and up to Stanmore. The feel of them vibrating the house was disquieting. It was funny, but he had lost the taste for smoking too. Was it because he had had a cigarette just before *it* happened, the one that had fallen out on to the line? Perhaps he was meant to give up smoking before it really took hold. Everyone said it was best to give up young.

He spent a lot of time in the cloakroom, sitting and thinking. Tina thought he was at school, but he went to school no more now than he had done in the old sledging days. He sat in the cloakroom with the electric fire on and blankets round him. Nothing had been done about the bell, though when a new rope was attached to the existing length it would pass through the trap in the dark part of the passage by the old Science Lab where no one but Jarvis went, and Jarvis was still in Russia. Tina had had a postcard from him with a picture of the Kremlin, posted five weeks before. She looked at it and said every postcard she had ever seen from Russia was a picture of the Kremlin and she did not believe there was any other kind.

Jasper always thought of the accident and Damon's death as *it*. He found that if he made himself think about it before he went to sleep at night, remember Kevin and Chris flapping about chicken-like, the man who shook them, Damon's quiet escape, the entry of the train under the tunnel portal and, last and continuously terrible, that cry and that *thing* passing the window. If he thought hard about all that last thing at night, he would not dream about it, this was an infallible method for stopping dreams. When he dreamed, he woke up yelling. If Tina heard him she never came in, and on the whole he was glad she did not, as he would have been ashamed. But he had no one to talk to.

Bienvida had covered up her ears and said if he mentioned it again she would scream so that she couldn't hear. She was round at their grandmother's, telling Cecilia with perfect truth that Tina had no boyfriend at present, so Cecilia of course believed she probably had two.

The newspaper story, when it appeared, was not just a disappointment to Tom, it was a shock.

'What did you expect?' Alice said.

'Not a send-up. I didn't expect a send-up, which is what this is. That woman who came to interview me gave me the impression she was going to write a serious article.'

'They say all publicity is good publicity.'

'I don't see how it can be if something says, or implies, you're only playing in the Underground or the street because you can't play anywhere else, and says you've no qualifications and insults you. What's an auto-didact anyway?'

'Someone who's self-taught.'

'You see? It isn't even accurate. I'm not self-taught, I just didn't take my degree. And why does she say those sort of snide things about Peter and Jay being gay, it's just perpetuating old homosexual persecution, as if it isn't just as OK to be gay as straight. You see where she implies *I'm* gay too, by association with them I suppose. I wonder if that's libel; I wonder if I could sue her for libel.'

'If you think being gay's OK why is it libel for her to say you're gay?'

It seemed he had expected the article to bring money in. At least the writer had taken pains to find out how much the wireless system he wanted would cost and had precisely itemized it. With misgivings, Alice saw him await the post, expecting it to bring him cheques sent care of the newspaper. His paranoia had become very marked. He thought everyone was against him. Everyone, that is, but Peter and Jay – and Axel. To Alice's astonishment and vague dismay, Tom had struck up a tremendous friendship with Axel.

It began one evening after one of their quarrels. The subject was the usual one, Alice persisting he return to college and in her determination to go on to a conservatoire, Tom retorting that she was trained enough, she should apply for an audition with some northern orchestra while he found, as he would soon find, a way to make big money. When he had told her she did not love him, if she loved him she would go back to busking with him, return to the way they had been when they were so happy, and she had been without a single answer to that, he jumped up and said he was going to knock on 'the new guy's' door. He was sure he was lonely up there, and he was going to take him out for a drink.

Alice was appalled. 'I won't come.'

'No, don't. I'd rather you didn't. I don't want you sitting there making sarcastic remarks about my ignorance and apathy and any other of my inadequacies that may come to mind.'

This was unfair as Alice had never uttered a word of criticism of Tom in anyone else's presence, but all she said was, 'You don't even know if he'll come.'

She was sure he would not. A man who had refused to make love to her under the same roof as her accredited lover, even when he was not present under that roof, would hardly start going out to have matey drinks with him. So she was very surprised when she heard Axel's voice as he and Tom passed down the stairs together, surprised and chagrined. If Axel was going out with Tom, would it not have been natural for him to come in here and speak to her first, just say hallo to her? She could not bear not to see him. As she heard the front door close she went across the passage into the big, empty, unfurnished Staff Common Room and watched the two men from the window.

It was too dark to see much. The light from a street lamp showed them both to her at the gate. She gazed at Axel, as if concentrating like this would photograph him and keep his picture with her. They disappeared into the dark and Axel's retinal image with him. Alone, she thought of him, as she always thought of him when alone, of his face and the things he said, but not of their love-making because that would be more than she could stand thinking of. It was as if doing that would make something swell and explode inside her or she would collapse or begin screaming the way the hawk had once screamed.

After that Tom and Axel saw each other constantly. She had always suspected that Tom, in spite of his love for her, a love which if they were married would have been called uxoriousness, was nevertheless what is known as a 'man's man'. He was the kind of man who preferred men's society and would like nights out with the boys. He would never be unfaithful because the life he enjoyed would not take him into the company of women. But none of that accounted for Axel's friendship with him. She could have asked Axel but she did not. She watched them go out together, down to the pub or to some club of which Axel was a member, and she was jealous. She envied Tom because he was out with Axel.

Another strange thing was that Axel seemed to have forgotten all about his principle of no love-making under Tom's roof. They had met twice more in Alice's office building and then Axel, taking her home in a taxi, had said, 'We won't do that again.'

'What do you mean?' A small hoarse croak of a voice like a very old woman's.

'What do I mean?'

She thought he was going to force her to explain. She shook her head, feeling sick.

He laughed. He took her face in his hand and looked into her eyes and touched her nose with his nose. 'Oh, Alice, not *that*. I only meant, home is best.'

'But you said you wouldn't . . .'

He shook his head, pointed to the back of the driver's head, though the glass panel was closed. With a shrug, he said, 'Needs must when the devil drives.'

She did not know what he meant.

'That place, your office, I shouldn't like to be – caught.'

She was surprised, for without much evidence for this she had thought him afraid of nothing. But she had not argued, she was too happy that what she had feared for that appalling moment was not true. He wanted her, he still wanted her. Although they had only just made love, had indeed made love twice, the idea that this would now take place at home, in her room or the Art Room or in Five, filled her with excitement. It would be more frequent, it would be more spontaneous, it would happen as the result of chance encounter and rapturous impulse. From clandestine sex, it would become what she wanted, a love affair.

He seemed to have forgotten about the taxi driver, or was only interested in what the man might hear, for he took her in his arms and began kissing her passionately. It seemed strange, after what had happened, their extremely uninhibited, *astonishing* love-making, to think that this was the first passionate kiss he had ever given her, the first kiss of true feeling. But so it was. It was quite different from those sensuous and lascivious teasings with lips and tongue that she expected from him. She abandoned herself to him, as if she could be one with him, as if she could lose herself. She grew weak, yet a great energy and power possessed her.

The only television set in the School was Tina's. It was an old black and white set, which was why it was seldom watched, even by the children. Tom and Alice never watched television or bought newspapers and it would not have crossed Jed's mind to do these things. The bomb attached to the underside of the car which went off and killed the MP who was driving it, they knew nothing about. Bienvida and Jasper might have seen news coverage of the car exploding in the Mall if they had been able to watch their grandmother's television, in which case Jasper would certainly have recognized the face of the man who had been arrested. But Cecilia was not at home. Cecilia was in Willesden staying with Daphne.

'It sounds awful,' Cecilia had once said, had said in the days when this staying in each other's houses began, 'it sounds awful but I sometimes wish we didn't live quite so near each other. Then, if you see what I mean, we'd have more *reason* for going away to stay.'

This was said soon after Tina had made that suggestion about her and Daphne. It was during the time when Cecilia nervously believed that everyone they knew must be thinking things.

'I shouldn't worry,' said placid Daphne. 'Look at the young, they're always staying in each other's places. Peter's more often away than he's at home and as often as not it's with someone in the next street.'

Cecilia was comforted, though she knew she was not young and Daphne was not and different things were expected of them. But she had gone on staying with

Daphne and Daphne had gone on coming to stay at Lilac Villa. It was so nice, it was something she would have missed bitterly in spite of what Tina said. They looked after each other. Daphne looked after Cecilia in Willesden and Cecilia looked after Daphne in West Hampstead. And as the years passed this looking after became a more and more important part of the staying in each other's houses, so that Peter, looking in one day while his mother was with Cecilia, called it 'intensive care'.

Daphne had been sitting in front of the television and Cecilia had just put a cushion behind her head and brought her a cup of tea and two biscuits on a plate. She had put a small table at Daphne's elbow. The pills Daphne took for her blood pressure were in a coffee saucer and there was a small medicine glass of water beside them. This was because Cecilia had read somewhere that you should never swallow pills with any liquid but water.

Peter said, 'I didn't know my mum was in intensive care.'

'You should see how she looks after me when I stay with her.'

Cecilia had been in Willesden since Saturday and would go home on Wednesday. She and Daphne called it a long weekend. She had the bedroom that was known as 'hers', just as Daphne when at Lilac Villa had *her* room. Daphne had bought daffodils, forced ones with elongated stems, and put them in a vase by her bed. Another thing she did was to creep into Cecilia's room just before they watched the nine o'clock news, turn down the bed, arrange Cecilia's nightdress on top with the sleeves spread out and the waist nipped, and place a chocolate in a paper case on the pillow. It was usually a white chocolate because Daphne had once heard Cecilia express a preference for this kind, which she could remember when it first came in, and remember too how surprised she had been to find that chocolate did not have to be brown to taste like chocolate.

They made a point of listening carefully to what the other said with regard to tastes and preferences so that they would know what to buy for presents and how to give surprises. Sitting down to watch the news, they had, not tea this evening, but a small whisky and water each because Cecilia said it helped her to sleep. They had the magazines they had bought that day, *She* and *Country Living*, though they were too old for one and too urban for the other, and *Where Angels Fear to Tread* which Cecilia was reading but not enjoying half as much as *A Passage to India*.

The first item on the news was the arrest of a man for the Mall bombing. Yesterday they had shown the sort of bomb it was, not Semtex this time, as in the case of the 'Bayswater Bomb', but a kind of gunpowder. The powder was called magnesium flash, which was tightly packed into a tin and set off by a match-head fuse. The tin was linked to the car's petrol tank to cause a tremendous fire as well as the explosion. Daphne had said that she could not understand the police and the BBC because by now even she, who was very unscientific and not even much of a cook, had learned from all these diagrams how to make a workable bomb. The man who had planted it, who had 'allegedly' planted it, was shown leaving the magistrates' court between two policemen. His name meant nothing to them.

'I'm sure I've seen that face somewhere,' said Cecilia.

'The older I get,' said Daphne, 'the more I think people get to look like other people. I never did when I was young but now I can hardly look at a face without thinking how much it looks like someone else.'

'I don't know anyone who looks like *him* but I think I've seen him somewhere. Not many people have repaired hare lips and noses like spoons, do they?'

'That's something to be thankful for,' said Daphne.

19

The room was cold and the bed not much warmer. Alice was beginning to know the view from this pillow very well, she waited there so long. Axel's cameras had returned here from the Art Room and cluttered the window sill. He had a book on the bedside shelf. Last time she was here it had been Gurdjieff's *Meetings with Remarkable Men*, this time it was *Thus Spake Zarathustra*. She had never read either, had no idea even what kind of books they were, fiction or non-fiction.

Axel seemed to live out of his suitcases. Both were always open on the floor. He might keep some clothes inside the cupboard, she did not know, she had never looked inside. Some days before he had brought the painting of Mary Zambaco in here from the Art Room. She remembered what he had said, that she resembled it a little, that the likeness was what made him like her. He had not said 'love' or 'want' but 'like', a tame word, a word which frightened her.

She lay looking at the picture, which Axel had hung on the wall where a world map in Mercator's projection used to be. That same inner honesty which made her feel so miserable in Madame Donskoy's presence, forced her to admit she was not really much like Burne-Jones's Mary. She was unable to tell herself, without self-delusion, that he had brought the painting in here because it reminded him of her.

The door opened and Axel came in. His face was set in grim lines, he looked suddenly older. The hands that held the newspaper had crunched and crumpled it, his knuckles white and shiny. He said nothing.

The front page of the paper had a photograph half-filling it of an ugly man with a broad upturned nose. When he saw her looking, Axel tore the page in half, screwed up the rest and flung his coat on top of it. He turned his attention to her and his face changed. She had the uncomfortable feeling he had attended to the business of his life and now had a little time to spare for her. A smile began, curling his mouth, and she knew he was thinking how keen she was, how she could not wait, but got her clothes off at the first opportunity and waited there, hot for him.

For the first time he did not bother to undress, only took off his jeans. 'You don't mind, I hope. I'm cold.'

Afterwards, he sent her back to the Headmaster's Study and when he called for her an hour later he had Tom with him and they were all set to go to the pub. Tom ate in the pub these evenings, so she did too. They had forgotten about economy. More often that not, anyway, Axel paid for all of them. He asked Tom if the newspaper article had brought forth any donations but Tom had to say it had not.

'You should have let me do some shots of you,' he said. 'I'd have made a better job of it than that newspaper photographer.'

It was a damp evening, more like April than February, the kind of weather when people say it is warmer out than in. The winter had passed without snow or frost or much rain. Only Axel seemed cold, his black overcoat drawn round him like a narrow, cylindrical cocoon. He drank brandy, quite a lot of brandy, but it had no apparent effect on him. Alice, across the table from him, was learning something: how much concentration it can take, what an amount of control, to keep one's hand from reaching out to touch another hand. She pushed her leg in between his legs, just to feel his flesh, the swell of his calf, but he

264

suffered this only for a moment before shifting his chair back and drawing himself to one side.

There was black powder on his hands, he hadn't bothered to wash his hands before coming out. She wondered what he had been doing in that room after he had sent her away. Watching his hands brought her to a high degree of sexual excitement.

'What's that on your fingers?' Tom said.

Axel turned his hands over, looked at the palms, seemed surprised. 'It's stuff they used to use to make the flash on old-fashioned cameras.'

'Is that what yours are? Old-fashioned?'

Axel said nothing. He had a way of simply not answering if the question was not acceptable. He became deaf. She was beginning to feel that he was making her half of a couple with Tom, withdrawing himself and isolating them. Then, as she watched him, she became aware of something else: that he was seriously upset, that something had happened to shock or distress him.

It was not herself. It was nothing to do with her. A sudden flash of knowledge that she had not the power to upset him, never would have, made her shiver. It passed and a little confidence came back. She remembered how, less than two hours before, he had made love to her. He didn't *have* to make love to her, he must want her.

While he was away, fetching more drinks, Tom said, 'I'd never have thought of him as a moody person.'

She shrugged. She was watching Axel at the bar, his hands as he took the glasses, the shift of his shoulders, the gravity of his glance.

'You missed your cue,' Tom said nastily. 'You should have said that was my province.'

Axel set the glasses in front of them, went back for his own. He said to Tom, 'Would you like to be my assistant?'

'Assistant at what?'

'When the photographer came to take your picture, didn't he have someone else with him? Someone to carry cameras and tripods? A helper? In fact, an assistant learning the business?'

'Yes, I suppose so. Yes, he did.'

Instead of repeating his request, Axel said carefully, not looking in her direction, looking across the smoky room towards the windows, 'You see, I've had a blow. You could say I've had a loss.'

Tom looked uncomfortable. 'I don't mind giving you a hand.'

'There would be money in it,' Axel said coldly. 'A lot of money.'

A porter at Covent Garden saw a ghost in the station in 1955. This apparition, six feet tall, slim, was wearing a light grey suit and white gloves. Others confirmed the sighting. It is not known what made them believe this was not a living man in a grey suit and white gloves.

During the building of the Victoria Line the diggers sometimes saw a black shape in the tunnel. Although the complete The Lord of the Rings *trilogy was not published in paperback until 1968, the year of the opening of the Victoria Line, the three parts had been in hardcover and in libraries for more than a decade. Was the shape the diggers saw a Balrog? Or was it because they or one of them had been reading Tolkien that they imagined they saw a Balrog?*

A Balrog, according to J. R. R. Tolkien, is a vast black shape that appears in subterranean places.

Dressed for shopping, belonging to a generation that put on 'good' clothes to go to Oxford Street, Cecilia set out in a tweed skirt and new cashmere jumper, the brown broadcloth topcoat that even Tina admitted to be smart, brown gloves and pumps as shiny chestnut-coloured as a conker.

She carried her brown leather handbag and a shopping bag of a kind rather superior to the usual plastic carrier, a hessian bag with a red design round its border.

It was Saturday and, as arranged between them during Cecilia's stay in Willesden, they were to meet at Bond Street station to buy Daphne a spring costume at Selfridges. Daphne always bought her clothes at Selfridges. She continued to call a matching skirt and jacket a costume, though Cecilia had once or twice told her this was a suit. Cecilia did not persist, understanding what Daphne meant when she said 'suit' sounded to her like something men wore. She had feelings like that about words herself, not the same feelings but close enough for empathy.

On the way to the station Cecilia was going to call on Tina. It was late in the morning and Cecilia did not anticipate any unwelcome revelations. She did not expect to see the children, who in any case had been to tea the day before. They would be out with Brian. Cecilia meant to get a shopping list from Tina so that she could bring her what Tina called 'goodies'. As she walked along she thought about the little dead boy. Jasper's new wary silences she attributed to his reading about the dead boy in the papers.

Brian's car was outside Cambridge School. The children, or just Jasper, refused to go in the Underground since the accident to the boy who had been on the roof of the train. There was a van parked at its tail but this meant nothing to Cecilia, who was noting the precocious flowering of shrubs which her brother had planted and which still remained in the School garden among the weeds and elderberry and sycamore suckers. The camellia had big red flowers like roses, 'very showy' was the way they put it in the plant catalogue. She could remember buying it for Ernest all those years ago, and the little one with mauve flowers the following year. She could never forget the name of that. It was called a Daphne and she and her Daphne had bought it together, amused by its name. She opened the gate and went up the path; as she reached the front door it opened and Brian came out with Jasper and Bienvida.

She talked to them for a moment, looking all the while at Jasper. She was anxious about Jasper and she watched him for signs of a return to his old intense, serious or cheerful, *busyness*. It was because of this careful study she gave to Jasper's expression that his face was more than usually imprinted on her mental eye. She carried the image of it with her as she walked across the hall, past the cloakroom which, if she no longer shuddered at, she could not pass without awareness, to tap on Tina's front door.

Tina opened it and said, 'Hallo, Ma.' Then she said, 'This is Daniel. He's come to pick up his stuff.'

This was perfectly true, not a ploy to make Cecilia believe things were other than they were. Tina did not tell lies, though she acted them. Daniel Korn had left his CD player, some of his clothes, an electric toaster and a barbecue tripod at Tina's when he moved out. Now that he had acquired a flat instead of a room, he had come in a borrowed van to collect his property and he and Tina were having an amicable cup of coffee in the kitchen.

Daniel Korn said, 'Hi.'

Cecilia said, 'How do you do?' and lifted her eyes and looked at him.

The face imprinted on her inner eye reproduced itself somewhat enlarged before her. It was as if she were looking at Jasper once more. Or as if this was Jasper grown up, a shortish, stocky, neatly made man with a smooth oval face, what when she was a girl they called on girls a lovely complexion, hair as black as Chinese hair and looking as if painted on, bright black eyes, black crescent eyebrows.

Tina said, 'Ma?'

When she got no answer she said, 'Are you OK, Ma? You're looking a bit pale.'

Cecilia said she was quite all right. She said it twice. 'I'm quite all right.'

She went through the motions. What would Tina like her to fetch from Selfridges? Would Tina be in when she came back at, say, five? She spoke slowly and abstractedly. A thought came between the words and their utterance, a simple negative reassurance: it can't be. It did not reassure. She fell silent. She thought, I must be alone, I must think about this alone.

The shock – it was like a blow, enfeebling her legs – had made her sit down. She got up, still holding on to the table.

'Aren't you going to have your coffee?'

'I don't want to be late for Daphne,' Cecilia said.

The glance that passed between Tina and Daniel Korn, or which Tina gave and he received, a smiling, knowing look, though not without kindness, was not lost on Cecilia. But it did not touch her, either with anger or shame or embarrassment. She was beyond all that. She could hear a sound in her head now, a dull booming that did not lessen when she was out in the street, and because of what she had recently been reading and watching, she thought of Mrs Moore hearing the boom in the Marabar Caves. That had been a real sound and what she could hear was her own blood pumping, but her reaction to it was the same. There had come to her a dull but perfectly clear awareness that life had no meaning, that there was no morality, ethics did not exist, values had departed if indeed they had ever been.

Daniel Korn was Jasper's father. She knew that beyond a doubt. All these years Tina had been taking money from Brian who believed, who had been led to believe, Jasper was his son. He had been deceived, and she had been and the children had been, for now she had no doubt Brian was not Bienvida's father either, and Tina did not care.

Tina, if confronted with this, would smile and shrug and ask what did it matter.

Nothing mattered, then. And Cecilia, making her way towards the station, crossing the railway bridge, walking mechanically and without looking where she was going, but knowing the way because she had done it ten thousand times before, thought of her youth and her past and what had mattered. So it all meant nothing? When she was a girl Tina would have been ostracized; when her own mother was a girl, Tina would have been an outcast. But now everyone knew her, everyone smiled. It was not that they forgave, for there was nothing for them to forgive. Nothing.

Three bicycles were dropped on to the line from a bridge between Leytonstone and Snaresbrook on the Central Line on an April evening in 1951. The consequent short circuit delayed trains by only half an hour.

More than half a century before this a passenger fell from a train on the City and South London Railway, as the Northern Line was then called. The train was passing through a tunnel at the time and he was killed.

In November 1927 a porter tried to close the gate of a moving train at Piccadilly. He was carried to the tunnel portal and killed. Twenty years later a guard was killed when he fell from a westbound train travelling between Liverpool Street and the Bank, and in the same year a man died when his arm was trapped in the doors of a train at Lancaster Gate after he had tried to force them open. He was dragged to the tunnel portal and killed when it struck him.

On the bridge, on the slippery lichened boards, she paused to look, almost unseeing, down upon the unravelled skeins of dull lines and silver lines stretching out between here and Finchley Road. What would become of the children when Brian found out? Who would keep them? Tina was her only heir. The house would pass naturally to Tina. She thought that she would protect Jasper and Bienvida by making a will and leaving the house to them, not to punish Tina, but to keep the children from want. She would find a solicitor on Monday and make a new will.

Cecilia walked on and down the steps on the other side. She presented her Senior Citizens' Travel Card. She walked on to the platform. A new and terrible thought had come to her. If that morality which in her own youth had been hard and fast and inescapable, so that people said it had always been like that, throughout the ages, and always would be, what rules prevailed today that in the time to come, in twenty years' time, would amount to nothing too?

Almost the worst thing a woman could do in her youth was what Tina had done and constantly did. But it was all right now. The stigma then of illegitimacy, though admitted not to be the poor child's fault, was an ineradicable one. Who cared about it now? What Peter did was all right now, though her father had called it a sin so bad that it must not be mentioned, not even touched upon by euphemism or innuendo, in their house. So, this child abuse and this child pornography, which were the crimes of *now*, would these one day be all right too? In the years to come when she was dead, would they look back to smile indulgently on these horrors which to Cecilia had been the worst of sins?

Had been. She no longer knew. Tina, using a popular word, would have said she was confused. But Cecilia was not confused, she was not puzzled or in doubt. The division between right and wrong had been bridged, had melded, had fused, until there was no separation. She had never believed in God, only in rules that had seemed to serve her very well instead, but one by one those rules had been

271

broken and the world had not ended, only grown empty, become a nothingness. The boom in her head repeated itself. She listened to it. She felt the vibration, heard the singing sound, of the train approaching.

She felt divorced from herself. That was the way she put it, the only explanatory way there was. There was her body, which performed actions, stepped into the train, moved towards a seat, sat in it, and that part she called her mind, which seemed to watch her body from a distance, to tread the air on wings outside it, as if she were already dead. A huge desolation rolled upon her.

Other people were in the train. The days when she could have entered an empty car at this station were long past. But the faces might have been goats' and monkeys' heads on human bodies, they were as devoid of reason, of civilization, of *humanity*. The car began to fill up at Swiss Cottage and people were standing. She closed her eyes, retreating into that dark chamber which was her own Marabar Cave, empty, desolate, the booming dull now and distant.

It was the first time she had been in this train, descending the steep gradient, without thinking of the dead boy, without thinking of the boy and his terror, with compassion and with pity for his parents. That death was meaningless now, not worth a thought, of no account in a world where nothing mattered. Cecilia thought of chaos and the blood boomed in her head.

Only the partial emptying of the train, the displacement of people, brought her back and made her open her eyes. There had been the usual Baker Street exodus. The kind of sickness that comes when one is actually empty, when one has not eaten for a long time, was afflicting her. Her mouth filled with saliva. She felt for her handbag and could not find it. Her handbag was gone.

★

It sometimes happened, when they had arranged to meet like this, that Daphne and Cecilia got into the same train. That is, Daphne got into a train at Willesden Green, and two stops down the line Cecilia got into it at West Hampstead. This had happened now, though neither of them knew it. And Cecilia, for once, had not thought that this was something she must tell Daphne, had not longed as she had always longed in the past for Daphne to be there and to listen. After the first shock of discovery when all her feelings had been involved with personalities and their interaction, she had not thought of individual people at all. Those in the tube car with her had been so many beast-headed lay figures, incapable of good or evil, incapable of doing her a mercy or doing her harm.

But one of them had stolen her handbag.

The sensation common to all of us when we realize we have lost something important or valuable was what Cecilia felt, as of her inside turning and of a heaviness rolling down through her body, a monstrous child expelling itself without pain. Her head seemed to be released from her shoulders and to float above the rest of her with a spatial lightness, and there the common feeling ended. For an instant she was not there at all, she was not in the car, a second's blackness drew her into itself, a second of death, and then she was back in her seat, half-keeled over.

The seat was the one nearest to the door, with the steel pole to which standing passengers clung. Cecilia clung to it with her right hand, her right hand was all right, and dragged herself to her feet. Or to her foot, her right foot; the left leg was as dead as the left arm. No one took any notice of her. They said no one did in cases like this and with her new knowledge of the world, she was not surprised. I have always been very strong physically, she thought. She was upright, or almost so, and she was hanging on. The train came into Bond Street, someone outside pressed the button, and the doors opened.

273

Cecilia got out of the train. She limped out and fell. People took notice then. Hands came to help her up, to lift her, and suddenly Daphne was there. Daphne was holding her. Cecilia's face felt as it did after the dentist had given her an injection of anaesthetic in the gum. There was no feeling on the left side. Daphne was holding her right hand, sitting beside her on the bucket seats on the platform, and she wanted to put up her left hand to touch her frozen mouth but she could not move her hand, it felt as it sometimes had when she had lain on it in sleep. But this was not sleep. You woke from sleep and feeling returned to the numb hand.

She said, 'I have had a stroke. It was on the right side of the brain, thankfully, for the left side you know is dominant and damage there would be much more serious.'

She spoke as clearly as she could but to Daphne her speech was as incomprehensible as a mumble in a foreign language.

The appointment Jed had made with the vet was for Monday morning. He had wondered if this vet, a kind of general practitioner, would be competent to give Abelard a painless death but the vet said, sure, that was OK and would Jed like him to come to the house. Jed said, no, he would bring him.

Abelard was in the shed in the garden. Jed continued to weigh him and to feed him according to his weight. His weight increased because now he had no exercise, so his food had to be cut and out there, alone, he began to scream again. Tina told him that in the house with the windows closed she could not hear the screaming, but Jed could hear it. He was like the princess in the princess and the pea story who could feel the pea through twenty mattresses, only with him it was his hearing and not feeling that was sensitive. Twenty closed windows between him and the hawk could not have cut off that sound.

It was Saturday afternoon before it occurred to him that it was pointless what he was doing. The hawk was going to die on Monday morning and here was he still worrying about its weight, about restricting its feeding. At least he could make Abelard's last days of life happy. As he crossed the hall the phone was ringing, so he answered it. The caller was someone wanting Tina to tell her that her mother had been taken ill. Jed knocked on the front door of the Headmaster's Flat and Tina came running out to the phone, the smile wiped from her face and her cheeks suddenly pale.

It made Jed think of love, what it is and the strange forms it takes. He had loved others, his wife once, his daughter. He sometimes told himself, though suspecting hypocrisy, that he worked with the Safeguards from a love of humanity. But he had loved nothing and no one more than this bird whose screams for sustenance and for care now reached him with a dreadful, penetrating, bitter shrillness as he went out by the garden door.

Abelard became silent as soon as he was in his jesses and on Jed's wrist. Jed stroked his head. The great well of love inside him rose and overflowed. He was crying. He took Abelard upstairs and into his room. There when the hawk was on his perch he fed him all the meat that was to have been slowly rationed out. Abelard gobbled the food. His eyes flashed. Jed had no day-old chicks because, since Abelard no longer flew, these were not needed as rewards for prowess.

I'll get some on Monday, he thought, and then he remembered that on Monday Abelard would be gone. Abelard would be dead. The tears rolled down his face. The hawk's eyes were closed. Jed pushed his hand across his eyes and rubbed at the tears. He watched the hawk and the heavily hooded eyes, the poise of him and his balance. Abelard was so beautiful, he had so much dignity, such grace.

Presently Jed went downstairs again and phoned the vet's surgery to cancel that appointment.

It was clear what he had to do, it was simple. He need do nothing but keep Abelard with him. This was of all things open to him the one thing he most wished to do. It always had been and had always been denied him. But now – and he realized all these things by a gradual process rather like the inward flowing of a tide – now he could keep Abelard in his room and feed him unrestrictedly. He could make the hawk *happy*. He could make the thing he loved endlessly happy. And it would be nearly endless, there was no reason why Abelard should not live twenty, thirty years. Close, side by side, day and night, they would live together in this room or some other like it somewhere, in companionable silence. The hawk would never cry again.

In a happiness that seemed to have come in the simplest and clearest possible way, Jed sat watching the bird on its perch. He sat relishing his decision. After a long time, when Abelard opened an eye, Jed went to the cupboard and took out the meat he had intended for his own supper.

The school at Aldeburgh did not want Alice. They told her so when the audition was over, or rather before the time she thought the audition was over. They were kind and polite and rather distant.

She wondered what she had meant by thinking being in love made her a better performer. It now seemed a curious fallacy to which she had subscribed in a moment of madness. When she played with the aim of being chosen as one of the few post-graduates at the Britten–Pears School to be taught by an eminent violinist, she had forgotten all she had ever known of technique. One horrible discord she drew from the violin brought the hot blood up into her face.

She was ashamed, for she had indulged in daydreams of the kind Tom would have. She had seen herself as the pupil in Max Rostal's master class to which the public could come, playing before an audience in the Recital Room at Snape. Axel would have been there, watching her. She imagined his mocking expression displaced by one of pride.

She thought she would not have minded the great violinist's reproaches in public but would have borne them smiling, for a chance of playing and pleasing Axel.

20

'They're going to let me know.'

Tom was used to hearing those words from her. She came back from auditions and said that. Or she admitted flatly that they would not offer her a place on their course or subsidize her at the conservatoire or finance further lessons.

It was wrong to exult, but he could not help himself. She would join him now and become a musician in his street band. She could leave her job as soon as her failure at this most recent audition had been confirmed. The experts were cruel only to be kind and it was best to know before wasting more time and money. Everyone who knew anything about it said that if you wanted to be at the top, a star, you had to start as a child. You had to go to Chetham's or the Yehudi Menuhin School and have a hothouse training.

In this world you had to be a realist. Not everyone could get to the top, most could not. Second-class was an unattractive way of putting it and he thought of his – and her – position as the middle ground. That was what gave the most pleasure, after all, and provided the best entertainment. To look as stricken as Alice did and make such a drama of things exasperated Tom but had no effect on his love for her. He put his arms round her and held her, whispering kind, meaningless words and stroking her hair. She clung to him like a child and he thought, ambition took her away but she is coming back to me.

Later, when he told her he was going to the pub with Axel, she shook her head fiercely before he could make the various excuses he had prepared for getting her to stay at home. Talking about her to Axel was something he could hardly ever do because she was always there. He wanted to talk about her more now she was more his.

'You see, I think when the first disappointment's past she'll see this as all for the best.'

'Why so?'

'A lot of people would think themselves enormously lucky to get into an orchestra like mine. Alice would never have made it as a soloist. It's crazy, you know, people leave music school in this country knowing how to play the solo part in a Mozart concerto but without the faintest idea of the discipline you need for an orchestra. She isn't going to have to learn that now, or rather we'll all be learning together. It's the best chance she could have.'

Tom noticed Axel's abstracted expression.

'Sorry, I'm boring you.'

'Not at all. What are you going to have?'

'Same as always,' said Tom. 'Pint of bitter as usual.'

He would let Axel buy the first round and therefore the third. That way he would only have one round to pay for. He found Axel curiously easy to talk to. It was something to do with the man's silence, the intent way he listened, looking into your eyes, nodding sometimes. He said now, 'What do you think of Alice? I would have asked before except that she's usually with us.'

'What do I think of her?'

'Yes.'

'She's very beautiful.' Axel spoke dismissively, though the words he used sounded odd when uttered with indifference. They sounded like a contradiction in terms. 'I think you're right.'

'Right in what way?'

'To discourage her from these – how shall I put it? – high musical ambitions. She hasn't got it in her.'

Tom was astonished. 'How do you know?'

'Oh, I don't. I don't know. I'm no judge. But she did play for me once. I asked her and she played for me. I was disappointed. You don't mind my being frank?'

'No,' said Tom.

'That's why I think the best thing you can do is form some sort of band of your own with her in it, if you like. If *she* likes. As the case may be. I actually see Alice as a homemaker. You should take her away from here and get a home for her to make.'

He held the brandy glass in both hands and smiled over the top of it, making Tom think of some advertisement for liquor or for glasses or for things which are not offered for sale, cunning perhaps, guile, or just an understanding of the human heart. The illusion went and Axel looked friendly and pleasant again.

'How can I?' Tom said.

'Maybe you could get one of those government grants that are made to help people start small businesses. I don't see why a band isn't a business, do you?'

'Yes, and what you get is £40 a week,' said Tom bitterly.

'I was joking.' Axel's face changed. It became harder, it was no longer smiling, mocking or even cunning. It had become *businesslike*. 'Would you like to make some real money, Tom?'

Passengers were removed from the cars when fire broke out in a train between Elephant and Castle and the Borough on the Northern Line in January 1902.

A man was shot at in an Underground train between Baker Street and Swiss Cottage one day in August 1910. He recovered. One of the results was to install safety communication devices for passengers in all trains.

Twenty-four years later a runaway ballast train wrecked the signal box at Rayners Lane on the Piccadilly Line. And in the

following year an Auxiliary Air Force plane crashed across the
Northern Line near Colindale, caused a short-circuit fire in a
signal box and burned it down.

A serious fire in an escalator shaft at Paddington on Christmas
Eve 1944 killed no one.

Stonebridge Park station on the Bakerloo Line burned down in
January 1917. Twenty-eight years later it burned down again.
One passenger died from the fumes when fire broke out in a
Central Line train at Holland Park in 1958.

The ban on smoking came in 1985. It did not prevent the
worst of all tube disasters, with the exception of the Balham
bomb: the King's Cross fire of November 1987.

The idea of moving back to Lilac Villa to look after
Cecilia frightened Tina. She lost her calmness, her cool. It
was as if all those characteristics that made her what she
was, placidity and being laid-back, taking life as it came,
an unworriedness, vanished as soon as she heard Daphne's
news.

She wouldn't do it, she couldn't do it. A host of reasons
for not doing it jostled at each other. She was picking the
best of them when Daphne said, wonderfully, almost incred-
ibly, 'If you don't mind, Tina, I'm going to stay here and
look after your mother. It's what she would like and, of
course, I should like it. The doctor says there's no need for
her to go to hospital, she's not immobile.'

'My God, of course I don't *mind*,' said Tina. 'I think
you're marvellous.' Relief made her generous. 'We'll come
and see her tomorrow, shall we? Me and the kids?'

Cecilia lay on the sofa in her living room, the one that
could be made into a single bed. The stairs were rather
steep in Lilac Villa and there was no reason why she should
be forced to use them. Leaning on Daphne and using a
stick, she could limp to the lavatory. After a day or two
she sat up in an armchair and the physiotherapist came to

start teaching her exercises that would help her regain the use of her left leg.

She was very happy with Daphne. She was grateful, but her gratitude was not of the kind that is overwhelming. It was more a feeling that Daphne had only met the high standard of conduct she, Cecilia, would have expected of her. It was rather like that which subsists between a devoted, long-married couple. Desertion, letting-down, failure to rise to this testing occasion, these things are not possible. Daphne had done what she would have done, had their roles been reversed. Daphne loved her as she loved Daphne. The strange thing was that Cecilia, since she had been ill, found it quite easy and indeed a source of happiness to use that word, inwardly and out loud though not in Daphne's hearing, about her relation with her friend. Substitutes for it, those were what would have been wrong. She liked to say quietly, while she half-dozed, Daphne and I love each other.

People had crowded round while she sat there on the grey bucket seat beside Daphne. There was, miraculously, a doctor among the alighting passengers. He went up the escalator and spoke to the station staff and someone appeared with a chair, into which they put Cecilia and carried her up to street level. It was then that Daphne proved her worth. She took Cecilia home in a taxi and called her own doctor. So Cecilia avoided being taken to hospital and, if paralysed down her left side and with her face distorted and speech numbed, was at least in her own home.

She was not confused or disturbed in her mind, but she had forgotten things. There was a great blank between seeing Brian with the children and sitting on the Bond Street platform with Daphne. Cecilia did not quite know but had a feeling that several bad things had happened in that blank time. It was those bad things which had brought on her stroke, of this she was sure, though she had no memory of what they were. There was something wonderfully strange about knowing that the hour in which she had been stricken, perhaps mortally stricken, certainly irredeemably, whatever bright and encouraging things the physiotherapist might say, was a lost hour, a tiny piece cut out of her life just as the hard-pumping blood had cut a minute piece from her brain.

A double shock, Cecilia thought it had been, without recalling more, which had raised her blood pressure too high. It had dropped again, the doctor said. The doctor was pleased with her. Daphne cooked the things she liked to eat and got books for her from the library. Cecilia went back into her sofa-bed in the evenings and they watched television together. Though they had never done this before, they held hands. Daphne pulled her chair up against the side of the bed, took the paralysed hand in hers and held it. There was no movement in that hand but there was feeling.

Cecilia's face got better first, within days. The second time Tina came with the children they could understand everything she said. Daphne had been able to understand almost from the beginning. Peter called in on the way home from the hospice, looking shaken, and told them a sad story of a boy of twenty who had died the night before in his arms.

'I don't think people ever actually do die in someone else's arms, do you?' said Daphne after he had gone. 'I didn't like to say so because he was so upset, poor boy. But it would be very uncomfortable for the patient and very hard to gauge exactly when to sort of get them into your arms, if you see what I mean.'

'I expect they mean they put their arm round them when they see they're going.'

'Yes, I suppose that's it.'

'Do you believe in eternal life, Daphne? Do you think the soul leaves the body at the point of death and goes off to a place of bliss?'

'No,' said Daphne.

After a while she said, 'You *are* talking well. You're nearly back to normal.'

'I expect you'll say it's not very wise, Daphne, but I would like to look at my face. I can take it, really. After all, at my age I hope I'm past vanity. If you'll find my handbag for me, there's a mirror in my powder compact.'

Daphne did not look very hard for the handbag because it was as Cecilia said and she thought it unwise for her friend to see the distortion of her mouth. And Cecilia understood this. She had not, as Daphne believed, forgotten about asking for the bag, only decided not to repeat her request and thus avoid causing Daphne distress.

The old woman appeared asleep and there was this handbag on the seat beside her, asking to be taken. Nicholas Mann, unemployed, clever, sharp and penniless, living in his sister's flat with her and her boyfriend, took it. Nobody saw him take it or if they did they preferred not to say. He got out at Baker Street.

Almost the first thing he did was remove Cecilia's wallet containing cash and three cards: one credit card, one charge card and a cashpoint card. He also took out her cheque-book. The rest of the contents of the bag and the bag itself he put into the first rubbish bin he came to in his progress along the Marylebone Road.

He had already noticed that Cecilia was not in the habit of signing herself with her full name but with the initials C. M. The same signature was on her cards. Written on the chequebook, on the back cover, were four digits which Nicholas Mann thought might be Cecilia's secret cashpoint number. In this he turned out to be correct. He went to Brighton where he checked into an hotel. He spent a lot of money during the rest of the day on meals, drink, clothes and personal accessories. Then, fearing that the loss of the cards must already have been reported, drew out at the cashpoint all the money Cecilia had on her current account and spent the evening in the casino. Luck was with him and he trebled Cecilia's money, returning to the hotel with £1,400.

Next day he phoned his sister and told her he would not be coming back. Since her boyfriend, with whom she was very much in love, had said if Nicholas stayed he was going, he had had as much as he could stand, this made her very happy, so happy that when the boyfriend said he had run out of condoms but would go out and get some, she said not to bother, let's not bother with that any more. It was the first time she had ever had sex without using a contraceptive and she conceived at once.

After Alice had left for work, Tom went along to the Art Room as arranged, where Axel had said he wanted to talk to him. The first thing he saw when he entered the room was a rope. It was a long, tough-looking but thin rope, tightly wound up into a cylinder shape. To one end of it was attached a steel ring bolt. Axel was sitting at the drawing table. It was cold and he was wearing his long overcoat. On a sheet of paper on the table he had been drawing some sort of plan or chart.

He said to Tom, 'Did you mean what you said about being prepared to be my assistant?'

Tom hesitated. Then he said, 'If the money's good.'

'It may involve – let's say stepping over the wrong side of the law.'

'So long as it's non-violent.'

'Oh, it's *non-violent*,' said Axel, as if the very idea were bizarre, as if Tom had said so long as it doesn't involve going up in a space probe.

'Are you going to tell me what it is? I mean, I presume

there is something, you're making me some offer? This isn't all academic?'

That made Axel laugh. 'You've seen the rope. That's not an academic rope, is it? It's not an illusion, you can't do the Indian rope trick with it.'

'The what?'

'Never mind.' Axel changed tack, in the way he had. He said, 'I don't know how well you know Jarvis.'

'Not very well. I like him, you couldn't help liking him. He's my landlord, that's more or less it.'

'He's never talked to you about – well, the esoterica of the Underground?'

'I don't think I understand what you mean.'

'He's never talked to you about the disused parts of the Underground, the old shafts, for instance, some of which are vertical tunnels coming up through London buildings?'

'I've never been interested in trains, the tube, all that,' said Tom, 'except for playing music there.'

'So you don't know what a Signals and Communications Room is?'

'I think I can imagine.'

Axel handed Tom the piece of paper on which he had been drawing. It was a plan, but of what Tom had no idea. There were lines that might have formed the outline of a build-ing, there was something shaped like a greatly elongated pot. While Tom was looking at it, Axel said, 'I want to take a photograph of something in the Signals and Communica-tions Room. The room is marked on the plan with a cross.'

Tom could see it as a small circle, a spider in the midst of a web. 'Will they let you?'

'If by "they" you mean London Transport Underground, I haven't asked them. I don't bother asking permission for things when I know the answer will be no. I have to do it without asking and I want you to help. That is the thing I want you to do.'

286

'Yes,' Tom said slowly. 'Yes, I see.'

'I don't suppose you do see. Not yet. There won't be any breaking, though there will be entering. There won't be any burglary or picking of locks. I'll explain exactly what I'm going to do and you have to do in a minute.'

'Can I ask you something?' said Tom, and because that sounded weak and, indeed, childish, did not wait for an answer. 'What do you want this photograph for?'

'I'm a photographer.'

'That's not an answer,' said Tom, more than usually bold. 'Photographing things the authorities want kept secret sounds more like the action of a – well, a spy.'

Axel laughed again. He took his plan back and wrote some words on it, made another cross.

'If you agree there'll be a considerable monetary reward.'

'I suppose I've already agreed,' said Tom.

'You haven't asked what the monetary reward will be.'

'No, I haven't.'

'Does ten grand sound all right?'

'Ten thousand pounds?' said Tom. He must have misheard. 'Did you really say ten thousand pounds?'

'I expect I could make it a bit more.'

'*You* could? Don't you mean your employers, bosses, masters could?'

'If you like.'

Tom stared at him.

'You'll have to trust me,' Axel said, 'and I'll have to trust you. I've proved I trust you by telling you all this. I've burned my boats, queered my pitch, whatever you like to call it, telling you I want to take this photograph – well, photographs. You could phone London Transport, make an anonymous phone call if you like, and that would be the end of it. So by telling you what I have, I've really put myself in your hands. I want you to put yourself in

mine and trust me about the money. You'll get a thousand
now, when you agree, and the rest when it – when the
task is done. OK?'

'I must think about it.'

'Don't think about it for too long.'

'I'll tell you tonight.'

The fire began when a lighted match fell through an escalator.
This escalator led from the Piccadilly Line platforms to the main
ticket hall concourse under the mainline station forecourt. The
time was 7.25 in the evening, the date 18 November 1987.

Dense obliterating smoke filled the passageways. People later
described it as a black hell. Passengers arriving by train smelt the
smoke and tried to crush back into the cars, but there was no room.
Trains left people stranded. Others went through without stop-
ping, though the trapped people banged on the windows as it
passed. One man said, there was plenty of room in the train but
we could not get in.

One view was that trains pushed air into the tunnels and
fanned the flames, another that trains impeded the wind.

Thirty-one people died in the King's Cross fire.

The worst accident on the Underground before this was on 28
February 1975, when a train hit the end of a tunnel at Moorgate
station, killing forty-three people.

Later in the day Tom met Jay and a friend of his called
Mark at Tottenham Court Road and they went down the
escalator to the pitch they had booked. It was in the
concourse that is circular and tiled in coloured mosaics.
Peter was ill, Jay said, at least he was not well enough to
stand up to hours of playing.

Mark was a saxophonist. He had brought his saxophone
and his new true-diversity wireless microphone system as
well. Tom was taken aback when he heard what it had
cost. They set up in the mosaic area, which might have

been designed as a concert hall specially for them, Mark said, laughing. He laid down his saxophone case open on the tiles in front of them. The microphone, Tom found, was very light and easy to hold and when he sang the sound was stunning. It seemed not to come just from his throat and lungs but from the walls and the very air itself, filling up the tall round room and flowing through the entrance and exit passages. Tom sang folk songs, ending with 'Scarborough Fair' because he liked the bit about the one who lived there and was once a true love of his.

One or two people passing looked taken aback by the sound and one woman actually flinched, but most people loved it. Tom sang 'Auprès de ma Blonde' and a French party, who looked like students, gathered round and joined in. All the voices and the saxophone and guitar amplified to the system's full capacity fetched one of the station staff down the escalator to move them on. He tried to move them *off*, but even he couldn't say they were playing to the annoyance of passengers. They set up again further along the passage and Tom sang the Toreador Song from *Carmen* for the benefit of his French audience.

From where they now were he could see a pair of those grey doors Axel had said would lead into the disused part of the Underground, to half-lit tunnels and narrow unlit passages, old lift shafts and shafts where staircases once ran up. He kept thinking about what Axel wanted him to do, what he had agreed to do, though it was not too late to back out, and he could not see anything wrong about it. It was odd, considering how she had left her husband and her child, but he always felt Alice was somehow more of a moral person than he was. He would have liked to talk to Alice about this and hear her views. But Axel had made him promise to tell no one, not even Alice.

They packed up just before five, which was early for them, but it had been a good day, they had taken over

£20. Tom got Mark to promise to join them again – with his wireless microphone system – and then he thought of going along to meet Alice from work.

He knew more or less where she worked and the name of the company, though he had never been there. He knew the street but not the number. It was too far to walk if he was to get there in time. He went along to the Central Line going east. The platform was jammed with people and after a moment or two a voice came over the public address system apologizing for the absence of trains and explaining that there had been an 'incident' on the line. This meant another body, a suicide.

More people kept coming on to the platform. Could you get to a point where the pressure would push people over the edge on to the line? He imagined a choked escalator, and a water image came to him, the escalator like a waterfall that poured into a full pool. Water would drip over the edges, heave, swell and flood. Jarvis had told him there were stations where a warning bell rang to stop this, but the occasional claustrophobia from which he suffered began to affect him. A headache was beginning. He struggled back through the mass of people and made for the westbound platform. It was ten past five and Alice would have gone.

Months had gone by since he was home so early. Alice was not in the Headmaster's Study nor in Four. Even if she had been at home he was not allowed to consult her about Axel's plans. He was going to do it anyway, wasn't he? The two of them were to get into one of the disused parts of the tube and Axel would take his photographs. Axel had not told him how they would get in nor who these photographs were for.

Russia? It seemed ridiculous. Since Jarvis went to Russia, there had been a continuous detente, a loosening of all those tight bands that bound the satellites of Eastern Europe to their mother planet. Some Middle Eastern country, then? Why would any country want photographs of the London tube? Tom remembered, while a student, being threatened by an official with having his camera taken away from him when he got it out in a railway station in Italy. And wasn't there a rule in some countries about not taking pictures of their territory from aircraft? So perhaps wanting photographs of London Transport's signals system was not so bizarre as it seemed, perhaps all countries wanted such photographs of their enemies' or possible enemies' secrets.

It was inescapable, though, that all the time he thought about it he had this feeling he was being taken for a ride. Possibly it was only the money that worried him, the chance he might not get the money. Tom resolved that if he said yes and the promised £1,000 was not forthcoming, he would withdraw. But it was not just the money. It was more as if Axel thought he was a fool who would accept any story. As soon as this idea came to Tom he dismissed it. He had no reason to think Axel did not respect and trust and like him. Other people might call him paranoid. He knew he was paranoid, he did not deceive himself, but this was the reverse of that. Axel liked him, Axel had nothing against him.

Tom lay on his bed and slept for a while. He was tired. There was the occasional tube passenger who passed them and made a comment about beggars or about their being too lazy to take proper jobs, but busking was hard work. Tom sometimes felt worn out by evening.

When he woke up it was nearly seven. His left hand was numb, as it often was on waking. There was no sign of Alice. He put his head round the door of the Headmaster's Study but she was not there. Jed's door was open a little way and Tom could see the hawk in there, asleep on its perch. The room smelt like the aviary of a bird of prey, which was what it had become.

He went along to the Art Room and knocked on the door. There was no answer so he knocked again and looked inside. Someone had been there but not for a long time. The empty whisky bottle on the drawing table looked as if it had been emptied days before and a winter-surviving fly had drowned in the dregs of one of the glasses. Tom knocked at Five. He opened the door and Alice got up off the bed and stood looking at him.

It was cold in there, no heater was on, and she was still in her outdoor things, the old navy-blue coat and the thick shawl. He said, puzzled, 'Were you waiting for Axel? Were you looking for him?'

'I must have gone to sleep.'

'I wondered where you were,' he said.

He thought she looked strange, weary and worn. She was holding one hand up to her mouth, speaking through the fingers. 'I'm cold,' she said, and then, 'I don't know what I'm doing in here.'

That made him laugh. 'Well, I certainly don't. Come on. You always feel cold when you wake up, you know that. I expect you're hungry too.'

'I'm not hungry,' she said, but she allowed him to lead her from the room and downstairs to where he had made Four warm and had spread out an Indian takeaway and had a bottle of red wine breathing. He helped her gently out of her coat and wrapped her once more in the shawl. She was deathly tired, he could tell, and he thought he would talk to her about giving up that job. A train rattled down beyond the wall and he drew the curtains to shut it out. She turned to him, 'Oh, Tom, oh, Tom!'

'What is it, darling? What's wrong? You can tell me.'

She went into his arms and held him as he held her. 'I'm so tired of it all, this life.'

'We won't stay here much longer,' he said. 'We'll have a home of our own.'

Later, after they had eaten, and she was listening with closed eyes to a Haydn symphony, Tom heard Axel come up the stairs. He said he would be quick, he would be straight back, but she gave no sign that she had heard him. He went upstairs to Five where the door was ajar and told Axel he would do the job – so long as he got the money.

Axel smiled, said he was pleased and gave Tom a £1,000 in £50 notes. He had it all ready, which amazed Tom. His worry receded when he had the notes in his hand and this made him certain that all he had been worrying about, all the time, had been money.

21

Every evening, when she got home from work, she went
to Axel's room to wait for him. This was the fifth time she
had waited in vain, or she believed it would be in vain
when the time came to 6.30, to a quarter to seven. Of
course she knew very well he would hate her pursuit of
him, her waiting for him like a dog, but she could not help
herself.

Tom had told her he would be away for a whole night.
He was going to Bristol to see a man who had a secondhand
dynamic microphone for sale. He had not explained why
he could not come back in the evening, it was only a two-
hour train journey, but she had not asked or cared. The
first thing she thought of was that she and Axel might
have that night together. The idea of a whole night with
Axel as a marvellous possibility had replaced musical aspira-
tion. It was all she wanted, a night with him – then a life
with him.

Wrapped in her shawl, her coat on, she sat waiting for
Axel in his unheated room. Once, when she went there the
first thing she did was put the heater on, but now she told
herself not to prepare, not to turn down the bed, not even
to take her coat off. If she did those things Providence
would be tempted and he would not come. So she sat
shivering in a coat and shawl not warm enough to keep
out the chill.

Sometimes she got up and walked about. She was
tempted to look inside his suitcases. She told herself mad
things, that the time in which she was doing things in his
room she should not be doing was the only time she
would not want him to come. There would be ten minutes,

half an hour, of not wanting him. While looking in his suitcases she would be hoping for him *not* to come, so therefore he would come. Was she prepared to pay the price of his anger?

She listened. The house was silent. Then footsteps began to mount the stairs. She froze and waited but the footsteps did not continue up the second flight. It was Tom coming in or Jed. She thought she felt much the same about Tom now as she did about Jed, a friendly, impatient indifference. She would have hugged each of them equally, except that Tom was clean and Jed smelt of stale meat. That made her laugh hysterically. She laughed to herself in the empty room.

Tom was a comfort to her. She hugged him and cried in his arms as she might have hugged her father, if she had had that sort of father. Guilt overwhelmed her and made her dislike him, though it did not keep her from clinging to him, from holding him in the night. She would have said she had no physical feeling for Tom left, yet paradoxically her feeling for him was *all* physical, for his warmth, his touch, his arms round her, his body near her in bed in the dark. Once she had reassured herself by recalling the things they had in common, the way they could talk and confide in each other. Now she did not want him to speak or to speak to him, only to have him there to hold.

In Axel's suitcases she felt sure was contained his secret life, his past, his history, all of which she knew nothing. While in here, her eyes often went to Mary Zambaco on the wall. She had grown jealous of the picture, believing that if she looked like that he would love her.

The cases lay open. A folded garment lay on top of the contents of each, obscuring the tantalizing things beneath. If she touched those open cases, he would know. He might even have placed objects in certain positions to catch her out. Perhaps a hair had been laid carefully between a cloth surface and a sheet of paper, a piece of fluff nearly invisible on white cotton.

She listened, heard the silence, heard a train go down to Finchley Road. The things in the cases would smell of him, all had been handled by him, bore his hairs or his sweat or the residue of his breath. They drew her to them. She was the girl in the Bluebeard story, longing to search forbidden places, longing to find out, even though finding out would be her destruction.

Silence prevailed. A firm resolution not to touch anything in the room took her back to the bed, to seating herself on it, gripping her left hand in her right. How many such resolutions had she made in the past year and broken them as soon as they were formed? To go back to Mike that first morning. Not to become Tom's lover. To put music first before everything. Not to go to Kensington and meet Axel.

Her head turned away from the suitcases, strained sideways like a lever turned, she looked towards the cupboard. She held her breath, jumped up, opened the cupboard door. A leather jacket hung inside, a pair of jeans over the bar of a cleaner's wire hanger, a dark sweater on another and, shimmering a little in that dim place, bright with the light it gathered to itself, a long white dress.

Clothes did not interest her much. It was as if she knew she could not afford them and might never be able to. But this dress demanded attention as a work of art might, its snow-white perfection, its embroidered panels, its lace, the fine tucks that covered the broad spaces of the lawn of which it was made. Alice was reminded of her own wedding dress, a plainer confection, but also white and tucked, a ridiculous travesty, the waist made high to conceal her pregnancy.

But this one, in Axel's cupboard – could it be intended for herself? She stared at it but did not touch. A belief that if she touched it with her perfectly clean fingers she would leave a mark, made her draw back her hands. Could it be a present for her? She did not want to think of other reasons for its being there, other women who might wear it, who might have worn it. Without touching, she brought her face close to it, her eyes, she stroked it with her eyes and saw the tag hanging on a loop of white cord from one of the long lacy cuffs. No one had ever worn it, it was new.

She closed the cupboard door just in time. The door opened and Axel's hand came round it, the hand with the gold-and-silver ring. He came in.

'Why are you standing there in the cold?'

'I'm waiting for you.'

'Put the heater on.' He kicked the switch. 'I'll be glad to get away from this cold.'

Terror struck her. 'What do you mean, get away? You're not leaving?'

'Not just yet.' He smiled. 'Not till Friday. I think I'll go on Friday.'

She was silenced. She watched the bar of the old-fashioned electric fire turn from grey to a dull pink, to orange. As it heated it made a sporadic crackling sound. He had sat down opposite her, in the chair. His hands, his thin wrists, dangling from the sleeves of his dark overcoat, looked cold, bluish, and the ring loose between the joints. She wanted to take one of his hands but she dared not. She dared not speak now, not after what he had said. A cold panic silenced her, she seemed to have forgotten how to speak.

He turned away and warmed his hands at the heater. She found a voice, remoter than her normal one, no more than a distant whisper. 'Where will you go?'

Instead of answering, he said in tones that were teasing, that were full of laughter, 'Shall I take you with me?'

'You don't mean that.' She had begun to tremble.

'Don't you know by now that I never say what I don't mean? I may tell lies but I don't say things unless I mean them.'

It was like a revelation. She seemed at last to see things clearly, to see what suspicion and distrust had made her miss before: that his laughter was sincere, not a teasing malice, that he might really love and want her, that he might, against all the odds, be good and kind. But he had also said he was mad. Was that a thing he meant?

'Can we really go away from here together, Axel?'

'Why not?'

'Where shall we go?'

'Over the hills and far away. I'll fix something.'

She felt she could touch him now, the time had come for that. She put her hand on his knee. He brought his hands away from the hot bar and leant towards her. Their faces were close.

'I was going to say to you,' she said, 'that Tom will be away on Thursday overnight.' Her voice dropped. She told herself that she was wrong when she believed he liked to make her embarrassed. It was all in her head. 'I thought – I mean, that we could have the night together. But it doesn't matter if we're going to go away.'

He said in a businesslike way, 'I shan't be here on Thursday night anyway. I've arrangements to make. I told you I have to fix things up.'

'Shall I tell Tom?'

'Tell him what?'

'About us.'

'For Christ's sake, no.' His vehemence startled her. She pulled back. She had never heard him speak so roughly. Perhaps she had never heard him speak with *such real feeling*. 'Don't say anything to Tom. Not till Friday, maybe not even then. He'll know when we're gone. Promise me, please, Alice.'

'I'll write a letter resigning from my job but I promise not to say a word to Tom till Friday.'

He pulled her to her feet and kissed her gently. She was warm now, a little sweat on her upper lip. He unwrapped the shawl and began to undo her coat. It seemed to her that he was looking at her tenderly, appreciatively, and hen she was naked with a breathless, barely controllable, aamiration.

She wanted to say to him that he was everything to her, the very beat of her heart, but she thought he would laugh.

'I love you,' she said.

She said it every time they met.

Because the theft of Cecilia's credit card, chargecard and cashpoint card was never reported, Nicholas Mann was able to go on using them with impunity. He knew that he had emptied her current account but this did not stop him drawing a cheque for £500 which, backed by the credit card and the chargecard, he presented to a secondhand car dealer as deposit on a five-year-old Ford Fiesta. The rest of the cost was covered by a hire purchase agreement that Nicholas Mann had entered into quite serenely.

Driving himself back to London, he checked into an hotel in the Edgware Road. He had no more wish to return to his sister than she had to have him back. By now he understood that, for some reason or other, the owner of the handbag had not reported its loss. Sometimes he speculated as to why this should be, but not often. He was in no state to think. He had embarked upon a death wish-fulfilment roller coaster, though he would have said himself that he was happy.

He drank. He bought cocaine from a man in a bar in Noel Street. Most of the time he was on a giddy high. If he had any wish it was that the owner of the things he had stolen had been a man and not a woman so that when the shop assistant made that phone inquiry, checking on the presenter of the credit card in the case of expensive sales, she would not be obliged to say when she had given the number and the cost of the purchase: 'It's a lady.' It meant that he could not dare to buy things that cost more than £100.

Luck remained with him, the gambler's quixotic, inexplicable luck. He even made money on the fruit machines and passed dizzy hours in amusement arcades. He went to the dogs, put £100 on a greyhound that won at odds of seven to one. The cash he took back to his hotel room, guarded it and counted it carefully like a miser. The room was full of things he had bought, not things that he wanted but which he had bought on the credit card for the sake of using it: electric shavers and hair dryers and bottles of cologne, silk scarves and sunglasses, videotapes of TV series, sterling silver cigarette lighters and agate eggs. He even bought a telephone answering machine because he saw one for £79.99. He lounged in an armchair among all this, drinking vodka and watching dirty Italian videos.

The only things he used real money for were taxis and gambling. Two weeks after his spree began he spent much of Wednesday night in the Formosa Casino, where he made a little fortune at blackjack, lost most of it and made himself stop when he was down to £600. Nicholas had a last drink at the bar, a double vodka kir, a concoction of Stolichnaya Imperial, champagne and cassis, his own recent invention.

There were no taxis but he was not far from the hotel. He walked down Castellain Road to the bridge at Warwick Avenue and there, taking the south bank of the Grand Union Canal, began to make his unsteady way along Maida Avenue. When he came to the dark bit this side of the church they were upon him. Three of them had followed him from Formosa Street. They knocked him down and kicked him. They took his wallet, containing something over £600 and all Cecilia's cards.

He groaned, so they knew he was conscious. With no wish to kill him, only to make a safe getaway, they tipped him over the railings. But they had supposed the tow-path wider than it was, a broad walkway, not a mere narrow kerb between embankment and water.

At teatime in Lilac Villa, Cecilia, Jasper and Bienvida watched television. Now that Daphne was with her all the time and there was no six o'clock phone call to be made, Cecilia could watch the early evening news without interruption. She sat on the sofa-bed, restored to its sofa state from nine until nine, with her feet up and a rug over her legs. She wore the cameo brooch Arthur Bleech-Palmer had given her pinned to the collar of her dress. The children were at the table but both on the side from which the screen could clearly be seen. Daphne waited on them all. There was a homemade chocolate sponge with white chocolate icing and toffee ice-cream.

The first item on the news was Romania and then there was something about people who were HIV positive, which Cecilia hoped Daphne would stay out of the room long enough not to see, and then an account of a man's body pulled out of the canal at Little Venice. The man had been called Nicholas Mann, was unemployed and of no fixed address. None of them was much interested even when the newscaster said police were treating the case as murder. They wanted to get to the bit about the Duchess of York's baby, or Bienvida did, in spite of Jasper's sneers.

Cecilia was no longer able to walk the children home. Still, as Daphne said, it was only round the corner and Jasper was accustomed, it appeared, to roving about all over London. Cecilia did not like to ask Daphne to go with them. She managed to accompany them to the door herself, leaning on her stick and with Daphne holding the paralysed arm. Halfway there the thought struck her that it would be nice to give them some spending money each, say a pound coin each, and she asked Daphne, for only the second time since her stroke, if she would fetch her handbag.

Daphne sat her down in the chair just inside the front door and went to look for the bag. She came back empty-handed, saying she could not exactly lay her hands on it, but produced two coins of her own. She helped Cecilia back to the sofa after Jasper and Bienvida had gone and Cecilia had another piece of chocolate sponge with white chocolate icing.

'That white chocolate will be my undoing,' said Cecilia.

'I can't imagine it will hurt you.' In the months to come Daphne often remembered how she had said that.

'It's a beautiful cake. I know you say you can't cook, you're so modest, but you're a much better cook than I am. I wonder why you couldn't find my handbag.'

'I'll have a proper look in a minute.'

'I don't seem to have seen it for ages. Not since before this trouble. I don't know *when* I last saw it. You know the one I mean, don't you? A dark brown leather. If only I could remember what happened before I I was taken ill.'

Daphne could remember. Or, rather, she could remember everything that had happened on that platform, and there had been no handbag. Returning to the scene of it, she saw herself sitting on the grey bucket seat with Cecilia and the doctor bending over them and the people around. Why hadn't she looked for that handbag, at least asked where it was? Unthinkable now that Cecilia, like some young girl of today in jeans and pocketed jacket, would go out without a handbag.

There had been a shopping bag, rather a smart one of

hessian with a red printed border. That was why she had not inquired. She had assumed Cecilia's purse and keys were in the shopping bag. Oh, there had been so much else to think of, the most important thing to get Cecilia home to her own house before they could carry her off to hospital.

She said, 'I'll look for it, Cessie. It must be somewhere.'

If it was lost, which meant stolen, could she possibly deceive Cecilia? Daphne knew there would not only have been money in the handbag but keys and credit cards and even Cecilia's long-unused driving licence. There would have been a chequebook. That brought a wave of fear breaking over her. She went about the house, making a show of looking for the bag. The show must have been made for herself or so that Cecilia downstairs could hear her busy footsteps.

In their long, deep friendship they had not been open with each other. They belonged in a generation which had been conditioned to conceal, to place courtesy above all, not to talk about distasteful things, to put others before oneself, even though this might give rise to resentment. But somewhere between them had been an inner honesty, an unspoken trust, a sense that each could rely upon the other and not be let down. They had acted too on the principle of each putting herself in the other's shoes, or as Cecilia who was the reader put it, being like Mrs Doasyouwouldbedoneby. Daphne, in Cecilia's shoes, would want to know. She would want the credit card company to be told and the bank, new locks fitted to the doors perhaps. She told herself it was no good hanging about, putting off the evil day, and she went down to Cecilia and told her.

The same thing happened to Cecilia as had happened to her. Daphne could tell. A wave washed through her, of shock and panic, but in Cecilia's case it was much stronger and more physical. After all, the lost things were Cecilia's. She leant back on the sofa and closed her eyes. After a while she opened them and said, 'How long is it?'

'I'm afraid it's nearly three weeks.'

'Someone must have taken it while we were on the platform.'

'Oh, surely no one would do that,' Daphne cried. 'Not seeing you so ill. Oh, surely not. People are not as bad as that, are they?'

'Daphne, I know it sounds silly and unlike me, but do you think I could have a drink?'

'Of course you could. I'm sure it won't hurt you. What would you like? Sherry? A little whisky?'

Cecilia said she would have a glass of dry sherry. Daphne had one too. She said she would phone the bank and the credit card companies in the morning and Cecilia said thank you and laid her hand on hers.

Three hours later Daphne was telling the doctor that the shock had brought on Cecilia's second stroke. The doctor thought she was being kind in disagreeing. She was so relieved at not having to find a hospital bed for Cecilia at eleven at night and that this capable old woman would keep her at home and nurse her that she told Daphne rich food and alcohol had brought on Cecilia's vomiting and it was that which had sent up her blood pressure.

Cecilia lay asleep on the sofa-bed which had become a bed again.

Tom had spent hours in the Art Room. This was to make Alice believe he had left for Bristol. He and Axel had eaten a meal together but had drunk nothing. Axel had said it would be unwise to drink. At some time during the evening they had gone across to Five. Axel had packed his backpack with the camera, a torch, a pair of leather gloves, some tools and a bunch of keys.

The contents of the backpack Tom had not actually seen. It stood there, propped up against the side of the bed, a very large khaki-coloured thing on a frame. Tom went to lift it, just to feel the weight because it looked heavy, but he had hardly raised it an inch from the ground when Axel said sharply, 'Don't touch!'

Tom had the rope in his own pack. It was long, far too long for their purpose, Tom thought, but Axel said it was better to be on the safe side. As it was, he had cut half of it off and put the other half in the bicycle shed, up at the end where the roof was still intact. At some point during the evening the sound of music reached them from downstairs. It was Alice playing the violin in her room immediately below them. Tom did not recognize the music, it was very likely the solo part from a Mozart concerto, and it sounded to him infinitely sad and forlorn.

Axel behaved as if he could not hear it. He said, looking at himself in the mirror, '"Mr Verloc, who by a mystic accord of temperament and necessity, had been set apart to be a secret agent all his life."'

'What's that?'

'Conrad.'

The music had stopped before they went down. Someone had turned off the electrolier. The house was still. The streets were not empty but they saw only three people between Cambridge School and the alley that led to the bridge and they were all men on their own, walking home fast.

It was a damp night. A pale moon had a fuzzy look, as if it had been soaked in water. The wooden steps seemed more than usually slippery as they crossed the bridge. A light condensation like dew lay on the grey metal lattice-work. They were on their way to West End Lane to pick up a taxi, it being too late to catch a train. Each carried a backpack, Axel walking with balanced deliberation as if his was very heavy. They looked like students starting out on some trip across Europe, for Axel, for the first time in Tom's experience of him, was not wearing the long dark overcoat but a thick black sweater.

They had a long time to wait. Two taxis came, both without their lights up but only one with a fare. The third had its light on. Axel asked the driver to take them to Oxford Street, anywhere in Oxford Street would do. He closed the glass partition between them and the driver, said to Tom in a low voice, 'It's wiser. We can walk from there.'

Tom looked at Axel and away. His unease strengthened, became something which took hold of him. It was the first time this had been put directly into words, that what they were about to do might get them into trouble, might be against the law and reprehensible. And yet of course he must have known it was. It was not just a lark, an adventure that at worst would merit a reprimand from some London Transport policeman, like busking did.

He said, 'You're only going to take a photograph.'

Axel gave a short laugh. 'Don't think about it.'

He could back out now, there was still time. The money Axel had given him was still untouched and he could return it. Tom, shifting uneasily in his seat, thought it was not the £1,000 or the £9,000 to come that stopped him, but simple fear of Axel's reaction. No, not fear, not quite, more embarrassment, awkwardness, he did not want the man's disgust, his incredulity. How weak I am, thought Tom.

The taxi dropped them a little way west of the Circus. They started walking. Tom asked if it was much further and for answer Axel pointed to his own backpack, which weighed two or three times what Tom's did, so Tom said no more and they plodded down New Oxford Street. Axel led the way along High Holborn and turned right through Little Turnstile into Gate Street and Twyford Place.

It was all new to Tom, who had never been there before. The place was, of course, lit, but not very brightly and it was quite deserted. They entered a street behind a building Axel said was the Soane Museum. It was a mix of late-Victorian houses, now all offices, and small, purpose-built blocks. An alley between the last in the row of these houses and the first block seemed to be where Axel was heading and at the end of this narrow passage he stopped at a solid-looking door, inserted a key into its upper lock and another into its lower. Inside, three feet away, was another door. Another key from Axel's ring unlocked it. They were in a small entrance hall. Tom switched on his torch and Axel switched on his. The torch beam showed him a counter with two phones on it, a small computer terminal on a shelf behind, notices on the wall that it was too dark to read.

'I don't want to use the lift,' said Axel. 'We'll walk up.'

The stairs were steep but quite wide. Tom was very aware that for the first in his life he was on premises he had no right to be on. He was trespassing. There were seventy-two stairs to the top and on the way they passed through three floors. The first landing had a sleek decor, carpet-like tapestry on the walls and tapestry-like carpet on the floor, a melange of blues and blacks. The next floor up, after another fourteen stairs, was a metallic cavern with etched gilt panels grown shabby and tarnished. The name of a publisher Tom had never heard of glimmered from the wall in the light of his torch.

At the top they came out into a hallway that seemed much more utilitarian than any floor they had passed. The floor was not carpeted but tiled. The walls seemed to be painted a dull buff colour. Doors to rooms stood open, it was rather as if they had come into someone's flat, for playing his torch inside one he saw a bed and in another kitchen fitments.

Afterwards Tom was to tell himself he had a sick feeling at this point. A sense of impending disaster laid a cold touch on him. But afterwards he was equally sure he could not have felt this, he could not have foreseen. There had been nothing up till then to warn him. The name of the publishing house meant nothing, struck no chord out of his past, the blue and black carpeting, even the faint smell that pervaded the whole building, a citrus yet chemical smell as of fruit-scented soap, none of that evoked anything.

It was impossible that he had been less than innocent. He must have approached this decisive spot in contented ignorance, even jauntily.

Along the passage they passed the lift. It was the merest chance that made Tom direct his torch beam on to the wall facing the lift doors. The wide circle of light showed him, lettered there in black and chrome, followed by an arrow pointing to the right, the name: Angell, Scherrer and Christianson.

He swung the torch beam down. Axel's own torch beam made a circular pool of light ahead of him. Tom directed light up once more. He nearly cried out that this was Alice's company, this was where she worked. Some realization, although of what he did not then know, stopped him. He felt as if on the brink of an awful chasm. Later on, when he was recalling it and his premonitions, he thought that what had stopped him shouting it out was the sight, ahead of him in the torchlight, of the bunch of keys swinging from Axel's hand.

Mechanically, he went on walking. He went on following Axel. They came to a narrow flight of stairs, at the top of which was a door. There was no need to find a key to it. The key was in the lock. Axel unlocked the door, opened it and stepped out. A rush of damp air came to

308

meet Tom. It felt cold and sharp, striking him backwards, though the night was quite mild. He followed Axel out into the night.

They were on the roof. It was dark but vaguely moonlit, and beyond and below the flat expanses ahead of him the street lights glowed yellow and misty, so that the roofs were like a vast raft floating on a shining sea. Underfoot was tarmac. All kinds of excrescences bulged or protruded out of it, posts and funnels, chimneys and ventilators. Attached to the top of a tank was a television dish, to another an aerial. Axel led the way across the roof, keeping to the centre, away from the edge and the railing that was only high enough to keep a small child from falling over.

Tom had a stunned feeling. It was as if he had entered, down there, a zone that paralysed all emotion. He could think of practical things, he could calculate, but feeling had been turned off. He could calculate that they must be proceeding across the roofs of those Victorian houses of which the solicitors' office building was the last in the block. He was quite used to the darkness now. It was far from absolute darkness and it almost seemed light to him. Ahead and to the left, protruding from another roof, that of a block behind this street, he could see a kind of turret. It was about ten feet in from the edge which on this level and this building was bounded by a low brick wall with a concrete coping. All this his mind registered, perhaps more lucidly than it would normally have done.

Axel vaulted the wall and Tom followed him. All the time he could see Axel ahead of him, a different Axel in these different clothes, thin and tall and carrying the heavy pack. He must have been here before to know the geography of the place. Perhaps he had been many times. *He had keys to Alice's office.* The building they had entered, the building whose stairs they had climbed, belonged to the company for which Alice worked.

Tom repeated this to himself several times. Stopping when Axel stopped and swinging the pack from his back when Axel swung the pack from his, he saw again the place they had passed through, that top floor which he had thought at the time seemed like someone's flat, a private apartment, if not a very luxurious one. He saw the open door and the bed inside. At once, the image changed to Alice sitting on a bed, waiting on a bed. Waiting for Axel.

Axel was looking at him. He was giving him a long, intuitive look. It was light enough to see that. 'What's wrong with you?'

'Nothing.'

'Right, then. Good. We aren't going to sit here all night, admiring the view, I hope.'

Tom thought, I must speak. I must say something, ask, do something, and *now* before we do any more, go any further. Emotion returned as his body, his mind, his inner self, adjusted to shock. He had fixed his eyes on that bunch of keys that Axel, apparently careless of them now he and Tom were in and up here and more than halfway to accomplishment, had dropped on to the flat metal lid of the tank where he was sitting. Axel saw him looking. He did something strange, something Tom thought he would not do to anyone no matter how much hatred he felt, and Axel had no cause to hate him.

The long thin fingers reached for the bunch of keys. He picked them up, tossed them once in the air and caught them, like a boy playing fivestones. His smile widened, he was almost laughing. The look he gave Tom was knowing, it was contemptuous. It told Tom everything. He had no need to ask, he *knew* now, and Axel knew he knew and did not care. For a moment he thought Axel was going to reach across to him and pat his shoulder. He *was* going to, but Tom jumped to his feet, opened the backpack and, taking out the rope, began to unwind it.

'Is it down there you're going?'

Axel nodded. He walked to the turret, the rim of which was about four feet high, and looked down inside it. Tom said, 'Will it be dark?'

'In the shaft it will. Not in the tunnels, not entirely dark. Some of them may be, the small ones. It's all disused down there but it's not abandoned, they inspect it, they patrol it. The point is it's all the ninety-year-old stuff with the old tiles and the old brickwork and the shafts where the stairs used to be and the lifts. Except for the Signals Room — that's modern, that's in use. You could say it's the heart or the brain of the system.'

'And that's what you'll be photographing? Will you use a flash? Won't there be someone on duty? I mean some electrician or signals operator or whatever.'

'You ask too many questions.' Axel was taking a small case of tools from his pack. There was a screwdriver, a hammer and a spanner. 'Yes to the first and I'd use a flash for what I'm doing if it was broad daylight. There won't be anyone on duty. What would they be on duty for? The trains don't go through here till six, remember?'

He had a way of speaking to Tom, which Tom had not really noticed before, though it had surely been there, as if he thought him stupid, but as if that stupidity instead of angering or exasperating him, was only a source of boredom. Tom felt his own anger beginning to rise. But he made an effort to control it and helped Axel bolt the rope end to the metal rod which, apparently without purpose, made a division between this section of the roof and the ten-foot-wide perimeter. One end of the rod was attached to the parapet, the other to the side of a small corrugated iron hut. It felt as solid as rock and as safe as the top parallel bar in a gym.

The two sections of the metal ring were joined and bolted together round the rod and Axel turned the nut

311

hard with his spanner. He took the hammer and struck the nut two hard blows with it to tighten it further. Tom, holding the torch for Axel to see by, thought he might as well not have been there, he was no use, he was superfluous – well, he held the torch.

Axel put his gloves on. He put the tools back in the case and the case into his pack.

'I may need them down there,' he said when he saw Tom watching him.

He fed the rope into the turret mouth. He's really going to go down there, into the dark, not knowing what's there, Tom thought. The grudging admiration he felt was able to co-exist with his anger. Axel was going down there, sixty feet down that shaft, just for the sake of taking a photograph.

Axel swung one leg over, then the other. He got a purchase for his feet on the brick interior and held the rim of the turret with his hands. The rope hung between his arms and between his legs. As he moved something in the pack made a liquid slurping sound. Tom could tell he had done this before or something like it. He was athletic, he was an expert, and he was excited now. There was a light in his eyes, a gleam of exhilaration, and he was suppressing laughter, the laughter of joy. The upturned face was that of a happy man, a man who has just received a piece of good news or promotion or a promise from a lover. Alice's lover, thought Tom. As if to show his coolness and his expertise, Axel adjusted the strap of his backpack first with one hand, then the other.

'See you in – let me see – twenty minutes. Maybe twenty-five. It shouldn't take more.'

Tom leaned over, bent over, and watched him go down. Axel looked up once, unsmiling, a glare of a look, then dropped his head. His hands passed over each other, over and over, down and down, his feet moved down and down against the brick side of the shaft. He dwindled into the dark. Tom withdrew the torch beam and backed away.

He was alone on the roof, lifting his eyes to the sky.

22

It was twenty minutes to three.

Up on the roof it was very quiet. Most of the traffic down there had stopped. Occasionally cars passed along High Holborn, but the sound was remote. Tom fitted the pieces together, Alice's coolness towards him, her occasional affection – confiding in a kind father or brother when the lover is cruel – her inexplicable absences, the yearning look he now recalled seeing in her eyes when they were all out together and she stared at Axel. That first meeting with Axel at the top of the stairs, that *alleged* first meeting. He recalled it now as awkward and staged and he seemed to recreate an electric current passing between them. They had known each other before that, there had been secret meetings, there had been meetings *here*.

He screwed up his face in pain. Until then all his emotion had been involved with Axel. Now he thought of Alice, of Alice herself, and pain passed through his head and through his chest as if claws had seized him. He bent double and rubbed his hands across his chest, stretched his neck and rubbed his head, as if this were physical, as if it was some body blow Axel had struck him. The bed downstairs that he had seen through the half-open door, he knew they had used that bed and knew too that Alice would not have been with Axel as she had been with him, not passive and compliant and smiling, but – Tom found he could not confront the way Alice must have been with Axel. He could not bear the image of Alice naked before Axel. A sound that was half sob, half groan, came from him and he grasped the metal bar, hung on to it, rocking himself back and forward.

The ring-bolt that attached the rope to it caught his eye. He could undo that bolt and let the rope drop down. It would be a fitting revenge on the man who had taken Alice from him and thought so little of him as to bring him here and to *trust* him. Tom looked around for the tools before he remembered Axel had taken them down with him. No doubt Axel had taken them down because he foresaw just such thoughts as these coming into Tom's mind. That would not prevent him from pulling the rope up and leaving Axel without the means of exit from the disused tunnels.

Tom found himself shaking at the thought of it. If there were no London Transport staff down there at present there would be by six. Axel would be discovered, arrested, maybe charged with spying, sent to prison.

"'Mr Someone, who by a mystic accord of temperament and necessity, had been set apart to be a secret agent all his life.'"

He had never been much good at learning by heart, but he could remember that, all of it but the name. It sounded in his head like a prophecy. He stood there in doubt, grasping the rope with both hands, thinking of Axel now, imagining him down there in the dark, with his torch and his camera and flash, by this time approaching the Signals and Communications Room.

Would there be lights on? Were lights always kept on, even in those distant, unused reaches? And how far was it that Axel had to go? Half a mile or only a hundred yards or less? Tom imagined the room that was his destination, seeing it as some vast CD player, panelled with rows and rows of control buttons.

The kind of revenge he contemplated did not appeal. It was not revenge he wanted, or not only revenge. He thought of Alice waiting for the imprisoned Axel. He imagined her talking to *him* about Axel, confiding in him, talking about their love and what they would do when Axel came out. That was certainly how it would be, he knew that. He did not want Axel in the role of martyr.

She is my life, he thought, I can't live without her, she has saved me but I have to go on being saved, I'll need saving all my life. I need to be kept in the safe place she makes for me. Alice, Alice . . . He spoke her name aloud to the night. His anger was delayed but it was there, it was rising. He felt it begin to spread through his veins, the way strong spirits seem to do. There was no room for Axel in this world while he and Alice were in it. He envisaged life without Axel and it appeared like a happy vision, the two of them joyous and innocent again, the serpent driven from the garden. In a double sense they would make music together again, for it seemed that even their music had been corrupted and diminished by Axel's presence. It was not only revenge he wanted but the end of Axel, his abolition, his destruction.

As soon as the thought took form and stood before him, Tom knew what he had to do. But do it how? He looked at his watch, brought it close to his eyes and made out the time: twelve minutes to three. If he was going to do it he must act quickly. Uselessly, he struggled with the ring-bolt again. It was tools he needed and had no means of getting. If not a spanner, the next best would be a weapon.

Tom played the torch beam across the roof. There was nothing, only the pipes and chimney-like projections, ventilators which even at this hour kept up a steady hum, the hut which he guessed was the shelter for a hatch and a ladder going down into whatever building this roof covered. What had he expected? A toolshed for someone employed below to come up to in his lunch hour and do a little useful carpentry?

Axel was a strong, athletic man, very probably a man who had undergone the kind of physical training the SAS are said to be put through, '...set apart to be a secret agent all his life'. The idea that came to Tom, of bending over the mouth of the shaft as he came up, of striking at him, punching his face and attempting to prise open his hands, very likely would not work. Axel would go on climbing up, weathering the rain of blows, and once out would exact his own revenge.

Unless Tom had a weapon. A blunt instrument was what they called it. Or perhaps even a sharp instrument. Then he remembered the kitchen. A fleeting picture had come to him of Axel and Alice, entwined in each other's arms, making their way to that kitchen to pour wine or even, incongruous but perhaps apt, make tea. The kitchen. He saw a heavy pan or a rolling pin. Could he get back down there and up here again in the time? It was nine minutes to three. Axel would be back a minute or so before three.

He went across the roof the way they had come, across the low wall, the raft that sailed on the sea of dim lights, past the television dish and the aerial, the chimneys. The moon had gone, had set or else been swallowed up in cloud. The sky looked red, a dirty dark red, from reflected chemical light. Tom found the door, let himself in and went down the steps. There was a light switch and he put the lights on. What did he care? He wasn't going to waste time with a torch.

He passed the lift with the lettering facing it, the lettered name that had told him, and came to the kitchen, where he switched on the light. Last time he had seen it he had not known, he had been secure in Alice's love. The premonition had come immediately afterwards. A terrible urge came over Tom to break things, to tear the place apart, overturn the table, pick up the big china bowl from that shelf and smash it to the floor. He breathed deeply, briefly clenched his fists.

317

The kitchen was very small. He had been stupid imagining cooking equipment, fire-irons. There were just three drawers beneath the counter, above cupboards. The first one was empty, the second full of paper sheets with printing on and diagrams that looked like instructions for using equipment, the third held cutlery. There was nothing very suitable but time was running out. Tom hesitated, then took out a long serrated knife.

At the door to the roof he looked at the time again: four minutes to three. He put out the lights behind him and ran across the roof, vaulted the low wall. It would have been no surprise to see Axel there waiting for him, but Axel was not there. His eyes went to the ring-bolt. The rope hung inert. When Axel began to climb there would be a twitch on the rope.

Time had never passed so slowly. Tom went to the turret, the mouth of the well, and looked down. He switched on his torch and thrust it as deep as he could into the shaft. The light penetrated a long way down but after a short distance showed nothing, became a bleary yellowish fog. The brickwork which, well-like, should have been covered with lichen or even ferns, was smooth, brown, darkly stained. Tom withdrew the beam, lifted his face to the sky. It had become a slightly ruffled, smoky canopy, the dirty red of blood-soaked cloth.

It occurred to him then that Axel might not come up. He might find another way out, an unlocked door, a negotiable shaft, a usable stairway. Tom knew Axel would have no compunction about leaving him up here. The thought was intolerable, the idea of Axel's escape, of going home and finding the smiling Axel there. Tom was for the first time aware, in memory, of the bright blueness of Axel's eyes. As he imagined himself baulked of retribution, he saw the rope twitch.

He not only saw it twitch but heard the metallic clatter

the ring made as a weight on the rope pulled it against the bar. Tom grasped the saw. The point of it looked sharp, efficient enough to stab at Axel as he began to surface.

But there was a better way. Tom gasped because he had not thought of it before, because thinking of it now might be too late. He took hold of the rope in his left hand, his weak hand. It was not too late. Doing it now might even be *too early*. He must time it right, wait for Axel to reach as high as the lowest point the beam of his torch had reached.

Tom began to saw.

He paused and looked over the edge, shining the torch down. The rope twitched and pulled, slackened, twitched, pulled, as down there, silent, unseen, Axel ascended. Would he speak? Tom hoped that he would speak so that he could answer. It would be good to answer Axel's hail with a cry of what he was doing, what fate he had in store for the man on the end of the rope. He was halfway through the rope, it was hard going with the now-blunted saw edge, and the thought came to him that the knife might break or buckle on the toughness of it.

The rope twitched and pulled, slackened, twitched, pulled. Then something happened very fast. The last threads, at least a third of the rope's thickness, pulled, strained, unravelled with a creaking sound and snapped. Before the last strand gave, Tom managed to grasp the rope end in both hands and hang on. Axel's weight dragged him to the turret and the well mouth. It would have pulled him over but for the protective wall.

Tom held on in this desperate tug-of-war. His bad hand burned. He pushed his toes against the wall, leaned back, wishing he need not lean back, wanting to look over, see Axel and then, when they were face to face, let go.

It was impossible unless he wanted to go over too. Both hands were burning, his heart pounding. His body had become a great throbbing pulse. He opened his mouth, let out a roar which seemed to echo and reverberate off the sky and, with this sound, this expression of hatred and rage, let go of the rope and threw up his hands.

He did not see the tail of it go over. He had shut his eyes. The cry Axel made was louder than his own. It was the most terrible sound Tom had ever heard and something he thought he would remember all his life, a scream of terror and despair, which did not stop but seemed infinitely prolonged, curling and throbbing up the shaft, reverberating on many desperate notes, at last dying away on a thin wail of anguish.

Tom had passed his arms round himself, was clutching his body as if to prevent its disintegration, its falling apart. He rocked himself from side to side, held his breath, waiting for the sound of the man on the end of the severed rope striking the ground. He heard nothing, it was too far down. But he waited, finally opening his eyes long after this impact must have taken place.

A profound silence succeeded Axel's scream. Even the distant traffic and the whispering, humming ventilators seemed hushed.

For quite a long time after it was all over Tom sat on the tank, bent over, with his head in his hands. He was shaking and his heart was behaving strangely. At one point he thought his heart had actually stopped but then it began again with a lurch he felt like a punch in the ribs.

The shaking took a long while to stop. He knew he was recovering when he began to feel cold. It was a mild night, very mild for the time of year, but the cold had reached him now, slipping on to his skin through his clothes. As soon as he got up, came back to life really, stood and looked about him, his eyes fell on the ring-bolt.

He began to think. The sight of the ring-bolt made him

start thinking, he had to. It was almost painful. He pressed his fingers against his temples, as if rubbing at his brain. *He must think.*

Some time, though possibly not for a day or two, Axel's body would be found and beside it the backpack containing the smashed camera and also the rope. The assumption might be made that Axel had the rope for some quite other purpose and had entered the tunnels by one of the doors, with the help perhaps of an accomplice, but they would certainly suspect he had come down the shaft and investigators would soon be up here.

Tom thought, I have done murder, I have killed someone, I am a murderer. It made him feel dizzy. What he had done seemed to set him apart, and now the first shock was past, it exhilarated him. The weak do not do what he had done. It seemed to show him the unwisdom of tampering with people like himself, of the folly of coming between such a one as himself and the woman he loved. But even as this passed through his mind Alice's image came before him and quelled this self-congratulation. Alice, he said aloud, Alice. He shut his eyes on the picture, shook it away, looked at the ring-bolt.

If there had been a way of undoing the nut he would have done it rather than saw through the rope. But there had been no means of doing this. On the other hand, he had not searched, he had not had time. Two things appeared to Tom highly significant. If the ring-bolt was found they would know Axel had come down on the rope and that an accomplice had cut the rope. They had only to find out where Axel had lived and whom he knew, which they rapidly would, and then he, Tom, would be found. Alice would know and that seemed to him the worst thing. Without the ring-bolt and the frayed rope-end protruding from it they might very likely assume, when they found the body and Axel's possessions around him, that their owner had brought the rope with him for some other purpose.

He returned to the door and the stairs. This time he was afraid to turn lights on. He had killed a man and the world was changed. Already the world was hunting him. Back in the kitchen he searched the drawers and the cupboards underneath them but failed to find a spanner. No one, after all, keeps spanners in kitchens.

Nor in bedrooms. Tom could not have brought himself to go into that bedroom. He went down a flight of stairs by torchlight and on the floor below found a suite of offices. It was in one of these, no doubt, that Alice worked. The scent of citrus was strongest here. On the wall facing the lift doors Angell, Scherrer and Christianson was lettered once again. He searched the offices one after the other. There was not going to be a spanner. If he found one he was convinced it would not be an adjustable spanner and it would be the wrong size.

The last door opened on to a pair of lavatory cubicles, two wallbasins and a hand-dryer. Tablets of orange-coloured soap lay on the side of each basin and he knew it must be from here that the smell emanated. On top of the dryer, left behind perhaps by a plumber, lay a hammer. Tom put the light on in there. It was windowless and in the middle of the building. The fan that started up automatically made him jump, it roared so loudly.

The light revealed no more tools. Tom took the hammer and went back. A lot of time had passed, he could not imagine what he had done with the time, so much of it flashing away while the minutes during which he had waited for a twitch on the rope had lingered, infinitely drawn out. His watch showed him a quarter past four.

Once, years ago, he had seen his father loosen a nut with a hammer. There was a knack to the way you struck one of the facets of the hexagon. Axel had *tightened* the nut that

322

way. Tom balanced his torch on the wall of the turret, its beam directed on the ring-bolt, and began to attack the nut. Nothing happened. He thought he could have got a better purchase, something to hold on to, if the rope had still been there, but if the rope had still been there he would not have been doing this.

He took a rest, then tried again. It was while he was striking ineffectually at the nut that the notion came to him that Axel might not be dead. Axel might only be terribly injured. True, it was sixty feet down, but Tom thought he had heard of, read of in newspapers, people falling far greater distances than that and surviving. That dreadful cry meant nothing. *He could only have cried out while he was still alive.* The idea of Axel being still alive was monstrous to Tom, unthinkable. Unthinkable, but *possible.* It was all the more reason for getting this ring-bolt off. He imagined the terribly injured Axel coming out of a coma in hospital and telling people about the man who had been with him, telling them to go and look on the roof.

Time was still scurrying past. Time had changed its nature since his act of cutting the rope, for during the minutes or probably only seconds he had waited for Axel to begin his climb, eons had passed. But now, as in the hymn they had sung at school, a thousand ages were flashing by like an evening gone. He saw that it was now a little after five o'clock.

The first tube trains would begin running through Holborn around six. It might be that the first thing the staff responsible for this would do, was enter the disused tunnels and begin a morning inspection. Perhaps, on the other hand, this only happened every other day or twice a week, say, and this morning was not an inspection morning. There would be time for him to go down into the street, hang about somehow till nine and when the first shops opened buy a spanner. But by then, or soon after, the

Angell, Scherrer and Christianson people would be coming into the building, *Alice would be coming into the building.*

The roof would be closed to him until the following night. Tom thought about it. He knew that once out of here he would be afraid to come back, at no matter what hour of day or night. Nor could he, at present, go home. Alice thought he was in Bristol. Tom realized that he still had a little while, he had an hour, for it was unthinkable that anyone could discover Axel's body before, at the earliest, 6.30.

Like it or not he must search the whole building for a spanner: go back down there, not stop because he had found a plumber's hammer in a cloakroom, but search cupboards, see if there was a basement or even a cellar and search that. Go down to the publishers' offices and search them, go down to the blue- and black-lined boxes and search.

He got up and started across the roof. Passing the hut to which the rod was attached, he examined the place where the rod was fastened to the corner of this small solid building. There was no help there, no possibility of detaching it. But suppose he were to try entering the building under this roof? Better the devil you don't know than the devil you do, thought Tom. For all he knew the rooms immediately below him were full of tools, they might even be the storerooms of some motor maintenance company or engineering firm.

He tried the door to the hut. It was not locked. As he had supposed, a trapdoor filled most of the floor inside. He pulled on the handle but the trapdoor was bolted on the inside. So much for exploring the motor mechanic's paradise he had envisaged below. Tom looked round the inside of the hut. Shelves filled two walls on which stood cans blackened with oil and grime, other cans that had recently contained coke, a triangular plastic pack made for holding sandwiches, a glass jar full of nails and an adjustable spanner.

If it had been a laughing matter, Tom would have laughed. He had searched the building once, might have searched again in vain, had planned a raid on another unknown private building, while all the time a spanner was under his nose. He reached for it rather gingerly, as if its presence here were too good to be true, as if it might vanish at his touch. His hand closed round it and felt its cold, solid reality. It had been carefully maintained and there was even a dribble of oil still on it.

In less than a minute he had the ring-bolt off. Although it was light enough up here to use the spanner, see his way about, find things, although dawn was coming, it was still too dark to read the time. Tom switched on his torch, noticing that the light was growing feeble, the battery was running out. His watch showed him twenty-five to six.

He was still unsure what to do until Alice had left the house. Remove himself, certainly, from these environs as soon as he could, get into the first tube train that came, go somewhere, anywhere. He switched off the torch, conserving it for later, for passing through the building. The ring-bolt, the serrated knife and the hammer he put into his backpack, he wiped the spanner and replaced it on the shelf inside the hut and, as an afterthought, wiped with the welt of his sweater the metal rod to which the ring-bolt had been fastened.

Having checked he had left nothing behind, Tom made his way across the roofs between dish and aerials and ventilators to the door. The air seemed colder and a little breeze had got up. He closed the door behind him, stood for a moment at the top of the stairs in the pitch-dark, then switched on the torch. The light it gave was now very dim. He saw 5.45 and did not look at his watch again.

His first call was the kitchen where he replaced the knife

325

in the drawer, having wiped its handle. By the pale gleam
of the torch he found the head of the stairs, went down
and along the passage to the little orange-scented room
where the lavatories and washbasins were. There he
switched off the torch and put the light on. It was safe to
do that, but even so the roar of the fan starting up once
more made him jump. He wiped the hammer and holding it with his jacket sleeve between it and his hand, laid it
carefully on top of the hand-dryer. It made a small
metallic click. Tom found that all sound he did not directly make himself alarmed him. He switched off the
light but the sound of the fan continued. A few minutes
must pass before it died away. He began walking back
along the passage to the stairs and as he came to them,
as he set his foot on the first stair down, two things
happened.

The torch went out and everything beneath him blew
up in a tremendous roar.

The sound was enormous, enduring, broken as thunder
is broken. The building rocked and the stair under his
feet shifted. Waves of noise rose up in great crashing
breakers beneath him. At the same time it was as if
warehousefuls of furniture were being hurtled from the
roofs of towers and cannon were expelling iron balls
across infinite battlefields and avalanches tumbling rocks
into the depths of mountain passes. He clung on to the
banister while the explosion roared in his ears, burst and
reverberated, throbbed and echoed, coughed, rumbled,
gave to the house a final push and slid into a series of
tremors.

The tremors grumbled and whimpered. It was as if the
place was shivering with fear of what it had undergone.
Tom stood on the stairs, realizing he was still alive, he was
still *there*. He trembled as the building trembled. Having
not breathed as it seemed to him for the endurance of the

explosion, he now breathed quickly and shallowly as it, adjusting itself, began to breathe again.

He took a step down, then another, blind in the absolute dark.

23

One night, when Arsenal were playing at home, a bomb went off in a tube train car on the Piccadilly Line.

The bomb had been taped to the underside of seats. It exploded at nine o'clock at Wood Green where the train terminated, blowing out the sides of the car but not utterly destroying it.

The car had been quite empty. What the bomber had forgotten was that most people using the line would get out at Arsenal for the football, as they did.

That was in 1976. A short while before, a man got into a train at West Ham and as he did so the duffle bag on his shoulders began to smoke. No one but the bomber was hurt and he was shot while escaping.

All things considered, there have been remarkably few bombs in the London Underground.

Jasper, legitimately at home because his Easter holiday had begun, was beginning to recover from his traumatic experience. He had spent the previous evening with Jed, first collecting from the depot in Barnet where they were 'processed' the day-old chicks with which Abelard's diet was varied, then feeding them to the semi-somnolent and now rather fat hawk. Jasper found himself fascinated by these scrawny, yellow, miserable corpses, born to be fodder. They were very different from the fluffy golden Easter emblems that had currently appeared in the shops. One day, he thought, he might come to understand the adult world in which both kinds of chick existed, one to be adored and cooed over, the other swiftly slaughtered – how? – and mashed up into bird and animal-feed. He did not understand it yet.

That Abelard had his permanent home in Upper Six Jasper had not fully realized till now. Of course he was aware that the screaming had stopped, but had supposed only that the hawk had grown out of it. People often told him he would grow out of things, some of them the things he best liked about himself. The removal of Abelard meant the bicycle shed would now be empty. Jasper had cast wistful eyes on this shed from the moment of his arrival at the Headmaster's Flat, but Abelard had already been in residence.

He saw it as a summer retreat. There were other possibilities not yet gone into. It might smell revoltingly of hawk and have to be cleaned, an operation in which he was not well-versed. In the morning, after Tina had gone round to Lilac Villa with Bienvida, having waited for their departure with that habit of secrecy he had got into even when there was no need for it, Jasper went out to investigate the shed. He ran, ducking his head, because it was pouring with rain.

It was larger inside than he had thought. Someone, perhaps Jed himself, had made an attempt to mend the roof. The smell of hawk was there but not strong and not at all unpleasant. It looked as if the place had been swept. There were various objects of interest on some shelves at the back, old suitcases, a pair of very large lace-up walking boots, something that might be a tent, and, of immediate appeal, a coil of rope.

Feeling very pleased, Jasper uncoiled the rope and was gratified to find it much longer than he had thought at first. It was very long. It would do.

Dawn had come.

As soon as he was out in the street Tom had realized he should get himself as far from there as soon as possible and as fast as possible. Something had happened nearby, in one of these streets perhaps, or up in Holborn. He knew by then it had not been an earthquake, it had been a bomb.

The explosion had seemed to come from the depths of the building he was in, but this was deceptive. There was no sign anywhere of damage, of debris. The street was silent, empty. He made his way back into Kingsway, walking quickly but not running. Cars were parked down here and cars were moving, not many yet but enough to show the city waking into life. The only person he passed was a ragged man carrying an empty bottle. Tom looked back and saw him stuffing the bottle into a wastebin.

There should have been sirens by now, police cars coming and perhaps an ambulance. But coming where? He came to Holborn Underground station but it was closed. The time was twenty past six and it was still closed. Rain had begun to fall. It was no more than a thick mist, a soft grey drizzle. Tom thought of what Axel had said about taking taxis; he shuddered when he thought of Axel.

He would be very conspicuous walking along High Holborn with his backpack at this hour. But if a policeman stopped him what would he find? Only the ring-bolt and a torch. Tom dropped the ring-bolt into a bin attached to a lamp standard. Now he only had the torch, an entirely innocuous thing to be carrying. The rain, though fine, began to soak through his clothes and drip from his hair.

Chancery Lane station was open. A train going to Ealing Broadway came in and Tom got on. Only one other passenger was in the car. As the train approached Holborn a voice on the passenger address system announced that it would not be stopping there. The reason given was 'signalling problems'.

Tom felt stunned. He could not think, he was trembling. That word 'signalling' had done it. It was the Signals and Communications Room that Axel had been going to photograph, or *said* he had been going to photograph, somewhere down here in the old labyrinth of tunnels near Holborn. Tom pushed his fingers through his wet hair. His cold wet fingertips he pressed against his forehead, which for some reason had become burning hot. He did not want to think, he dared not.

Instead of getting out of the Jubilee Line train he had changed on to at Bond Street, at his usual stop, Tom went on to Kilburn. The idea of going home was horrible. He rang Peter's bell but there was no answer, so, without thinking, avoiding all thinking, trying instead to make music in his head and hear that, he trudged up to the hospice where Peter still sometimes worked nights.

He was there behind the desk, perhaps only temporarily alone, listening to a radio that played very softly.

'What's wrong? You look awful.'

That was quite something from Peter, whose death's head stared out from its thin parched covering. Seeing him, his perpetually weary look, made Tom realize how tired he was, how exhausted to dropping point.

'Can I stay here for a bit, Pete? Can I sit somewhere?'

Peter asked no questions. He was one of whom too many questions had been asked and he did as he would be done by.

'Sure, you can go in the TV room. There won't be anyone in there for hours.'

He told Tom where it was. The room smelt almost intolerably of stale cigarette smoke. Some of the residents smoked heavily, fifty or sixty a day, they were past being harmed by it. Tom sank into one of the armchairs. Then he shifted on to the settee and rolled on to his face, his head in his arms.

After a while Peter came in, walking slowly, the way he did now, and with his head bowed.

'All right?'

Tom said he was.

'I go off at eight but there's still an hour to go. You can stay on anyway. I've just heard the news. Someone put a bomb in the tube. It was timed to go off at six this morning when the first trains start.'

'Was anyone – was anyone – hurt?' Tom whispered. 'Was anyone killed?'

'They're not sure. It's a bit of a mess down there.'

Alice went to the Art Room and to Five, looking for Axel. It was early still and she was not worried. He was unpredictable, he would always be, and she must not expect otherwise. She could not tell whether his bed had been slept in, for he never made it.

She looked out of the window at the river of train tracks and saw a silver train, scored all over with black and red graffiti, come up from Finchley Road, and stop in the station. Axel might be on it. Tom might be on it, but hardly yet. She did not believe that story about Bristol, though not caring whether it was true or not. Whatever he was doing, he was not seeing another woman. Very likely his absence was something to do with her, some clumsy surprise he was creating, some consolation, some gateway he was opening for her into a world of compromise and second best.

Rain was falling steadily. Water lay in pools on the platform. From the Art Room window she could see people with umbrellas up. Cars moved sluggishly through puddles. Alice went back to the Headmaster's Study and wrote a note to Tom. It was as brief as the one she had written to her husband. She read it and tore it up. The superstition about tempting providence made her do this. If she had a note prepared and waiting for Tom, Axel would not come or, if he came, have changed his mind. If she was not ready for him, still had things to do, he would come soon, impatient for them to be off.

The morning passed with infinite slowness. The phone rang at lunchtime, and, thinking it would be Axel, she went down to answer it. It was her mother.

'Have you heard the news?'

'What news?' Alice said.

'The IRA have tried to blow up the Underground. Well, they haven't said it's them but it must be. Don't you ever listen to the radio?'

'Not often.'

'The bomber blew himself up. That's one thing to be thankful for, he won't do that again. He's in bits. They didn't put it like that, though he must be. They said he can't be identified. Mind you, he didn't do all that much damage. He thought the bomb was bigger than it was, you know, would do more than it did.'

'You didn't phone to tell me about a bomb in the tube, did you?'

'I have to have a reason, do I, for speaking to my own daughter? The fact is I thought you'd like to know Mike has got a girlfriend. She's twenty-five. She's a computer programmer and she lives somewhere in west London. The really good thing is she absolutely adores Catherine. I think it's nice he didn't get anyone until the possibility of his divorce was well in sight. I mean, he'll only have a year and three months to wait, won't he?'

She heard someone come into the house at about four. She listened behind the door of the Headmaster's Study and heard a furious wiping of wet shoes on the doormat. The door open an inch, she watched Tom come up the stairs. He did not look in her direction, perhaps the crack between door and frame was not visible, but went straight into Four.

A little later, footsteps could be discerned on the top floor. Axel was back. She thought that only for a moment.

The footsteps were at the other side of the building, near the Science Lab. It was only the children playing.

The rain had stopped. The sky was a great dome lined with concrete. It was the colour of grainy stone and looked as hard. She had never before lived in a place from which you could see people approaching at such a distance. If someone came by tube and took the bridge, you would see them on the top and coming down the wooden stairs five minutes before they got here. Axel had not told her where he was going, she had no idea where he might be. She only knew he must be coming back because his things were still here.

Or she thought they were still here. They had still been here at eight this morning. The awful thought came to her that they might be gone, he might have come back for them very quietly, stealthily, while she was in the Headmaster's Study after her mother's phone call. Anxious as she had been, taut with fear, she had nevertheless fallen asleep on the bed for a few minutes. The night before she had hardly slept. Suppose Axel had come while she was asleep, had come, had collected his things, and crept away?

She went upstairs. The children had gone and there was a smell of cigarette smoke. She opened the door of Five. It was exactly as it had been that morning. The unmade bed, the tumbled bedclothes, recalled to her the many hours she had spent lying there, waiting for Axel. She lay down on it now, realizing with something like a feeling of comfort, that this was the only place for her to be, the only place to wait. She told herself she must have more faith. He had invited her to go with him, she must cling to that.

When she woke it was dark. She got up and looked out of the window. A silver-segmented worm of a train was running down from West Hampstead to Finchley Road. Three people, all women, were crossing the bridge, three

334

black silhouettes between the Lego struts. She pulled down the blind. The room was just as it had been, the two cases open on the floor, the cameras on the table, *Thus Spake Zarathustra* by the bed. She looked at the place he had reached, only a few pages into the book, and read: *I teach you the Superman. Man is a thing to be surpassed.*

It was hours since she had eaten or drunk anything. She began to go down and stopped on the fourth stair when she saw Tom waiting for her at the bottom.

'He won't come back.'

She did not have to ask whom he meant. It was plain. Everything was plain and clear in his wounded face.

'Why has he left his things then?'

Slyness changed his expression. He hesitated, but only for a moment. 'He doesn't need them where he's gone. They'll be safe here for a year.'

'I don't believe you.'

'Come in here.'

He opened the door of Four and, when she tentatively approached, took her by the arm and pulled her inside. She stood rubbing her arm where he had hurt her. There was a bottle of wine on the table, cheap red wine from which about half had already been drunk. She knew what was coming, or had some idea, and she filled the glass he had already drunk from and drank it down.

'I know about you and him,' Tom said. 'He doesn't care for you, not a bit, not the way I did. He told me to tell you he's gone, he's gone – ' she noticed the tiny hesitation while he improvised ' – abroad. You won't see him again.' He watched her, looking for signs which did not appear. She was quite still and impassive. 'When I found out,' he said, 'I thought it would be all right after he'd gone, but it's not. It's all over. *You're* all over.' He turned his head a little, not looking at her. 'You're all over for me, loving you. I don't care any more, it's spoilt.'

335

He spoke like a child. He sounded younger than Jasper.

'I don't want to see you again.'

'That's all right,' she said. 'I don't want to see you.'

'You haven't a chance with him, I just want you to know that.'

She said again, 'I don't believe you,' and she did not. Axel would not have confided these things in Tom. It was a ploy to punish her for her infidelity. She suddenly saw how absurd she was being, assuming the worst because Axel had not yet returned from wherever he had been. He would come tomorrow – only she had to get through till tomorrow.

The risk that he would not let her out of the room had to be taken. He had that look on his face it wore when he was about to break something. She felt dazed. The wine she had drunk on an empty stomach had gone straight to her head. She opened the door under his staring eyes, walked out, closed it behind her. He did nothing.

The empty feeling which came as she was halfway to the kitchen was unconnected with hunger or the wine. It was a draining of the spirit. Everything seemed to be falling away, every prop, hope, comfort, and what would remain was something very small and naked and vulnerable. There would be Axel. She held on to that. In the fridge she found some salami, some tomatoes, in a biscuit tin a newly opened pack of crispbread. Her hunger had gone but she ate some of the crispbread dry and a tomato with it.

Afterwards, she was half afraid to go up again in case Tom waylaid her, did her some violence. Perhaps from breaking plates it was only one more step to breaking people. She went past his door very quietly, holding her breath. In Five she thought that the next thing to happen would be that he would come up here. She turned the key in the lock, fell on her knees and began searching Axel's luggage.

In the first case, under his clothes, T-shirts, socks, briefs, was a photograph of a girl in a frame. It was a studio portrait and the frame was silver, badly tarnished. The girl looked like the girl in the picture on the wall. The photograph was in black and white, so you could not see if her hair was red or dark. The long white neck was swan-like, the expression in the large eyes apprehensive. In one corner in a bold hand was written: *To Axel with all my love, Alice.*

The blood came rushing up into Alice's face. They shared a name, she and this girl. She remembered things, how when they first met he had lingered over her name. Pressing cold hands to her hot face, she thought of this beautiful girl, that he might be with her now. She went on searching, feverishly now. Inside a box labelled *Diazonium Supports, Instant Access Systems* she found bundles of letters. Alice, though sick and gasping with jealousy, did not think anything had happened to warrant her reading Axel's letters. If he has not come back by tomorrow I will read them, she thought. Under the letters was a colour print torn from a magazine. It was a reproduction of a painting, though not the one up on the wall. A line of print under it said: Edward Burne-Jones, *The Beguiling of Merlin* (model: Mary Zambaco).

The girl in the painting was looking down on a recumbent man in black robes. She was inordinately tall with disproportionately long legs, long hands and a very small head. A semi-transparent gown clung to her body. Snakes writhed through her hair. Alice found this picture very disturbing; she turned it face-downwards, put the photograph frame on top of it and closed the lid of the case. She found she was breathing shallowly, as if she had had a shock.

There was nothing but books in the second case, and not many of those. Or so she thought at first. The book she opened was a volume of Skrebenski portraits, having had a flash of certainty that she would find the girl inside. In a way she was there but not printed on a page. A photograph lay between the endpapers.

It was of Axel and the girl together, a clean-shaven Axel a few years younger. They were in a garden where there was topiary and stonework, and they leant against a stone balustrade with cypresses behind. Alice gasped because they were so much alike, they had the same pale oval faces, large dark cautious eyes, red mouths, high foreheads. Both were tall and thin, the girl only a few inches shorter than Axel. On her hand, that rested on Axel's shoulder, was the ring he now wore. Alice turned the photograph over, though by now she hardly needed to read what was written on the reverse: *The twins in the garden at Temple Stephen.* The hand which had written those words had been elderly and shaky, a parent's or, more likely, grand-parent's.

So she was only his sister. The relief of it was like a glass of water to someone feverish with thirst. She was liberated from jealousy and felt at once light and almost carefree. Might the dress also be his sister's? She opened the cupboard and looked at it, gleaming there in the dark recesses. Perhaps he had bought it as a present for this girl. Alice found she did not mind how much Axel loved his sister, his sister Alice.

This time she investigated the rest of the cupboard. The dark sweater was gone, he must be wearing it. In its place, pushed along to the extreme lefthand side of the rail, was his long black overcoat with the long black scarf draped over it. Under the hem of it, on the floor of the cupboard in the far corner, was another large, square package, like the one inside the suitcase but contained inside a bag of clear plastic.

Back in her Bluebeard's wife role, but curious now

338

rather than jealous and fearful of what she might find, Alice scrutinized this package. She lifted it out of the plastic bag, loosened one corner of the brown paper, then the seam along the top, managing to unwrap it without tearing the paper. Inside was nothing but a cardboard box, labelled *Magnesium Flash, highly flammable, handle with care.* It was only another container for a substance used in photography, the contents long used up and the box now a repository for more letters.

This was the first object in the room that she had actually interfered with. Everything in the cases she had taken care to replace exactly as they were. She was sure Axel would know someone had touched the stuff in the cupboard. She began searching the room, opening drawers. Inside one she found a roll of Sellotape. She re-packed the box and taped it, making a package precisely as it had been before, and replaced it in the plastic bag.

For the first time she was aware of a strong smell of petrol in the room. She could not tell if it was new or had always been there. It seemed to reach through her mouth and nostrils to bring pain to her head, and made the temptation to stay all night in there less insistent.

He would be back during the night. She went downstairs to the Headmaster's Study, took off her clothes and got into bed. She could see her violin in its case and she squeezed her eyes tight shut. When the bed lamp was off she opened her eyes into the dark and the violin had disappeared. The sight of it now always made her wince, made her feel bruised. Music was to be amputated from her life and Axel would have to replace it.

It was not yet ten and she was sure she would not sleep but she did not know what else to do. There was silence from the room next door, as if Tom had gone out. Lying there in the dark, listening to the trains passing, resolving at any moment to get up, put her coat on and go down to ask Tina if she had any sleeping pills, she fell into a profound, heavy sleep.

Cecilia slept most of the time. The doctor said it was the best thing for her, then that she would try to get her a hospital bed, it was too much for Daphne. The children no longer came. *That* was too much for Cecilia.

She still liked watching the news, propped up on pillows, her dead hand in Daphne's hand. Together they looked at the film of subterranean caverns, pitted and pock-marked by blast, a room full of control panels not too badly damaged. There were stains on the cavern floors that looked as if they might have been made by flying blood, but Daphne said it was only oil.

Repairs were under way and trains would be running normally through Holborn by tomorrow. The bomber had not been identified. The newscaster gave an impression of caginess and caution when he talked about it. The way he spoke made them not want to know more. Another bit of film came on and this time Cecilia said, in her thick mumble that only Daphne could interpret, that some of the stuff on the floor looked like *hair*.

'Just fibres,' said Daphne. 'Like rope, you know, or coconut matting.'

Neither could imagine why there should be coconut matting in the Underground.

The IRA had said they did *not* do it.

'They've never done that before, have they?' Cecilia asked.

'I don't think so, but they may have done; I'm not an inveterate news-watcher like you, Cessie.'

'You know I shall have to go into hospital when they find me a bed, don't you?'

Daphne said if they did it would be over her dead body.

★

Alice slept all night. Just before she woke up – or she thought it was just before she woke up – she dreamed that Axel had come back and broken her violin. He snapped the bow across his knees and destroyed the instrument with a hammer. She watched without trying to stop him.

This dream was succeeded by a series of half-comprehended impressions, some known to be real, others in the area of dream or fantasy, as she dipped again into sleep and again surfaced. Footsteps moved about overhead, then ceased, sounded as if someone were dancing, then became normal footfalls. She awoke to silence, then to the sound of a train running past, and wondered if all of it had been unreal.

It took a few moments before she understood the footsteps meant Axel was back.

Had she heard them a minute ago or an hour ago or during the darkness of the night? She listened, heard nothing now. If this had been Mike or Tom, she would have waited for them to come to her. With Axel she could not wait, except to make herself presentable. She was not jealous of his sister, but his sister had been beautiful, comparisons must be made. She combed her hair, washed her face and, staring at herself in the glass, thought how worn she looked for twenty-four, how tired.

It was quite late, after ten. She went upstairs, confident she would find him stretched out on the bed. She was so sure that she knocked on the door. After a while she opened it, surprised that she could, that it was not locked.

He had been back. The cases were gone. His cameras were gone. She put her hand over her mouth to stop herself crying out. The cupboard doors were open and the contents gone, the white dress gone.

There must be a note, there must be something for her. She looked round the bare empty room, at the open cupboard, the unmade bed, the pale, blank sky outside the window, the walls. Mary Zambaco gazed back at her, with that fey, mysterious stare.

Axel was not the kind to write notes, farewell or explanatory letters. Somehow she knew this, without evidence for it. She thought, he came here to do something, something to do with his sister, and he has done it, accomplished it, whatever it was, and gone. It had nothing to do with me, I was incidental, a step along the path perhaps, part of a means to an end. That was all.

She closed the door and began to go downstairs. She was experiencing something very frightening, and experiencing it for the first time in her life. Time had stopped and there was nothing ahead of her. Medieval people believed that you could reach the end of the world, which was a cliff edge. If you took another step you fell off into space, into chaos. It was not quite like that that she felt, for a falling off, a plunge into chaos, would be welcome. Rather, she was unable to do anything because there was nothing to do, nothing ahead, even to sit alone with her thoughts was impossible, for she had no thoughts. The feeling extended to physical things, paralysing her, so that walking down these stairs was like wading through mud, a hard task, to be thought out and concentrated on; putting her hands up to her head was like lifting weights.

Tom had gone and her music and now Axel was gone. The only possession she had ever had which was truly hers, her baby, she had left. But when she thought of that, shutters in her mind closed, slid across each other, blanked and cut off the images. A blankness took over and the screen was wiped clean.

The phone rang. Not anticipating Axel, not anticipating anyone, she lifted the receiver. A woman. Alice heard the woman's voice bleating away, asking questions, uttering exclamatory remarks, had reached the point of hearing it asking why she didn't speak, before she realized it was her mother.

She said, 'I'm sorry,' and then, 'I'm still here.'

'It's just that I thought you'd like to know Shelley has moved in with Mike. It seemed the best thing, so now they can have Catherine back from Julia.'

It took her a moment to adjust to these names, to understand who these people were. She heard her mother extolling this Shelley's virtues, what a good housewife she was, a *cordon bleu* cook, and with some kind of nursery nursing diploma. Catherine *adored* her. Had her mother told Alice Catherine was walking now?

Alice said in a voice that sounded like someone else's, like the voice of a man with a cold, 'You owe me £1,000.'

'What? What did you say?'

'You bet me £1,000 I'd never get into any orchestra. Well, I never shall now. That's all. It's over.'

Her mother gave a little dry laugh. 'You mean you owe *me*. What's the matter with you? I was going to give you that money when you succeeded, not when you failed, thank you very much.'

Alice put the receiver down gently. The phone rang again almost at once. She did not think there was anyone else in the house, except perhaps the hawk on its own. Tom had gone out to play. At another time she would have smiled at this form of words but she did not smile. While she was coming downstairs, though it had not much registered at the time, she had seen Tina and the children going out by the front door.

She let the phone ring. She would never speak to her mother again. Perhaps she would never speak to anyone again, it seemed likely. He had come back in the night, in the small hours, and taken his things and gone.

She would have thought, five minutes before, that such a thing as hope was gone for ever. But hope came like a tiny beckoning finger, a child's finger. Tom had said so many things about Axel, about her and Axel, as if he knew everything. Suppose he had taken Axel's things himself, hidden them, to sustain a fantasy about his departure. Alice began exploring all the empty rooms in the house, starting on the top floor. The Science Lab first, then the Art Room, down to the Handwork Room, the Staff Common Room, down to Remove. She had come close up to the cloakroom door. This door she had passed a hundred times without curiosity, without the inclination to open it.

It would be like Tom to hide Axel's things in here. To punish her, to make her feel as she did feel. She opened the door to the cloakroom. It was not empty, there were cushions on the floor and bedding and an empty Coke can, but Axel's suitcases were not there. She did not feel disappointment, only a fleeting speculation as to how she might have felt if they had been.

Down from an aperture in the ceiling hung a rope. It hung in the centre of the room to within six inches of the floor. A vague memory came to Alice of hearing how some old man had hanged himself in here. She had heard hanging called a quick death. If she saw no future, only the edge of the precipice in front of her, had no conception of what to do next, how even to fill an hour, perhaps it was because there was nothing to come, that she had been led here for this moment, this finality.

She took the rope carefully in her hand. She touched it gingerly, as if it were alive, might slither from the ceiling and a head appear to bite her. It lay lightly across her palm. Surely it must be easy to make a noose, for all sorts of people did it, they hanged themselves by far less effective means, with belts and scarves and shoelaces. Some kind authority had brought her here and put this rope, these means, into her hands.

In the construction of a noose she got as far as turning

344

the rope back on itself and making a single twist to hold the loop. It became necessary to hold the rope more firmly. She grasped it, gave a tug on it, and from above, high up over the roof, came the single toll of a bell.

She did not hesitate, she did not wait in wonderment. A great desperate, wild excitement gripped her, an intense sensation of nothing mattering any more, that the absolute end of things was at hand. Doomsday had come. This was the end of the world and she was in it, seeing it. With that, she seized the rope in both hands and, pulling with all the force she had, dragging on the rope, reaching up as high as she could, dropping to the floor as low, she began to toll the Cambridge School bell.

24

Jarvis heard the bell as he was crossing the bridge. His plane from Moscow had come into Heathrow ten minutes early, at 9.25, there had been no trouble with baggage collection or customs, and the Piccadilly Line train had moved off the moment he stepped into it. Jarvis thought the graffiti on the cars had got worse while he was away. It was everywhere and multi-coloured. He even saw some *inside* a car. Solomon's carpet, woven of dirty-coloured threads.

He changed on to the Jubilee at Green Park and got to West Hampstead after a journey from the airport of just an hour. Although it was slightly quicker to go home south of the station, he took the bridge. He wanted to look down on all those lines from the bridge, reassure himself it was all still there, and if defaced – if, as he had read in the newspaper on the aircraft, bombed – nevertheless indomitable.

As he reached the halfway mark and had seen a train run below his feet down to Finchley Road, flashing silver beneath the slats, the bell started. It took him a moment or two to understand that it was *his* bell. He tried to line up a view of the campanile through the metal bars of the bridge, failed, ran down the steps.

The bell was tolling at a great rate. It clanged out over West Hampstead like a tocsin, like an alarm, a great ringing designed to warn a populace of fire, invasion, imminent catastrophe. People had come out on to the balconies of the flats, others were in their front gardens. Jarvis could see that many of them had no idea where the sound was coming from but that some knew very well and gazed in wonder in the direction of Cambridge School. By now he could see the bell tower clearly and the bell inside it furiously rising and falling as its tongue rang out the deep brazen clangour.

Jarvis ran on. He was carrying two cases and a backpack but he ran. The front door was not locked. He dropped his cases, the bag from his back, threw open the cloakroom door. Alice, seeming fastened to the bell like some heroine of romance, some bellringer's daughter proclaiming that Bonaparte had come, an invading army had come, turned to him a white face and glittering eyes. He took a step towards her. With a long shudder, she flung the rope from her and fell sobbing into his arms.

Trailing up Priory Road from Kilburn High Road where she had been to buy socks for the children in a closing-down sale, Tina, up early for once and with Jasper and Bienvida in tow, heard the bell as she turned the corner. She did not immediately know what the sound was or where it came from. Jasper and Bienvida knew. Jasper was awe-stricken. He even thought for a moment the bell must be ringing of its own volition or for some atmospheric reason. Then the loud continual clanging made him indignant. It was *his* bell, and whoever it was ringing it, for he knew it could not really be the bell doing it on its own or the damp air or supernatural forces, had no right to do so.

Bienvida was staring at him in an accusing way, as if he were ringing the bell himself. Tina said, 'Where's it coming from?'

'It's our bell,' Jasper said.

'You mean the old School bell?' Tina started remembering. She had a vague recollection of hearing it before, long ago, when she was younger than Bienvida was now. It was a memory she associated with tangles in her hair, with her mother coming upstairs and trying to ease the knots out of her long fair hair. 'Oh, Christ,' she said, 'Ma'll hear it and it'll bring up all that old stuff about her brother.'

She began running in the direction of Lilac Villa. The children exchanged glances, Jasper shrugged, and they followed her.

But Cecilia had not in fact heard the bell. She died just before the first peal rang out.

She was on the sofa-bed that became a bed during the hours of daylight, propped up by two pillows and two sofa cushions, and Daphne was sitting beside her on a stool, asking her what she would like for her lunch. It was much too early for lunch but things moved at a leisurely pace in Lilac Villa and Daphne liked plenty of notice before preparing half a scrambled egg or a very small cup of soup, which were the only things Cecilia ever wanted to eat these days.

Cecilia said egg, or Daphne thought she said egg, but it was very difficult to understand anything she said. It became more difficult every day. Cecilia's mind was full of vague images and memories, her whole mental process had become most of the time like one of those dreams where nothing makes sense, but this dream of hers was audible only. She could not see it, this past she conjured up, the people who inhabited it and spoke. What she could see, and still see quite clearly, was her own drawing room, the window with the white sky, and Daphne sitting beside her, looking not a year older than she had on her wedding day when Arthur Bleech-Palmer gave each of his wife's bridesmaids a cameo brooch. Cecilia got Daphne to pin the brooch on her every day and she thought this pleased her friend.

About two minutes before the ringing began, Cecilia was stricken with a pain in her side. It was like she imagined having an electric drill pushed into you might be and at the same time like the pains of labour, which she

348

thought she had forgotten. She did not tell Daphne she had a pain but taking hold of her hand, said, 'Dear, I have loved you all my life with all my heart.'

Daphne, who thought she was trying to say something about scrambled eggs, leant nearer. 'I didn't quite get that, Cessie.'

The grip on her hand began to slacken. Daphne laid the hand back on the blankets. A sound came from Cecilia the like of which Daphne had never heard before, a rattle from the depths of her, and, thinking she wanted to clear her throat, Daphne quickly went behind her and tried to raise her upright in the crook of her arm. Cecilia's head lolled and with wide-open eyes she subsided softly on Daphne's bosom.

'Oh, Cessie,' said Daphne, 'oh, Cessie, Cessie, my dear.'

Somewhere out there, from the direction of the School, a bell began to ring. It came so appositely, so like a knell for Cecilia, that Daphne cried out. She stood up, holding her hands up to her face, listening in horror to the tolling bell, the rapidly clanging, roaring, hysterical bell.

Another bell rang, the one on the front door.

To answer it, to do anything about it now, seemed a superfluous act. Daphne continued to stand there, listening to the bell, with her hands up over her face and the tears dripping through her fingers. The front doorbell rang again, the way it does when someone keeps a thumb pressed on it. This time Daphne had to go. Numbly, she let in Tina, Jasper and Bienvida.

Bienvida was actually at the drawing room door. 'No, no, don't go in, not for a moment. Oh, that awful bell! What is it? Why doesn't it stop?'

'Why not go in, Auntie Daphne?'

Daphne believed you should never mention death in the hearing of children. But what could she do? They were all looking at her with innocent wonderment, knowledge gradually dawning on Tina's face.

349

'Oh, Tina, Tina,' she said, she had to say it, 'your mother's gone. Just this minute. She died in my arms.'

Without a preliminary sob or hiccup, Bienvida burst into howls. The bell rang on, then stopped with a double clang and a rattle.

After the funeral, when Daphne had gone home to Willesden, Daniel Korn came over in his van and helped Tina move all her things back to Lilac Villa. Tina intended to do what Jarvis had done with the School and let rooms. The biggest room on the top floor had already been taken by Jed, who wanted more space. Tina had put him well out of the way because the hawk smelt so strongly and she had an idea that smell, like heat, rises.

Jarvis's publisher was quite keen on the new book he was contemplating, *Metro Networks in the USSR and Eastern Europe*. He was nearing the end of the last chapter of his complete history of the London Underground. Tom intended to stay on at the School and a drummer he was working with called Archie was going to take Five when the lease on his room ran out. Jarvis knew he would have no trouble finding tenants for the Headmaster's Flat, the hard part was all the deserving people he would have to turn away.

Tom had said nothing to him about Axel, he never mentioned Axel to anyone. As for Alice, she was in no state to talk. It was Tina, over a cup of tea at Lilac Villa, who asked him if Axel had left owing him rent.

'Who's Axel?' said Jarvis.

'That fellow with the beard who went to Heathrow to see you off, the one who came to live in Five and the Art Room.'

'I don't know anyone called Axel. He must have been a squatter. I'm surprised we haven't had more of them.'

'He went around with a bear,' said Jasper, but no one took any notice of him.

Jarvis said that if he was going to do this new book, the one about Russia and Eastern Europe, he ought to go off to Berlin and ride the U-bahn, he ought to see what happened when the line reached the Wall. What he would like to do, when the time came and they had pulled the Wall down, was ride in the first train to run through from Friedrichstrasse to Marx-Engels Platz, from the West to the East without a change. He talked happily about dates and plans, having apparently forgotten about the man who had squatted in his house and not paid him a penny.

It was not so easy for Jasper. He said nothing, but he thought a lot. Up in his new bedroom, which was the one Daphne Bleech-Palmer had when she stayed, he sat on the window seat, from where he could see the trees on the Heath but not the silver trains, and sometimes thought about the man and the bear. Now they had a big colour set he and Bienvida watched television much more and one evening he had seen Ivan's face on the screen, the sewn-up lip and spoonbill nose, while the newscaster talked about him being sent for trial on charges of bombing and murder.

Jasper remembered Axel, the first time they met, asking him about lost stations and secret ways of getting into the tube and Ivan the bear man saying they were three of a kind. Ivan was a professional bomber and had no doubt taught Axel about explosives. It seemed to Jasper quite likely that Axel had got into the tube by one of those secret ways and been responsible for blowing it up. Or trying to blow it up, for he had evidently not been very successful, and Jasper thought it was going a bit far, those experts whose comments he had heard saying the bomber had aimed to wreck the entire system. Out of madness, or revenge, or mindless hatred.

Occasionally he dwelt on what had happened to Axel. What did happen to you when you blew yourself up?

People on television said a lot about bombs but they never said that. Jasper imagined bits of Axel scattered all over the tunnels, his hair and his teeth, and somewhere among the debris that ring he wore. They had never identified those bits, they still had no idea who it was and perhaps never would have. Jasper had decided to say nothing to anyone, not even Bienvida, but keep it as the second great secret of his life, the first being how he had sledged alone on the great long runs.

Jarvis finished his book on a pessimistic note:

It is not long since London Transport was making a small annual profit, but things have changed and the changes are due to railmen's strikes, to unscheduled re-building and to increased spending on safety measures. For instance, the District Line trains, all seventy-five of them, recently had to be taken out of service after electric motors broke free from car bogies. Doors were opening on the wrong side of cars, the side without a platform, there were accidents, and thousands had to be spent on finding a fail-safe system.

Blackfriars Bridge over the District and Circle Lines has been rebuilt and the cost was £3 million more than expected.

One of the plans for cutting costs is to stop all tube services on Boxing Day. At present London Transport is paying its employees double time for working on 26 December.

The numbers using the London Underground are declining: only 765 million last year and there will be fewer this. One of the results has been a loss of £10 million in ticket revenue. At the time of writing the Underground faces a cash shortfall of £40 million.

This was so depressing that he added a few lines he was sure his publisher would make him cut out.

On the face of it, this does not look like the time to enlarge the system by building new lines. And yet it is only by such enormous outlay as this would entail that the London Underground can recoup its losses and instead of a slow, ignominious death, go on triumphantly to a future in the twenty-first century.

No qualms troubled Tom about using Axel's money. In a mail order catalogue he had seen an advertisement for a wonderful device and had sent off for it. This was a music-maker called a Voconverter 5000. You sang into the microphone and it played back the same tune to you, transformed into the sound of any one of thirty musical instruments. When the tune was recorded you could lay four more tracks on top, using different instruments. It cost £400, but he could afford it. He imagined playing it back in the tube, the start of a revolution in busking.

Down in the cellar, he contemplated Axel's property. He had put the cameras into two plastic carriers and all the rest into the two suitcases. The lot, covered by a dust sheet formerly used by some decorator of long ago, stood in the sooty compound where Ernest Jarvis had once kept his coal.

Tom could not imagine anyone would come trying to identify those cameras. One was a Nikon, the other an Olympus with a telephoto lens and looked enormously expensive. He decided to keep them and accordingly took them upstairs to the Headmaster's Study, where he put them inside the cupboard. Tom had moved into Alice's old room after they took her away. It was bigger and got more light than Four.

He had made up his mind to take Alice back. After all, no one knew better than he that Axel was dead. When he visited her in the psychiatric ward he tried to tell her she was forgiven but she never made him any answer or even seemed to know who he was. They said she would get better, it was only a matter of time, to give it time. The drugs they were using were marvellously effective in cases like this. When she was all right again he thought of asking if the two of them could take on the Headmaster's Flat, but since she was not all right yet he rather welcomed the delay occasioned by Jarvis's departure the day before for Berlin.

He was alone at the School at last. It was a mild, dry evening, which would suit his purposes. The previous week some people in the flats had lit a fire on the ground between their block and the train lines. There had been a great deal of smoke but it had not lasted long and no one had complained, though this of course was a smokeless zone. If they could do it, so could he.

The presence of Axel's things in the School, in his keeping, had worried him daily, ever since he put them in the cellar. That Jarvis might return without warning had not occurred to him, though what warning there could have been he hardly knew. He was on tenterhooks a lot of the time for fear Jarvis would go into the cellar, find the cases and the cameras and start inquiring.

All sorts of ideas for disposing of Axel's property kept passing through his mind. He even thought of dumping the cases at some railway terminus or taking them to Heathrow where, abandoned, they would certainly be stolen. But most of the things inside the cases were marked in ways which identified them as Axel's, the books with his name in them, the collection of photographs, which Tom had not even glanced at. There were two heavy parcels, wrapped in brown paper, one of which contained letters from some female relative, possibly a sister. The other was a similar package inside a plastic bag which he did not trouble to open. He could remove all Axel's signatures but how could he be certain of not having missed one? Axel's fingerprints might be on file and all those things would be covered with his fingerprints – and, now, with Tom's.

Fire was the best way. He returned to the cellar and fetched the cases up into the hall. Searching the School for paraffin reminded him of how he had searched the Angell, Scherrer and Christianson building for a weapon and then for a spanner. There were half a dozen oil heaters in the School and paraffin must be somewhere, unless now in the spring it had all been used up. Cans of petrol he found, two of them in a kitchen cupboard, but he was afraid to use petrol, he didn't want to set fire to himself. Eventually, he found a can of paraffin in Remove beside Jarvis's fireplace.

He went outside with the cases. The lawn would do, somewhere at the end by the rear fence. To the fate of the books, the letters and the photograph of the girl Tom was indifferent but it seemed a pity to burn the white dress. Still, he dared not keep it. What could he do with it? He smiled wryly to himself when he thought of bestowing it on Alice. He prepared the basis of a bonfire with newspaper and with sticks gathered from all over the garden, over which he poured a trickle of paraffin.

The sky was clear and the air was still. April had been a lovely month, like high summer. Tom heard a train coming and saw its silver sides flash between the open boards of the garden fence. He took the matches out of his pocket. Then he tipped the contents of the suitcases on to the ground, put the dress on the pyre he had built and then Axel's own clothes, the jeans, the trainers and the black overcoat.

He put a match to the wood and paper. Because of the paraffin it caught quickly and flames shot up, eating the white dress and the overcoat. They burned very fast. Tom found himself a long stick, a fallen branch from one of the big trees. He threw on the books, watching with satisfaction while the fire consumed them. It relieved his mind to think of the flames eating up Axel's signature, licking and swallowing his fingerprints.

The smoke was dense, white and choking. But it would

soon be over, leaving a few handfuls of grey ashes. He would stamp on the ashes and grind them into the ground, smooth earth over where the fire had been. He threw on the first parcel of letters, pushed it with his stick as the flames caught it, then the other box, the last thing to be destroyed.

As the flames approached the tightly taped package inside the plastic bag, Tom came close to the fire to see it consume the last of Axel.

On his way to join the Safeguards for that night's Central Line duty, Jed caught a southbound train at West Hampstead. It passed the end of the School garden just in time, the last car slipping along the rails as the magnesium flash, tightly compressed, met the fire and burst its bonds.

The black powder, metamorphosed into gas, went up with a brilliant flash and an enormous explosion. It leaped across the tracks with a roar, taking stones with it and bricks and tree branches, grasping everything in that garden, living and inanimate, in its fierce chemical breath, and hurling what it snatched into the air. Flames leapt, doubled back, and shot with a screaming hiss into the sky.

The train went on unharmed down to Finchley Road.